CRITICAL A

SILF'

"A brilliant, awkward, relentless, ıventional hero who will not take 'no' for an answer, sav ıe day. Get me Special Agent Gordon Stone for every difficult case and watch this man work."

—Chuck Rosenberg, former US Attorney,
Eastern District of Virginia

"This is a fascinating story about real people, complex issues, and a world of many complicated challenges. It's an interesting read that keeps you focused and anticipating the next page. I liked it and recommend it."

—Chuck Hagel, former Secretary of Defense
and US Senator

"A truly innovative thriller with a refreshingly unique protagonist who will quickly have you rooting for him. A fast-paced tale told with imagination, fused with a realism that only insiders from the investigative world can bring. It will keep you guessing from page to page. Highly recommended."

—Kimberly Prost, former Ombudsperson for the
U.N. Security Council Al-Qaeda Sanctions Committee

SILENT KILLER

TRACY BURNETT
& ROSS WEILAND

SILENT KILLER

DOWN & OUT
BOOKS

Down & Out Books
3959 Van Dyke Road, Suite 265
Lutz, FL 33558
DownAndOutBooks.com

Cover design by Xing Burnett

ISBN: 1-64396-413-5
ISBN-13: 978-1-64396-413-3

For Lisa & Jeanne

PROLOGUE

Captain John Finch stared into space, his eyes unfocused. He reached over to a small wooden table, blindly turning off his alarm, which had not yet rung. It was 0429 hours. Finch smiled as he sat up in bed, trying to remember the last time he'd needed an alarm to get him out of bed at his 0430 wake-up time. He stretched his arms to the ceiling, then bent forward and grabbed his ankles, his forehead touching his knees in perfect pike position. He held that pose for thirty seconds and then stood up, awake and ready to roll.

He dressed quickly in physical training gear and left his private quarters; one of the perks of being the ranking officer for this assignment. Finch broke into a run as soon as he was outside and headed to the airstrip. The US Army owned him, but this morning ritual was his. For the next thirty minutes, he would run and sweat along the mile-long length of the airstrip to clear his head and prepare for the day.

The strip existed outside of an internally fenced US perimeter within a Nigerian base camp established and occupied by the US military. Inside the US perimeter were sleeping quarters, a medical facility, and a small mess hall known as LittleMess. LittleMess had a kitchen and dining area. A small attached lounge, known as the pub, consisted of a beer fridge and some beat-up furniture. Through a door on the far side of the pub was an office with a desk and conference table, around which four or five soldiers could meet, plan operations, and engage in after-action debriefs.

The larger, busier mess hall open to all was on the main base, outside of the US section. It was referred to as BigMess, and Finch instructed his team to eat most meals there. They were here to train the Nigerian Army, after all, and Finch believed breaking bread with their Nigerian counterparts was a necessary step.

His morning ritual complete, Finch walked into BigMess in search of coffee. Finch loved physical training, but he loved his morning coffee even more.

Finch nodded to a group of new Nigerian regulars he was still getting to know, grabbed a coffee, and approached a table crowded with his Special Forces brethren. Everyone grunted some form of greeting to their boss. Finch smiled at them and said, “Good morning, gentlemen. Hope everyone is well rested and well fed.” That got a few insincere laughs. “Intel meeting in fifteen at LittleMess, then straight to brief the Nigerians on today’s training.” He sipped his coffee and let out a contented sigh. “Any questions?” There were none.

Finch and his team were in Nigeria to train Nigerian Army regulars in anti-terrorism tactics for use against Boko Haram and other similar organizations that had sprouted up in this part of the world. While not classified, the team’s mission was discreet. It was not a secret that the US Army supported the Nigerian armed forces with training and equipment, but it didn’t exactly print recruiting posters of the effort either.

United States Armed Forces outpaced the rest of the world in their ability to bring destructive force to a particular place at a particular time, and as with countless other discreet deployments of US forces throughout the world, this one had expanded beyond mere training of a foreign army. It was inevitable that when Finch’s team arrived, they would, in reality, assume a leadership role beyond that of a simple training coordinator.

The result, as any forward-deployed soldier could tell you,

was that US forces frequently became the focal point of a terrorist organization's wrath in that particular foreign country. In Nigeria, that meant Boko Haram, which had existed at various levels of influence since 2002. Teams like Finch's had been around almost as long, assigned to various regions in Nigeria to provide training to Nigerian forces and support their efforts at suppressing a terrorist organization that had murdered tens of thousands.

Finch's job was to train Nigerians how to repel these groups so Nigeria could continue to grow, evolve, and maintain its status as one of the United States' most influential allies in the region. Boko Haram and groups like it used violence, threats, fear, and intimidation to try and obstruct Nigeria's journey.

Inevitably, units like Finch's immersed themselves in the ebb and flow of their surroundings. Connecting with the local community was a critical and invaluable part of their mission. Whether it was a steady supply of fresh eggs from a local chicken farmer or a piece of intel about a bad actor's activity, Finch, his team, and the Nigerian Army depended on these local relationships. And while the fresh eggs were terrific, the most valuable contribution was information about the bad guys.

This human intelligence, or HUMINT in the Army's vernacular, allowed Finch's team and the Nigerians to enjoy multiple successes in the field. This did not sit well with Boko Haram, who viewed those assisting the Americans as betrayers of biblical proportion, worse than the Americans themselves.

While Boko Haram enjoyed significant influence throughout Nigeria and ran several operations in Cameroon, their leader, Abubakar Shekau, had a vision of the group's rebirth to the north into Niger, Chad, and Sudan, eventually leading to Libya and Egypt. Shekau was said to entice his followers with visions of dipping their toes into the Mediterranean Sea after Boko Haram expanded its power, influence, and control across Northern Africa.

But Boko Haram could do none of that while fighting the

Americans at home. To achieve his vision, Shekau would first have to remove the American Army from Nigeria.

At the briefing in LittleMess, Finch listened intently as his intel officer explained the latest information received from JoJo, a HUMINT source who had been hanging around the base for several months. No one seemed to know how he got the name JoJo, but he got it, it stuck, and everyone seemed comfortable with him and the information he provided.

JoJo had arrived with a compelling story. Three years ago, Boko Haram kidnapped his sister, and he had not seen nor heard from her since. He was angry and wanted payback. A US intel officer had conducted a standard introductory intelligence interview with JoJo. Regardless of the local population's cooperative attitude, sources still had to be vetted. JoJo's story checked out. What JoJo did not know, but US Intelligence was able to determine, was that JoJo's sister had been killed. Who'd done it remained a mystery.

It had fallen to Finch to deliver the news to JoJo. JoJo's attempt at stoicism was betrayed by a few silent tears, which dried quickly to be replaced by resolve. "Boko Haram murdered my sister," JoJo said. Finch made a mental note of the anger he sensed pouring from JoJo. If this guy actually had good intel, Finch thought, he could be a huge benefit to the US mission.

JoJo did have good information, and upon receiving the news of his sister's death, he began sharing it. He provided intel on several low-level Boko Haram gatherings, allowing the US/Nigerian forces to destroy a number of valuable targets. Using the United States' drone capabilities, Finch's team eliminated several Boko Haram soldiers and successfully navigated the capture and interrogation of several more.

JoJo's information continued to be significant and substantial, and his credibility with Finch and the team skyrocketed. Over time, JoJo became a welcome and valued part of the team, and whenever he came around, he brought an air of goodwill and sense of mission accomplishment. On one occasion, JoJo brought Finch information requiring immediate action. This mission sounded like a pretty straightforward snatch-and-grab—JoJo had identified a camp with active Boko Haram soldiers—but without time to scout the area and see the target, Finch's team would go in blind, relying only on JoJo's intel and what they learned in real time once on scene. Finch needed to clear the mission parameters and make sure his chain of command was fully aware of the circumstances.

While the team prepared for its assault, Finch contacted his commander, Colonel Bartsall, at United States Africa Command (AFRICOM) in Stuttgart, Germany. Bartsall was a seasoned operations officer, probably with a general's star in his future. Finch explained it was a low-risk operation with straightforward ingress and egress. Even if the intel was bad, availability of a quick and silent exit made it worth checking out.

Bartsall did not like it, but with only minimal reluctance, he greenlit the mission. Finch and his team, along with some select Nigerian trainees, proceeded. When they arrived at the camp, Finch could not help but smile. "It's fish-in-a-barrel time," he whispered to his Nigerian counterpart.

Finch gave the execute command, and amid flash-bangs and smoke, the team took the area, capturing three Boko Haram soldiers. Finch and the Nigerians had caught them unaware, not a single shot fired.

Back at base camp, the after-action debrief was short and sweet. The mission had gone flawlessly, and JoJo's place on Finch's team solidified.

Three weeks went by before JoJo emerged again from the Nigerian jungle, bringing new intel to Finch. "What brings you back today, JoJo?"

For the next ten minutes, JoJo explained there was to be a gathering of high-level Boko Haram leaders. It was not yet known where the meeting would take place. It would be a secret location and heavily guarded. No chance for an unsupported ground attack like the last mission. JoJo gave Finch a wide region where the meeting was likely to take place, but he would not be able to provide exact coordinates until the participants were there and the meeting was underway.

"Damn, JoJo," said Finch. "You're givin' me a woody. When is this happening?"

"Best guess? Four days, Captain Finch," JoJo said with a shrug. "Maybe five."

"You're a goddamn hero, JoJo." Finch stood and extended his hand to JoJo. "Go do whatever the hell it is you do. We'll be ready. Just get me those coordinates."

"Four days, Captain Finch. I'll be back."

Finch contemplated this new intel, digesting it. Even if JoJo was only half-right, a successful mission could cripple Boko Haram leadership. He spread the word to his US team to gather for an intel briefing. At the briefing, he explained the information JoJo had provided. The excitement was palpable. Not knowing exactly what they would be up against caused only the slightest pause. Considering the general security of the meeting site, all agreed that if JoJo's intel proved accurate, an eye-in-the-sky should light the place up, then Finch's team could go in and pick up the pieces. Finch left the team to start preliminary planning and headed back to his quarters. He needed to call Colonel Bartsall.

"Another no see 'um?" asked Bartsall.

"Yessir," replied Finch. "But, sir, we've been down this road before with the HUMINT. Time after time, he has absolutely delivered. That op three weeks ago that delivered three targets to your doorstep? That was this guy. If he's right on this, we could put Boko Haram out of business."

"All right, Captain, let's not get ahead of ourselves on—"

"Sir," interrupted Finch. "Shekau could be there."

There was a pause on the line as Bartsall contemplated what Finch said. Abubakar Shekau. Boko Haram's leader. If they knew where he would be and when, this could be an extraordinarily big deal. "You've got a few days. Start planning and get ready. Let's see what this guy brings you. We'll get a bird up when the time comes. Keep us posted, Captain."

"Roger that, sir," Finch replied.

"And, John, this is need-to-know. No details to the Nigerians until you're on your way. Just make sure they're ready to go."

"You got it, Colonel. I'll keep it vague."

"It's happening," Shekau said to Mahmud Adamu, his deputy and closest confidante.

Adamu nodded respectfully. "His will be done," he said.

"Yes," responded Shekau. "His will indeed." He paused a moment, looking directly at Adamu. "You know what must happen? After?"

"Yes. It will be taken care of."

"It's going to work," Shekau said. "Your brilliant plan, after all this time." He grabbed his deputy by both shoulders, holding him at arm's length. Staring intently into Adamu's eyes, he whispered, "It's going to work."

With a hint of genuflection, Adamu turned and left the room.

Shekau sat, alone with his thoughts. The United States for far too long had meddled in the affairs of Boko Haram. It was time for the US to be embarrassed, humiliated, and politically compelled to leave Nigeria. Shekau could deal with the Nigerian Army, but the Americans were like an open sore. They brought money, weapons, technology, and sophisticated military skill into the equation. He did not have the resources to deal with the Americans directly. He needed them gone.

Adamu's plan truly was a genius counterintelligence maneuver, though it had been costly. Not in dollars so much as in the lives of his brethren. Some had been captured by the Americans.

Some even killed. But if the plan worked, it will all have been worth it. If the Americans left Nigeria, Boko Haram would be reborn, its expansion into northern Africa all but assured.

Other than Adamu and himself, only one other person knew about the plan that was in motion, and Shekau had only met the third member of their conspiracy a few times. He did not even know his real name, only that the Americans called him JoJo for some unknown reason. Adamu had introduced him, and Shekau was immediately impressed. JoJo was not a typical Boko Haram soldier. Sure, he was a believer, but not one born of desperation. He was educated, for one thing, and a thinker. It had been his suggestion that to truly establish credibility with the Americans he would have to provide them with information that could actually hurt Boko Haram interests.

Yes, Shekau was impressed. Plus, the man had a credible story. His sister had been killed in a car accident three years ago, and that was spun until history was rewritten as a kidnapping and told to help secure the man's place with the Americans. Then, for a while, everything JoJo did would hurt Boko Haram. It was a heavy cost, but necessary to build trust with the Americans.

Now, when the time was right, Shekau would strike at the Americans without lifting a finger, firing a weapon, or being anywhere near the catastrophe that would send the Americans out of Nigeria. JoJo would have to be dealt with, of course. That was unfortunate, but also necessary. If the plan came to light, Shekau would lose everything—his position within Boko Haram, and most likely, his life.

After his meeting with Shekau, Adamu went to meet JoJo. He gave JoJo no indication that the plan's final phase was now in play. To JoJo, it was just another meeting, just another mission. Adamu placed a slip of paper into JoJo's hand, saying, "Give that to the American leader. Tell him the meeting has already begun and ends around one thirty. We can't give them too much time, so you'll have to plan your arrival at the base.

Eleven o'clock should do it."

Adamu had prayed daily that his calculations were accurate. The amount of intelligence the Americans allowed on the internet was stunning, but there was no guarantee of its accuracy. The drone was key. It had to get within firing range, but not close enough for its cameras to "see" the target. The drone would come from the north, while the foot soldiers, JoJo's contacts, would come from the east. The "meeting" needed to end before the soldiers arrived, requiring the drone to get the job done.

JoJo nodded. He knew what he had to do.

Adamu said a prayer for his loyal soldier, knowing he would never see him again.

Six days had passed when the Nigerian gate guard called to let Finch know JoJo had returned. Finch asked the guard to bring JoJo to the US section immediately. He glanced at his watch—1104 hours—and went to the section entrance himself to greet JoJo. His relief was eclipsed only by his curiosity about what JoJo had to tell him. JoJo appeared a bit flustered, and Finch invited him to the pub. They sat at the table outside of Finch's office.

"I was about to send out a search party," said Finch.

"Much apologies, Captain Finch. Very, very sorry. But no time." He shoved a slip of paper into Finch's hand.

Finch examined the paper, which revealed only a latitude and longitude. "Okay, that's our location. Tell me you know when."

"Now, Captain Finch. Big meeting already begins. Over soon. Around one thirty."

Without missing a beat, Finch poked his head into Little-Mess. "Saddle up, boys. We're doing this now." He looked around LittleMess for Omar. Omar's real name was Corporal Dean Bradley, but even now, if you were in the Army and your name was Bradley, everyone called you Omar, after the legendary general.

"Omar, take JoJo over to BigMess and get him some chow," Finch instructed. Stepping back inside the pub, he looked at JoJo. "You're a good man, JoJo." He extended his hand, and JoJo obliged him with a firm handshake. "When this is over, you and me are going to celebrate, okay? You head to BigMess and get a hot meal. Omar'll walk you over, and I'll see you when we're back. Time for me to get to work."

"Thank you, Captain," said JoJo with a smile. With a slight bow, he left.

Finch called Colonel Bartsall. The situation was critical, and Finch needed a decision now.

"Captain Finch, I thought you forgot about all us desk jockeys up here at AFRICOM. It's been six days, son, whatcha' got?"

"Sir, we are mission critical. We've got a location, but, sir, the time is now. The meeting has already begun. It's happening now, and the window closes at 1330."

"Any word on Shekau?"

"Not confirmed, sir. There's a chance, but we won't know until we get there."

"Sounds like that might be too late."

"Yes, sir." Finch paused. "Sir?"

"Speak your mind, John."

"Sir, I know this isn't ideal, but we are out of time. My guys can hit the road in ten, but neither us or your bird will have time to put eyes on the target before this meeting is over. You know I believe our guy, sir. He has never—never—given us bad intel. It's a hot target right now, and my recommendation is to light 'em up and we get there when we get there."

Finch got an uncomfortable silence as a response. He was about to repeat his recommendation, with more colorful language, when Bartsall broke the silence.

"Make it happen, Captain. Tell your ground team to haul

ass. They needed to be there yesterday. If you somehow get there before the drone, paint it. If not, we'll go with the coordinates your source provided. My bird will be airborne in less than thirty minutes. We'll go full throttle. If we can't get into a recon position by 1320, we'll launch with preprogrammed coordinates. I won't wait for you to paint the sonuvabitch, so at 1320 you need to be clear of the target. Radio silence until then. Got it?"

"Roger that, sir. We're on it. Launch at 1320."

"John?"

"Yessir."

"I'd really like to be amazed with your speed and have your team there first."

"Understood, sir.

"Good luck, John. Happy hunting."

As soon as Bartsall got off the call with Finch, he called Sand Creek, the classified drone hub of Western Africa located at a small air base attached to the Ouagadougou Airport in Burkina Faso, northwest of Nigeria. "It's go time. Get that Reaper in the air right now. Coordinates are on the way."

At Sand Creek, a ground crew jumped to life. They were used to sending up surveillance drones all over western Africa, but a Reaper was different. An MQ-9 Reaper hunter-killer drone was the most advanced and most lethal unmanned aerial vehicle the world had ever produced. They did not call it the Reaper because it took great pictures.

Finch's team moved with the speed of a seasoned Special Forces squad. No choppers this time. Stealth was the key right up to the moment the Reaper unleashed hell. If all went exceedingly well, his team would get there first and confirm, then paint the target where the meeting was being held, ensuring a direct hit from the Reaper. Then his team would mop up, gather any intel they could find, confirm any dead, and bring any left alive back to base camp. If they were lucky, Finch thought, Boko Haram would assume its rightful position as a pimple on the ass end of history, never to be heard from again.

No choppers, but the two four-door Toyota Tacoma pickup trucks racing through the back roads of rural Nigeria might still get noticed. That could not be helped. But after an hour's drive, they would stop ten klicks from the target and hump the rest of the way through jungle. To paint the target in time for a 1320 Reaper strike, they would need unobstructed eyes on the building not later than 1318. Finch knew that would be a stretch, even for his elite team. They were not jogging by the base airstrip today. He hoped conditions on the hump would be good and they would get there in time for the fireworks at least.

Far from the commercial jets at Ouagadougou, a Reaper jumped to life as a launch pilot got the bird airborne. Halfway around the world, a US Air Force warrant officer stepped into a small, windowless room at Creech Air Force Base in the desert a few miles outside of Las Vegas. The warrant officer settled into an ergonomic pilot's seat, put on a headset, and opened communications with the launch pilot at Ouagadougou. The launch pilot turned over control of the Reaper to the warrant officer, who grabbed the stick between his legs and pulled back. Their Reaper climbed to 25,000 feet before banking south toward the preprogrammed target location. The warrant officer leveled the Reaper, checked all systems, avionics, and weapons—definitely weapons.

His orders were to proceed to the programmed coordinates "with all due speed" and be prepared to unleash holy hell on the target with a launch order from AFRICOM. With the systems all checked out, he edged the Reaper's speed close to its maximum three hundred miles per hour. "Off we go, into the wild blue yonder," he sang, wondering who pissed off who today.

***

Finch's two pickups left the road and pulled into a secluded clearing. They had made it in less than an hour, ahead of schedule, but a ten-klick hump with gear through the jungle provided a tough path on which to make good time. Finch looked at the team. Everybody was out of the trucks, assembled and ready to go in seconds. Finch directed an affirmative nod toward the Nigerians. Could be a good group, he thought.

"Sir," he said to the Nigerian team leader. "With your permission."

The Nigerian offered a salute, which Finch returned before addressing the team.

"Gentlemen, you've all been briefed on the way here. You know what's at stake. We're going to have to push hard to reach the target and paint it by 1320. Otherwise, we're mopping up after the Reaper has done its work. We're quick and quiet. Radio silence until the drone strike. Let's haul ass."

With smiles all around, the team entered the jungle.

At Creech, the warrant officer rechecked his systems. The normal routine called for him to get there, do some recon, take some pictures, see what he was blowing up. Today's mission was not normal, and he knew he would not get there in time to see the target through the Reaper's cameras. But if the ground pounders moved faster than anticipated, they might have a chance to confirm the target and put a laser on it, "painting" it and virtually guaranteeing a hit within an inch or two of the red dot, whether the Reaper could see the target or not. That made for great video in the debrief, but he knew those "ifs" were unlikely. He would be shooting blind if he got the launch order, with only programmed coordinates to guide the strike. There was not much to do until then. He checked the time. Not much longer.

* * *

At AFRICOM, Bartsall sat anxiously in the command center. He looked at the digital clock synced with Nigeria time for about the thousandth time, then looked up at a screen showing the Reaper's location. So fucking close, he thought. This was no movie, and Bartsall did not have real-time satellite video of Finch's ground team, though he knew generally where they were. The open question was when they would arrive at the scene. When the clock reached 1315 hours, Bartsall picked up the phone, already linked with Creech. "Let me talk to the pilot," he said.

Finch checked his watch—1316 hours. They would be there in minutes. They had made amazing time through some dense jungle but would not get there before the scheduled Reaper strike at 1320 hours. It looked like mop-up and intel gathering for his crew today.

Bartsall was patched through to the pilot of the Reaper. "Reaper 1, this is Colonel Bartsall at AFRICOM. We are a go on my command. Ground forces are approaching. Assume launch attitude and proceed with weapons check."

"That's affirmative, AFRICOM. Weapons are go. Proceeding to launch attitude."

An endless minute ticked by. Bartsall checked the clock again—1318 hours, two minutes to launch. He got up out of his chair. Just as he was about to speak, the warrant officer broke the tension.

"AFRICOM, Reaper 1 is in position. Coordinates are locked in. No eyes on target. Repeat, no eyes on target. Ready to launch at your command."

"Understood, Reaper 1," responded Bartsall. "Stand by." 1319 hours. "Dammit." he shouted at no one. "I need more time." With arms crossed and brow furrowed, Bartsall made the call—he wanted to see this target. He wanted to see it and confirm what it was. Five more minutes. The drone would not get close enough for pictures, but maybe Finch's team was close. If they could get there, confirm and paint the target, Bartsall would get the warm fuzzy feeling he so desperately sought. "I'm giving ground another five minutes," he told the pilot at Creech.

"Roger that, AFRICOM. Maintaining launch attitude and continuing toward target. Launch time now 1325 local."

Finch's team regrouped at the edge of a small village. Finch looked at his watch. Something was wrong. It was 1322, but there was no sign of an attack. They had heard no explosions, saw no smoke or fire. There was nothing that would indicate a missile had just destroyed a building in the village. That is not good, thought Finch. Time was critical, and the target should have been hit two minutes ago.

He considered breaking radio silence and contacting Bartsall. Instead, he signaled to Smitty, a US Army sergeant, to come to him. "Grab Donk and head to the target site," he whispered. Donk was a Nigerian soldier who had proven himself with the Americans on prior missions. He was one of their best. "See what you can see. Slow and steady, okay? You do not need to be seen out there. Maintain radio silence unless there's a problem. Stay outside the blast radius. No one on my team is getting blown up today. If you can paint it, paint it. Got it?"

Smitty gave Finch a thumbs-up and disappeared.

It was 1325 hours and still no word from AFRICOM. The warrant officer reconnected with Bartsall. "AFRICOM, Reaper 1 affirming weapons are hot and we are in position to fire. No visual confirmation of target. We are at launch time. Reaper 1 is standing by."

"Roger that, Reaper 1. Stand by," answered the colonel.

***

Smitty and Donk stayed in the shadows as they approached the outer perimeter of the target. Something was off. It had all the appearance of a traditional Nigerian village going about a typical day. Smitty saw no Boko Haram guards, there was no established security perimeter, and certainly no indication of a secret Boko Haram meeting. Smitty considered breaking radio silence to contact Captain Finch. Instead, he said, "Donk, are we in the right place?"

Donk shrugged. "Target coordinates are right up ahead. Let's go see."

It was 1326 hours.

At AFRICOM, Bartsall brought the phone back up to his ear. He could not wait any longer. He was shooting blind, relying solely on Finch's HUMINT source, Finch's belief in that source, and the coordinates the source provided. But if Shekau was there, that would be a general's star for sure, Bartsall thought. Even if Shekau did not make the meeting, it would be a big win for the good guys. He checked the clock—1327 hours. "Reaper 1, this is AFRICOM. Mission is go. Launch approved."

"Affirmative, AFRICOM," the pilot responded. "Please confirm, we have not reached target site and have no eyes, repeat, no eyes."

"Mission is go, Reaper 1," replied Bartsall. "Launch now."

The pilot's grip on the stick tightened imperceptibly. With an easy squeeze on the trigger, the Reaper belched death from above. "Missile away."

It took only a few seconds for Smitty and Donk to find a secluded spot with a clear line-of-sight to the target. Smitty raised the handheld laser designator to his right eye. He was about to trigger the laser and paint the target when Donk grabbed the designator out of his hand.

"What the fuck?" asked Smitty.

"That cannot be the target. Look again," Donk said, handing

the designator back to Smitty.

"Oh shit," said Smitty as he looked again. He stood up in a daze, the designator dropping from his hand. As it hit the ground with a smack, Smitty recovered from his shock and scrambled to radio Finch. "Abort! Abort! Abort!" Smitty screamed. "Cap, it's a fucking—."

An explosion rocked the village. Finch never heard the end of Smitty's call.

CHAPTER 1

What would be a landmark day for any other federal agent was an exercise in misery for Special Agent Gordon Stone. He sat, restless and uncomfortable, in the crowded auditorium inside the Albert V. Bryan US Courthouse in Alexandria, Virginia. Wesley Jay, the US Attorney for the Eastern District of Virginia (EDVA), was on stage addressing the capacity crowd. Jay extolled the virtues of his office and its extraordinary success in managing the Eastern District's "rocket docket." The court's namesake had coined the term in the seventies, District Court Judge Bryan himself. What it meant for Jay and his stable of Assistant US Attorneys (AUSAs) was that they were forced to be one of the most efficient offices in the country when it came to prosecuting cases. They gathered annually to recognize the most successful investigations and prosecutions of the preceding year. Lawyers, law enforcement, and family members filled the auditorium. For an office that had prosecuted some of the most notorious spy and terrorist cases in the country—not to mention the occasional political scandal—the yearly awards ceremony always attracted a full house.

"Copied by many, mirrored by none," said Jay. "We bring justice to the American people more quickly and effectively than anywhere else in the country. I take great pride in that fact and hope you do as well."

Gordon tried to listen, but his discomfort just being there

compelled him to tune out Jay's speech. It wasn't that he did not want to be there. On the contrary, his greatest desire was to be able to sit in the audience, listen to Jay, and enjoy a career highlight. Gordon was being recognized for his work as lead agent on an application fraud case with the Food and Drug Administration Office of Criminal Investigations (FDA-OCI).

But Gordon did not fit in. He liked people, but he had trouble relating to them and was painfully aware of his social awkwardness. Way back in elementary school, he had been diagnosed with high-functioning autism, at the time referred to as Asperger Syndrome, or colloquially as Asperger's.

Gordon appeared just like everyone else, but when it came to basic human interaction, it took a great deal of effort for him to engage with most people. It was always hard and frequently exhausting. Small talk, humor, and sarcasm often flew past him. Therapy had brought him a long way, but still, those who did not know him thought he was aloof. Some actually found his behavior offensive.

"Damn Asperger's," he said to himself.

The true irony, he knew, was however damning Asperger's was to his social status, it was also his superpower, allowing him to focus on a particular topic—or investigation—to the point where he could see things no one else could see. He could anticipate what others viewed as unexpected. That focus bred unparalleled intuition, which was what made him a great investigator.

That was why he was here in this crowded hall, surrounded by people he did not know. He *was* a great investigator. But he was most definitely not a great socializer, and he was uncomfortable. As much as he wished he could enjoy the ceremony and embrace the praise of his peers, his Asperger's would not allow it. In fact, a big group setting surrounded by strangers? That was pretty much the nightmare scenario.

Gordon's brain was wired differently. At least that's how Katherine, his longtime therapist, described it. He thought differently, acted differently, saw the world differently than most. She emphasized repeatedly to him he was not broken, just different, and Gordon knew it was okay to be different. Most of the time, that was enough. But even now, as a successful thirty-two-year-old federal agent, he could still feel broken. He hoped today would not be one of those days.

"The work we do—check that—the work *you* do for this country is, simply put, extraordinary," Jay continued. "We put more cases before a judge than anyone else, and that means when it comes time to recognize our best work in a given year, the competition is tight. I salute those of you sitting in this room. Your work, your intellect, your dogged pursuit of justice places you at the top of what we do here. You are the best of the best. Thank you for all you do for our organization, our district, and our country." Jay smiled to his audience. "Now then, let's hand out some hardware."

CHAPTER 2

Applications fraud. Mundane terminology for a case that may have saved hundreds, or even thousands, of lives. It involved an NDA, or New Drug Application. Gordon had been the duty agent when the call came in from the FDA's Consumer Complaint Coordinator. They had received a hotline complaint from a doctor whose patient had died unexpectedly after treatment with Nextemol-4, a new antibiotic that had been on the market for six months after the FDA had signed off on the manufacturer's test results demonstrating Nextemol-4 was safe and effective.

Nextemol-4 was the creation of PharmaCorp, Inc., a multinational drug manufacturer with its US operations headquartered in Richmond, Virginia. Upon development of Nextemol-4, PharmaCorp hired Jenner Testing, Inc., a drug trial research organization named for Dr. Edward Jenner, who discovered the smallpox vaccine, to conduct drug trials. PharmaCorp also tapped RxMonitor, a PharmaCorp subsidiary, to act as third-party overseer of Jenner's trials. Nextemol-4 was designed to treat community-acquired pneumonia and could revolutionize treatment around the globe. Much was at stake, and PharmaCorp was in a hurry.

Jenner determined the most efficient means of testing Nextemol-4 was in rural areas with older populations prone to developing pneumonia. Jenner hired doctors from around the country to administer Nextemol-4 and report back results, paying $2,500 for every patient who agreed to participate. That was no small incentive for many doctors practicing in poor, rural areas. In some cases, that incentive proved too big a temptation, and doctors created patient files for townsfolk who were not suffering from pneumonia and manufactured fictitious results for treatment that never took place.

As the testing continued, several of these doctors began reporting dramatic increases in positive results from patients treated with Nextemol-4, which led to a dramatic increase in test subjects. Such increases should have been, and in fact were, recognized by Jenner as well as RxMonitor as potential red flags. Both companies saw the unusual increases, but both were also keenly aware of the importance of Nextemol-4 to PharmaCorp. Jenner failed to make inquiries and kept writing checks, all willingly funded via their contract with PharmaCorp. RxMonitor wasn't about to put the brakes on its parent company's biggest release in decades and, instead of providing real oversight of the testing process, merely questioned those cases where negative results were reported. PharmaCorp, its figurative head firmly buried in the sand, had no interest whatsoever in questioning Jenner's results or RxMonitor's oversight.

With testing complete, PharmaCorp submitted its application for approval of Nextemol-4 to the FDA based on largely fraudulent test results. Hence, application fraud. Absent any awareness of wrongdoing, the FDA approved Nextemol-4 for distribution.

On its own, Nextemol-4 caused no harm. It simply did not work as an antibiotic to treat community-acquired pneumonia. Absent effective treatment, however, patients being prescribed Nextemol-4 started to die.

Gordon entered the picture with nothing more to go on than one doctor's complaint to the FDA that his community-acquired pneumonia patient, who he was treating with Nextemol-4, PharmaCorp's new wonder drug, had quite unexpectedly died.

Gordon's first investigative stop was the FDA's Center for Drug Evaluation and Research, which coordinated all drug manufacturers' requests for FDA approval. When Gordon explained he needed to speak with someone about the approval process of Nextemol-4, he was referred to the Office of New Drugs. To Gordon, that was the most appropriately named government office he had ever seen.

The director at the Office of New Drugs was knowledgeable, a bit salty, and liked to talk. He guided Gordon through the minutia of Nextemol-4's approval process and set him on a detailed and exhaustive investigative path, where Gordon discovered a spike in pneumonia deaths around the country. Examining the treatments of the deceased patients, he found that an excessive number of them had been treated with Nextemol-4. He interviewed nearly a hundred doctors with experience administering Nextemol-4. A startling number had already stopped using the drug because their patients were not responding to it. Some legal wrangling got him a subpoena for Jenner's doctor-participant records, and he started interviewing.

It did not take long to discover that many participating doctors had played fast and loose with their test results, but Gordon recognized the fraud did not start nor end with the doctors. Working his way backward through the testing phase, he found data that any legitimate analyst would have questioned. That led him to RxMonitor, where through "a dogged pursuit of justice," as US Attorney Jay put it, Gordon found an overseer who had actually questioned Jenner's results and raised concerns with PharmaCorp. That overseer had been reassigned and told to shut up.

It was a big case, with big dollars attached, and Gordon's work took it all the way to the top of PharmaCorp. Their new signature product did not work, and they had lied about it. People had died relying on Nextemol-4's ineffective treatment. Others would live because Gordon's investigation took Nextemol-4 off the market, allowing sick patients to use other, effective antibiotics.

Gordon's intense, process-driven focus was the driving force in the investigation. He could have stopped with a handful of doctors willing to sacrifice their integrity for $2,500 per patient, but he knew there was more at stake. In the end, fourteen doctors lost their licenses and went to prison. Jenner Testing was shuttered, and RxMonitor was absorbed back into PharmaCorp. PharmaCorp's CEO was forced to resign. The executive vice president who reassigned the RxMonitor whistleblower hanged himself while doing time at a Federal Prison Camp in Pensacola, Florida. PharmaCorp was issued several civil and criminal fines, and a pending class-action suit would cost the company hundreds of millions of dollars. PharmaCorp survived on the international stage, but its US operations were shut down. Whatever illusions the company had of joining the Big Pharma community vanished with Gordon's investigation.

Gordon, having checked all his investigatory boxes, put his files away and moved on to the next case. That is, until he got the call directly from US Attorney Wesley Jay that he had been selected to receive the US Attorney's Investigative Excellence Award. And now, he sat surrounded by people he did not know, well outside his comfort zone. Being here at all was uncomfortable. Being here as an award-winning focal point was beyond the pale. So, Gordon sat, sweating in his suit, staring down at his black Vans Authentic Core Classics. At least his feet were comfortable.

Gordon's right leg started rhythmically pumping up and down. He placed his right hand on his knee in an effort to stop the leg. Instead, his hand, seemingly with a mind of its own, began tapping the knee in sync with the pumping leg. Gordon sensed the inquisitive stares of the attendees on either side of him.

Instead of acknowledging them, he forced himself to think of Katherine, his therapist and rock. One of two people in the world, aside from his mother, who truly understood him. He and Katherine had planned for this, worked on this. “Start with Pokémon,” Katherine had said, a reference to the video game and its characters that Gordon had been obsessed with as a child.

Gordon began reciting names. “Abomasnow, Abra, Absol, Accelgor,” he mumbled to himself, an image of each character sprinting across his mind. “Aegislash, Aerodactyl, Aggron.” He closed his eyes. With each passing name, US Attorney Jay’s speech was further reduced to a muffled buzz. His pumping leg slowed and then stopped. His tapping hand followed. His mumbled recitation of Pokémon names went silent.

His lips continued to move ever so slightly, but the sound existed only in his head.

CHAPTER 3

Gordon's mother, Norma, found tremendous relief in Gordon's Asperger's diagnosis. She believed it likely his father, George, was also high-functioning autistic, albeit undiagnosed. She knew her son and husband were not abnormal, just different. They saw the world through a different lens, and she loved them all the more for it. Gordon's initial therapy was less treatment and more *how do we live with this*. At some point, the therapy slowed, then ultimately stopped. Norma, George, and Gordon were living with it, and that was that. In time, Gordon's parents developed a thorough understanding of his Asperger's. Norma, in particular, was insistent that any limitations resulting from his condition could, at a minimum, be stretched and potentially overcome. She looked no further than George to know what was possible.

George was a tenured college professor, and his accomplishments, despite his lack of normal social skills, helped Norma lay the foundation for Gordon to succeed. Education, and the associated process-driven environment to achieve each step along the way to becoming tenured college faculty, had allowed George to become a successful professor, meet and fall in love with Norma, have a family and create a life.

Gordon's parents encouraged him to pursue education with whatever intellectual vigor he was capable of. He would exist, survive, and even thrive in modern society regardless of Asperger's.

And indeed, Gordon proved to be a gifted student. He did not test off the charts, but when focused on a particular subject, Gordon typically found himself at the top of the intellectual heap. His favorite subject was chemistry, and he pursued a double major in college of chemistry and education, the assumption being that he would take up the family business and teach high school chemistry.

In the academic environment of college, Gordon thrived. Order was all around him—syllabi, reading lists, assignments, lab work. All necessary steps to achieve a chemistry degree and teacher's certification. It was high-level box checking and reflective of his approach to the world around him.

Where things fell apart for Gordon was the doing as opposed to the learning. Teaching required interaction. Part of his education curriculum was a semester of student teaching, a necessary prerequisite to his certification. For a week, he merely observed his cooperating teacher, his CT, but his observations left him troubled. High school students befuddled him. Their questions rarely made sense. They were frequently off topic. They often ignored the material covered in lecture. Many did not complete assignments on time. Gordon did not understand. It was simple: follow the process, complete the steps, check the box, move on.

CHAPTER 4

Ten Years Ago

The weekend before his second week of student teaching was a restless one for Gordon. In week two, he was scheduled to teach his first sophomore chemistry class under the watchful eye of his CT. He spent hours perfecting his lecture notes.

When he arrived at the chemistry classroom, something was wrong. His CT was not there. The assistant principal walked into the classroom behind Gordon. "Mr. Stone, there's been an accident," he said. Gordon's cooperating teacher had been T-boned in an intersection on his way to work that morning. He would be okay, but an extended hospital stay was expected. For the next couple of weeks, Gordon was on his own.

Gordon took his position behind the table at the front of the classroom as students trickled in. "Good morning," Gordon said. "I'll be teaching today's class." He looked down at the iPad he used to project class material onto the Prometheus Board behind him and dove into his lecture. It was fairly straightforward material introducing gases in chemistry—pressure, temperature units, Graham's law, molar volume, etc. Gordon excitedly got into the flow of his lecture. He was alive, everything made sense. He wondered if this was how his father felt when lecturing a captivated college class.

But this was not a college class. This was tenth grade. To

most of his students, chemistry was just a college-prep requirement. Where Gordon thrived in the process and order of chemistry, most of the class simply did not care. To the surprise of nobody except Gordon, the interruptions began three-and-a-half minutes into the lecture.

"What's a mole?"

"Who's Graham?"

And to a robust round of laughter, "Can I go to the bathroom? I'm feeling a little gassy."

When the bell finally rang, its tone signaled relief to Gordon. The lecture had been a disaster. With all the interruptions, he had never even gotten around to the lab portion of class. He shouted out tomorrow's homework as the students filed into the hallway. When the door shut behind the last student to exit, Gordon sat at his CT's desk, wondering how he was supposed to reach these kids. He did not know the answer, but he recognized a mounting fear building inside him that he had to do it all over again tomorrow.

Time slowed over the next two weeks as Gordon grew more and more disillusioned with teaching. High school had been bad enough when he was a student. "How could it be even worse now?" he asked himself. By the middle of the second week, he was wrecked. Student teaching simply was not working. All the things he held dear—processes, formulas, order—meant nothing to the class. He could not reach them, and the endless interruptions prevented him from ever completing a lecture.

During his last class, Gordon became aware of the growing commotion in front of him as the class's disinterest got the better of them. Their volume grew as they tuned Gordon out. Gordon kept going until he realized he had lost control of the class. He stopped talking. His right hand drifted from the tablet mid-formula, dropping lifelessly to his side. He approached his CT's desk and sat down. The commotion amongst the students continued. Gordon turned his chair to face the corner of the room, his back to the class, and stared at the wall. Unconsciously, he began pumping his right leg, up-and-down, up-and-down, faster and faster. His leg kept pumping right through the bell, and Gordon kept staring at the wall. That's how the assistant principal found him.

Gordon was twenty-two years old, about to graduate from college, and his teaching career was over before it had even begun.

In the aftermath, Norma shed a few tears but was undeterred in her quest for Gordon to live a good life. She now knew he would not be a teacher, but she did not know how to move on from this meltdown. She made calls, searched, asked questions, and found Dr. Katherine Anne Kewley, a clinical psychologist specializing in executive functioning and emotional intelligence.

Norma met with Katherine to discuss Gordon. When Norma described his Asperger's as a "condition," Katherine bristled.

"Mrs. Stone, I try—"

"Call me Norma, Doctor. I'm a middle-school teacher with a son about to graduate college who suffers from Asperger's. He'll be on his own soon, and he needs help. I want to be able to sleep at night knowing my son is okay."

"Norma it is, then. And please call me Katherine. First things first. I try not to refer to Asperger's as a condition or something a patient suffers from. Autism, in all its variations, is, medically speaking, a disorder. Frankly, I don't much care for that terminology either. All of it comes from a place where people who have Asperger's, or high-functioning autism, are not considered normal. That has a negative connotation regardless of how you define normal." Katherine paused, collecting her thoughts. "I call it Asperger's. It's not a condition. It's not abnormal. It's just different. I'm not going to cure your son. What I will do is help him recognize how he can better take care of himself in a world that sees things differently than he does. I will work with him to make him more comfortable with who he is so he can better self-manage his Asperger's and function in the world around him. If that's something you'd like me to explore with your son, then I will be happy to take him on and start him down that road."

Norma stared at Katherine, and a smile began to spread across her face. "When can I bring him in?" she asked.

CHAPTER 5

"Special Agent Gordon Stone." shouted US Attorney Jay.

"Fennekin, Feraligatr, Ferroseed, Ferrothorn," Gordon muttered.

"Agent Stone?"

Gordon paused as the question hung in the air. He took in the silence that had embraced the room. He was Gordon Stone. He. Was. Gordon. Stone. Why were they calling his name? What was happening?

Realization of where he was and why swept over him. The awards ceremony. His application fraud case, closed so many months ago. With only a distant memory of his pumping leg and tapping hand, Gordon, with some effort, reluctantly pulled himself out of his seat and made his way toward the stage with trepidation.

Gordon stood on the stage, not really hearing Jay describe the case or his investigation of it. He awkwardly managed a handshake with a polite nod as Jay presented him with a plaque recognizing his exceptional performance. Gordon fixated on the plaque and was only partially cognizant of several camera flashes as a photographer documented the presentation. The ornate plaque boasted a raised image of Lady Justice, blindfold on, scales in one raised hand and sword in the other, the sword tip resting at her feet. Something was wrong.

Lady Justice had become loose on Gordon's plaque, and she

stood at an odd angle, just a few degrees off center. With the camera flashing, Gordon reached down to his plaque, applied pressure and twisted her back into alignment. With a contented smile, he looked up. The photographer looked across the stage as the next award recipient made her way toward US Attorney Jay. A robust round of applause reached Gordon's ears, and with a gentle push from Jay on Gordon's shoulder, he nodded in acknowledgment and shuffled off the stage, returning to his seat.

Once back in his seat, Gordon shut his eyes and, with the slightest of head nods, continued his mantra: "Finneon, Flaaffy, Flabebe, Flapple..." The mantra worked its magic on his brain. He actually opened his eyes between Lampent and Landorus but kept going. There was no more leg pumping or hand tapping, but Gordon made it all the way to Passimien before the ceremony was over. And while the ceremony might be over, he would find little relief at the reception in the foyer outside the auditorium.

What he did find was a large waiter's tray loaded with bottled water on a stand. He grabbed a bottle and quickly retreated to a quiet corner. Unlike ten years ago when he'd melted down in front of a high school chemistry class, this time, Gordon sat facing the crowd. He took comfort from the corner at his back, and Katherine had taught him that facing the problem would help him deal with the problem. In this instance, simple observation of the growing crowd exiting the auditorium made him aware of his surroundings and his place within them.

Facing the crowd also allowed him to scan the sea of people in search of his boss, Assistant Special Agent in Charge, or ASAC, Peter McNeely.

Along with his mother and Katherine, McNeely was the only other person in the world who understood him. McNeely had been the first to recognize that Gordon's innate ability to focus on a particular subject and religiously stick to a process and methodology might provide him with the foundation to become a successful criminal investigator. And that had certainly panned out. More than anyone else, even Katherine, McNeely was responsible for Gordon being front-and-center today. Gordon smiled at the irony. He could certainly do without awards ceremonies, but McNeely knew his ways. He let Gordon be Gordon. He let Gordon work alone, but was always there when Gordon needed an assist or a different way of looking at a case. And more than once, McNeely had intervened to alleviate a situation where Gordon's intense, process-driven approach had rubbed prosecutors and other investigators the wrong way.

McNeely had a soft spot for Gordon. His own son died at a young age from childhood leukemia, and while McNeely had done the best he could with his son's short life, he knew well what it was like when the rest of the world looked upon someone differently. He was empathetic to Gordon's Asperger's and knew his particular characteristics were the superpower that made him a great agent.

Gordon continued to scan the room, trying to spot McNeely. Instead of his boss, however, his eye found Sophia Pressman. Pressman was a girl-next-door beauty with an edge sharpened through years of working the federal court beat for *The Washington Post*. Federal crime and national security were her specialty. He had met Sophia once before, early in the application fraud investigation. At the time, he ignored her reportorial advances. But he remembered her being nice and not pushy. She hadn't badgered him when he refused to comment on his investigation. And she was pretty.

His experience on that front was practically zero. Any relationship was difficult for him, but a romantic one seemed nearly impossible. He never dated in high school, and while he was studying at American University in Washington, DC, he had focused on his schoolwork. He had kissed a couple of girls—more accurately, they had kissed him—but it had never gone anywhere. He had been on a few dates since college, but they were not much fun. Like Katherine said, most people saw the world differently than Gordon. That was fine as far as he was concerned, but it did not help him at all when interacting with women.

Sophia caught Gordon staring at her and crossed the room to his corner. “Finally ready to talk to me, Agent Stone?” she asked.

He appreciated the directness of her question—no small talk here—but was unnerved by her rapid advance across the room. He had nothing against reporters, but he had not spoken to her during the investigation for two reasons. First, it would have been inappropriate to comment on an ongoing case. Second, and the real reason, was when he focused on an investigation, he really focused, to the exclusion of everything else. Sometimes when he fixated on a case, he would even forget to eat. It made him an exceptional investigator, but not a great interview subject for a reporter.

Smiling at Gordon’s fluster, Sophia saw US Attorney Jay out of the corner of her eye and deftly excused herself before Gordon got a single word out. Gordon stayed in his corner. He was not reciting Pokémon names anymore but remained somewhat flustered at all the day’s events. He sighed and exhaled as he raised his water bottle to take a drink. A tap on his shoulder caused him to jump, spin, and splash water on himself.

“Hey, boss,” Gordon said. “You startled me.”

“I can see that,” McNeely said, handing Gordon a napkin to dry himself off. Gordon patted down the front of his now wet shirt and thanked his ASAC for coming. “Wouldn’t miss it, Gordo,” McNeely said. “You earned it, even if you don’t really like being at these things.”

He hated when anyone called him Gordo. Anyone, that is, except McNeely. For some reason, when the large, barrel-chested, round-headed black man said it, it seemed right and okay, and Gordon did not mind in the least.

“Helluva job on this case, helluva job. I know you don’t like all this," McNeely said, gesturing around the room, "but you saved lives, and goddammit, I'm proud of you."

For the second time in less than two minutes, Gordon was surprised by McNeely when the big man stepped in close and gave him a hug. He was even more surprised when he found himself hugging back.

CHAPTER 6

As the two men separated, McNeely stepped back from the embrace, arms extended, hands grasping Gordon's shoulders. Gordon still wore a look of resigned bewilderment. McNeely gave Gordon's shoulders a firm squeeze. "Look at you," he said. "Special Agent Gordon Stone and a US Attorney's Award for Excellence." McNeely was smiling now. "You look like your dog just died, son. I know you hate these things, but you do understand this is a good thing, yes?"

Gordon focused on McNeely, looking him in the eye. "I do, boss. I just..." his voice drifted off.

"You just what? You just wish you could enjoy this. Ya' wish you could be nawwwwwwmal." McNeely dragged out the word, and a hint of a smile appeared on Gordon's face. "How many times do I have to explain it, Gordo?" McNeely waved a hand around the room before returning it to Gordon's shoulder. "This is fucking bullshit. This is a goddamn circle jerk with the fine folks of the EDVA," McNeely said, emphasizing every letter. "You know what's not bullshit? What's not a circle jerk?" After a pause, McNeely continued. "Come on, Gordo, say it with me."

"The work," they both said.

"Goddamn right," McNeely said, and with a final squeeze, released his grip on Gordon's shoulders. "Tell you what," McNeely added. "Why don't you take the rest of the day, maybe call your shrink. See if you can have a convo with her this afternoon."

"I was going to go back to the office," Gordon protested. "Do some of the work."

"Take the day, Gordon. Call the doc," McNeely said.

Gordon knew the conversation was over. "Will do, boss," he said as he turned to leave, reaching into his pocket to dig out his cell phone.

He was only a few steps away when McNeely called out. "Hey, Gordo." Gordon turned to look at his boss. "Congratulations, Agent Stone!" McNeely practically shouted. Gordon smiled and walked away.

In his car in the parking garage, Gordon dialed Katherine. Her machine answered and he left a message. "Hi, Katherine. It's ummmm, me. Gordon. I was wondering if you had any time this afternoon? You know, just a few minutes would be fine, not a whole session or anything. Anyway, I had that awards thing this morning. The room was packed, and everybody was looking at me, and there was this reporter, and I spilled water everywhere, and well…I got to the Ps, Katherine. Can't remember the last time I got to the Ps. Well, yes, I can. It was July, three years ago, when I—never mind. Anyway, if you've got a minute. Ummmm…my boss made me call."

He hung up, exasperated. He only met with Katherine monthly now, and his next appointment was twenty-two days away. He had not needed an unscheduled visit in years.

When Katherine got Gordon's message, she found time to see him despite her full schedule. He had been doing very well. So well, she was going to suggest cutting back to quarterly visits at their next session. She listened to his message a second time to make sure she heard it right. "He made it to the Ps," she said aloud in her office, shaking her head. Gordon had to be quite agitated to make it that far through the Pokémon characters.

Picking up the phone at her desk, she dialed Gordon. He picked up immediately, as he was still in the parking lot, sitting and waiting for Katherine's call.

"Hey, Gordon," Katherine said. "You okay?"

Gordon walked Katherine through the awards ceremony and everything that happened.

"Listen, Gordon. You made it through it all. You used the techniques we worked on, and you got through it. Sometimes it's going to be a little hard, with a few bumps. But you did it. You got through it. You survived." She let that sit with Gordon for a moment. "Listen, I've got some time this afternoon. Can you be here at two?"

"Yeah, I can be there. Thanks, Katherine. Just a few minutes."

"Sure, just a few minutes. I'll see you at two."

Gordon arrived at 1:55 p.m. and sat in the waiting area. At precisely two, the door to Katherine's office opened, and she greeted him with a warm smile. "Hey, Gordon, how are you?" Gordon knew this was not small talk. Katherine oozed sincerity, and when she asked, "How are you?" she well and truly meant it. Gordon thought she was very good at her job.

"I'm okay," he answered. "Still a bit rattled from earlier."

"Well, come on in. Let's chat."

Katherine ushered him into her office. A wooden desk sat beneath a window at the far end, with two formal chairs in front of the desk. He had not sat in either of those chairs since his first trip here after his student-teaching meltdown so many years ago. Back then, he was a scared twenty-two-year-old who had famously blown up any chance he had to follow in the academic footsteps of his parents. He could remember distinctly sitting in the chair on the left, rubbing his hands together and staring at his shoes. His mother had sat on the right and done all the talking. The conversation was a buzz in his ears. He could not have told you who Katherine was or what she looked like or what was said. He'd just nodded his head when Katherine asked, "Does that sound okay to you, Gordon?"

He'd started weekly visits that lasted for a long time. After a while, weekly turned to every other week, then monthly. He never sat in that formal chair again.

Just inside the doorway, a section of the office was arranged like a small living room. Two big, comfortable stuffed chairs on a thick, soft carpet. A small side table sat beside each chair, big enough for a cup of coffee or bottle of water. And lamps that were adjustable and could aim just the right amount of light at any particular spot. He did not know how it worked, but when he sat in the big stuffed chair and talked with Katherine, the rest of the office melted away and time flew. Their hour-long sessions—really fifty minutes, Gordon teased—always ended too soon for him. Sometimes, he felt like he could sit in that chair and talk with Katherine forever.

"Have a seat," Katherine said, motioning to one of the cushioned chairs. "You want some water?"

"Better not. Wouldn't want to spill it on you."

Katherine smiled as she turned to him. "Gordon Stone. Is that a joke? Are you making a joke about your episode today?"

Gordon blushed but did not respond. Only then did he realize he had, in fact, been making a joke. It was even a pretty good joke, he thought. *These chairs really are amazing.*

Katherine took her seat in the chair opposite his. "So, what's going on, Gordon? Tell me what happened."

Gordon walked her through his morning. The crowd, the award, the cameras, the US attorney, the leg pumping, hand tapping, and Pokémon recitation. He told her about the reception and about Sophia Pressman and ASAC McNeely, about spilling water and hugging his boss. When he was done, he was almost sweating.

"How do you feel about all that?" Katherine asked.

"I hate it," he answered. "I hate that I get so rattled by it all. I hate that I have to recite characters from a kid's video game just to cope and get through it. I hate that I can't talk to people.

I hate that my only friend is my boss. And I hate that I feel this way and that I'm never, ever not going to feel this way. I hate that I had to call you, that my boss gave me the afternoon off to do so." Gordon paused. "I hate all of it."

He looked up at Katherine. She saw a tear running down his cheek and handed him a tissue. "All of it? You hate *all* of it?" she asked.

He nodded.

"Huh," she said. "You know, you can't help how you feel. Right now, you feel bad because of the situation you were in. That's okay. It's okay to feel bad. None of these feelings are wrong. This is who you are. This is how you do it. And it's okay. Today, you *managed the situation.* You handled it. Was it a little rocky? Sure, so what? You're self-aware, Gordon. You know your Asperger's makes you who you are. And it's okay. We'll keep working, and you'll keep getting better at managing the situation."

Intellectually, Gordon understood all of this. Nevertheless, it frustrated him at a human level. If he was that smart and that self-aware, why was this still a problem? Why was he unable to overcome his differences and be comfortable interacting with high school kids, or receiving an award, or just making regular conversation with people?

"You know," he said, "I applied to the FBI once. I was twenty-eight. Got an interview, but they wouldn't take me. You know why? Because of this." He pointed to his head. "Because of the *differences* up here."

Katherine frowned at him, shaking her head. "Oooooh, the FBI. Think about that for a sec. Look where you are. A special agent with the FDA's Office of Criminal Investigations. An award-winning special agent, no less." Katherine paused to let him absorb her words. "Did you ever consider that maybe, just maybe, the reason you're where you are today is *because* your brain works differently? *Because* your focus and how you see the world drives you? *Because* your devotion to process allows you to see things others can't see?" Katherine paused again and lowered her voice. "Did you ever consider that maybe the FBI screwed up when they didn't hire you?"

Gordon managed a weak smile.

"Why were you at that ceremony today, Gordon?"

"To get an award."

"But why did you get the award?"

"For that fraud case. A company was selling a useless drug and people were dying."

"Okay, but why you? Why you, Gordon?"

"Because I figured it out."

"*You* figured it out. *You* solved the case. Why did you solve the case?"

"That's my job."

"Your job? C'mon, Gordon. I read the news. You're not writing parking tickets. You sent a bunch of bad people to prison and brought down a corrupt company that was killing people. How did you do that?"

He thought for a moment.

Katherine stared at him silently.

"I did the work."

"That's right," Katherine said, leaning forward in her chair. "You did the work. You did the work like hardly anyone else can do it. You were diligent, you were focused, you were smart, you were relentless. You wouldn't stop, *couldn't* stop, because you had to right a wrong. Gordon, that is who you are. The person who doesn't like crowds or attention or social settings is the same person, maybe the only person, who solves that case. You have high-functioning autism. Sometimes that's going to throw a hurdle or two in your way, and we're going to keep working on that. But look how far you've come. Think about it, Gordon."

Gordon sat quietly staring at Katherine. Slowly, he shut his eyes, remembering. Ten years ago, his mother first brought him to see Katherine. He came in every week, sitting in this exact chair. After a couple of months, his fog began to clear, and he started remembering his meltdown as a student teacher. Surprising himself, he was able to begin talking about it with Katherine—what happened, why it happened, and about how to manage it when it happened again.

Together, they came up with the calming technique of reciting the Pokémon characters' names. Gordon was shocked at how that simple trick worked to calm and relax him. It also made him smile. For a near-friendless boy with an active imagination, the characters were a pleasant childhood memory for him. Reciting their names was a warm and soothing exercise.

Three months into therapy, he and Katherine determined it was time for him to get a job. Academia was out, but Gordon's chemistry degree got him an entry-level position as an inspector at the Food and Drug Administration. Looking back, Gordon realized the job saved him. And changed his life forever.

CHAPTER 7

Nine and a Half Years Ago

Gordon thrived as an FDA inspector. His job was to ensure industry providers complied with the myriad of FDA rules and regulations governing the food and drug industry. Most found it thankless paper pushing. Gordon embraced it. He knew he was only checking boxes, but it was simple and process-driven. Top-to-bottom inspections of a food processing facility, reviews of corporate quality-control logs—methodical, detailed, mind-numbing work was his comfort zone.

It had not taken long for his co-workers to stop asking him to lunch or happy hour. Gordon wanted to interact, he wanted to socialize, but his student teaching experience was still fresh, and he was not yet prepared to fully engage with others. Of course, his colleagues did not know of his Asperger's. To them, Gordon quickly became "that guy." Kind of strange, just sat by himself doing the work.

On site visits, Gordon worked and worked and worked. He did not make mistakes or slow the team down. He would tackle whatever assignment was given, and if you needed help and were willing to ask, Gordon would do that work, too.

His first site inspection was three weeks into his FDA career. The inspection team traveled to the small Philadelphia suburb of Montgomeryville, about thirty miles north of the city, where they would inspect the Moyco Technologies Itch-Away Foot Powder production facility. Gordon's job was to confirm Moyco's quality assurance data. For Itch-Away Foot Powder, that meant confirming the test results recorded in Moyco's quality assurance ledger met FDA requirements.

Gordon sat in a conference room with his FDA manuals and checklists and examined Moyco's ledger. Its cover was discolored and worn from life in a lab, where it was exposed to spilled coffee as well as the variety of chemicals used to manufacture the powder. There was a bit more care taken when the ledger was open in the lab, as the hand-written test result data on the inside was the truly important part of the ledger. If that data failed to meet FDA requirements, Moyco could not sell its product.

Gordon was tasked with reviewing the last two years of test results. He went to work, applying a strict adherence to the requirements in the manuals. In his mind, a facility passed or it failed. There was no argument. There could be no argument. Follow the rules and you passed. If you did not follow the rules, you failed—period, paragraph, end of story. Gordon did not care which box he checked, as long as it was the right box according to the rules. It was the purest process he had seen since his days in the chemistry lab in college.

Gordon spent several hours going through two years of ledger entries. He examined the chemical composition of Itch-Away recorded in the ledger and verified it was within the FDA parameters for a safe and effective product.

Late in the afternoon, he closed the ledger and packed up his materials. His checklists were complete. Everything had been documented. He was done. Only then did he notice a Moyco executive pacing outside the conference room. Gordon picked up the ledger and left the room, handing the ledger to the executive. "You're all set," Gordon said. "See you in two years."

He never saw the relief that washed over the executive's face, as Gordon was already headed out of the building.

Two years later, right on schedule, Gordon was back in Montgomeryville, back in the conference room, once again checking Moyco's QA ledger to verify that the composition of Itch-Away Foot Powder was still within required FDA guidelines. This time, an executive secretary delivered two volumes of data for Gordon's review. He picked up Volume 2, noting its relatively pristine cover. It had not been in use in the lab long enough to be soiled by coffee and chemicals. He opened Volume 2 to verify the most recent quality assurance test numbers. The pages were crisp, still holding the familiar new-paper smell.

Gordon worked his way backward through Volume 2, finding that all the most recent tests were within requirements. He shut Volume 2 and grabbed Volume 1, its cover stained, abused and generally beat up. He began the verification of the data that had closed out Volume 1 after his previous inspection two years ago.

All the data checked out, but there was something that bothered him. Volume 1 did not seem right, even though everything was within FDA specifications. He went over the new data again, and then a third time. Everything checked out. Gordon rubbed his eyes. Why was this bothering him? What was he seeing? "You're checking boxes," he said to himself. "They either pass or they fail. You just check the box."

But Gordon was Gordon, so he re-opened Volume 1, flipping back to the old data he had confirmed on his first visit to Moyco. Yet again, the data was good to go, like it had been two years earlier. Everything pointed to Moyco Industries producing Itch-Away Foot Powder within FDA regulations.

He rubbed his eyes again. Maybe it was time to move on from the simplicity of this job. Maybe he was ready for that. Before wrapping up, and because it still nagged at him, Gordon made a photocopy of the data in Volume 1 that he had confirmed two years ago. He packed up his materials and made a mental note to talk to Katherine about finding a new job. He had been an FDA inspector for more than two years. Maybe it was time to move on.

The breakthrough did not occur until he was back at his cubicle in the FDA's Maryland office. The data was good. Moyco was in compliance. Gordon just had to sign and submit his report. Then it struck him.

The smell.

Gordon remembered opening Volume 2 and inhaling the new-paper smell. Volume 1, on the other hand, was not new, as its worn and stained cover could attest. Yet when he had opened Volume 1, those pages smelled the same as Volume 2; the same new-paper smell. But that did not make sense. The new-paper smell of Volume 1 should have faded over the years in concert with the wear and tear of the cover.

Gordon pulled out the copy of old data he had made today from Volume 1. That data should match the data in his report from two years ago. He pulled up his first report and compared the numbers. They did not match. Both sets of data were within FDA parameters, but they were different numbers. They should have been identical.

His pulse quickened as he realized there was only one reason the data did not match. Moyco was lying about the quality assurance test results and had created a new version of Volume 1 of their QA ledger. It still had the new-paper smell because it was new. They had banged up the cover for appearances, but it was not the same ledger he had examined two years ago.

Moyco had a ten-million-dollar contract with the Department of Defense to provide Itch-Away Foot Powder to US soldiers deployed around the world. If they stopped production, they would be in breach of contract and would not get paid. To preserve their government contract, and their corporate viability, they doctored their QA ledgers to show their tests met FDA requirements; requirements that ensured the buying public they were purchasing a product that worked.

When a lab tech recording faked results into Volume 1 managed to spill a solvent on it, destroying it, Moyco was in a bind. They bought a new ledger and "aged" the cover for appearances, then created new data that fit FDA requirements and filled in the new Volume 1. Moyco would keep producing the ineffective powder, keep creating fraudulent QA test results, maintain their FDA approval and, most importantly, keep their ten-million-dollar contract with the Department of Defense.

Gordon stared at the two-year-old report from the first Moyco inspection on his computer screen. He felt his heart rate tick up a few notches. He reconfirmed the data in the report did not match the data he had copied today from the new Volume 1. His heart rate increased a bit more. He stopped checking boxes and opened another window on his computer, pulling up the FDA Employee Home Page. He clicked open a map of the FDA's White Oak campus in Silver Spring, Maryland, a few miles north of DC. With his finger tracing a path on the computer screen, he found what he was looking for and launched out of his chair.

Gordon ran out of his office, down three flights of stairs. No chance he was waiting for an elevator. He ran out the door and across the sprawling lawn between his building and his destination. This was standard Gordon being Gordon. He'd found something wrong, and it had to be fixed. Right now.

With his head down, he pulled open the glass door at the entrance of the FDA's Office of Criminal Investigations, DC Field Division. Before he made it to the security desk, he crashed headlong into the largest man he had ever encountered, ending up on the ground in a daze.

Extending a large, meaty paw, Assistant Special Agent in Charge Peter McNeely helped Gordon to his feet. "Son," said McNeely, "you're in an awful big hurry. Anything I can help you with?"

After helping him up, McNeely invited Gordon upstairs to his office. He had to remove a stack of papers from the chair in front of his desk so Gordon could sit.

"Coffee? Water? Soda?" McNeely asked.

"No thanks," Gordon replied, already on the edge of his seat. He wanted to talk, needed to talk, right now.

"It's all right, son, tell me your name," McNeely said.

"Uhhh, I'm Gordon Stone. I work over in inspections. I need to tell you—"

"All right, all right." McNeely raised his hand, palm facing Gordon; a non-verbal cue to relax and slow down. "I'm Assistant Special Agent in Charge Peter McNeely with the FDA's Office of Criminal Investigations. Now first, tell me if anyone is in danger, is anyone hurt?"

"What?" Gordon looked perplexed. "No. What? No, nobody is hurt."

"Good, that's very good. Now then, Mr. Stone, we've got all the time in the world. Let's just take a breath and start at the beginning." McNeely's tone was soothing. His deep baritone voice had a calming influence. For the first time in several minutes, Gordon felt his heart rate slow. He told his story.

When he finished, McNeely looked at him, taking his measure. "Mr. Stone, that is quite a story. Tell me again why you were so troubled by your second inspection? You said yourself it met all FDA requirements. What made you go back and look at your first report?"

Gordon thought for a moment, looked McNeely directly in the eye, and said, "Sir, I—It wasn't really the data, not at first. The data was good. I checked all the boxes. It just..." Gordon paused. "It was a feeling. Then I realized it was the smell. The first volume of the ledger. The pages still smelled new."

In McNeely's line of work, they might have called it a hunch or a sixth sense, but a feeling was the same thing. All the best ones had it, that gift for knowing when to latch on to a case and see where it leads. This kid had it in spades. And he didn't even know it.

"Mr. Stone," McNeely said, "I'm going to jacket a case on Moyco Technologies and their Itch-Away Foot Powder. I don't usually investigate cases these days. I'm more of an overseer. But I like this case you've brought me, and I'm going to take the lead on it. It's not life-and-death, but it's a good case. And you're going to be my SME. Do you know what that is?" McNeely didn't wait for a response before he continued. "That's subject matter expert, and you're it. So, I'm going to need your help. Is that something you're interested in?"

"Y-Y-Yes, sir," said Gordon.

"Good. Who's your boss over there in inspections? I'll give him a call, make sure he can spare you."

It was the last day Gordon ever spent as an FDA inspector. McNeely's investigation turned into a ten-million-dollar fraud case and a six-month tryout for Gordon. OCI worked it jointly with the Defense Criminal Investigative Service, since the Defense Department was the primary victim of Moyco's fraud. It never went to court. Moyco was caught and ultimately agreed to settle the case.

As the case wrapped up, Gordon wondered what was next for him. He was certain it was time to move on, to see what was next. When McNeely asked if he might like to be a special agent and investigate fraud, Gordon could not say yes fast enough. A job as a criminal investigator with the FDA Office of Criminal Investigations? That was a dream come true.

At the center of that dream was ASAC Peter McNeely. Gordon had no way of knowing McNeely would become a mentor, teacher, big brother, father figure, even a friend. He could not know that McNeely would join Katherine and his mother as the only people Gordon trusted implicitly. What Gordon did know was that he would happily call McNeely his boss and could not wait to get started.

CHAPTER 8

A vibration in his pocket interrupted Gordon's trip down memory lane. He opened his eyes to find himself still in Katherine's office, still sitting comfortably in the big stuffed chair. "Look how far I've come," he said, more to himself than Katherine. He reached into his pocket and pulled out his vibrating cell phone. Work was calling, and in many ways, it was a welcome interruption.

Katherine allowed herself a quiet sigh and rolled her eyes, a reluctant approval for Gordon to answer the call. On the other end was McNeely. Gordon was needed in the office. Now.

"That's time anyway," Katherine said.

"Fifty minutes," said Gordon. "You can owe me the other ten."

Katherine laughed. "Two jokes in one session, Gordon. Very impressive."

Gordon smiled as he rose out of the comfort of the chair. "Thanks, Katherine. See you next time."

As he walked to the car, he caught himself whispering, "This is who I am. This is who I am."

CHAPTER 9

Frank Sharp paced in front of his desk. Observant onlookers would notice a well-worn path across the carpet there. Sharp, the Director of the FDA Office of Criminal Investigations, was not happy. In his right hand, he held his cell phone, only just disconnected from a call with the FBI. Sharp's left hand was multitasking. Between his index and middle finger, he squeezed the stem of his eyeglasses. He'd removed his glasses during the call so that his left hand's thumb and index finger could firmly pinch the bridge of his nose. It was Sharp's noble, yet futile, effort at beating back the spiking pain behind both eyes, which were now closed as he continued to pace.

"Sonuvabitch," Sharp muttered. "Sonuvabitch!" Shouting this time as he opened his eyes and threw the cell phone across his desk into the soft cushioning of his desk chair.

Sharp had been speaking with FBI Assistant Director of Counterterrorism Dan Pendleton, whom Sharp considered a condescending, arrogant prick. "Typical," Sharp said, sounding defeated. He put his glasses back on and stared at his closed office door. Just as he was about to shout for his office manager, he heard a knock.

Four knocks, actually—precise, solid, evenly spaced knocks.

"Come," Sharp said.

The door opened with purpose and Donna Sinclair marched straight to Sharp's desk. She placed a bottle of water on the desk and held out two Advil.

"Everything all right, Frank?" she said.

"Goddamn FBI." Frank took the Advil in his right hand and reached into his front pants pocket with his left.

"Language," said Donna with a smirk, holding out her hand.

"That one was on purpose," Sharp said, peeling a dollar from the money clip he pulled from his pocket. He handed it to Donna, then opened the bottle of water and swallowed the Advil.

"Counts just the same," Donna said.

"That was Pendleton over at Counterterrorism," Sharp began as he slumped into his desk chair. "He was calling to request"—Frank made air quotes with both hands—"twenty OCI agents for the JTTF. Twenty! Can you believe that?"

The Joint Terrorism Task Force was the FBI-led body created to combine the skill sets of all the nation's law enforcement into a single, ass-kicking, terrorism-busting, no-nonsense criminal investigations enterprise. In many respects it had worked. The JTTF enjoyed a solid track record of foiled terrorism plots, most of which had never been made public. In reality, it was task forces and not one single entity. While the task forces around the country were led by the FBI, whose assigned agents occupied the top tiers at any JTTF, they were staffed with investigators from other federal, state, and local law enforcement organizations from the particular region.

The first JTTF was born in New York City in 1980. It consisted of ten FBI special agents and ten New York Police Department detectives. The next twenty years saw slow growth in the concept. After the 9/11 attacks at the World Trade Center and the Pentagon, JTTF growth exploded to more than one hundred task forces around the country over the next decade.

Pendleton's request for twenty FDA-OCI agents could not be ignored. The formal request would go to the FDA commissioner, who would call Sharp directly to relay the request. He did not yet have an appropriate response for the commissioner, but twenty agents accounted for nearly ten percent of his investigative team. Sharp was angry. Turning twenty of his gun-toters over to the FBI would cripple his operational capability. The FBI had approximately 35,000 employees of which about 13,000 were special agents. Sharp had a handful more than two hundred. With them, his job was to keep the public safe from threats against the food and drug supply in the United States. Nobody in the general public had ever heard of FDA-OCI, and they were largely clueless that Sharp's little shop headquartered in suburban Maryland saved countless lives every year. But that did not matter to the FBI. The grand-freakin'-poohbahs of law enforcement had come calling, and Sharp had to play ball.

He looked at his office manager. Donna Sinclair was a vigorous seventy years of age. She had been at OCI since it was created in 1993, and as far as Sharp was concerned, she could run the place. She knew where the bodies were buried, and how to keep them buried. Sinclair was equally loved and feared, but above all, respected by the directors who had sat in Sharp's chair.

Sharp, like Peter McNeely, was a veteran US Secret Service agent when he left those prestigious ranks to come to the FDA. They'd both come at the request of the first OCI Director, Jim Pine, who had been their Special Agent in Charge at the Secret Service's Washington Field Office. Pine had come out of retirement to build the new OCI, and he'd recruited heavily from his old office.

Having grown tired of the topsy-turvy schedule demands of working a protective detail, both Sharp and McNeely sought a life that did not require them to have a "go-bag" packed and ready for imminent departure at all times. When Pine called, they both jumped at the chance to build something new and important at the FDA. Sinclair had been at Secret Service as well—a smart, knowledgeable secretary who always seemed to be there when Special Agent Sharp or Special Agent McNeely needed some help or guidance finding their way through the

Secret Service labyrinth. The US Secret Service was a sink-or-swim agency that could prove treacherous to young special agents. Sinclair had pulled both Sharp and McNeely from swirling waters on more than one occasion, and when Pine needed an office manager, Sharp and McNeely were quick to recommend Sinclair for the job.

"Senior staff," Sharp said, looking at Sinclair. "My office."

"Johnson and Pete too?" she asked. Steve Johnson was the Special Agent in Charge (SAC) of the OCI's Washington Field Office, located three floors below, and the immediate supervisor of ASAC Peter McNeely.

"Johnson, yes. McNeely, not yet. He hates this shit anyway."

Sinclair held out her hand again.

"Dammit." Sharp laughed, reaching into his pocket and peeling two more dollar bills from his money clip. "Those were *not* on purpose," he said.

With pursed lips and raised eyebrows, Sinclair took the money and said, "They'll be here in five." She did an about-face and retraced her steps out of Sharp's office.

With his senior staff, along with SAC Johnson, sitting around his conference table, Sharp explained the FBI's request of twenty OCI agents detailed to the FBI to support the JTTF.

"We can't give 'em twenty, and we can't just say no," Sharp said. "What are our options?"

"We've got to do our part," said Sharp's deputy director.

"Fuck 'em. Give 'em nothing," countered the assistant director in charge of Medical Devices Investigations.

The conversation went on for several minutes as the senior staff considered the impact of losing twenty agents to the JTTF. Sharp watched and listened. He knew they could not simply say "no" to the FBI. If they did and some whack-job, lone wolf managed to lace Tylenol with cyanide...well, that was a career-ender for everyone in the room. That had happened in 1982, before OCI was even an idea. Seven people died, and the age of secure, tamper-proof medicine packaging had begun in earnest.

If that happened now, word would leak from the FBI that they had tried to get FDA-OCI to support the JTTF to prevent the tragedy. *But OCI Director Frank Sharp wasn't interested.*

So, declining the request outright was not an option. But Sharp also knew he could not afford to give them twenty, or even five, of his investigators. He had his own mission requirements to think about, too. The conversation died out and the senior staff looked at Sharp.

He sighed. "All right. We'll give them one agent. Pendleton will wet his pants, but I can take the heat for that. I need a name or two from each of you on my desk tomorrow morning, and I'll pick one. And no problem children," Sharp emphasized. "Whoever the lucky winner is needs to be squared away. I'm giving them one guy, so it can't be a slouch. Questions?"

After a pause, SAC Johnson provided his first input of the entire meeting. "Why not give 'em Stone?" Sharp looked up, interested. "Stone is solid," Johnson said. "Hell of an investigator. He just won that award at EDVA. He's a bit of an oddball. Works alone, doesn't socialize. No one dislikes him, but no one really likes him either. Except Pete. Stone's always been kind of a pet project of Pete's. He'd be onboard though. It's actually an opportunity—go to work for F-B-One, the big boys at JTTF."

Sharp smiled. "Donna," he shouted.

"Yes, sir," answered Sinclair, magically appearing at the office door.

"Get McNeely up here, quick as you can."

Five minutes later, McNeely greeted Sinclair. "What's up, Ms. Donna? How are you today?" When Sinclair did not return his smile, McNeely got serious. "Uh-oh. Should I let myself in?" he asked, pointing to Sharp's office.

Sinclair bit her lip and nodded. "Go on in, he's waiting for you," she said. As McNeely reached for the door, Sinclair warned, "You're not going to like it, Pete."

McNeely paused, sighed, and without looking back, opened the door.

CHAPTER 10

It was another hot afternoon in the small Nigerian village of Ireti. Okunola Adeyami watched as his younger brother, Kambili, slid under the family truck, putting on the finishing touches to a new transmission. "Another new transmission," Oku noted. The old Toyota Land Cruiser had served the family well, but was overdue for retirement. Oku reminded himself to discuss buying a new truck next time he talked with his older brother, Jummal.

Jummal worked in the United States for a big food company. He made a lot of money and regularly sent some of it home. He'd been away for several years now, but Ireti remained Jummal's home. As the eldest son, he would one day inherit their father's title of Village Chief, and when that time came, Jummal would return.

In the meantime, Oku fulfilled Jummal's duties on the home front. That meant serving as his father's aide in all things. Oku did not mind. In fact, he embraced it. People in and around Ireti looked up to him and knew him to be a young man of influence with the chief. But Oku respected tradition and history too. Whenever he heard a whisper that perhaps he should become chief, he always—always—defended his elder brother's path. Jummal was the smartest of the three boys. Neither Oku nor Kam had any intention, or desire for that matter, to attend university, and certainly not as far away as the United States.

Kam was perfectly happy fixing things and had no shortage of work around Ireti. And Oku thoroughly enjoyed being his father's right-hand man. He loved being on the inside of the village's political theater.

Oku was a natural leader but did not suffer from the same wanderlust as his older brother. He would not mind visiting the United States one day, but living there, being educated there, making a life there—all of which Jummal had done—held little interest to Oku. One day, he would serve Jummal when Jummal became the chief. He would serve until Jummal had a son, who would replace Oku. Then he would retire, a village elder statesman, dispensing advice, opining on the comings and goings of Ireti, staying faithful to the Adeyami family and supporting Jummal and his son as they led the village.

But right now, he needed Kam to finish fixing the truck so he could drive their father to a morning meeting on the village outskirts. Someone had tried to divert a stream and managed to flood his neighbor's property. Threats had been issued, bloodshed was a real possibility, and the chief was needed.

"Hurry up, Kam," Oku said. "The chief waits for no one."

Kam slid from under the old truck. "He'll wait plenty when this transmission burns up. Did you talk to Jummal yet? It's time. This bucket will get you where you're going, but you may be walking home."

"I'll ask him next time he calls. Maybe Father will let us go to Lagos for a night and get him something new."

Kam climbed to his feet with a smile. Lagos was Nigeria's largest city, and Kam had not been there in years, certainly never unescorted. "You make that happen, brother, and I will personally come and get you when this bucket finally expires, wherever you are. Keys are in it."

"You'd better come get me anyway," Oku said, pointing at Kam with feigned irritation. "Father can walk back. He needs the exercise."

As Oku pronounced the last syllable, the air rushed from his lungs as he was lifted off the ground. Kam nearly collapsed in hysterics.

"Plenty of exercise carrying you around, tiny man," shouted the chief as he clenched his middle son in a bear hug and held him in the air. The chief was a large, powerfully built man with a personality that filled a room whenever he entered. Everyone in Ireti called him "Chief," and it was a sobriquet well-earned and respected. Chief had led his fellow villagers out of shacks and off of dirt floors. He inspired his people and was beloved, and not without reason. His little slice of Nigerian backcountry had electricity, modern plumbing, computers, internet, and basic infrastructure. Many families had a car or truck, and cell phones seemed to be showing up everywhere. Homes with concrete foundations had replaced huts and nobody went to bed hungry.

"Careful," said Oku with a smile, "you throw your back out again, and I'm taking over. Jummal will have to find another village to run."

"Ha!" laughed the chief, releasing Oku and setting him gently to the ground. "Soon enough, soon enough. But not today. Is this beast ready?" he asked Kam, looking at the truck.

"Best I can do. It doesn't have much left to give," Kam responded.

Squeezing his youngest son's shoulder, the chief said, "Well done, Kambili. Let's figure out what's next after dinner tonight." Looking at Oku, he asked, "You ready?"

"Yessir, let's go. See you tonight, Kam. And remember…" He paused, then whispered, "Lagos."

"Lagos," Kam repeated to himself, as his father and brother left a dusty trail behind them.

Ireti lay in the opposite direction. It was small—500 people—and humble. A plaza, where the community gathered on special occasions, doubled as a diminutive soccer field where a boys' team defended Ireti's pride on the weekends and all the village children learned the basics of the nation's favorite pastime. Surrounding the plaza were a handful of modest concrete block buildings. At the center stood the largest, which served as the municipal building, where the chief had his office.

But the newest and most modern building was the chief's pride and joy, not to mention his greatest accomplishment as leader of Ireti. A school. And not just any school, but a school for girls. Fifty of them and still growing. Girls of all ages and grades, and four full-time teachers. Any girl from Ireti was allowed to attend for free, and any girl from the surrounding villages was welcome for a small fee. Only a few years ago, an all-girls school in the middle of a remote Nigerian village would have been unheard of. For the most part, any sort of formal education for girls would have been unheard of.

But Chief Adeyami and his wife, Kikiogoluwa, changed all that. Because along with their three sons were two daughters, Abebi and Abiona.

Kiki stood only five-feet tall, but her spirit matched, and perhaps surpassed, the chief's outsized personality. She was a force of nature whose mission in life was to see all of her children, including the two girls, enjoy every opportunity to live full and meaningful lives. So, they built a school where girls could thrive and move beyond traditional village roles.

Their efforts in building up Ireti had already lifted the village out of the Nigerian backwater and transformed it to a place people were proud to call home, but they both knew Ireti's journey did not end with them. They wanted to ensure future generations of Ireti villagers were intelligent, worldly, and capable, and would have the wherewithal to maintain the shining light Ireti was becoming.

These ambitions took root in their decisions to send Jummal to college in the United States, to send their second oldest child, daughter Abebi, to the University of Nigeria across the country in Nsukka, and to build the new school so other young women could follow her there. Abebi was the first girl from Ireti to attend the University of Nigeria. If Kiki and Chief had their way, she would not be the last.

When Jummal graduated from Georgetown University in Washington, DC, he convinced his parents to let him stay in the United States to attend graduate school at the Darden School of Business at the University of Virginia, then beyond that, to stay and work professionally in the US business world, sending a healthy portion of his pay back home. Jummal began his career at Field-Town Foods, Inc., a large, Manhattan-based food brokerage. He started as an entry-level broker in the wholesale food industry, but his professional growth was rapid. Before he knew it, he had become a recognized leader in the organization, and a vice president known for his depth of knowledge of the wholesale food markets. He would come back to Ireti and assume the mantle of chief one day, but until then, there was much to learn, see, and do in the West.

Abebi's path was different. After receiving her degree and teacher's certificate, she came home and took great pride in her position on the faculty at the new all-girls school.

On this day, she was teaching fifth-grade math. As the girls settled into their seats, Abebi shared a smile with a precocious student in the front row—the youngest of the chief's family, her sister, ten-year-old Abiona.

Abebi was about to begin class when she was distracted by a long, guttural howl from a feral dog outside the classroom window. Looking out at the dog and into the street and plaza beyond, Abebi saw no activity. The dog appeared to be baying at nothing at all.

As she turned from the window, Abebi heard a faint, high-pitched whine, much like the sound from her hearing test during her annual physical at the national hospital in Abuja last year, a privilege she enjoyed as the chief's daughter.

As she made eye contact with her baby sister and prepared to begin the lesson, she sensed a vibration in the window behind her.

In an instant, they were gone.

Abebi, Abiona, the other students, the teachers, all turned to vapor, the school a pile of rubble burning in a sizable crater.

CHAPTER 11

Oku cursed at Kam under his breath. Not even halfway to their meeting, and the "new" transmission had blown with a bang. Not only would they have to walk home, but they would have to walk the rest of the way just to get to the meeting.

Except the Land Cruiser did not stop. It kept going. Oku took his foot off the accelerator and hit the brakes. He looked at the dash. Everything appeared to be in working order. He looked at his father. "What was that noise?" he asked.

The chief turned in the passenger seat and looked behind them. A tower of black smoke rose from an area he knew well—the village center. "Turn the truck around, Okunola."

Closer to Ireti's center, everyone saw or heard the explosion and headed toward the plaza. Shock and desperation filled the gathering crowd as the villagers tried to make sense of what happened. Parents succumbed to their worst fears, and more than one perished as they climbed into the burning crater in a selfless but hopeless attempt to find their daughters amidst the devastation.

Oku and the chief pulled into the plaza, finding chaos. Kam ran to the Land Cruiser. "It's gone, the school is gone," he shouted through the mayhem.

The chief stepped from the truck and grabbed Kam by the shoulders, squeezing tight. He stared at Kam until his youngest son calmed down. Oku ran from the other side of the truck.

The chief swallowed his initial shock while maintaining his grip on Kam, never breaking eye contact. When he spoke, it was to both his sons. "We need to get control of this and get those people away from the fire. Find your friends. Get them to help. We need to encircle the fire and keep people away. Go, now." The chief released Kam, and he ran off with Oku, instructions received.

Once his sons departed, the chief approached the fire, continuously barking orders to anyone who would listen. Duty prevented him from processing what happened; he needed to act. Forcibly pushed to the back of his mind was the recognition that his daughters were dead.

Through the course of several minutes, the chief and his sons, along with a small group of friends, managed to form a perimeter around ground zero. They tackled more than one grieving parent heading into the inferno and prevented other villagers from getting too close. The chief orbited the perimeter, in charge and seemingly in control.

Distracted by everything going on around him, he failed to see a piece of debris, tripped and stumbled to his knees. He placed his hands on the ground to push himself back to his feet. As he did so, he glanced to his side into the burning rubble that had been the school where one daughter worked and the other learned. In that instant, he acknowledged what he knew to be true—the daughters he loved were gone. The school he built for them was gone. All the young girls attending the school, Ireti's promise to the future, were gone. He sensed his mind giving way to unfathomable grief. He could not push it back anymore. Before he succumbed, he had one thing left to do.

He pulled a cell phone from his pocket and hit number one on his speed dial.

CHAPTER 12

Jummal Adeyami rose from his seat at the large table in the executive conference room of Field-Town Foods, Inc., in midtown Manhattan. As he strode purposefully to the front of the room, he could not help but smile and nod his head with a slight affirmation. Jummal was, by all accounts, financially and professionally successful. As a vice president at Field-Town Foods, he was in charge of the firm's wholesale food division. Not exactly a lion of Wall Street, but a long, long way from Ireti.

Jummal knew he had done very well for a son of a Nigerian village chief, but his place in the world remained unsettled. He'd come to the United States for an education at the age of seventeen, stretched his stay through college and graduate school, and now a career. But the call from Ireti was always there—sometimes buried deep, but always there—beckoning for Jummal to come home. It was his duty, his family responsibility as the oldest son of Chief and Kiki Adeyami, to one day assume the mantle of chief. But until that day came, Jummal would take Thoreau's advice and "suck out all the marrow of life" that he could find.

But while he was satisfied and reasonably happy, Jummal longed for more excitement than the wholesale food markets provided. Until he figured out what came next, however, Field-Town Foods allowed him to send a great deal of money back to

Ireti and provided him with an education in how American business really worked.

His job enmeshed him in the US food industry. He had learned much earning his college degrees, but Field-Town Foods had shown him how the system really worked—the secrets, shortcuts, and workarounds necessary for corporate survival. Jummal's food-industry network reached across the country. If a growth season resulted in excess broccoli production, he could set up sales with grocers from coast-to-coast in order to move that excess supply. He would both earn his commissions and direct the national rebalancing of broccoli's supply and demand.

As he guided his colleagues through a PowerPoint presentation, the phone in his coat pocket vibrated. He did not miss a beat in his presentation, but recognized it was unusual to get a call on his personal phone during the workday. Except, that is, from the endless stream of telemarketers that seemed to pursue him relentlessly. He wrapped up his presentation, and the phone vibrated again as he fielded questions from the senior staff. He had been thorough, so there were not many questions. After a few minutes, he was on his way back to his office.

The phone vibrated again, but he ignored it as he set the notes from his presentation on his desk. He removed his coat, hung it on the back of his desk chair, and stretched his arms toward the ceiling, relieving the built-up tension from the presentation. With a satisfied groan from his stretch, Jummal reached into his coat pocket and grabbed his phone. He placed it on the desk as he sat. "Let's see who was interrupting," he said.

He was surprised to see his father's number on caller ID. The chief never called him during work, only at home on the weekends. And there were no calls from telemarketers. All three calls had come from his father, and there was one voicemail message. Something was wrong. With trepidation, Jummal played the message from his father. It was short and frantic, and filled him with anxiety.

"Jummal, this is your father. There's been a terrible accident. Call me at once. We need you to come home."

He gently placed the phone down, shut his eyes, and put his head in his hands.

CHAPTER 13

Jummal lifted his head from his hands and stared at the wall. *Is this it for me? Am I to finally go home?* He shook his head with a modest admonishment. He understood his duty as the chief's eldest son. If the time to fulfill that obligation had come, then so be it. He would return and support his village.

Jummal looked at the phone. With a sigh, he picked it up and called his father back.

"Jummal, my brother," answered Kam, weariness in his voice.

"Kam, where's Father? What's going on?"

"Did you get his message?" Kam asked.

"I just heard it. Sorry, brother. I was in a meeting. What's happening? Why are you on Father's phone?"

"Jummal, listen. Father is okay. He's just...well, he's spent. We're all spent."

"What the hell is going on, Kam?"

There was a long pause on the line. "They're gone. The girls. Abebi and Abiona are dead."

Jummal stood at his desk. "What the hell are you talking about?"

Kam collected himself halfway around the world. "They're gone, Jummal. The school exploded. Abebi and Abiona were there."

"Dead?"

"Yes. Everything is gone. They're all dead. There's nothing left but a big—" Kam was cut off. Jummal could only hear a muffled conversation on the line. With the phone in his right hand pressed to his ear, he rubbed his temples with his left.

"Hello? Hello?" Jummal queried. He waited breathlessly until a voice returned.

"Jummal." Jummal recognized his father's baritone immediately. "It's time, my son," he said. "You need to come home."

CHAPTER 14

"The F-B-I." Gordon paused between each letter as he whispered to himself. Technically, he knew he was still an FDA-OCI agent. But the JTTF was an FBI owned-and-operated group using FBI processes and methodologies, all the leading-edge law enforcement hardware, and the FBI crime lab with access to every forensic tool that currently existed.

Others poked fun at the FBI, and the organization certainly had its eccentricities. There was an "FBI way" of doing things, they could be rigid in their processes, and they were just about the only cops left who wore coats and ties to kick down a door. But they were the F-B-I, the most sophisticated law enforcement organization the world had ever known. They had their own legendary training facility in Quantico, Virginia, and their resources were seemingly endless.

Gordon had applied to join the FBI a few years after he got his start with FDA-OCI, attracted to the FBI's rigid structure. The application process consisted of multiple phases, the first of which was a three-hour test in three parts. He sailed through the Logical Based Reasoning and Figural Reasoning portions of the examination. The third part, however, was a Personality Assessment. Gordon got through the personality assessment, but his Asperger's raised a red flag. Following the test, applicants engaged in a meet-and-greet with a single FBI special agent. He got through that as well, but the quirks associated with his Asperger's were noted by the interviewer.

Even with the anomalies that were noted, Gordon qualified for phase two of the application, but he was in the middle of the pack. Phase two included a writing assessment and a structured interview with three special agents. The writing assessment was child's play for him. He easily identified the pertinent areas of each presented hypothetical and was concise and fact-based in his written analysis. The structured interview, unfortunately, did not go nearly as well.

Gordon was a good interviewer at FDA-OCI, not because he had mastered any particular technique, but because his own authentic self, made him so. His was a methodical, straightforward, process-driven style, direct, but with no mastery of the subtleties of effective interviewing. He could not lie to a subject or be intentionally manipulative or threatening. He could assess the subject and the surrounding circumstances, but had trouble adjusting his tone and approach to best deal with those circumstances. He was unpolished and quirky, and subjects would often lower their guard, underestimating him. Most people he interviewed believed themselves to be smarter than Gordon, and that was their downfall. Because they did not perceive him as a threat, they would talk uninhibited, eventually implicating themselves. This was not intentional on Gordon's part, it was just who he was and how he was perceived.

But in phase two of his FBI application, Gordon did not ask the questions—the three special agents across the table did. While it was a structured interview and every applicant was asked the same set of questions, the anomalies from phase one of the process came up.

With the spotlight on him, Gordon attempted to explain his Asperger's. He sensed his dreamed-of future with the FBI slipping away, and could not stop himself as he tried to explain how his failed attempt at teaching lead him to therapy with Katherine and eventually to the FDA. He did not even notice when his foot started a rhythmic tapping on the floor.

His interviewers just nodded a lot and took notes. When it was over, they thanked him and each one shook Gordon's hand. But it was most definitely over. Gordon knew it before he left the building because he was not asked to schedule a physical fitness test, the last phase of the application process. The formal rejection letter came a week later. He was deemed "not qualified" to be an FBI special agent.

And while his current assignment to the JTTF was not the same as being hired by the FBI, at age thirty-three, it was probably as close as Gordon would get to the storied organization. He was thrilled, but anxious too. His track record as a criminal investigator had led to the JTTF opportunity, and he promised himself that his Asperger's would not get in the way.

The JTTF was a hard-charging task force staffed with FBI agents and seasoned law enforcement officers from across federal, state, and local governments. It was not a touchy-feely environment. The pressure was always on to bring results, and nobody extended a helping hand or a warm embrace to newbies. The JTTF's potential had always outpaced its actual results. JTTFs from around the country had scored some notable victories in their fight against terrorism, but still missed every now and then. When that happened, the collective JTTF could take a beating in the press and on Capitol Hill.

Gordon was assigned to the DC JTTF, hosted by the FBI's Washington Field Office. It was composed of several different groups, such as the International Group, where Gordon had been assigned, the Domestic Group, and the Cyber Group. No desk, computer, or phone waited for Gordon when he arrived, and his presence appeared to surprise everyone.

Armed only with his FDA-OCI badge and government-issued personal identity verification card, it took Gordon four phone calls and ninety minutes to get through security. Issued an unescorted visitor's badge once security figured out he was supposed to be there, he finally stepped through a magnetometer and was in. He smiled and allowed himself a brief instant to embrace the moment before acknowledging he still had no idea where to go or who to see. Losing the smile, he started to walk. He turned left down a long, narrow hallway. Like a mirage on the desert horizon, a crowd of dark-suited men and women appeared at the opposite end of the hallway. Gordon could tell these were agents, maybe his JTTF colleagues, and he wondered if they could point him in the right direction.

But the gaggle did not notice him. They were all talking, one or two into cell phones, the others to one another. They moved deliberately and with purpose, focused on the task at hand, ignorant of the new guy they were about to physically overwhelm in the narrow hall. Gordon recognized he would get no help from this mob and ducked into an open doorway to avoid being trampled. Inside, another dark-suited agent was talking with a receptionist sitting behind a counter. Sensing his presence, the agent turned to face him.

Gordon wore the same suit from the awards ceremony, which he had not cleaned and now included a heavy dose of wrinkles in the pants and jacket. The two men stared at each other. Gordon blinked first and lowered his eyes.

"Can I help you with something?" the man asked.

Unbeknownst to Gordon, he'd stumbled upon B.F. Dillon, ASAC of the Washington Field Office and overseer of the DC JTTF.

"It's my first day," Gordon mumbled.

"Speak up, son. I can't hear you."

"It's my first day," Gordon repeated. "I'm, ummm, not sure where to go."

"Jeeeesus. What scrap heap did they peel you from?"

Gordon awkwardly continued to stare at the ground. Finally, he said, "I'm from FDA-OCI. Just detailed here to the International Group."

"Wow," Dillon said, shaking his head. "You need to find your SSA, Sean Swayz. Head upstairs, end of the hallway on the left. He'll get you set up." Dillon turned back to the receptionist and resumed his conversation with her.

Gordon realized he had been dismissed and backed out of the doorway. The hallway was now empty, and he looked for the stairwell that would lead him to the International Group and his Supervisory Special Agent (SSA).

A sign with an arrow pointed him in the right direction—up the stairs, down the hall, last door on the left. Inside the International Group's suite, there was a bustle of activity. On the right, a receptionist's desk blocked the entrance to a corner office. In front of Gordon was a busy "cube farm" with twenty occupied desks. A walkway circled the perimeter of the cube farm, with two perpendicular cut-throughs dissecting its middle. To the left were a glass-walled conference room and two rooms with no windows. Interview rooms, thought Gordon.

Gordon reported to the receptionist, who escorted him to Swayz's corner office. Looking up from a thick stack of paper on his desk, Swayz gave Gordon a top-to-bottom once-over. While not as brusque as Dillon, Swayz was certainly less than impressed with what he saw. The two men shook hands and introduced themselves to one another.

"Well," said Swayz, "welcome aboard, Agent Stone. You're going to need a polygraph and security clearance upgrade before you can do anything, so get started on that today. Liz will set you up to get your Task Force Officer credentials," he said, nodding at the secretary standing in the doorway. Speaking to Liz directly, Swayz added, "Have Joe set him up on the range." Turning back to Gordon, Swayz said, "You'll need to re-qualify. Still have your firearm from...where are you coming from, Stone?"

"FDA, sir. Office of Criminal Investigations."

"FDA huh? You carry a firearm at FDA?" There was a hint of mockery in Swayz's tone.

"Yes, sir," Gordon answered, not noticing the slight.

"Good, what is it?"

"Switched to Glocks three years, seven months ago."

"All Glocks, all the time," said Swayz. "I kept my Sig when we made the switch," he added, referring to his Sig Sauer P226 with some arrogance. "Privilege of rank, I suppose."

Gordon had only ever pulled his firearm while executing search warrants over the years. He had never actually pointed it at anything other than a target on a gun range. He carried a weapon because he was told to, but he did not consider it an essential tool. And he could not have cared less if it was a Glock, a Sig Sauer, a Smith & Wesson, or any other manufacturer. But he also knew that was just him and many agents had stronger feelings about their particular firearms. Swayz was apparently one of them. Gordon tried to connect with Swayz on that very point.

"Yes, sir. I liked my Sig Sauer, but they wouldn't let us keep them when we changed vendors," Gordon said.

Swayz gave a knowing nod. "Slaves to the bureaucracy, Agent Stone. Poly's in the basement. When they're done, they'll send you to security to start processing your clearance. That may take a month or two, but we'll get you to work supporting some ongoing cases. We're full up at the moment, so we'll set you up in one of the interview rooms. Once there's an opening, you'll get a cube in the bullpen. May take a while." With that, Swayz returned to his paperwork.

Gordon stood. "Thanks, sir. I'm looking forward to working here."

"Yep. Welcome aboard. Glad to have you with us," Swayz said without looking up.

Gordon stopped at Liz's desk on the way out. He made arrangements to get his new TFO credential and reserved time on the gun range. Invigorated, he left the International Group's suite in search of the basement and the polygrapher.

CHAPTER 15

Weeks of torturous waiting followed Gordon's eventful first day. He had passed his polygraph, and his security clearance upgrade from Top Secret to Top Secret/Sensitive Compartmented Information (TS/SCI)—a requirement for anyone working on a JTTF—was being processed. He could not do much substantive work, certainly not on his own cases, before his TS/SCI came through. Instead, he was stuck working in support of other agents' cases. No one in the International Group had been reassigned yet, so he remained stuck in one of the suite's interview rooms. He did not mind being alone, but he hated doing grunt work in a support role.

The International Group kept itself busy, so the interview rooms got a lot of use. Gordon frequently found himself packing up and moving out to make way for someone's ongoing investigation. In those instances, and with nowhere else to go, he retreated to the basement. He had noticed an old break room a few doors down from the polygrapher on his first day. The vending machines and microwave were long gone, and all that remained was a cafeteria table and a couple of chairs. That was fine with him. The room was quiet and solitary, his immediate needs met.

As usual, Gordon did not quite click with his new colleagues. He did not really fit in and was not getting to know anyone particularly well. He went to lunch with the group a few times early on, but skipped the happy hours. Eventually, as always, the lunch invitations stopped coming and Gordon ate alone. He wished it could be different, but this was familiar territory at least, and he was comfortable by himself.

While unperturbed by the social aspect of his new job, Gordon grew increasingly anxious about the actual work. Days and weeks were slow and tedious since he did not have his own cases. His supporting work for his colleagues was uninteresting and unsatisfying. More and more as time ground ever forward, Gordon found himself in his secluded basement break room, even when the interview rooms in the suite were not needed. He had found his retreat, his safe zone, his corner.

And there he waited, comfortable where he sat but desperate to get out. "This will all change," he told himself, "once my clearance comes through and I get my first case."

CHAPTER 16

Jummal sat stoically at his desk, rehashing the morning's events. Abebi and Abiona...dead? It did not seem real. His sisters were dead? Any remaining thoughts about his presentation to the senior staff were long gone. He stared at the phone, remembering something his brother said about the school exploding. That did not make any sense. *Schools don't just explode,* Jummal thought.

A wave of grief crashed over him. Abebi and Abiona were dead. It was true. Kam said it, and Jummal knew it was true. Abebi, in every sense his peer and his equal. Not only his sister, but a woman he admired and looked up to. And Abiona, the family's precious jewel. The last to arrive and the sweetest thing he knew to exist on this earth. Both gone. Jummal sat silently for several minutes, oblivious to the tears flowing freely down both cheeks.

When the tears finally stopped and dried, leaving only a salty residue, Jummal signed on to his computer and booked a flight home to Nigeria. He stood, rubbed his eyes, and gathered himself. He walked down the corridor to the corner office of Buddy Harris, his boss. Bypassing Harris's assistant, Jummal rapped on the closed door and, without waiting for a response, let himself in. Harris was on the phone.

"All right, good. Hey, let me call you back. I've got someone in my office," he said, hanging up the phone. "Jummal, great job this morning." He looked up and saw Jummal for the first time, noticing something was off. "Everything okay? You look a little flushed."

"No. I'm sorry...no," was all Jummal could manage.

"Hey, hey, partner. Come in, have a seat. Talk to me. What's going on?"

Jummal sat. He hesitated, collecting himself again. Saying it made it all real and true, and Jummal could not get the words out. Instead, he shook his head and looked down. A few remaining tears appeared.

"Whoa, Jummal?" said Harris, coming from behind his desk and putting a hand on Jummal's shoulder. He passed Jummal a tissue with his other hand. "You okay, big fella?"

Jummal looked up into his Harris's eyes. "They're gone. An accident...an explosion." He took a deep breath and exhaled. "My sisters in Nigeria. They're dead."

Harris squeezed Jummal's shoulder and sat on the edge of his desk. "Jesus," he whispered. "My God, Jummal. I'm so sorry."

The moment lingered in silence between the two men. Finally, Harris spoke. "Tell me what you need."

"I have to go home."

"Yes, of course. We'll get it set up. When do you need to go?"

"I'm already booked on the 1:00 a.m. flight tonight."

"Good, good. Listen, take all the time you need. Go home. Take care of your family. Take care of yourself, Jummal. When you're ready, you call me, okay?"

Jummal nodded.

"My God, Jummal, I'm so sorry to hear this. Just go. Don't worry about work, don't worry about time away. Just focus on your family. We'll figure out the rest later."

"Thank you," Jummal mumbled, rising from his seat.

"You okay to get home?"

Jummal nodded. Looking up, he said, "Thanks, Buddy, I really appreciate this."

"Don't worry about it. Go take care of your family. Call if you need anything—ride to the airport, anything, okay?"

Jummal nodded again. "I'll call in a week or two when this is sorted."

"No problem. Take whatever time you need," Harris said. He put his arm around Jummal and walked him back to his office, where Jummal gathered his things.

"Did you take the train in this morning?" he asked.

Jummal nodded.

"Let me get a car to take you home."

With the ride ordered, Harris took the elevator down with Jummal and waited with him on the curb. The car arrived and the two men shook hands.

"Take good care, Jummal," Harris said.

"Thanks, Buddy," Jummal said, climbing into the car. The two nodded at one another as the car pulled away.

Jummal's mind wandered during the ride. He was going home to Ireti to take his place by his father's side. He knew he would have to come back to the United States to close out his personal affairs and clean out his apartment, but was that it? Was he really returning to Ireti forever? *I'm not ready.* In his heart, he knew he would never be ready. But he also knew that was not his choice. He respected his family and his village. Ireti was in his soul. Whether the time was now or ten years from now, his destiny was settled. He would be Ireti's next chief.

CHAPTER 17

Two six-hour flights, separated by a seven-hour layover at London's Heathrow Airport, had been somber for Jummal. His typical *joie de vivre* had been ripped away. He ate and slept little and spent most of both flights staring out the window into the void.

His father and brother Oku met Jummal at Murtala Muhammed International Airport in Lagos. The Toyota Land Cruiser Jummal had helped the family purchase with his first bonus check from Field-Town Foods was showing some wear. Understandable, as it already had more than 100,000 kilometers on it when Jummal bought it.

Oku saw Jummal looking at the old truck. "Might be time for a new one. Kam keeps it running, but it owes us nothing." Oku drove, their father up front in the passenger seat. Jummal had the back seat to himself. He fought off the jet lag and perched in the middle of the seat on its front edge, his head partially crossing the plane into the front cab. Oku focused on the four-hour drive back to Ireti while their father shared what he knew.

He described the explosion and the destruction of the school, and the horrors of the aftermath. His father seemed to age before Jummal's eyes as he shared the story of the devastation in the village, the life draining from him with every word. His eyes welled with tears as he mumbled, "At least they didn't suffer," referring not just to his daughters, but to all the girls and staff at the school he'd built. He collected himself. "I'm glad you're home, son," he said. "We need you now more than ever."

Jummal gave his father a slight nod and sat back in his seat. The information overwhelmed him. In shock, saddened, and resigned to his fate, he felt himself fade and finally succumb to his exhaustion.

He woke with a start, his heart racing as Oku pulled up to the site of the devastation. Kam was there, opening the chief's door first, then Jummal's. The brothers shared a long embrace as dusk settled over Ireti.

"Come, Jummal," their father interrupted. He guided Jummal to the edge of the still-smoldering crater where the school once stood. Villagers who had gathered to mourn gave them room, with deferential nods to the chief and his eldest son.

Looking into the abyss, Jummal summoned tears he had not believed he had left.

"Let's walk, Jummal," the chief said, grasping Jummal's arm at the elbow.

As they slowly walked around the perimeter of the crater, Oku assumed a position behind his father and older brother. Oku's place was no longer by his father's side, and he willingly gave way to Jummal. *As it should be,* Oku thought.

Jummal took it all in. Being here brought home with force that he would never see his sisters again. He recorded the scene in his mind. The finality of it triggered something deep inside of Jummal. This was his home. These were his people. He was their future chief.

As they walked, his father spoke of expectations for Jummal, and of the eventual transition of the chief's authority to him. Jummal feigned rapt attention, a trick he learned from endless meetings in corporate America. He nodded in all the right places and mumbled appropriate affirmations when he sensed a pause in his father's monologue. But his focus was on the simmering crater. Palpable heat came out of the hole in waves, as if the dead were reaching out to the living from under the broken concrete and ash. He listened and heard his father, but his focus was internal. *What's next?* he thought. *For me? For Ireti? What's next?*

Jummal shivered and turned to his father. "A funeral," he said, interrupting.

"What?" asked the chief, caught off guard.

"We have to have a funeral. For Abiona and Abebi…for all of them," Jummal said, looking into the crater.

"Of course, son. That will come." The chief looked perplexed, unclear about Jummal's meaning.

Jummal turned back to his father. "We will mark this day, Father," he said, tears welling yet again. "We will mark this day and we will remember it forever. Remember *them* forever," he said, his voice rising as he turned back to face the crater. "A piece of Ireti's soul has been taken from us. It is our worst day." Jummal was almost shouting now, facing the crater as though the dead could hear him. "But it will bring out the best in all of us, in all of Ireti," he said, turning back to his father, his chief.

Oku stared wide-eyed at Jummal. "Yes, brother," he said with unhidden pride.

"We will honor them, Father," Jummal continued. "Abebi, Abiona, all of them. We will honor them and mark this day."

The chief stood silently, staring intently at Jummal. He was beaming. There was even a hint of a smile. "Yes, son. A funeral," was all he could muster. Then, after a pause, he said to his sons, "Let's go home."

"Just a few more minutes," said Jummal. He stepped off on his own, approaching the gathered villagers. Some he recognized and exchanged brief greetings with. To others, he offered a warm nod and a comforting touch on the arm or shoulder in silence. This was Jummal's destiny—these people, this village. It was a sacred moment on newly sacred ground.

When they finally arrived home, Jummal shared an extended

hug with his mother. Like the chief, Kiki seemed to have aged significantly. She was visibly tired, but Jummal still saw the familiar twinkle in her eye. The spirit there was alive.

When the two finally parted, the chief stepped in and hugged his wife. "Our son is ready," he whispered in Kiki's ear. "He's going to heal Ireti."

CHAPTER 18

Over the next several days, Jummal and his mother worked side-by-side making arrangements for a mass funeral and burial ceremony. The service took place in the village square. The typical Nigerian service—a festival-like atmosphere with music and dancing—was subdued, given the crater just a few hundred feet away still smoldered in some spots. There were many prayers, representing Nigerians of both Christian and Muslim faiths.

The burial itself was a sight to see. Following the service, the victims' families led all in attendance in a silent procession around the crater. When they reached the back side, the furthest point away from the square, the chief and Jummal greeted them. The two were dressed in wide-sleeved funerial robes. Intricate and colorful embroidery wound its way around the sleeves and across the chests of their robes. They stood in front of a darkly stained and highly polished wooden cart festooned with bright flowers and loaded with clay urns. The round urns rose to narrow necks before opening wide at the top.

The night before, Kam and Oku had climbed down into the crater, loading the urns with ash from the ruins. There had been no bodies, no remains, to recover, but the ash was symbolic, representing the remains of the departed. They filled an urn for each victim and loaded them onto the decorated cart. Now, the chief and Jummal passed out urns to victims' surviving families. When they were finished, two remained. Jummal lifted one from the cart and raised it to the heavens before kissing the side of the urn and passing it to his mother. "Abebi," he whispered.

The chief joined Kiki in the procession, and Jummal lifted the last urn to the sky, kissed its side, and passed it to his father. "Abiona," he said with tears in his eyes. The chief cradled the urn in his arms, weeping at the memory of his precious baby girl.

Jummal took his place at his father's right side and followed the families back around the crater to the square, where a crowd encircled a roped-off area. The victims' families were escorted inside the enclosure. At its center, a shallow, two-meter square hole had been dug in the earth.

After a brief service representing both Christian and Muslim faiths, the chief and Kiki approached the hole. The chief hesitated, tightening his grip on Abiona's urn. The words would not come. He looked up at Jummal, eyes glistening, and shook his head. Jummal understood and stepped forward.

"My friends," Jummal shouted to be heard by all in the square. "My friends, we gather today to remember who we have lost. And most importantly, to never forget them, what they meant to us, and what they meant to Ireti. They were—" His voice caught. He collected himself and continued. "They were everything. We remember them, today and forever, as we lay the foundation for a new Ireti, marking this day. Our village square becomes Memorial Square. Let us never forget what we have lost."

Jummal turned and nodded to his father.

The chief walked to the side of the hole, raised Abiona's urn to his lips, and kissed it softly. "Precious child!" he cried out as he turned the urn over, dumping the ash into the hole. The chief fell to one knee. Kam and Oku rushed to his aid, while Jummal tended to Kiki. The chief recovered and was lifted to his feet by his two youngest sons. Kiki took her turn at the side of the hole, raising Abebi's urn. She looked up and whispered, "My darling girl." She turned Abebi's urn and sprinkled the ash into the ground.

Each family took their turn saying goodbye to loved ones, sprinkling the symbolic ash into the hole. Next, the villagers were allowed into the enclosure, and those who wished laid flowers atop the collected ashes. By the end of the ceremony, the hole had become a mound of colorful petals, as beautiful as it was tragic. The crowd dispersed, retiring to homes to honor those lost in their individual ways. Some had parties, some mourned somberly. Many stories were shared, and many more tears were shed.

The night Jummal had come home, he asked his mother how to have a funeral for an entire village. She had no idea, but knew they would figure it out. Now, at home after the ceremony, he hugged his mother. After a moment, he pulled away partially and gripped her shoulders. "We marked the day, Mother. We honored them all."

Kiki reached up and placed her hands on her son's cheeks. She gently pulled him down and kissed his forehead. Then, looking Jummal square in the eyes, she smiled. Her eyes twinkled. "You will be a great chief, my son." Kiki hugged her eldest once more before she said goodnight and went to bed. The chief was already asleep.

Jummal went outside and around to the side of the house. Kam and Oku were waiting for him, sitting at an old wooden picnic table in the dark. The chief allowed beer in his house, in moderation, and Kam pulled cold Star Lagers from a cooler, passing one to each brother. He held his bottle out to his brothers, who followed suit and clinked the bottle necks together.

"Abebi and Abiona," Kam said.

"Forever," added Oku.

The brothers took long drafts from their bottles. Jummal let out a refreshed sigh and looked at his brothers. *I'm right where I'm supposed to be.*

"Now then," he said. "Let's figure out what happened."

CHAPTER 19

The Africa desk at *The Washington Post* was a buzz of activity surrounding the total destruction of a small girls' school in Ireti, Nigeria. When the story first came across the wires, it did not attract much attention. Disasters in Africa were, sadly, not all that uncommon, and an explosion in a backwater village no one had ever heard of, while tragic for the loss of life, did not capture world-wide attention beyond a day or two. The working assumption was a natural gas explosion or some sort of industrial catastrophe.

That changed when pictures of the site started to appear. There was nothing left but a huge crater and smoking debris. Gas explosions were bad, but this was wholesale, targeted devastation with no survivors. All any witness could say was that they heard a huge explosion, felt the earth shake, and when they arrived at the scene, the school and its occupants were gone, vaporized, leaving a burning crater and little else.

As photographs of the site began their viral infection across the internet, it did not take long for the realization this was a military attack to take root. Stories first appeared in the little-read blogs, then the second-tier news sites, and finally the mainstream media. Experts appeared on news programs describing the types of weapons that could cause such destruction, the potential delivery mechanisms, and who across the globe had such capabilities.

Any notion of terrorism was quickly dismissed. Terrorists might strap C-4 to their chests and run into a city bus station, but none had the capability, nor motivation, to carry out the type of mission that caused the devastation in Ireti. Only a government would possess such capability. But why would any government destroy a small girls' school in the middle of nowhere?

CHAPTER 20

Jummal enjoyed the time spent with his brothers. It had been years since they had spent this much time together. There was implicit trust among the three, and Oku and Kam guided Jummal on his return to village life, with Oku catching him up on the inner workings of Ireti.

This time was essential, Jummal knew, in order for him to successfully take over for his father one day. There was a pace and beat to village life, and Jummal had to re-familiarize himself with the comings and goings of Ireti. It had all happened so fast, but here he was, back home, spending time with family and apprenticing as the village's next chief. Oku would one day serve as his right hand, and Kam as a trusted advisor. They would have a say in Ireti's future, but Jummal would be the decision maker, the chief.

Jummal could do it, could be chief, but in his heart of hearts he knew Oku was the better brother for the job. While Jummal had been getting his education and earning a living in the United States, Oku had assumed his position by their father's side, watching and learning how to manage a thriving Nigerian village. Jummal admired his brother's strength of character, his charisma, his leadership. Oku was a natural. But for the twist of fate that made Jummal the firstborn, Oku would have made an exceptional successor to their father. That was the example Jummal had to live up to, surpass even. It was not at all clear to him he could do so.

The brothers kept themselves busy during the days following the funeral. There was much work to do in a village still grieving from unspeakable loss. But at night, after dinner, after their parents had retired for the evening, the brothers continued their ritual of gathering at the old picnic table. They might have a beer or two, or they might not. It was fellowship, brotherhood, and family. Every night, the conversation inevitably turned to their sisters and the school. Still, no one knew what happened and speculation was rampant. They questioned if Boko Haram could have wrought this wanton destruction on their family and their village.

Boko Haram had attacked Nigeria before, with young girls a frequent target. But this was not their style. They kidnapped girls for their nefarious purposes, but just killing them for no apparent reason? And on such a scale? That did not make sense. Could it be an attack on their father's progressive views on the place and education of women and girls in the village? Could their remote village have risen so much in stature that it had drawn Boko Haram's ire? The terrorist group had certainly not said so.

Those same progressive views had been responsible for lifting Ireti from being yet another backwater Nigerian village and connecting it with the rest of the world. The chief's leadership led the village from the relative Dark Ages and into their own Enlightenment. Ireti would always be a remote Nigerian village, but for a long time, before technology had spread across Nigeria's outlying areas, if you lived in the region and needed to make a phone call, you came to Ireti. If you needed to look something up on the internet, you came to Ireti. Such connectivity had become more common in Nigeria's remote communities, but Ireti had been first. And that was because several years ago, on a trip to Lagos, the chief had stepped into a store with a sign that read "MTN South Africa." For over an hour and through his sheer force of will, the chief engaged a clerk to teach him all he knew about cell phones, cell towers, the internet, and wireless connectivity. One thing led to another, and before long, MTN South Africa built its first cell tower outside of a Nigerian metropolis on the outskirts of Ireti. It connected the village to the rest of the world, and was MTN South Africa's first step toward becoming Nigeria's leading internet and cell phone service provider.

Every evening after saying goodnight to his brothers, Jummal, who had grown used to near-constant internet access while in the United States, would scour the Web searching news sites from around the world and reading blogs, hoping for answers. The Nigerian government had proven essentially useless and of no help whatsoever beyond a brief statement of a possible "gas explosion."

It was that same internet access that prompted more than one villager to post pictures of the site, which of course went viral overnight. This did not escape the notice of Boko Haram's leader, Abubakar Shekau. The entire world would soon see what happened in Ireti and would want to know who was responsible.

"Push the story," Shekau ordered his deputy, Mahmud Adamu. "Your brilliant plan is working, Mahmud."

Adamu logged onto his laptop and began the next phase of his plan. He sent emails, posted on social media, wrote comments in blogs. He even used some of the pictures of the crater that were exploding across the internet. Hundreds of emails, postings, and comments that were unattributed to Boko Haram or anyone else. But they all asked the same question: Why was America attacking Nigeria? Soon, expert analysts popped up seemingly everywhere speculating the United States military was responsible, for who else could wreak such targeted devastation. The world was rapidly coming to the conclusion the United States was responsible for the destruction of the girls' school in

Ireti, and the United States was not denying it. Boko Haram's plan to discredit the US military presence in Nigeria was working better than they could have possibly hoped.

The pictures seemingly confirmed the stories. Even the untrained eye could recognize this was not gas or some sort of industrial accident. That the United States was neither confirming nor denying responsibility did not matter. The beast that was the 24/7 news cycle had to be fed. "Why is the American military in Nigeria?" "Why is the US dropping bombs on its primary African ally?" "Was this a manned mission?" "Was a drone used?" "Were ground troops involved?" And on and on.

Jummal witnessed all of this unfold as he surfed the Web each night. *The Americans?* he thought. *It can't be.* In an instant, Jummal was proven wrong.

In Washington, DC, the apple cart tipped. Whatever misguided hope the Pentagon had that the story would die a quiet death disappeared when the photos appeared and the story spiked. The longer the Department of Defense tried to ride this out, the worse it would get. In the Pentagon press room, the Department's Public Affairs Officer read a statement:

> *"At this time, the Department of Defense is investigating a possible mishap that led to the destruction of a small school in the village of Ireti in Nigeria. We are cooperating with Nigerian officials and ask that all Americans keep their thoughts and prayers with the victims in Ireti. We do not believe this incident to be a result of terrorism or terrorist activity in the region. Upon conclusive investigative results, appropriate action will be taken against those responsible. The United States and Nigeria share a long history of promoting democracy and freedom in this part*

> *of the world. Those shared sentiments continue and will continue into the future. At Nigeria's request, the United States will reduce the number of US military personnel, who have operated in the region to train and support Nigeria's growing defense forces. As this is an ongoing investigation, the Department will have no further comment at this time."*

The spokesperson left the podium and the press room to a cacophony of unanswered questions. For all the statement did not say, it spoke volumes. Within minutes, Russia and China released statements pointing the finger squarely at the United States. The Pentagon strategy was clear: admit nothing, take some body blows, let the matter die of its own accord.

It was a page one story in every major newspaper in the country and led all the network and cable news broadcasts. Words and phrases like "Pentagon mendacity," "cover-up," and "drone strike" appeared in almost all of the reports and articles. Soon, not just those in Ireti, but people around the world wanted to know exactly what happened to the small girls' school in Nigeria that was wiped off the map. All eyes looked toward the United States.

Recognizing they would get nothing more from the Pentagon, the press corps quickly mobilized on Capitol Hill. There were 435 men and women serving in the House and 100 in the Senate, and each one of them stood ready to answer the press corps' siren song. Those on the political left wrung their hands and demanded an immediate ban of all drone flights and a recall of all US troops in Nigeria. Those on the political right pounded the table and called for an increased military presence around the globe. Because it happened so quickly, there were many members from both political parties who came out strong, but on the wrong side of things from their party's perspective. Party leaders did not have enough time to get their positions straight. It was chaos, and the 24/7 news beast was sated for several days.

The harsh reality—the truth—never became entirely clear. The drone strike theory, though widely believed, was never acknowledged. The epic intelligence failure would remain classified for the next thirty years, at least. The Pentagon moved on, and so eventually did the politicians and the press corps. The world soon followed. Boko Haram's scheme to rid Nigeria of US military had worked flawlessly.

CHAPTER 21

Jummal felt as though he was reliving his sisters' deaths every day. The frustrating lack of real answers ignited a slow burn in his belly that began to consume him. *A US drone strike killed my sisters? Wiped out all the girls in my village?* He dreamt of drones flying in circles high above his village, out of sight and sound and releasing holy hell on the school, killing his sisters. He woke in cold sweats and could not understand how the United States had forsaken his tiny village. His shock turned to a simmering anger, aggravated by the fact there seemed to be absolutely nothing he could do about it. Every minute of every day, he wondered why the US would not say what really happened.

Jummal was not alone. Oku and Kam felt the same way. Kam said it first. "What would America do if we blew up one of their schools? Think we'd get away with that?" Neither brother responded, as they all knew the answer. With tears in his eyes, Kam drove his right fist down into the table, hard. "It's all bullshit," he hollered to no one in particular.

Jummal and Oku stared at their younger brother.

"Bullshit," Kam mumbled again, flexing his hand.

"You're bleeding, Kam," said Oku, noticing blood dripping from two split knuckles.

Kam looked down at his damaged hand. "Fuck," he said, shaking his head for being so foolish.

"Go get that cleaned up," said Jummal. "It's time to call it a night."

"All right, brothers," Kam responded. "I'll see you in the morning." After a pause, "Sorry about this," he added, looking at his hand and shaking his head.

After Kam left, Oku said with a smile, "I remember when you punched the side of the house a few years ago."

"The inexperience of youth," Jummal responded. "And it was more than a few years ago. I don't even remember what I was upset about, but I remember the broken finger."

"I get it, ya' know. These last few days, I've wanted to scream and beat something, too."

"I know, Oku, I know. Me too. I suggest something other than the house or the table, though."

Oku scoffed. "If I punched the table, we'd have nowhere to meet. And if I punched the house—"

"I know, I know," Jummal cut him off. "We'd have no place to live." He threw up his hands in mock surrender. "Let's call it a night."

Jummal went to bed restless and stayed that way all night. Only fitful sleep came, and it came with images of him landing blow after blow at iconic American monuments like the Washington Monument and the Gateway Arch in St. Louis, then watching them explode and crumble to dust. He woke early the next day but stayed in bed, staring at the ceiling. He laughed at himself, remembering his dream. He had never even been to St. Louis. And he was certainly no terrorist capable of such destruction.

Like his parents, he was progressive and hoped to continue their work in advancing Ireti into the future. He traveled to America to learn and grow, and grow up. But he knew he would return. He knew his hidden wish for Oku to become chief was idle fancy. His deep reverence for his familial duty drove him. Oku might be better suited to lead, but that was irrelevant. He was here now, ready to repair and rebuild Ireti.

Ready to continue his father's dreams of what Ireti could be. His village must never live through something like this ever again. This was wrong, painfully wrong. He would fulfill his duties as chief and cover Ireti with a protective embrace. But not just Ireti. He must extend his embrace beyond his home village. This was a crime against all of Nigeria, against everything that made Jummal who he was. He was infused with his newfound sense of duty. He would protect Ireti, and he would protect all the other villages like it. He would ensure nothing like this would ever happen again in Nigeria.

Nearly a month had passed since Jummal received the call at work. It had been a little more than three weeks since the memorial service. The United States government had issued its non-denial denial, essentially an admission on the world stage. The brothers continued to meet at the picnic table. Inevitably, the conversation turned to the drone strike on the school and how no one outside of Ireti seemed to care. The story had already become old news.

Jummal called his office, explaining to his boss what was happening with him and his family, that his destiny was to assume leadership of Ireti. He said he would be back to close out his affairs but would not be coming back to work. Jummal's boss refused to accept the resignation notice, instead giving Jummal an extended leave of absence. "Take six months," he insisted. "All this is still too new, too raw. Just take some time. Do what you need to do, figure it all out, then we'll talk some more. No need to decide the rest of your life today, okay?"

Jummal did not see the point, but it was not worth arguing. Whether he quit his job today or in six months was of no consequence. His place was here, at home in Ireti.

CHAPTER 22

Though there was no official admission, the world knew the United States was responsible for a drone strike that destroyed the small school in Ireti. And for all the posturing and all the headlines, very little was going to happen. American troops were leaving Nigeria; little more than a slap on the wrist for nearly sixty dead girls and their teachers. Barely an acknowledgment that Jummal's sisters were killed for no reason. Jummal's anger simmered, never boiling over, but always was there. A constant companion.

The chief's office was in the municipal building across the square from the newly placed memorial. Jummal had begun accompanying the chief to work every day and shared the office with his father while he learned the ins and outs of being the village chief. His years in the United States going to college and becoming a successful businessman were paying off. Jummal was a natural with the bureaucracy required to successfully manage a progressive African village, inching its way to modernity. The *organization* of Ireti had never been better. The calendar was updated regularly, the chief was never late and never missed any meetings. The transition from father to son was progressing smoothly. From the business end of things, the chief could not have been more pleased.

But something was missing.

"Jummal," called the chief.

"Yes, Father?" Jummal replied without looking up from his desk.

"Jummal, stop for a minute."

"I'll be right with you, Father."

"Jummal, stop what you're doing. Look at me."

Jummal looked up at his father with slight annoyance. "What?"

The chief sighed. He stood up and walked to the office door, pulling it shut. He slid an extra chair next to Jummal and took a seat.

"Jummal, I feel it too," he said.

"I'm sorry?"

"That rage inside you. I feel it too."

"The what? Rage? What are you talking about?"

"I'm talking about how you feel about what happened to Abiona and Abebi, about what happened to Ireti." The chief adjusted his position in the chair. "Did you know your mother still cries every night before bed? Every night. I ran out of tears, but your mother...she still cries. For all of us."

"I have no more tears left, Father. I'm just so angry all the time."

"Yes, son, I have seen it. You don't laugh, you barely smile anymore. You are like a machine, learning to be chief. Now, don't get me wrong, you are doing great things here and you will be a great chief. But there is so much more to being chief than keeping the books and managing the village. At our heart, at Ireti's heart, is us—people. Human beings. Anger feeds on Ireti's heart, Jummal. I understand because I'm angry too. Part of me died that day, and I fight my own anger, my own rage, every day. Some days it almost consumes me. But you have to fight it. You can't let the anger win."

"How?" Jummal shouted. "How do I fight it? Do I forget? Just move on, become chief, have a family and don't worry about it?" Jummal caught his breath, then said more calmly, "The world forgot about Ireti, Father. The United States *was my home*. They forgot. Or they don't care. Nobody cares. Abebi and Abiona died for nothing. They were killed for nothing. Nothing! Look at my eyes, Father. There are no tears. Fight the anger? Anger has already won! Every second of every day, it's with me. Smiling, laughing, crying? Never again. I can't rid myself of it. I can't. I can't..." Jummal's voice trailed off into silence.

The chief grabbed each of Jummal's shaking hands in his. He stroked his thumbs gently over the tops of Jummal's hands until the shaking stopped.

"Jummal, look at me." The son looked into his father's eyes. "The anger will always be there. Forever. We can't beat it, but it can't beat us either. Anger cannot win, Jummal. It might be winning now, but you keep fighting. Keep fighting," he said again, voice raised and squeezing Jummal's hands hard. "You think of the girls. You find your strength through them. How would they want you to live, Jummal? Would they want your anger to win? Would they?"

"No, no," Jummal said. "Of course not."

"Then that's how you fight. You think of Abebi and Abiona."

"It's hard, Father. I think of them every minute of every day. I think of Ireti and the sacrifice our village made. And it doesn't fight the anger, it makes it worse. I need to do something. I have to do something or I will lose this fight."

"Then do something. Figure out what you must do and do it. Soon, Jummal, very soon, it is you they will call 'Chief.' The funeral? The memorial there outside? That was you, Jummal. That was you doing something. That was you fighting. But it doesn't end there. Your duty—to your sisters, to this village, to yourself—is to keep fighting. Ireti is counting on you, Jummal. I am counting on you. And not just to be the town manager balancing the books. To be the chief. The chief, Jummal. I know you can do it. I saw it that night when you took control, and in the days following when you led Ireti in its mourning. You did that, my son. You. I was so proud. In the middle of all that sadness, I was never prouder. My son, the next chief." He stood up with a smile on his face.

Jummal looked up at his father, the barest hint of a smile emerging. "I will try, Father. I will keep fighting. I will figure out what I must do," he said.

"I know you will, my son. We will fill that hole in your heart, just like the bulldozers filled the hole in the ground outside. All of us are broken, but we will rebuild." He paused. "Ourselves, our school, our village."

That night at the picnic table with his brothers, Jummal sat quietly thinking about his father's words, ignoring Kam and Oku. *Rebuild ourselves, our school, our village. How does one rebuild himself? By doing something. But what? Rebuild the school? Maybe someday, but who was left to even go? Who would come to teach? There was an idea there, perhaps, but it was not clear. The village then? Ireti is still here. Changed forever, but still here. Broken, yes, but fixable? With time, Ireti would recover. Protect the village. Father's job. My job. Protect the village. How? Not just Ireti, but all the small, nameless villages throughout Nigeria. How to—*

Jummal looked up at his brothers. They had stopped their conversation when they realized Jummal was lost in thought. "Solving the world's problems, big brother?" asked Kam.

"No. Just Ireti's, and maybe Nigeria's," he answered.

With their big brother's attention, Kam and Oku rekindled their conversation. Inevitably, talk turned to the drone strike. Jummal noted his own anger remained. Receded somewhat with his thoughts, but still there. Like his father told him, it would always be there, engaged in a permanent battle within Jummal. But he knew he would fight it, and he knew he would beat it down in the end. He also knew that would take time, maybe a lot of time. Right now, he had to figure out what he was going to do to fight it.

He was not alone. Oku and Kam carried the same burden,

had the same questions, and wondered what they could do about it. So far, the answer was nothing. What could three brothers in a small Nigerian village do about a US drone attack that was only peripherally acknowledged by the attacker?

"I can't keep talking about this," said Kam. "Every night we're out here and every night it's the same thing. 'What are we going to do? What are we going to do?'" he said, mocking their nightly ritual. "Look, you need me to fix a transmission, I'm your guy. But this is out of my league. I'm going to go crazy if this is all we talk about for the rest of our lives. You two need to figure this out. I'm with you. I'll do whatever you need me to do. I'll follow you to the ends of the earth to make this right. But we all know I'm not the one good at figuring this kind of thing out. You tell me what you need me to do, and it's done. That's my promise to my older brothers."

"Well, chief?" said Oku, looking at Jummal.

"Not yet," Jummal replied.

"Okay, okay. *Jummal.* It's time to put all that education to work. You know me and Kam will be there for you. Whatever you need. But let's be honest—if anyone's going to figure this out, it's you, Jummal. We all know it. We're all angry, but you're the one who has to figure this out. Not today, not tomorrow, but you'll figure it out. And we'll be there to help you with whatever you decide."

Jummal looked at Oku, then at Kam. He knew they were right. It fell to him, the eldest brother, the future chief, to figure this out. He and his brothers were not born to radicalism, just the opposite, in fact. But all three understood they must take action. They must respond in some way or their anger would consume them. The sheer devastation of the drone strike on Ireti and their family, and the utter lack of accountability for it, was an outrage. An outrage that extended only to Ireti's borders, but should have extended to the rest of the world. The world had to know the people of Ireti would not allow themselves to be forgotten. The world had to feel their anger and know that what happened in Ireti could not be tolerated and could never, ever happen again.

"Okay," Jummal said. With a solemn nod of his head, he added, "It's been a long day. One of many. I have to think."

With that, Jummal left his brothers and went inside to go to bed. He lay on his bed, staring at the ceiling. Thoughts and ideas germinated. It was like a football match with thirty balls instead of one, all bouncing back and forth, over the net, into the net, in bounds and out of bounds. And Jummal stood on either side of the pitch, playing against himself, sometimes kicking lasers that rocketed into the opposing net, and sometimes stumbling and whiffing, missing the ball entirely. But the idea was there. The answer was there. Jummal knew it. He also knew he had to keep moving, keep attacking, keep striking balls toward the net until he found the right one. The right ball. The right answer that would tame his anger and allow him and his brothers to move on.

Jummal made a decision and sat up in bed. His decision would have been unthinkable only a day earlier. Maybe he was still in shock. Maybe he was overwhelmed. After all, there had been an attack on his country and his village, on his family. Had he been "triggered?" It did not matter. Jummal knew what he had to do. He stood up in the room he had grown up in and crossed the room to his old dresser, which looked worn and small. Facing the mirror hung above it, he asked aloud, "Is this how it begins?"

Perhaps so, he thought. *Perhaps so.*

CHAPTER 23

The next morning, Jummal woke up with a plan. Not really a plan, he thought, but an idea that might lead to a plan, or at least the beginnings of one.

Babatunde was step one.

Babatunde, or Baba as he was known, was a village resident. He was popular in Ireti because he was the local connection familiar with the workings of the black market in the region. He could procure items for his fellow villagers that no one else could. If you needed a particular medicine that was hard to come by, you went to Baba. If you needed an unusual birthday present at the last minute, you went to Baba. When Kam needed a hard-to-find part to fix a car, he went to Baba. And Baba came through, almost always. He was well thought of because his prices were fair. He did not gouge, and even if you were short, you could trade for his services. People liked Baba, and he had come through for Ireti on many occasions, most recently when Jummal needed sixty urns practically overnight. Baba lived on the edge of the village and might not get invited to a fancy dinner at the chief's home, but if you were in a tight spot and needed something fast, he was the man who could get it for you.

Jummal knew little of Baba's world. Conceptually, he knew what the black market was and how it worked, but only from an academic viewpoint. He had never dealt in those circles. As the chief's eldest son, growing up, it was inappropriate. In America, it was illegal. Now a grown man back in his village, he knew full well Baba was an integral figure in the machinery that made Ireti go. He also knew, like his father, when he became chief, from time-to-time Baba's services would be needed for the good of Ireti, and he would not hesitate to call on him.

Now was one of those times.

Jummal told no one of his plan when he left that morning. He walked to the edge of town rather than drive—more time to think and figure things out. Baba's house was a single story, concrete block house. Nothing fancy, but solid and clean, respectable even. Jummal approached the door, but instead of knocking, shouted, "Baba, are you there? Hello, Babatunde, are you home?"

Jummal heard a muffled "around the back" in response. He made his way around the house and found Baba in the backyard, tending a garden of all things, not at all the appearance of a seasoned black marketeer. But that was Baba.

"Jummal!" Baba shouted in surprise. "I didn't expect to see you way out here on the edge of nowhere." With a frown, he added, "Don't tell me you're here for more urns. I saw your ceremony, you know, off in the distance. It was a beautiful thing you did. Ireti needed it."

Jummal was taken by the sincerity in Baba's voice. It did not make today's request any easier. "No, no urns today."

"Then what can I do for you? Are you chief yet? Apologies and no disrespect, if so."

"No, no, not yet. I've still got a lot to learn."

Baba smiled. "Not much more. I heard how you took control after the explosion. You saved this village, and you'll make a fine chief. So, what can I do for you?"

Jummal hesitated. He had to do something, and he had to start somewhere. Baba could help. "I need to talk to someone in Boko Haram."

Baba stared at Jummal, saying nothing. Jummal held his stare. Baba blinked first.

"No. No way, man. Chief or no chief. I don't deal with Boko Haram. They leave me alone, and I stay out of their way. Everybody's happy...and alive. Anyway, I don't even know anybody in Boko Haram."

"C'mon, Baba. You can get me a meeting with someone. I know you can. It's for Ireti, Baba. I've got to do this. For my family, for our village. For me."

"No, no, no, no, no. Chief, I don't know what your game is and please don't tell me. But these are dangerous, scary people. What do they have that you need, or that Ireti needs? I'll tell you. Nothing. Nothing but blood, heartache, danger, and every other bad thing."

"I just need a meeting with someone connected. Just a meeting. I'm trying to figure some things out, and I think they can help me."

"Boko Haram don't help anybody but Boko Haram. They don't give a shit about you, me, this village—nothing but Boko Haram."

"Baba, listen. I've got to do this. I've got to have this meeting, or I can't move forward. Ireti can't move forward. Maybe you can't set me up directly, but I know you know someone who can. One of your black-market contacts, one of your suppliers, someone who owes you a favor. I need this meeting. Ireti needs this meeting. Will you help me?"

Baba stared at Jummal for several silent seconds. The silence, Jummal knew, meant Baba would help. If the answer was going to be "no," the conversation would have already ended. Baba shook his head, but said, "Okay, Chief. Sorry, Jummal. I'll see what I can find out for you. But this is between you and me. I accept no payment and no one else can know. I'll do it because whatever you are now, you're going to be my chief. And if you tell me Ireti needs my future chief to have a meeting with Boko Haram, then I'll try to make that happen. But, Jummal, these people are seriously bad guys. This isn't a case of penicillin falling off a truck in Lagos. Boko Haram is murder and mayhem and nothing good. If anybody ever asks, you didn't walk out here, and we never had this conversation."

"My brothers are in this too. They have to know. I speak for them. They'll respect your conditions."

Baba shook his head. "The brothers Adeyami. I hope you all know what you're doing."

"So do I, Baba. So do I."

Jummal's pulse was rapid on his walk back to the village center. He shuddered from a non-existent chill in the air that seemed to crawl up his spine. He hid it well, but his conversation with Baba unnerved him. He was scared, and it was only just beginning.

Baba watched Jummal walk away. As soon as he was out of sight, Baba went inside his house and started preparing for a trip. He would head north and east, further into the interior. Maybe he would get lucky and catch a ride along the way. He did not like anything about this job, but he would leave today and hope he could be done with it before the week was out.

Baba got lucky and did find a ride, at least for part of the trip. Nevertheless, it still took him a day and a half to find his source. Uzi was a thug and a bad guy, but he was as close to Boko Haram as Baba was willing to get. His real name was Uzoma, but at his insistence, everyone called him Uzi. Baba had done business with Uzi twice before when the village had needed medicine. The deals went smoothly, but Uzi scared him. This was a bad guy. Baba kept it professional, did not stick around unnecessarily, and disappeared as quickly as possible after the deals were done.

He did not believe Uzi was a real Boko Haram soldier, rather, that Uzi operated on the periphery of that group. But if he was not Boko Haram himself, he certainly knew people who were. Uzi quickly agreed to meet the future chief of an area village. To Uzi, a village chief meant one thing—money. They set up a time and place, and Baba made his way back to Ireti.

Baba's trip took three days. Once back in Ireti, he did not go to see Jummal right away. He hoped Jummal had changed his mind. Baba waited two nights before discreetly sneaking his way into the village under cover of darkness. It was pitch-black when he knocked on Jummal's window. Jummal, for his part, was barely sleeping and opened the window while Baba was still knocking.

"It's time, Jummal. I got you a meet. Are you sure you want to do this?"

"Let me get dressed. I'll be out in five minutes."

Jummal crawled out the window three minutes later, insisting they get moving quickly. The two of them moved almost at a jog. Jummal was surprised when they reached Baba's house but kept going further and further down the road, beyond the outermost limits of Ireti. They were still jogging when Uzi emerged from the darkness, surprising Baba and terrifying Jummal.

All three men came to a rapid halt. Uzi sized up Jummal, who tried hard to control his breathing and calm himself down. Baba made the introductions before receding into the darkness.

"Well, Future Chief, I'm led to believe you require our services. What is it, exactly, that you're looking for?" Uzi asked.

Jummal steeled himself. He was terrified and fighting hard to not show it. Finally, with some effort, Jummal began. "Yes, I am the future chief of Ireti, the village just down the road here. You know our village?" he asked.

"Sure. Drone strike. School blown up. Little girls dead."

The way he said "little girls," with a hard "t" and dragging out the "ir" reminded Jummal who he was dealing with. He shuddered.

"Right. Well, we don't know what to do."

"What to do?" Uzi laughed. "What you have in mind, Future Chief? Gonna fly some planes into buildings?"

"No, no, nothing like that." For the first time, he looked Uzi in the eye. "We need Boko Haram to teach us what we can do to respond, to fight back. To make sure this never happens again."

Uzi was about to burst into laughter when Jummal added, "We can pay you to teach us."

Uzi's transition was immediate. He went from bemused laughter to all business in a single breath. He recognized an opportunity with the young, future chief of Ireti. "I think we can help you. Give me a few days. I'll make some arrangements, and we'll set up a second meeting. We'll take care of everything. Rest easy. Baba will get in touch with you when we're ready." With that, Uzi disappeared.

Jummal stood in the road, staring into the abyss of night that would soon turn to daylight. He had to get home. He had to figure out what just happened, what he had done. Was he fighting his anger? Was the anger winning? He was not certain. All he knew was that he was doing something and that, at least, felt good. He turned and took his first step toward home. He was not scared anymore. He thought of Abebi and Abiona, and for the first time in weeks, he smiled. Not with any sense of joy at his sisters' memories, but with the satisfaction that came from movement, from taking action. Was this *rebuilding* anything? Jummal doubted it, but at least he was doing something.

There was no end to this path he had started down, not yet anyway. He was not sure where it would lead. All he knew was he was on a path, and he was moving. For now, that was enough.

CHAPTER 24

The next night, the brothers gathered in their usual spot. The high from last night's encounter with Uzi had begun to wane, and Jummal was anxious. This was unchartered territory, and Uzi was, as Baba had warned, a dangerous man. There were no agreements yet, no promises other than a second meeting once Uzi made "arrangements." Jummal had no idea what that might mean or when the next meeting would even take place. But he was not scared. He was doing something, and he needed to share that with Oku and Kam.

He explained the prior night's events—working through Baba, meeting with Uzi, the promise of a second meeting, and an "arrangement" to help the brothers figure out what they could do to make sure Ireti and other villages like it were never victimized again.

"I have money," Jummal told his brothers. "My work in America paid well, and what I didn't send over here, I put in the bank. So, if we have to pay, we can pay." He paused. "Oku, Kam, I can't do this alone. It has to be all of us. I had to do something, and this is what I came up with. Honestly, I don't know what this is or will be, but I know it's doing something. It's the first time I've felt, I don't know, less angry, less frustrated than any time since the funeral. I—"

Oku cut him off. "It's Boko Haram, Jummal. Boko Haram! How can they help us? Are they going to show us how to kidnap a bunch of schoolgirls and sell them off?" He stared at his brother, waiting for an answer.

"No, Oku, not that. Never that. Look, I don't know what arrangements Uzi will make. I've committed to nothing. I've paid nothing. But I'm *doing* something. And no, I don't know exactly what yet, but maybe they do. Maybe there's something they can show us that will point us in the right direction. Lead us down a path where we can figure out exactly what to do."

"Those are bad, bad guys, Jummal. They scare the hell outta me."

"Me too. We're not joining them, but maybe we can learn something from them. I don't know, but I had to do something. We were never going to do anything just sitting out here every night getting madder and madder." Jummal put his head in his hands. Was this game too dangerous? Was this the wrong path?

The brothers sat stoically, each contemplating within himself. Kam broke the silence.

"I'm in. I don't care if we dance with the devil. I am with you, Jummal, all the way. We've got to do something, and it starts here and it starts now. We'll hear what this Uzi has to say and we'll go on. I am in." Turning to Oku, Kam added, "And, Oku, you're in too. This is our brother. He's going to be our chief. And we are going to follow him to hell and back if that's what he needs us to do. That is *our* job and *our* responsibility. You and me, we support him." He pointed to Jummal without taking his eyes off Oku. "So, we're in, both of us, wherever this goes."

Oku looked down and raised his hands in mock surrender to his younger brother. "Okay, brothers, okay. I guess we're all in. So, what's next?"

"We wait," Jummal said.

CHAPTER 25

A week went by with no word, and the brothers started talking about finding Baba to see what was going on. As if conjured, he appeared around the corner of the house, startling the brothers at their table. All three stood.

"What's your news, Baba?" Jummal asked.

Baba hesitated, looking at the brothers.

"C'mon, Baba, what've you got for us?" Oku interjected.

With a sigh, Baba said, "Uzi is back. He's ready to meet again."

"Okay. When and where?" Jummal asked, sitting back down.

"Right now. Same spot past my house, like last time."

Jummal stood up again, and all three brothers moved to follow Baba.

"Hold on, hold on. Just Jummal. That was the deal."

Jummal nodded, then looked at his brothers. "It's all right. I'll see what he has to say and fill you in. It's probably going to be a long night, so go to bed, and I'll tell you all about it tomorrow." Then to Baba, "I guess we're running back to your house?"

Baba nodded.

"Ready when you are."

The two ran off into the darkness. They did not speak, but fell into rhythm with Baba in front. Jummal was anxious and excited to hear what Uzi had to say, but his emotions were mixed. He wondered what the chief would think—what his father would think. Would he approve? Jummal knew the answer, but forced himself not to dwell on it. He hoped his father would understand that he had to do something. It certainly would not hurt anyone to hear what Uzi had to say. Maybe he would learn something that would help figure out what to do *to rebuild, to protect Ireti.*

Again, in the darkness, they were almost on top of Uzi before they saw him. As before, Baba retreated, leaving Jummal and Uzi to themselves. Uzi stared at Jummal. Jummal stared right back, and was about to say something when Uzi said, "It's been a long week, Future Chief. I traveled all over trying to find the right people for what you want. These people don't always want to be found."

The dance with the devil had begun, thought Jummal, but he said nothing. Uzi went on and on about Boko Haram soldiers and trainers and bosses and money men. Jummal recognized the sales pitch, but also found Uzi's credibility growing. Uzi was the real thing, connected to some dangerous people who could help him and his brothers.

"I've talked to some people high up in Boko Haram," Uzi said. "They *emp-a-tize* with you."

Jummal wondered if Uzi just learned the word, or if someone in Boko Haram had instructed him to use it.

"Ireti got bombed. People died—women, girls. That's not what Boko Haram wanted for Ireti. Boko Haram wants to help you. They want vengeance for you against the infidels." Uzi left unsaid the leverage Boko Haram could gain against the future chief of Ireti if he started doing business with them.

The word *infidels* practically dripped from Uzi. Maybe he was a true believer, thought Jummal. Jummal himself did not care about infidels. He was raised in a progressive house with progressive parents. Was it just simple vengeance he now sought? Maybe it was, at a gut-wrenching, emotional level. His sisters were dead, after all. But no, it was not simple vengeance, not really. Certainly not only that. Jummal wanted to right a wrong and to make sure such a thing never happened again. What Boko Haram believed his motivation to be was of no consequence. And he did not care whether Uzi was a true believer or whether Boko Haram wanted to take vengeance on the infidels. All Jummal heard was that Boko Haram would help him. Someone, finally, was willing to help.

"How much?" Jummal asked, interrupting Uzi's pitch.

Uzi smiled. "To business, eh, Future Chief? Okay, how much?" he repeated. "Ten thousand American, and Boko Haram will teach you how to fight back."

"Done," Jummal said without hesitation. "I just need an account number to transfer the money to."

"Okay, Future Chief. I like this. No problem." He pulled a piece of paper from a shirt pocket and handed it to Jummal. "All the information is right there. As soon as we get the money, Baba will tell you."

"My brothers," said Jummal.

"What brothers?"

"I have two brothers. They'll need to be there too."

"Two, three, no matter. You just move the money soon." Uzi disappeared into the jungle.

Jummal's heart was racing. Another step forward. They were on the path. He took off toward home at a run. He had some money to move before daybreak.

Uzi's leisurely pace through the jungle was markedly different than Jummal's run home. He smiled. "Too easy," he said aloud. His smile grew. Uzi was not in fact a soldier of Boko Haram. He knew some people connected to the terrorist group, but Uzi's connections were, at best, loose ones. But he had worked with Boko Haram before. They paid him, and he was not about to say 'no' to one of their requests. But in reality, Uzi was little more than a thug and a scam artist, always looking to hustle. He'd pegged Jummal as an easy mark immediately. If the fool actually sent him the money, then he would have leverage over the future chief, and that could lead to more and more money. Maybe, just maybe, this $10,000 was only the beginning.

After his first meeting with Jummal, Uzi's plan took shape quickly. He did travel around Nigeria looking for his Boko Haram contact. He was not lying when he told Jummal they were often hard to find. When he finally tracked his contact down and explained what Jummal wanted, the contact said he would talk to Jummal for $5,000. On his return trip, Uzi simply doubled the fee. Boko Haram would get their $5,000, and he would pocket the difference. A very nice payday.

CHAPTER 26

Jummal was damp with sweat and coated with a thin layer of road dust from his dash home from the meeting with Uzi. He wiped his hands and face before opening his laptop. At this time of night, there was plenty of bandwidth, and he was able to log into his account back in the States. He quickly entered Uzi's account information and set up the transfer to something called the Nigerian Relief Fund. Ten thousand dollars electronically moved from halfway around the world in a matter of minutes. There was no buyer's remorse, no second guessing. Jummal just sighed, mostly relief but a bit of apprehension too. The dance had begun in earnest now, and the devil was his partner.

Two days later, Uzi logged into his bank account on his phone, curious to see if Future Chief had actually come through with the $10,000 fee. He smiled and shook his head when he saw the electronic deposit. With a few clicks, he moved $5,000 from his account to a Boko Haram account he had used before and had been instructed to use again if Future Chief came through with the money. *Too easy,* he thought, still smiling.

CHAPTER 27

In 2002, Boko Haram was born. In a few short years, two things happened. First, Boko Haram became recognized as a deadly international terrorist organization. Second, sophisticated law enforcement organizations around the world began to track Boko Haram's finances. When the Untouchables put Al Capone away for eleven years in 1931 for, of all things, tax evasion, it became evident that a new weapon had emerged in law enforcement to fight organized crime. The value of forensic accounting—of following the money—grew exponentially over the years and became an effective tool for investigating major criminal enterprises around the world.

In the United States, the center of the forensic accounting universe was the Financial Criminal Enterprise Network, or FinCEN. FinCEN was established within the Department of the Treasury in 1990, born to fight the trash bags of cash being laundered by the drug trade through the US banking system. That mission evolved and expanded, and after the events of 9/11, included a robust effort at tracking terrorist funding that touched US banks. When an account affiliated with terrorism was identified and funds moved into that account from a US-based account, FinCEN was notified, and the funds transfer was flagged as a possible contribution to a terrorist organization. When Jummal transferred $10,000 to Uzi's Nigerian account, red flags went up at FinCEN.

By nobody's definition was Uzi a major player. His connection with Boko Haram was loose at best, but it was most certainly real. His contact was a low-level Boko Haram soldier he had known since his teens. They had run many scams together over the years, usually low-dollar affairs, but occasionally with a bigger prize. In all the years they had worked together, Uzi and his contact had never bothered to change their bank accounts, except when Uzi labeled his account as Nigerian Relief Fund. He'd never bothered to remove the fake account name, and why would he? Whenever he ran a charity scam, the account name gave his marks the confidence to donate. He and his contact were little more than small-time hustlers who never dealt with amounts that would attract any real attention. And they were in Nigeria, with their banks based in Lagos.

They had no concept of FinCEN or anyone outside of Nigeria following their money, so Uzi would have been shocked to learn his account, because of numerous transfers to his Boko Haram contact's account over the years, was tagged as "associated" with terrorism. And both Uzi and his contact would have been surprised to learn that his contact's account was considered a "known" Boko Haram account, and thus an account actually used to fund terrorism.

Back in the United States, the computers at FinCEN took note of Jummal's transfer to Uzi. Ten-thousand-dollar transfers happened every day, and most were not criminal. But when Jummal's $10,000 went to Uzi, both US and Nigerian intelligence resources registered that movement of funds from an unknown US account to an account that looked like a charity but was known to be "associated" with terrorism. The red flag triggered an automatic notice from FinCEN to the FBI's JTTF in New York City—the site of Jummal's bank—"for actions deemed appropriate" and to the National Security Agency in Fort Meade, Maryland, for "informational purposes." At that point, FinCEN's job was complete and their file closed.

At New York City's JTTF, the referral went into a database

at the end of a long line of referrals. It could be months before it rose to the top and was actually reviewed by an analyst. The line was not nearly as long at the NSA, and the file would appear in the email inbox of an assigned analyst within a few days. That analyst would review the "informational" file and make an initial determination of whether anything further needed to be done.

Reviewing movement of such a low-dollar amount was not considered glamorous work and was handled by lower-level analysts who read hundreds of such reports every day, always on the lookout for any indicators that could determine whether the movement of the funds was indicative of an issue affecting national security.

The Jummal-to-Uzi transaction report sat in an electronic queue on the computer of Nora Williams. She had been with NSA for six years, long enough to know she should have moved up by now. She recognized that the work reviewing report after report was often mundane and regularly mind-numbing. But she also knew it was important work requiring thoroughness, diligence, and attention to detail, something she reminded herself every morning as she logged onto her machine. Nora was smart, dedicated, and did her job well, but she had not matriculated at an Ivy League university, and certainly not M.I.T. or CalTech. No, Nora Williams was a Golden Retriever from the University of Maryland, Baltimore County. She knew UMBC to be a fine school with a great reputation, but she also knew the real world, and without a pedigree, her advancement, if it ever came, would be slower than it should be.

It was just before her lunch break when the report popped up on Williams's screen. It was not a long report, so she rubbed her eyes and said to herself, "One more before lunch," and set about reading it.

The report from FinCEN included Jummal's and Uzi's account numbers, as well as Jummal's identifying information. FinCEN had no knowledge of who owned Uzi's account, only that it had been flagged as associated with terrorism.

The NSA, on the other hand, upon receipt of the FinCEN report, had linked the accounts with every reference to them that was available in their network. There was not much there, thought Williams as she read the report. She started with Jummal's account. That was easy. He had been in the United States for several years on a student visa initially, then a work visa. No problem there, she thought. He was from Nigeria and that was it. *Right up until he decided to send ten grand to somebody bad. Let's see who he is,* Williams thought.

Uzi's file was more interesting than Jummal's, to be sure, but it still contained nothing that jumped out to Williams. The guy was a dirtbag who worked on the periphery of Boko Haram, but did not appear to be part of them. It looked to Williams that Uzi was a con man who spent his spare time scamming well-intentioned US bank account holders into believing they were donating to a Nigerian charity, when in fact they were lining Uzi's pockets. She rolled her eyes at another sucker getting duped by Uzi from halfway around the world.

With nothing else to go on, Williams scrolled back to the top of the report. She read through Jummal's information once more and noted that under the heading "Recent Activity" there was a record of Jummal's trip back to Nigeria. *Poor bastard. Went all that way just to get hustled.* Under the heading "Status," Williams typed the word "victim" to describe Jummal.

Then she hesitated. Something lurked in the back of her mind. Something about Nigeria. With a touch of reluctance, and in an abundance of caution, under the "Case Disposition" heading, Williams chose not to "close" the case outright, but instead clicked a box that read, "Closed, Pending Action." She had a US address, bank account, and work visa information for Jummal, who was in Nigeria getting hustled by Uzi.

Nigeria. *What about Nigeria?* There was something there, just out of her memory's reach. She wanted to be sure. *It's my job to be sure*. Before she closed the case for good, she wanted to know when Jummal returned to the United States so she could send that information back to the FBI. FinCEN was not going to take that extra step, but Nora Williams would. Just to be sure.

"Just in case, Mr. Jummal," she said. She scrolled down to the bottom of the report, clicked the "Update" button, pulled her NSA ID from the slot in her machine, and headed to the mess, where last night's leftovers waited in the communal refrigerator.

Since Williams selected "Closed, Pending Action," the NSA's system did one other thing. As Jummal had been in the United States on a visa, which remained active, and since he was currently out of the country, the system flagged Jummal's visa for the US Customs & Border Patrol (CBP). When Jummal returned to the US, he would be required to provide CBP information on his whereabouts while in the United States. The CBP would let NSA know that Jummal was back in country and provide NSA with a current address and phone number. And because her name was already attached to the file, that information would eventually find its way back to Nora Williams.

CHAPTER 28

Jummal reflected for a moment. He had not hesitated to transfer $10,000 directly to Uzi. Was he being foolish? Probably. Naïve? Definitely. Generally speaking, Jummal considered himself neither foolish nor naïve, but when he'd run home from his meeting with Uzi, he was motivated. *Energized* even. The physical nature of those actions—the meeting, the running, signing onto the computer and moving money—had been…what? Therapeutic? "Therapy," he said. "This is my therapy. *Doing* something is my therapy."

A week had passed since the second meeting with Uzi. Each passing day brought increased skepticism from Jummal and an increased likelihood that Uzi had played him for the angry fool that he was—desperate to do something, anything, to ease his pain. He had known Baba for most of his life, even respected him for the complex role he played on the fringes in support of the village. But Uzi was an unknown. His only contact with Ireti was Baba, and Baba had little good to say about Uzi. He smirked ruefully at the recollection of Baba warning him not to get involved with Uzi. Baba had been right all along, but was doing what his future chief wanted him to do.

"No regrets," Jummal said. And truly, he felt no regret. The money was not nothing, but he had known many colleagues back in the States who spent thousands of dollars on their own *therapy*. Uzi had served his purpose. He allowed Jummal to do something, to respond, to take action. To recognize that doing something was his therapy. That lesson had come at a price, to be sure, but it had been worth it. "No regrets," he repeated.

Jummal thought of his sisters. Action was required. Then he thought of Boko Haram's history of kidnapping young schoolgirls. His stomach clenched. Boko Haram had brought shame to Nigeria. Jummal could not work with them. He had to take action, but not through them. He had to find another way.

That night, his brothers brought a sour mood to their regular gathering. Inactivity cast a moribund shadow as the brothers waited for Uzi's response. A response, Jummal now recognized, that would never come.

"Cheer up, brothers," Jummal said with measured excitement.

Kam and Oku looked up. "You've got news?" Oku asked.

"What did he say? Will they help us?" followed Kam.

"No," Jummal said. "Well, no, they won't help us, but yes, I do have some news."

Expectation practically screamed from Kam as he grabbed the edge of the table to steady himself. Oku simply stared at Jummal, waiting patiently.

"Brothers," Jummal said, "Boko Haram will not help us. I doubt we will ever see Uzi again."

"Bastard!" Kam shouted.

"Hold on, Kam, and hear me out." Jummal waited while Kam calmed himself. "Yes, Uzi is a bastard and a sonuvabitch. And yes, I'm fairly certain he stole our money, but listen." He let his words hang in the air for a moment. "I. Don't. Care," he said, emphasizing each word.

Kam was ready to explode again. Oku looked at Jummal. "Jummal," he asked calmly, "what do you mean you don't care?"

Jummal flashed a smile at Oku. He reached across the picnic table and gently grabbed Kam's wrist. "Listen to me Kam, Oku. I don't care that Uzi stole our money. Remember that morning when I told you about the meeting and how I sent the money to Uzi. Remember how you felt when I told you. Kam, tell me now, how did you feel?"

Kam stared at his oldest brother, who still held his wrist from across the table.

"How did you feel, Kam? How did you *feel*?" Jummal asked, almost pleading for Kam to understand, squeezing his wrist.

"I felt...*great*. I was excited. We were doing something for Abebi and Abiona. For the first time since the explosion, I felt like I was moving forward. Like I'd been stuck in quicksand and you'd pulled me out. I felt good, Jummal, really good."

Jummal released Kam's wrist. "Exactly, Kam. We were finally doing something, anything." Turning to Oku, he asked, "And what about you? How did you feel?"

Oku nodded. "Like Kam, I was happy for the first time in a long time. I was happy and excited and ready to run through a wall for you, big brother."

"Right, exactly right. My brothers, that night, it was like being hit by a thunderbolt. I think we all could have run through a wall, Oku, because finally, after the explosion, the funeral, the tears, the remorse, all that sadness for our sisters, we'd wrapped it all up and swallowed it whole. But instead of it tearing us apart from the inside out, now it fueled us, it energized us because we were *doing* something about it. Just that simple act of doing something, anything, made things better for an instant, made things right, yeah?"

Kam and Oku, smiling now, nodded to Jummal.

"But with each passing day, each passing minute since, we've waited and waited, doing nothing. Nothing except guessing about whether Uzi stole our money. Maybe he went to Boko Haram, maybe he didn't. Maybe he kept it all for himself. We'll never know. But he has stolen our money, I'm sure of it. But I don't care because it's only money. We've got more. What Uzi doesn't know, because he's a bastard, is that he has shown us the way. He's shown us that the way forward is us. Not the scum of Boko Haram, not thugs like Uzi, but the three of us. The brothers of Abiona and Abebi. I don't know how, but we will find justice for our sisters. We will find justice for our school and our village. We make sure this never happens again to any village anywhere in our homeland."

Jummal stood. "We will do something, and it is up to us to figure out exactly what."

Kam and Oku stood. Jummal grabbed them both on the shoulder and reined in his smile. He stared, alternating between brothers, with an intensity they had never seen. "We will find justice. Abebi and Abiona forever."

"Abebi and Abiona forever," the brothers echoed in response.

CHAPTER 29

The week that followed was alive with energy, ideas, and good cheer among the brothers. As they worked to brainstorm how they would find justice for Abebi and Abiona, their activity proved therapeutic for all of them. They were focused, motivated, and inspired as they accepted ownership of their quest. They met every night and thought about what to do every minute of every day. The euphoria drove them.

Some ideas were easy to rule out. They had no capacity for a responsive drone strike. They had no expertise in explosives or making bombs. They could not target a responsible party for assassination, as no particular party had been identified as being responsible. Jummal knew the answer would be found within the skill sets each brother brought to the table. Oku was a strong leader, but outside of village politics and assisting the chief, his operational skills were limited. Kam was motivated and an effective mechanic, but atonement for their sisters' deaths would not come from fixing a transmission. And outside of the village, all Jummal knew was the United States' food markets.

Jummal stopped mid-thought and burst out laughing. How could he have been so blind? The Americans had sent this deadly drone, yet they refused to take responsibility. They refused to even admit what they had done. The Americans must pay. The one thing Jummal knew better than most was the complex path food and sundry dry goods traveled as they made their way from farmer or manufacturer to grocer to homes in the United States of America. Jummal knew exactly what the brothers were going to do.

He looked at his phone. It was nearly 10:00 p.m. in Ireti, not quite 4:00 p.m. back in New York. His boss should still be in. He scrolled through his contacts until he found Buddy Harris's name. He touched the phone icon and waited for the international call to go through.

Harris sounded genuinely concerned when he asked how Jummal was holding up. They exchanged pleasantries and caught up, and the Harris finally asked, "Jummal, is there anything I can do for you?"

"Well, perhaps there is. You know what's happened here, at my home in Nigeria?"

"Yes, of course," Harris said. "It was all over the news. Are you okay?"

"We're managing. But there's something I need to do. We're going to try and rebuild the school. The school where my sisters were. It's gone. They're gone, and we need to rebuild."

"Of course, Jummal. Of course. What can we do? Do you need funding? I'm sure the company can help. It's certainly worthwhile."

"Well, no, not exactly. Buddy, we are a proud people. This village where I am from, Ireti, we built this village and the school from the ground up. It was part of us, part of who we are, and part of where we were going. Your willingness to help means everything to me. But I'm not looking for a donation. It's something else."

"Just say the word. Tell me what you need."

"Well, I haven't got all the specifics yet, but what I'd like to do is open a food wholesaler, with the intention of raising all the funds we need to rebuild the school. You know that's a part of our business I know well and can make work, but I need the seed money to get it going."

"Interesting. I'm listening."

"Well, basically, and again, I haven't worked through all the details, but with your backing, I'd open the wholesaler, build it up and run it until we've raised enough money to rebuild the school, then I'd turn it back over to the company. You could keep it going, sell it, shut it down, whatever."

"Uh-huh. Where would you put it?"

"Well, I was thinking about the mid-Atlantic region. Maybe right in Metro DC, where we could reach all the markets. Easy access to farm country right outside of the city center. Plus, I went to school down there and am familiar with how that city works. It seems like a natural spot."

"I like what I'm hearing, Jummal. It gets you your new school, the company can feel really good about helping you out, and when you hit your number, we've got a successful wholesaler to work with in DC. This could work, and you're right, it's a helluva lot more interesting than just writing you a check. I appreciate the thought you've put into this, Jummal. I can get you in front of our board with what you've told me, but you'll need a full-fledged business proposal to sell them on it. You do the legwork, though, and they'll buy in. Why wouldn't they? It's win-win. I'm going to need you back here to pitch it in person. When can you be ready?"

It had been seven weeks since the US drone had destroyed his sisters' school. "I need a month," Jummal said. "I'll wrap things up here and head back to the States in a couple of weeks. Then I'll go and scout out DC, see if I can find a spot, and start the groundwork. I'll finalize the pitch and be back to New York to deliver it in four weeks."

CHAPTER 30

The next morning when Jummal explained his plan to his parents, Kiki burst into tears and the chief wrapped Jummal in a bear hug. Kiki placed her hand on Jummal's cheek. "My son becomes the chief. And next time you come home, you come home for good." It was not a question, and Jummal could only nod in affirmation to his mother. The nod masked the twinge in his belly that came from not being forthright with his parents. They were proud of him, and he let them bask in it.

The plan he shared with his boss in New York and his parents in Nigeria, the plan that caused excitement and pride, was real. Jummal knew he would get the board's approval, open his food wholesaler in DC, and begin to earn money to rebuild the school. The rest of the plan he could not share. That was for later with Kam and Oku and no one else. He tried not to consider what his parents might think of his real plan, the whole plan.

That night at the picnic table, Kam and Oku were stoic. Tension resonated among the three of them.

"So, you're going back to the United States to open your store and raise money for a new school. That's your big plan?" Kam asked. "Sounds great for you, but I thought we were in this together. I guess I go back to fixing transmissions and forget about all this," he said, gesturing at his brothers and their regular meeting spot.

"Patience, little brother," said Jummal. "I'll give you all the details in a moment. I'm just waiting—" The lights inside the house went out, signaling their parents had finally retired for the evening. "Ah. Waiting for that," Jummal said. He leaned into the table, whispering to Kam and Oku. "Come closer, brothers. This is for no one but us. No one else can ever know. Yes, I'm going back to the States. And you two are coming with me."

He laid out the whole plan to Kam and Oku. When he finished, he sat back and looked at his brothers. He raised his eyebrows, silently asking to hear their thoughts.

Kam nodded. "Yes," was all he said.

Oku stared intently at Jummal. The silence lingered. Finally, Jummal flipped his palms upward and shrugged his shoulders, but did not speak. Oku slowly shook his head back and forth, pursed his lips. There was doubt there, concern even. "Okay," he said, countering his gestures. "We'll do this, Jummal. But I've got some questions."

"Let's hear them."

"First, how are you going to get us into the United States?"

"I'm working on that. I'm going back in two weeks. You two will come when the time is right, after I've got the shop set up and everything is in place."

"Okaaaaaay," Oku said. "But if you're over there and we're still here in Ireti, how will we know what to do? And when?"

"I'll call you, just like always."

"Jummal, you've never called me once in all the years you've been in the US."

"What are you talking about? We talked almost every week." Jummal realized his mistake as soon as the words left his mouth. "I called Father every week. Sometimes you were there, and we'd catch up on that call."

"Right," said Oku. "And you can't call on my phone—well, it's not even my phone, really, just Father's old one—because it won't take international calls."

The conversation came to a halt, Jummal and Oku lost in thought. Kam broke the silence. "Well, you can't call me. I don't even have a phone. I just borrow Oku's if I need one."

Jummal and Oku laughed. Kam smirked back at them.

"All right," Jummal said. "Phone calls probably aren't the best idea anyway. We're going to have to be discreet. We can't risk Father or Mother overhearing any of this." He thought for a moment. "Listen, we'll do it in writing. I'll set up an email account for this. When we talk about the plan, we'll do it through email. It's free, it's easy, and when it's done, we'll just delete everything. Oku, your phone has internet access, yes?"

"Sure, my window to your world."

Jummal looked at Kam.

"Don't worry about me," Kam said. "Oku will keep me posted, and I'll do what he tells me."

"About time," said Oku.

Kam reached across the table and punched Oku in the arm.

CHAPTER 31

The brothers went their separate ways for the night, each lost in his own thoughts. Jummal remained at the picnic table, motionless, contemplating. Slowly, he reached into his pocket, pulling out his cell phone. He set it on the table and stared at it for several moments, seemingly wishing the call he had to make would happen by itself.

He picked up the phone, took a deep breath, and called an old friend, Tayo Sani, in DC. They had been at Georgetown together and attended the same mosque in Virginia.

"*How far*, Jummal," Sani said, a common "hello" in Nigerian Pidgin. "You have come back to us."

"Not yet, Tayo. I'm still in Nigeria, but heading your way soon. Listen, I have no time right now, but I need a favor from you, and quickly."

"I'm at your service, Jummal. What can I do?"

"I'm coming back to DC, well, Virginia. I'll be setting up a new shop there. We're raising money for Ireti and a new school, and I need my brothers with me as soon as possible. This is where it gets a bit tricky. I don't have time to wait for passports and visas. I'll take care of that down the road so they'll be legitimate, but don't have time to do that right now. Do you know anyone who can help?"

"Hmmm." Sani hesitated. "You sure you want to do it that way? If they get caught, they'll be sent home and won't ever be able to come back. You'll be at risk, too, if the authorities put you all together."

"I understand, my friend, and I wouldn't ask if it wasn't important. You know I'm to be chief, right, so it wouldn't be the worst thing if we all got caught. It will soon be time for me to go home forever anyway. But I've got to get this business up and running so we can raise our money and get to work rebuilding Ireti. If I'm going to be chief, it has to be me and my family, and it has to be now. Can you help?"

"Okay, okay, I'm convinced. There's someone at the mosque who I think can help. Let me talk to him first. Give me a couple of days."

"I can't thank you enough, Tayo."

"Thank me by not getting deported. I'll reach out in a couple of days."

"That's a deal," Jummal said, and disconnected.

He went inside quietly so as not to disturb his parents. His laptop sat closed on his made-up bed. He recalled that he had been too lazy to make his bed when he woke up that morning, and knew his mother must have done it for him. He smiled, imagining the great care she would have taken, first removing the laptop from the unmade bed—where he had last used it—and then returning it ever so gently to the top of the bedspread. That was Mother, always going the extra step for her children. He shuddered. No more would Mother be able to take such care of Abebi or Abiona. Never again.

He picked up his laptop and went out to the kitchen. It was quiet. He sat at the kitchen table and opened the laptop. The glow lit up the otherwise dark room. He typed "yahoo.com" into his browser, and the homepage sprung to life. He clicked on the "create new account" button. A flashing cursor beckoned his input for a username. Jummal stared at the screen, fingers at the ready. After a moment's consideration, he typed in a username: Abebi_Abiona_Forever. A nice tribute to his lost sisters, he thought. He added the password "JumOkuKam" and sat back in his chair. He would use this account to communicate with his brothers once he got back to the United States. And once he and his brothers were done, the account would disappear forever.

Two days later, Jummal looked at the Virginia phone number Tayo Sani had texted. He took a deep breath and blew the air out through inflated cheeks. He hit the call button on his phone and put it to his ear. He shut his eyes as the phone rang—once, twice, three times. Jummal lowered the phone and was about to disconnect. He almost felt relieved. As his finger extended to end the call, he heard a slight click as the call was answered.

"Hello, this is Abdul Malik. How can I be of service?"

Jummal kept the conversation intentionally vague. Malik played along as they felt each other out. Jummal offered no real specifics about his plans, but plenty of innuendo about getting his brothers into the United States illegally. The specifics would come later, once Jummal was back in the US and meeting Malik in person at his mosque in Falls Church, Virginia.

CHAPTER 32

Two weeks later, Jummal felt like a beaten dog when his Delta flight landed at Dulles International Airport. He'd left Lagos some twenty hours ago, having left Ireti six hours before that. He was certainly tired, but also excited to be back in America after more than two months at home in Ireti. He had two more weeks to acclimatize and settle back into his American way of life before he took a train to New York to pitch his food wholesaler idea. He had sketched out a rough draft of his presentation, trying to anticipate questions and objections. In the next few days, he would perfect it and practice it over and over again, making sure everything was covered, every objection able to be overcome. It was going to be good, well received and accepted. He was confident. But there was plenty to be done between now and his presentation. *Abebi and Abiona forever*, he thought as he handed his passport and work visa to the US Customs agent behind the glass.

The agent scanned Jummal's passport and visa. Seeing nothing on her screen, she added a stamp to the passport and welcomed Jummal back to the United States. Unbeknownst to Jummal, and even to the agent behind the thick plexiglass window, when she had passed the barcode from Jummal's visa over the scanner mounted in her desk, the customs system that scanned and collected information from thousands of visas and passports every day auto-generated a notification. That notification went silently and quickly through a network that linked Customs with the National Security Agency.

A month ago, when Nora Williams filed Jummal's case as "Closed, Pending Action," she assumed it would make its way back to her whenever Jummal decided to come back to the United States. When that happened, she would input any updates, let the JTTF know Jummal was back, and close the case for good. She knew FinCEN had sent the case to JTTF in New York, and they would probably take a look in a month or two. It was a $10,000 charity scam. Not exactly at the top of the to-do list. They would get to it when they got to it. And if the JTTF needed her assistance at that point, they would let her know.

At the NSA, its system grabbed the Customs notification, assigned it a number, matched it to the information the NSA had on file, and sent it to an electronic stack of inbound notifications that required a human being to review. Williams, having previously reviewed Jummal's file, was automatically tapped to review this notification as well.

After logging into her computer at the NSA complex in Fort Meade, Maryland, Williams found the notification attached to the original file and waiting in her electronic inbox. She had a vague recollection of a wayward Nigerian who had been bamboozled by a con man. With a few clicks, she was reading about Jummal's latest adventures in international travel. As she read, she remembered that Jummal had left the United States and transferred $10,000 to an account associated with terrorism; a known bad guy's account. Jummal, probably a mark in a con job, was now back in the US, perhaps licking his wounds. She wondered briefly why the notification from Customs provided a Virginia residence, a house in Arlington, instead of Jummal's old stomping grounds in New York City. "Had enough of the Big Apple," Williams mumbled.

She noted Jummal's new Arlington address and added the phone number he had provided to Customs at Dulles. She looked at the accumulated new reports in her electronic inbox, shrugged, and closed Jummal's file. *Plenty more where that came from,* she thought. Upon closing the file, an automated "Referral for Action" went back to the New York City JTTF. The referral included Jummal's new address, added his phone number, and told whoever read the file next that this case was closed at the NSA.

Jummal's boss was fully on board with the idea of setting up a food wholesaler in the metro DC area. And he was confident Jummal would have no problem persuading Field-Town Foods's board of directors to approve the idea. He also really wanted Jummal to keep working for him at Field-Town Foods. With that in mind, he had authorized rental of a three-bedroom house in Arlington, as well as a car.

Jummal took a taxi from Dulles to an Arlington real estate office and picked up his house keys while the taxi waited at the curb. The taxi then drove him to a new development that was about half full, with plenty of construction underway. Field-Town Foods had taken care of everything, and when he walked into his new home, he found a cozy three-bedroom, completely furnished, with a full refrigerator. A note signed by Buddy Harris sat on the kitchen table, under a set of keys for the white Hyundai Elantra in the driveway. *Welcome back, Jummal,* it said.

Jummal smiled at the note, thankful for Harris's graciousness and the full refrigerator. He needed sleep after the flight, but first he had to make a call. Abdul Malik was expecting him, and they needed to meet.

CHAPTER 33

"*As-salamu alaykum.*" Jummal offered the traditional Muslim greeting to Malik when they met inside the Virginia mosque.

"And peace be upon you, as well, Jummal," he responded.

Jummal explained in greater detail that he was opening a food warehouse in DC to raise money for a new school in Ireti. It was a matter of honor that he, as the future chief of the village, and his brothers *earned* the money. But Jummal could not wait on the achingly slow pace that would get his brothers into the country legally. He needed them here now.

"Getting them here is easy," said Malik. "We'll bring them into Canada as tourists and then smuggle them into the States. The difficult part for you is keeping them here without getting caught, then either legitimizing them or getting them back home. I can help with that as well. It all costs, though, so you tell me what you need, and we'll go from there."

Jummal had no real idea what was necessary. Driver's licenses? Passports? Fake identities? Finally, he told Malik, "I need them here for a few months, maybe six. They need to be able to get around a little bit without incident. And they'll need to be able to go back to Nigeria the easiest way possible."

Malik nodded as if this were an everyday request. It was all very businesslike and professional and much different than his encounters with Uzi. Like Jummal, Malik was a businessman and Jummal could relate to him. He knew Malik would come through. Their burgeoning relationship gave Jummal the confidence he needed to dive in deeper.

"Mr. Malik, would it be possible…"

"What else can I help you with?"

"I'm going to need some buyers. Some women from the mosque would be perfect. And a van and driver to get them around. Not for long, you understand, but to get a project going."

"For the food wholesaler." Malik smiled. "Of course, Jummal. Just let me know what you need and when. I can get you as many buyers as you need, with a van and a driver. That's not a problem."

Jummal and Malik settled on a price, and with that business concluded, Jummal returned to his house. The familiar tingle, the excitement, the thrill of doing something had returned. It was not cheap, but Jummal knew it was money well spent. He smiled at the thought of reuniting with Kam and Oku, wondering what they would think of the United States of America. It was all in front of him now.

That night, Jummal laid in his bed, drifting in and out of a light sleep. He gave up around 3:00 a.m. and walked into another bedroom where the company had set up a small but functional office. Jummal pulled his laptop from his bag, wondering for the thousandth time if he should get a second laptop so he would have one at the new warehouse and one here in his home. He laughed at himself, knowing he would never make that purchase. *It's a laptop. You're supposed to carry it around.*

He powered up the laptop and sat behind the modest desk. He began surfing the internet, typing in "Nigeria" on a number of search engines to see what was happening back home. There was nothing, of course, about the drone strike on the girls' school in Ireti. That had been deemed "old news" weeks ago. Jummal bit the inside of his cheek until he tasted blood. He shook his head and closed his eyes. "No one cares," he whispered. And there it was—the frustration, the anger. The ever-present lump of it sitting in his gut, always there, never abating.

Attached to his anger was a newfound sense of isolation. He had been back in the US only a few days, but he had been going nonstop, and he had never felt more alone. Alone with his thoughts, fears, frustration, and anger. Alone with his plan. Oku and Kam were a part of it, but they were still 9,000 kilometers away. He missed them. He needed them here. Not just to execute the plan, but to do it together, the three of them, each with an integral part to play.

Jummal opened his eyes, squinting at the brightness of his laptop screen. He pulled up the Yahoo homepage, typed in Abebi_Abiona_Forever, added the password when prompted, then sat back in his chair.

There was nothing in the inbox. No surprise there. He'd told his brothers to do nothing until they heard from him. It was not yet time to reach out to them, as Jummal still had much to do. But it was late, and he was lonely. He missed his brothers. Needed his brothers.

He typed an email, but instead of sending it, he printed it. He knew it was too soon to communicate with his brothers. But pulling the printed email from the printer, holding it in his hands, feeling the paper with his fingertips, made it all real. He raised the paper to his face, shut his eyes, and breathed in deeply, taking in every scent the printed page offered.

"Soon, brothers," he whispered. He opened his eyes. The loneliness had abated. Jummal laughed at himself, crumpled up the email and tossed it into the garbage can under the desk. It was a process he would repeat several times before he spoke with his brothers again.

"Time to sleep," he said, getting up from the desk and returning to his bedroom.

CHAPTER 34

A week went by while Jummal prepared for his pitch to the board of directors. He took breaks by driving across one of the many bridges leading into the District and searching for a location for his food warehouse. He found a leasing agent that would rent him a couple of refrigerated trucks to move food in and out of the warehouse. Everything was lined up and ready to go. He just needed the board's approval.

As the end of a second week approached, Jummal had perfected his presentation. He was ready. An Uber took him to DC's Union Station, where he settled into his reserved seat on Amtrak's Acela train to New York City. Once there, his first stop was his apartment, where he stopped briefly to clean up and change into a suit. He paused only for the slightest moment, remembering the last time he had been here, nearly three months ago, packing a bag for an emergency trip to Ireti. The day his sisters were killed.

A quick cab ride took him to his old office at Field-Town Foods headquarters in Lower Manhattan. Sitting at his desk contemplating the presentation he was about to give, Jummal did not hear Buddy Harris come in.

"Welcome back, Jummal," Harris said, walking around Jummal's desk. Jummal stood and accepted the man's embrace. He hugged him back, a gesture of affection and thanks.

"I can never thank you for all you've done for me and my

village," he said. "It's not something I can ever..." He hesitated, finding the right word. "Repay," he finished.

"I'm just glad you're okay, glad you're back. And no thanks are necessary. You've given this company a rare opportunity."

Jummal looked at Harris.

"Heh, let me explain. Your idea, well, it's great for a lot of reasons. The two biggest are that it will allow this company to do a really good thing—help one of our own recover from an unimaginable wrong—and the other, of course, is that it makes great business sense. It's a chance for us to expand and establish a presence in DC. I've been prepping the board since we spoke on the phone. I did some research. Here, take a look at this." He handed Jummal a folder embossed with the company logo.

Jummal opened the folder and found pages of information on Ireti's history, the girls' school, and perhaps most importantly, cost estimates to establish the food wholesaler in DC. Jummal was dumbstruck and overwhelmed by his boss's efforts. The detailed cost figures he had thrown together, along with a potential value assessment of what the wholesaler could be worth after Jummal turned it back over to the company, should seal the deal with the board.

He looked up at Harris, speechless. "I don't know what to say," was all he could manage.

"Save it for the board. Go in there and bring it home."

Jummal nodded, and with a smile at Harris, said, "Let's go."

The board listened attentively as Jummal explained the motivation for the food wholesaler in DC. He described how he would set it up and run it, with all proceeds going to a fund that would pay for a new school in Ireti. He did not dwell on the drone strike, only the tragedy that had befallen his native country. Nor did he dwell on who was responsible, only that it happened and had devastated his village. He spoke of his sisters and the other students and staff who had lost their lives. He was eloquent and persuasive. More than one board member wiped tears away.

Ultimately, Jummal gave his resignation, telling the board that his duty was to assume his father's position as village chief, comparing the job to that of a small-town mayor in the United States, except one who was appointed for life and fully enmeshed in all the comings and goings of the town. He explained that once they had earned enough to pay for the new school, he would turn over control of the wholesaler to Field-Town Foods to do with as they pleased, and he would return to Ireti to take his place as chief.

It was an extraordinary and moving presentation. When Jummal finished, silence enveloped the boardroom as the members contemplated what they had just heard. They voted before Jummal even left the room. It was unanimous. The chairman stood and recessed the board, then walked over to Jummal and gently grabbed his arm. She thanked him and escorted him to the elevator.

"Just let us know what you need," she said, "and you'll have it."

CHAPTER 35

It had been almost three months since Gordon had been assigned to the International Group at the DC JTTF. Three long, tortuous months. Without his elevated security clearance, Gordon could not do much to support the JTTF, and so had done little more than grunt work on other agents' cases. Just about everything that came through the door was classified Top Secret, and without Sensitive Compartmentalized Information (SCI) clearance, Gordon was figuratively handcuffed in the work he could do. He certainly would not be assigned his own cases until his clearance application cleared what seemed to him to be a glacially slow FBI bureaucracy. Even with an expedited review requested by the JTTF, it was taking a long time. He called the security office religiously at 8:30 a.m. every Monday to check on his status. Each week he was told, "Not yet, Agent Stone. There's a pretty big backlog. We'll let you know." And each week, he would resign himself to another week of scut work.

The early weeks had not been too bad. He got his identification badge to get in the building, and when his JTTF credentials came through in less than two weeks, he was given access to the JTTF network. Then he took a seemingly endless series of required training on everything from sexual harassment in the workplace to cybersecurity threats. He even had the chance to drive south to Quantico and qualify with his Glock and a couple of different long guns he had not used at FDA-OCI. But until his clearance came through, his status was strictly second class at the JTTF, and he found himself more and more resigned to the vacated break room in the basement, alone and seemingly forgotten.

On this Monday, if his clearance still was not approved, he would reach out to ASAC McNeely and see if there was anything he could do. If necessary, he could ask McNeely to call the JTTF and let them know FDA-OCI would like Gordon back if the JTTF did not have any use for him.

When he arrived, Gordon did not even bother to go upstairs but proceeded straight to the basement break room. Another big case had taken over the interview room upstairs for the past two weeks, and he knew there was no spot for him in the group's spaces. He groaned in anticipation of making cold calls tracking down potential witnesses in that case—witnesses he would *only* track down, but would not be able to actually interview—for another week.

Gordon got comfortable in his chair at 8:20 a.m.—ten minutes before his weekly call to check on his clearance—and opened his email.

"Junk, junk, junk, junk," recited Gordon as he scrolled through a lengthy list of useless emails. Then he came to one that was not junk. This one came from the JTTF Security Operations Center, and it was encrypted. With hope, excitement, and a bit of trepidation, Gordon entered his encryption key code and the message opened. It was succinct:

Special Agent Gordon Stone/TS/SCI clearance application/approved.

He read the message again. Then a third time. Then a fourth. He sat back in the old cafeteria chair and slid back from the break room table. "Okay," he said to himself with a smile. He closed his laptop and packed it in his briefcase. He slid the few files and pads of paper he had with him in with the laptop. Then he grabbed his phone, shoving it into a front pants pocket.

"Okay," he said again and left the old, empty break room.

He rushed by the elevator and went straight to the stairs. He was done waiting. Up he went, almost at a run. There would be no more second-class status for Gordon. Through the door with the International Group sign, straight past Liz, the executive assistant, and right into the office of Supervisory Special Agent Dean Swayz.

Swayz was on the phone. "Sounds good, Don. Let's try and get a round in at Army-Navy this weekend. Hey, I've got to go. Someone just came into my office. All right, talk soon." He hung up and stared at Gordon, struggling to remember his name.

"Sir," Gordon said awkwardly.

"Stone?" Swayz responded, remembering. They had spoken little in the last three months. "How's my favorite broccoli cop?" Swayz chuckled.

"Sir?"

A pause lingered. "Broccoli, Stone. You know, the vegetable."

Gordon stood silently.

"Agent Stone, didn't you come to us from the FDA? Don't answer that. FDA. Food. Broccoli. Never mind. What can I do for you?"

For an instant, Gordon was thrown off by the conversation. Broccoli cop? What? He forced himself to focus. "Sir, my TS/SCI came through. I'm cleared to take cases."

"Sure thing, Stone. We'll get you in the lineup ASAP. Anything else?"

"No, sir. Thank you," Gordon said. He turned to go with a smile on his face. He did not see Swayz shake his head and roll his eyes.

Even with his clearance in place, Gordon was still not considered an FBI Special Agent. He was now a fully vetted, fully credentialed Task Force Officer (TFO). Not the FBI, Gordon knew, but pretty darn close. But not close enough, it seemed.

Days went by without a case being assigned. Instead, he continued to spend his days running down leads for other agents' cases. With his clearance in hand, Gordon was read into the casework and conducted preliminary interviews. The work was a notch above the table scraps he had been working prior to getting his TS/SCI, but not by much. As soon as any lead showed promise, the FBI case agent quickly swallowed it up, leaving Gordon with little more than a "thanks, Gordo" and sometimes not even that.

The days wore on and his enthusiasm again began to wane. Still without an office, still trapped in purgatory, sort of assigned to an interview room in the International Group section, but spending most of his time in the old basement break room. Still stuck in the corner.

CHAPTER 36

The case involving Jummal's transfer of $10,000 to Uzi sat untouched, buried in the New York JTTF's computer network until the same Customs notice that brought Jummal back to Nora Williams's attention at NSA pushed it up in priority at the JTTF. In New York, the case never made it to an actual JTTF agent. Instead, an intelligence analyst assigned to review, screen, and refer any notices from external agencies sipped his coffee and read the Customs notice about Jummal's re-entry into the country, along with the NSA's update. Jummal was now in Virginia. *That's an easy one,* the analyst thought.

He closed the New York JTTF file and forwarded the whole package to the DC JTTF. Because of the Nigerian component, the case was immediately forwarded to the International Group, where it arrived with no fanfare and initially received no human attention. The JTTF's network algorithm noted the low value of the $10,000 transfer and automatically filed the case into the electronic stack of "non-priority" cases to be reviewed for assignment by SSA Swayz.

Swayz referred to this stack as the Dog Pile. The cases were dogs and not fit for his FBI cadre to waste their time on. That is what he had TFOs for, the dogs. Swayz gave the file a cursory review. A transfer of $10,000 to an account "associated" with terrorism did not get him too excited. This one looked like a charity scam. There seemed to be little meat on this bone, but it still had to be dealt with.

Swayz scrolled back to the top of the file and noted the referral came from the NYC JTTF. *They could have killed it,* he thought. *Why send it to us?* Reading through the file a second time more carefully, he noted the victim of the scam, a Mr. Jummal Adeyami, was from Nigeria and sent the money from his US bank account to an account with ties to Boko Haram. Adeyami had recently returned from Nigeria and moved to Virginia. That explained why the case ended up on his desk.

A quick scan of Jummal Adeyami's background information revealed he had been in the United States for several years. He had a work visa and was here legally. *So far, so good,* thought Swayz. He worked at Field-Town Foods in New York City and was an executive vice president there. "Huh," said Swayz aloud.

"Liz," Swayz shouted through his office door.

"Yes, boss?" she answered, hustling to his doorway.

"Find uhhhh, what's his name from FDA." He paused, thinking. "The broccoli cop who was just up her a few days ago. What the hell's his name?"

"Agent Stone," Liz answered. "From FDA-OCI."

"That's him. Find him and get him in here, will you? Thanks, Liz."

"You got it, boss."

Liz walked down the hallway to the interview room to find three agents sifting through boxes of files. "Any of you seen Agent Stone?"

"Who?" they responded in unison.

Liz rolled her eyes and went back to her desk. She scanned the phone roster taped to a cabinet next to her phone. Finding Gordon's number, she picked up her desk phone and dialed.

It seemed to Liz that Gordon appeared almost instantly from somewhere as she hung up the phone. "Boss needs to see you, Agent Stone. Go on in."

With a nod and a smile, Gordon said, "Thanks," and walked into Swayz's office.

"Come on in, Stone, have a seat," said Swayz. "Got a case for you. Here's the file. It doesn't look like much, but we've got to close the loop on it. Subject is a businessman from Nigeria. Works in New York. Spent a couple months in Nigeria, came back and set up a residence in Virginia. Looks like he got scammed out of $10,000 by a fake charity. Call him, do a knock-and-talk, whatever works. I need you to confirm this case is a dog and kill it. We can't be wasting our time or our manpower on this small-time crap. Confirm he got hustled and close it. Understand?"

"Yessir," Gordon said with a smile on his face.

"Quick and easy, Stone."

"Quick and easy, yessir," said Gordon.

CHAPTER 37

With the case file in hand, Gordon retreated to the basement break room to read it. He read through it twice and made a decision. This was his first case with JTTF. No way was he going to do a quick-hit interview and shut it down. No, not his first case, and not after waiting three months to get it. He would not do a knock-and-talk, not yet anyway. Gordon had to do Gordon. And he was going to Gordon the hell out of this case.

He examined the file, methodically following the case from its roots at FinCEN, then to the NSA and the New York City JTTF. The NSA thought it looked like a charity scam, just like Swayz. But, Gordon noted, the NSA had not closed the case outright. Instead, whoever processed it flagged it so that when Jummal Adeyami returned to the United States, the NSA would be notified. The New York City JTTF had done nothing with the file except to transfer it to DC as soon as they learned Adeyami had moved to Arlington.

Admittedly, it did not look like much. It probably was, in fact, nothing more than a charity scam. The Nigerian Relief Fund certainly sounded fake. But why, then, did the NSA leave it open? Why not just close it out and be done with it? Gordon could not just do a knock-and-talk with Jummal Adeyami. He had to check the boxes and follow the process. He had a case, and he could see it through or he could go back to doing scut work and chasing leads on other agents' cases. That was an easy choice.

"Referred by Nora Williams," he said aloud, reading the file. No phone number. He looked at his watch—1:15 p.m. It would take him an hour to get out of the District and up to NSA Headquarters at Fort Meade. He would track down Nora Williams on the way.

CHAPTER 38

Having successfully navigated both DC traffic and the NSA's phone directory, Gordon arrived at NSA headquarters shortly before 2:30 p.m. Nora Williams met him in the lobby and escorted him back to the cube farm where she spent her work days.

"I need everything you have on Jummal Adeyami," Gordon said.

"Sure thing, Agent Stone, but I think you probably have it already. We pretty much send everything when we make a referral, but I can check to see if there's anything else, no problem." Williams pressed a few buttons and recalled the case file to her computer, staring intently at her screen.

"Yep, yep, looks like a classic hustle. We see it a lot. Guy comes over here on his student visa, likes what he sees and decides to stay. Then gets a little homesick, goes to see family, etcetera, and heads home. Except now, he's not some teenage ingenue, but a successful American-made businessman with loads of dough. And he gets hustled by someone, typically for a donation to one of a million needy causes over there. Let's see, this one's the Nigerian Relief Fund." Williams giggled. "NeRF, like those foam balls kids used to play with." She looked at Gordon, whose face was a blank slate. "Anyway," she continued. "Money changes hands and the guy returns to the US feeling good. Usually, it's for only a thousand or so. This one was pretty big at ten grand. That's why I remembered it. Not big enough to really grab anyone's attention, but bigger than what I've usually seen."

"What happens to the money?" Gordon asked.

"Well, let's take a look," Williams answered, skimming through the report. "You've already seen this, but it looks like our guy transferred the funds to this fake NeRF charity account that's associated with terrorism." Williams made air quotes with her hands when she said the word associated.

"What's that mean?" Gordon asked. "Associated?"

"Just that it's not a direct or known link to terrorist activity. Most likely it means there's some suspicion on the owner of the account, but nothing that puts him on a most-wanted list anywhere."

"That's it?"

"Afraid so," she said. "Looks like you got everything. Sorry about that. I guess you could have saved yourself the trip up here."

Gordon frowned, remaining silent, lost in thought. There had to be more. "I'm missing something," he said, finally. "If it's so clearly a charity scam, why did you flag it for notice when Adeyami came back to the States?"

"That's a fair question. Not really sure, to be honest. This guy looks like a victim who got conned out of a few thousand bucks. Maybe just an abundance of caution. I didn't want to assume anything since it was more money than I usually see moving around, and it went to an account associated with terrorism." Williams made the air quotes again. "Looks like a loose connection to Boko Haram, and we know those are bad guys. So, the flag went up and here we are."

Williams looked at Gordon, who just looked back.

"Tell you what, Agent Stone. Since you made the trip up here, let's see if we can go down this rabbit hole a little farther. Maybe there's something else."

"We can do that? That's possible?"

Williams smiled at Gordon. "Anything's possible at the NSA,

Agent Stone." She spun in her chair and faced her computer screen once more.

"Can you run his phone number? See who he's talking to?"

"We don't really do that unless there's a demonstrated reason. Ya' know, some sort of indicator he's a bad guy."

Gordon frowned. "I understand. I just thought there might be something more here and wanted to check it out."

"Well, let me see what I can find out."

Gordon gave her a quizzical look. "You *can* run his number?"

Williams smiled again. "I told you, anything's possible at the NSA."

His quizzical look remained.

"Okay," Williams continued. "That's a joke, by the way. But, yes, I can run it through MYSTIC. Don't ask me what that means 'cause I have no clue. It's a voice interception program that allows us to see calls from another country coming into the United States. If he's calling a bad guy we're already watching, MYSTIC will tell us. If he's calling Mom or his sweetheart or the office, we'll still get the numbers, but nothing about who's on the other end."

Gordon had heard of MYSTIC. The program had become public when a self-proclaimed whistleblower revealed it and other classified information held at the NSA to the world. He had read about it in *The Washington Post*. He remembered McNeely calling MYSTIC "some pretty scary shit."

"But you didn't run his number before?" Gordon asked Williams.

"Well, I only got his number when Customs sent notice he was back in the country. It's the number he included with his customs papers when he re-entered. And like I said, he looks like a victim here. We see it all the time. Naïve folks with money are easy marks for the bad guys."

"But we can do it now? See if he's talked to any *known* bad guys?"

"Sure," Williams said. "Just give me a sec." She pressed a few buttons and turned to Gordon. "Now, we wait." It took just seconds for the NSA's network to match outgoing numbers from Jummal's phone to numbers of "bad guys" NSA was watching.

"Whoa," said Williams. "What's this?" Three numbers had come back. Two were just numbers. Maybe a girlfriend and his office. But the third number listed included meta-data—the who, where, and when of that particular call.

"He's got one call to a number in Falls Church, Virginia, that we've flagged."

"Who is it?"

"Let's find out." Williams worked her keyboard. A minute passed, and for the second time in her conversation with Gordon, Williams was surprised. "Whoa," she said again. "That's interesting." She slid her chair to the side. "Come take a look at this."

Gordon stood and walked around the desk to face her computer monitor. He leaned on the desk, staring at the screen.

"This is who your man called. A man named Abdul Malik. We've been watching Malik for a while because"—she scrolled down her screen—"he's been affiliated with the Dar Al-Hijrah Mosque in Falls Church since before 9/11."

Gordon looked at Williams. "Dar Al-Hijrah. That's *the* mosque."

"Yep, the one and only."

Gordon nodded his head in affirmation. He knew the Falls Church mosque. Everyone in federal law enforcement in the metro DC area knew of the infamous mosque. Dar Al-Hijrah had historically been linked to multiple acts of terrorism, none more significant than the 9/11 attacks on the World Trade Center and the Pentagon. One imam from the mosque—who was alleged to have been a key organizer of al-Qaeda—was killed in Yemen by a US drone strike ten years after 9/11.

"Why are you watching Malik?" asked Gordon.

"Good question. No really good answer, not here anyway." She gestured toward her screen. "Looks like he's had ties to the mosque before and after 9/11. He must have been in contact with some bad people during that period for us to still be watching. It's kind of strange, actually."

"How so?"

"Well, the mosque got absolutely hammered after 9/11. A lot of bad guys went there. I mean, *really* bad guys. Terrorist bad guys. No doubt there was some hinky stuff going on there. But, it's not like everyone who worshipped there was a terrorist. Most of 'em were just normal folks going to church."

"Okay, what's that mean?"

"Well, they fixed it."

"They what?"

"They fixed it. Ummm, rebuilt it. Metaphorically. The mosque has been clean for years. No issues, no problems, no links to terrorism. Just an All-American mosque serving the local Muslim community. Not bothering anybody."

"I don't understand. You're still watching this guy's phone calls. Isn't he a bad guy?"

"Maybe yes, maybe no. I've got nothing on him here." She pointed to her screen. "But he's been around that mosque for a long time. Pretty good chance he's known some pretty bad people over the years. A 9/11 happens, maybe planned at this very mosque, we're gonna watch you for a very long time. Maybe forever."

"Huh," he said, mostly to himself. Williams gave Gordon a questioning smile. "Any chance any of those calls were monitored?" Gordon asked hopefully.

Williams's smile broadened. "Sure. *Ret-ro-spec-tive Re-triev-al*," she said, enunciating every syllable. "The RETRO tool inside the MYSTIC system records calls for thirty days. If your guy called Abdul Malik from Nigeria in the past thirty days, it should be there. Let's take a look." Turning back to her computer, Williams began typing. "Got it!" she said with some excitement. "Pull a set of headphones out of that drawer. Plug them into that speaker."

Gordon did as she instructed. Williams played the audio.

The call was a fairly vague conversation between Jummal Adeyami and Abdul Malik. Jummal spoke of his planned return to the US from Nigeria and his need to get his brothers, Okunola and Kambili, into the country to join him.

Gordon made a note of Jummal's brothers joining him back in the United States. That was interesting, though not particularly exciting. "Did you get anything on any family accompanying Adeyami on his trip back here?"

Williams did not even have to look at the file. She had practically memorized it at this point. "No family that NSA is aware of," she said. "He was flying solo."

CHAPTER 39

"Stone, c'mon in," Swayz shouted, gesturing Gordon into his office. "How'd that knock-and-talk go?"

"S-s-sir?"

"Your interview, Stone. Did you close that dog?"

"Well, sir, ummm..." Gordon stood awkwardly in front of Swayz's desk. He was getting uncomfortable.

"Spit it out, Stone. What's up?"

"Sir, I'd like to get a surveillance team assigned to take a look at our subject and possibly other co-conspirators," Gordon blurted out, meaning Jummal's brothers.

"Co-conspirators?" Swayz shook his head, staring at Gordon over the top of his glasses.

"Yes, sir," Gordon said nervously. "I went up to Fort Meade and—"

"You went to Fort Meade? To NSA?" Swayz was incredulous.

"Yessir," answered Gordon meekly.

"Jeeeesus, Stone. Did I ask you to go to NSA? No, I did not. I asked you to go to this guy's house, knock on his door, talk to him, make sure he wasn't going to blow up any buildings or strap dynamite to his chest so we could close this case. You'd get a nice fat closed case on your resume, and we could get on with our lives. Did you not understand what I asked you to do?"

"No, sir. I mean yes, sir. I mean—"

"And now you want a surveillance team for a $10,000 charity scam?"

"Well, ummm, it might be more than that."

"Agent Stone?"

"Sir?"

"Don't go to Fort Meade again unless I tell you to do so. Do you understand?"

"Yes, sir."

"Good. Excellent. Now get out of my office and go close this case." Swayz returned to the paperwork on his desk.

Gordon exited silently and retreated to the basement break room. There was something here. He knew it, but he could not yet see it. For the second time this week, Gordon decided to disobey Swayz. He did not close the case. If Swayz would not give him a surveillance team, he would do it himself. He was on his own. Just how he liked it.

CHAPTER 40

Gordon sat alone in his Jeep Cherokee, just another compact SUV in a cul-de-sac lined with them. It was 4:00 a.m. He had slept until three and pulled into the Arlington development about fifteen minutes ago. Breakfast, a coffee and sausage biscuit, lay on the seat beside him, untouched. He was not hungry and did not need the caffeine—not yet, anyway. He sat motionless except for the slight rise and fall of his chest and the blinking of his eyes, which were glued to 45 Sandy Spring Lane, the new residence of Mr. Jummal Adeyami, recently of New York, New York.

Technically, Gordon knew, he was doing nothing illegal. Nothing prevented him from parking in this cul-de-sac and looking out his window. In reality, however, he was, if not breaking, certainly bending, any number of federal law enforcement rules and procedures. One, the surveillance was not just unauthorized, but he had been ordered to close this case. Two, he was here on his own, with no available backup or even anyone who knew he was here. Gordon was being Gordon, and like his therapist Katherine said, that was just who he was. And he could not have been any happier. He was a Task Force Officer with the JTTF, and he had a case.

He had given himself until 6:00 a.m. before he would have to leave to avoid attracting any attention to himself as the neighborhood woke up. At 5:52 a.m., he stifled a yawn and started to think about leaving when the garage door at 45 Sandy Spring Lane opened. He watched as a white Hyundai Elantra backed out of the garage and pulled out of the cul-de-sac. He tried to curb his excitement as he pulled out after the Elantra and followed it into DC. When the car pulled into a non-descript industrial park section of the Union Market District, Gordon continued on, crossing the next intersection before turning around and returning to within sight of a warehouse. He saw the now-parked Elantra and noted the address.

The next several days proved exhausting. He stopped his surveillance of the Arlington house, which gave him an extra hour or so of sleep, but every morning he made the trip into DC, parking within sight of the warehouse. Every morning, Jummal showed up around 6:00 a.m., parked the Elantra and went inside. Gordon would then leave for his JTTF office, returning to the warehouse during his lunch break and again after hours. Each night, he would see Jummal emerge from the warehouse, get in the Elantra, and drive away. The first two nights, Gordon followed him back to Arlington. It appeared Jummal was just going home each night, so Gordon made the decision to continue watching the warehouse after hours. He knew he might miss Jummal doing something, but he was struck by the warehouse and wondered what could possibly be going on in there.

Gordon kept the warehouse under surveillance, sometimes for hours. Dinner was an afterthought. Sometimes he snuck in a Snickers and a Coke. Often, he stayed past midnight, watching and waiting for something—anything—to happen.

Finally, after several days, his doggedness paid off. On his lunch hour sweep of the warehouse, he saw two trucks backed into the warehouse loading dock. Both were being unloaded. He did not have a direct view, but after a few drive-bys, it looked as though the trucks were delivering furniture and other office or warehouse supplies. There were carts, dollies, file cabinets, at least one desk, chairs, and tables. Nothing remotely out of the ordinary and certainly nothing indicative of criminal activity.

He stayed well past his normal lunch hour. He doubted anyone would miss him at JTTF, so staying was worth the risk. The last item unloaded was wrapped in protective plastic. It was long and rectangular and appeared blue through the plastic sheeting. The delivery men did not take it inside. Instead, they set it on the loading dock. One of them went inside, and a few minutes later emerged with Jummal. That was interesting. Other than arriving in the morning or leaving for home at night, Gordon had never seen Jummal leave the warehouse. The three men talked, and Jummal pointed to the side of the warehouse facing the street.

The conversation ended, and Jummal went back inside. The two men pulled ladders from their truck bed. They knelt on the loading dock and carefully removed the protective plastic from the long, blue rectangle. "What is it?" Gordon asked himself aloud. The men lifted the rectangle and together carefully climbed the ladders.

Gordon smiled. "It's a sign." His smile broadened. A sign would have a name. Maybe even a number. He was closer than ever to finding out what Jummal was up to in that warehouse.

As the men hung the sign, Gordon slowly pulled away. He came to a near stop as he passed within clear view of the sign. A&A Foods was printed in large white letters across the blue background. Beneath the name, in smaller letters, the sign read A Field-Town Foods, Inc., Wholesaler. Gordon's heart sank. Field-Town Foods was the food brokerage company Jummal worked for in New York. Could this all be for nothing? Was this all a legitimate effort to simply open up a branch in DC? What was he doing, besides exhausting himself while he focused on Jummal, against JTTF orders, neglecting his real work?

Gordon drove back to the Washington Field Office. Back to the JTTF. Back to Swayz. Back to his quiet break room in the basement. On the drive, he went over everything he knew. Jummal had sent $10,000 to a bank account associated with possible terrorist players in Nigeria. Jummal had also called *the* mosque while in Nigeria. He had discussed setting up a business in DC and his brothers coming to help.

Jummal had done absolutely nothing illegal, Gordon admitted to himself. Even the NSA thought Jummal had been a victim of a charity scam. The call to Malik was interesting, but not illegal. Jummal could have been simply looking for help setting up this Field-Town Foods affiliate, A&A Foods. Malik was a free man, under passive surveillance for relationships he may have had leading up to 9/11. And how suspicious was that call, really? The man had not even changed his cell phone number in twenty years.

Maybe Swayz was right. This was a dog case that needed to be closed. *That's it,* Gordon decided. With a slight shake of his head, the decision was made. He would go back to A&A Foods this evening and try to do his "knock-and-talk" with Jummal before he went home for the night. Then he could close the case tomorrow morning and tackle the pile of leads sure to be waiting for him at the JTTF.

CHAPTER 41

As he made his way into DC that night, Gordon found himself somewhat melancholy. That in and of itself was unusual, as it was not an emotion he typically experienced. He followed the process. It led where it led. The end result was almost irrelevant. *It was my first case,* Gordon thought. *I wanted it to be more than it was.* That did not make sense, though. He wanted it to be more than it was? That was not how he operated.

But he had seen something in this case. Something that made him perform hours of surveillance on his own time, with no support, against orders. It had turned out to be nothing, and that was that. So why was he melancholy? The last time he felt this way was when his parents told him the Pokémon amusement park had closed and he would not be able to visit. He was sad then because he felt like he had *missed* something. Something important.

What did I miss here? Gordon shook his head. "Nothing," he muttered. There was nothing here. "You're not seven years old, and this is not Pokémon."

Lost in thought, he did not see the white panel van turning into the warehouse. He hit his brakes and skidded to a stop, barely missing the van. A honk from behind him snapped Gordon out of his stupor. He gave an apologetic wave in his rearview and pulled past the warehouse and into a streetside parking space. He took no notice of the driver behind him flipping him the bird as he went by. Gordon sat in his car collecting himself. *What just happened?*

He adjusted his rearview and side mirrors to reflect the warehouse. Two women wearing Muslim *hijabs*, exited the panel van and began unloading box upon box of unidentified goods and carrying them into the warehouse. As the women emerged from the warehouse, they climbed back into the van. Jummal followed them out and walked to the front of the van where the driver was standing, waiting for the women.

Jummal extended his hand and the two men shook. After a brief discussion, Jummal reached into his pocket and pulled out a plain white envelope, handing it to the driver. The driver looked into the envelope, nodded his head, and shook hands once again with Jummal before climbing back into the van and pulling out of the loading dock.

Gordon made a mental note that whatever melancholy he had been feeling had completely disappeared, replaced by a tangible excitement. He took a deep breath and looked back to the warehouse once more. Jummal had gone back inside. It was decision time, and this was an easy one. He pulled out into traffic and followed the van.

DC traffic was heavy and slow, and it was an easy tail. Even if the van's driver had been watching, Gordon was just another commuter making his way home in some of the worst traffic in the country. The van was in no hurry. It made its way, staying with the flow of traffic, not moving in and out in any attempt to find a speed advantage. Gordon stayed in sight, several cars behind.

The van left the District by crossing the Arlington Memorial Bridge, then made its way through Arlington, joining Route 50 before turning off into a Falls Church neighborhood and ultimately finding its way to the parking lot of the Dar Al-Hijrah Mosque. The driver and women got out and dispersed, going their separate ways.

This was something, thought Gordon, as he took down the

license plate number on the van before pulling away and heading home. Another link, perhaps, between Jummal and Abdul Malik? Something had been delivered, and it appeared money changed hands. Gordon had only seen the envelope, but it was pretty clear Jummal was paying for services rendered, whatever they were. Maybe, just maybe, this case was not the dog Swayz thought it was.

CHAPTER 42

Reenergized, Gordon was up early the next morning. He went back to the mosque to see if the van was still there. It was, so he watched and waited. Six o'clock came and went, then seven, then eight. Nothing had happened. No one had even approached the van. Gordon left for his job at JTTF. He had a new lead, and he would follow it. At lunch, nothing changed. The van stayed put, and no one approached it. He had run the tags and knew the van belonged to the mosque. What could the mosque be delivering to A&A Foods and what did this have to do with Jummal and his conversations with Malik?

That night, he returned to the mosque. All was quiet until 9:30 p.m., when two women wearing *hijabs* appeared from seemingly nowhere and gathered at the van. A man approached and unlocked the van's back door, and the women climbed in. The man was the same driver from yesterday. When he pulled out from the mosque, Gordon followed, thinking it could be a long night.

It was. Gordon followed the van as it made stops at seven different stores. Each time, the routine was the same. The women would get out of the van, three or four minutes apart. They would enter the store and emerge a few minutes later, sometimes with an armload, sometimes carrying a shopping bag, sometimes a shopping cart with a couple of items in it. They would return to the van and load up whatever they had been buying. The driver would move into the back of the van as the women brought the products out to him.

Gordon rubbed his eyes, asking himself whether this dance would last all night and, more worrisome, whether the routine had *anything* to do with his case. Both questions were answered when the van made its eighth stop. This time, it was not at a store but the A&A Foods warehouse, where the women dutifully unloaded what appeared to be everything they had spent the last four hours buying. Jummal appeared and handed an envelope to the driver, and the two men shook hands. It was 2:00 a.m. when the van finally left.

Gordon did not follow the van back to the mosque, but instead went straight home. This late, he did not want to be spotted tailing the van. Besides, he believed he now knew exactly what Jummal was up to. He was buying "loss leaders." What he did not know was why. The *why* made no sense at all, but he was determined to find out.

CHAPTER 43

Was Jummal running a scam? Why on earth would a successful food industry executive at a successful New York food brokerage company be pushing loss leaders at his start-up?

Gordon had no idea. None of it made any sense, so he reviewed what he knew. Jummal was opening some sort of food wholesaler called A&A Foods out of a warehouse in DC. The shop was affiliated with Field-Town Foods, where Jummal had been an executive for several years. He had recently traveled to his homeland of Nigeria, where he had been hustled out of $10,000 in some sort of charity scam. And now, someone at the Dar Al-Hijrah Mosque was, for a fee apparently, buying up various products from around the region and delivering them to A&A Foods.

Gordon had been with the FDA for nine years. He was familiar with loss leaders, which were products that retailers put up for sale at a loss; that is, for less than they had paid for them from their supplier. Diapers were a typical example. Essentially, a store would buy a load of Huggies for $10 per package, then turn around and advertise those same Huggies on sale for $5 per package. By selling the diapers at such a big discount, the seller was hoping customers lured into their store to take advantage of the great sale on Huggies stayed and did the rest of their shopping at the seller's store, whereby the seller quickly made up for the $5 loss they were taking on each package of

Huggies sold.

It was a legitimate sales and marketing technique, as old as the first grocery store. What appeared to be happening at A&A Foods, however, was the ugly side of the loss-leader market. A corrupt wholesaler could swoop into a store or market and clean the store out of all its underpriced Huggies at $5 a package. Then that wholesaler could turn around and resell them at the market price of $10 a package. If the shady wholesaler was savvy enough and hit the loss-leader sales just right, they could quickly turn the product back around, selling for a tidy and illegal profit.

Legitimate sellers fought this fraud by limiting the number of Huggies any one person could purchase. The corrupt wholesaler got around that by hiring cheap labor to go into a store *en masse* and buy all the product. Limit five per customer? No problem. Send in ten buyers and you walk out with fifty. Do that enough times in a big enough region and time it just right, and you stood to make a lot of money.

That was also the problem with the loss-leader scam. It takes a lot of time, planning, bodies, and money to gather up enough product to make it worthwhile, not to mention timing the market correctly so that buyers are interested in your product at the market price. Margins get very thin quickly, and if not timed perfectly, you end up with a warehouse full of Huggies you can't make any money from.

Jummal would certainly have the skill set and probably the means to support a successful loss-leader scam, but he would certainly need a lot more than a van load of loss-leader products. More importantly, why would he? Gordon asked himself this again and again. He was missing something. But it was there. He could feel it. His hours of surveillance had paid off. There was a crime here, and he knew it went beyond loss-leader fraud. And as much as he might have hoped, he could not run this case alone anymore. He needed help.

CHAPTER 44

Ever the process-driven investigator, Gordon knew that when he discovered actual criminal activity, he had to report it. In a move he regretted almost immediately, Gordon took the case to his supervisor at JTTF, SSA Sean Swayz.

Predictably, Swayz went ballistic.

"Jeeeesus, Stone." Swayz stood behind his desk, hands clenched in fists, his face red. "Kill. This. Dog. Simple, straightforward order. Did you not understand?"

"Yes, sir," said Gordon. "But there's something more here. Something is up. It doesn't make sense the subject would be running a loss-leader scam by itself. There's not enough money in it and it's hard to pull off. I know he's up to something."

"You don't know anything, Stone! You've seen some suspicious activity pointing to what? Food fraud? You don't even know if anything illegal has actually happened. You sure as hell can't prove anything." Swayz paused to catch his breath. "J-T-T-F, Gordo. J-T-T-F! That first T, do you know what it stands for?"

Gordon nodded.

"Let me hear you say it," demanded Swayz.

"Terrorism," Gordon mumbled.

"Bingo! You win the prize, Stone. Terrorism. Bombs, assassinations, nukes, nerve gas, hijacking. Do I need to go on? Do you understand what we do here? Terrorism, Agent Stone, strikes fear and terror in the hearts of everyday, God-fearing Americans. That's why it's called terrorism! Do you know what does not, in fact, strike terror in the hearts of God-fearing Americans, Agent Stone? Do you?"

Gordon tried to speak.

"Don't answer that, it was rhetorical. The sale of undervalued goddamn groceries does *not* strike terror into the heart of anyone on planet Earth. Therefore, it is by definition, *not* terrorism. Therefore, the JTTF does not and will not investigate this loss-leader market you're apparently so fond of. And more importantly." Swayz raised his voice another octave. "More importantly, I do not give a damn about food fraud," he screamed. "Close this sonuvabitch and get the hell out of my sight!"

Gordon practically ran out of Swayz's office, down the stairs to the basement break room. He did not even turn the lights on, but just sat on the old cafeteria chair quietly in the dark. There was no head-in-his-hands, no reflection, no regret. He knew there was more to what Jummal was doing. There was something going on at A&A Foods, and he knew what he had to do. He had to check the boxes. He had to follow the process. But right now, he just needed a friend. He pulled his cell phone from his pocket and dialed.

ASAC McNeely answered on the first ring. He had known and worked with Gordon for a long time, and he knew if Gordon was calling, something had gone off the rails at the JTTF.

"What did you do, Gordo?" he asked.

"I may have gone a little rogue," Gordon responded.

McNeely smiled. "Just 'a little,' huh?" Unlike Swayz, McNeely knew Gordon and how he operated. He knew Gordon's Asperger's made him a better investigator in many ways. Most importantly, he had traveled enough miles with Gordon to trust him implicitly.

Gordon told McNeely the whole saga. Almost immediately,

McNeely was all in. When he saw Gordon like this—fully vested in a seemingly hopeless case—he knew exactly what Gordon needed.

"Gordo, listen to me. If I was there right now, I'd put my arm around you. I'd build you up for a minute or two, and I'd make sure you understand that I have your back. Do you understand that, Gordon? I need to know that you understand that."

"I do, boss."

"Alright, that's good, that's good. And Gordon?"

"Yes."

"You know what you need to do, right? Let me hear you say it."

"The work, boss."

"My man, Gordon Stone," McNeely said with a chuckle. "Hey, Gordo?"

"Yeah?"

"Those JTTF boys have no clue on this, do they?"

Gordon smiled. "Not yet, boss. Not yet."

CHAPTER 45

Gordon stood up in the darkened break room. He walked slowly to the closed door but did not exit. Instead, he flipped the light switch and a half dozen fluorescents flickered to life, brightening up the room. Gordon paced, covering every inch of the room, step-by-step, almost in slow motion, mumbling to himself. His face was a panoply of expressiveness. Pursed lips. Raised eyebrows. A hand rubbing his chin. A head shake. A nod. Back and forth around the room, doing the work.

He stopped in the middle of the room. Arms crossed, he gave himself a gentle nod, pivoted on his heel, and sat back down at the table, staring at his phone. He picked it up, scrolling through his contacts until he found the right one.

Assistant United States Attorney (AUSA) Gabriel Jameson sat at his desk with his feet up on it. A brief in his left hand and a pen in his right, he looked at his phone with annoyance when it rang. It was the direct line into his office. "Now what?" he said aloud. He was about to let the call go to his message when he glanced at the display.

Stone, G. followed by a number he remembered well. Jameson had prosecuted Gordon's award-winning applications fraud case. He appreciated Gordon's focus and diligence. That investigation, when it landed on Jameson's desk, was tight and solid. It proved an easy plea bargain against multiple defendants. It was just the kind of work an AUSA loved to get from an investigator—clean, tight, no holes, easy win. Gordon had delivered.

Jameson put down the brief and picked up the phone.

"Agent Stone, it's great to hear from you. How's it going?"

"I need some help, sir."

Jameson smiled. Stone was nothing if not direct. No small talk and always called him sir. Out of deference, Jameson always referred to Gordon as Agent Stone.

"What can I do for you, Agent Stone?"

"I've got a case but need some help. Quite a bit of help, actually, sir."

"Do tell."

"I need grand jury subpoenas for phone subscriber and toll information, as well as a court order for a pen register. I'm going to need a warrant—no, sorry, two warrants—for a residence and a business, but I'm not there yet so those can wait. I'm probably going to need wiretaps or maybe a FISA warrant, too."

"Whoa, slow down Agent Stone. Why don't you tell me about your case first, then we'll get to what you need." Jameson was intrigued, but he had his own process to follow.

"Yessir, right. Sorry."

"It's no problem, Agent Stone. Tell me what you've got."

In painstaking detail, Gordon told Jameson the story. Jummal Adeyami in Nigeria, paying a con man with possible ties to terrorism $10,000. Jummal's return to the States, move to Virginia from New York, setting up a food wholesaler in the District. The contact Jummal had with *the* mosque in Falls Church and how the mosque was providing Jummal with buyers for retail goods and delivering products to Jummal's warehouse. He explained what a loss leader was and how it could be taken advantage of by repackaging and reselling loss-leader purchases as new for significant profit. And he described how once products were repackaged, the FDA or any law enforcement would have no way to trace the merchandise, even if they figured out the loss-leader scam.

"Have you seen him repackage or resell anything, Agent Stone?"

They both knew the answer. "Sir, I have seen no laws broken, but I know this business. All the indicators of a loss-leader scam are there. But, sir, there's something else here. To be effective, a loss-leader hustle takes a lot of planning and resources. Even if you get all that right, you still have to depend on the food markets and your own sense of timing. Usually, a loss-leader scam is a street hustle for a few hundred or maybe a thousand dollars. A large operation with real profit is difficult to pull off, even for someone like Jummal Adeyami, who knows this world inside and out. There's something else going on here because a loss-leader scam doesn't make any sense for someone like Adeyami."

"What's the JTTF say about this?" Jameson asked.

"They want me to kill it. It's not their kind of case. But there's something here, sir. I know this business from my days at FDA-OCI. There's more to this. And one other thing, sir. I think Adeyami may have brought his brothers into the country illegally. He mentioned them coming back to the US with him, but there's no record of them entering the country."

"And you've seen them, the brothers?"

"Well, no sir. I just know that in a conversation with a contact at *the* mosque, Jummal mentioned getting his brothers into the country. But I can't say if they are here or not at this time."

Jameson shut his eyes and took a breath. "Agent Stone, how did you hear this conversation? Don't tell me if it's classified. I don't have a *need to know*. Not yet, anyway."

MYSTIC and RETRO were classified systems at NSA. Gordon knew he could not talk about them with Jameson. "That came from the NSA, sir. I can't really tell you how."

"Understood, Agent Stone. That's fine. But there's not much

here in terms of illegal activity. None, in fact." Just speculation and suspicion, Jameson thought. But the speculation and suspicion were coming from Agent Gordon Stone. That was something. Jameson knew he never would have made the application fraud case without Gordon. He saw things no one else could see. Jameson had history with Gordon and trusted his instincts. Nevertheless, he had to have more.

"Agent Stone, you find me something, anything, with some substance to it, more than just a hint of criminality, and I'll jacket a case. But you've got more work to do before I can make that happen."

"Yes, sir. I'll do that. Thanks for hearing me out." Gordon abruptly hung up the phone. "More work to do," Gordon muttered, echoing Jameson. Gordon knew the AUSA was right. "Just like McNeely always says, you've got to do the work."

CHAPTER 46

For three more nights, Gordon continued to stake out the A&A Foods warehouse. And for three nights, he saw nothing. No deliveries, no mosque-owned van, no Jummal, nothing at all. Just a food wholesaler closed for the night with absolutely nothing going on.

Am I wrong? Gordon had begun asking himself on the second night. He did not think so, but the work was not turning anything up at all. He drove home after the third night at around midnight. Maybe his instincts were wrong. It was his first case with the JTTF. He knew he wanted there to be some substance to the case. The loss-leader aspect was still pretty strange, but the deliveries seemed to have stopped. Could he have been misreading this whole investigation? "One more night," he said to himself.

On the fourth night, everything about the scene at A&A Foods looked exactly as it had for the previous three nights, until 1:00 a.m., when the familiar white Hyundai Elantra turned into the adjacent lot. Jummal got out, and it seemed to Gordon he was practically running to the warehouse with a noticeable spring in his step. Something was happening, but what?

Jummal's extra energy passed to Gordon. He sipped a coffee and was energized, hoping against hope this was not just another delivery of loss-leader grocery products. But as soon as he thought it, the familiar white van from the mosque appeared and backed into the loading dock.

When this happened before, there had been an explosion of activity as the driver emerged and the women in the back of the van immediately got to work unloading it. Jummal typically appeared on the loading dock, overseeing the delivery and exchanging words—and money—with the driver. But not this time.

This time, the van went dark. The driver turned off the engine, but stayed in the cab. Stayed and waited. No calls, no cigarette—Gordon saw the glow of neither—hardly any movement at all.

A door from the loading dock opened, revealing a thin ray of dim light. Jummal emerged and jogged straight to the van doors. With a wave to the driver's side mirror, he opened the doors. Gordon could almost see his smile and sense his excitement as Jummal disappeared inside the van. Thirty seconds, a minute, two minutes. What was happening in the back of that van? Gordon held his focus, barely breathing, rarely blinking.

Jummal emerged from the van, then turned back toward it. Two men followed him out of the van. He grabbed each affectionately by the shoulder with his left hand and pointed to the lighted doorway across the loading dock with his right. The two men headed toward the door, and Jummal followed. When the three disappeared inside, the van driver, who had never left his seat, started the van, pulled out of the loading dock, and disappeared down the road.

Gordon was giddy. It was the brothers. It had to be. Gordon waited. More than an hour went by. His eyes never left the warehouse. Jummal finally came out, but by himself. No brothers in tow. Jummal climbed into his car. Gordon had a decision to make. He decided to stay on the warehouse for a little while longer, hoping Jummal was just going home for the night. With any luck, Jummal had put his brothers to bed in the warehouse and called it a night.

An hour later, Gordon yawned, finally coming down from the excitement of the brothers' appearance. He knew he had to determine if the two men were, in fact, Jummal's brothers. He was certain of it, but his certainty was not the standard. All was quiet at A&A Foods, so Gordon took the opportunity to flip back through his notes to his first conversation with Nora Williams at the NSA. In the recorded call Jummal had made from Nigeria to Malik at the mosque, Jummal had mentioned his brothers by name. Gordon flipped through his notepad. "There you are," he said when he flipped to the right page. "Okunola and Kambili Adeyami. Welcome to America."

Having reached the limits of his solo surveillance effort, he started his car and pulled away from A&A Foods. It was around 2:00 a.m., and he needed rest. He took a long route home. There was no traffic and the easy driving worked to clear his head. Without thinking about it, he crossed the Potomac River and drove through Arlington. He found himself circling Jummal's suburban cul-de-sac. Gordon's headlights and the streetlamps above provided the only illumination of the neighborhood. There were no people out and about, no dogs barking, no other cars moving around. Dark houses with garbage cans at the curb. As quiet as quiet could be. Gordon had a thought, but shook his head and turned out of the cul-de-sac. He needed rest. Tomorrow was going to be a busy day.

He managed a bit of rest, but found himself up, showered, making coffee, and out the door by seven. The arrival of Jummal's brothers seemed likely to impact Gordon's case. At the moment, he had no idea what that impact might be, but he knew today would be different than all the days prior. He reversed his route home from a few hours ago and drove through Jummal's neighborhood on his way to the office. This time, however, the drive did not clear his mind. Instead, there was plenty of traffic to work through, as well as pedestrians going through their normal morning routines. The drive served as a stimulant, adding to the coffee he sipped from a travel mug.

Jummal's cul-de-sac remained quiet, but nothing like the night before. One car backed out of a garage, and an elderly woman in a housecoat retrieved her now empty trash can from the curb, wheeling it back toward her home. Two emptied garbage cans rested at the foot of Jummal's driveway. *Looks like someone is sleeping late today.*

Gordon left Arlington and drove into DC. He turned into the parking garage used by the JTTF staff and turned off his car's engine, but did not get out. He sat perfectly still, eyes closed. He was tired. With only three hours of sleep, the drive and coffee had not been enough. He knew he had to go inside, but he would take a moment to steel himself. Sleep called, but he fought it off by going over the case in his head, his lips moving slightly as he replayed what he knew. He rehashed everything, from the moment Swayz gave him the case to his drive through Jummal's Arlington suburb just a few minutes ago. What was Jummal up to? Loss-leader fraud? Illegal immigration? Surely there was more.

His eyes popped open. "Trash cans," he said with a smile. Gordon knew exactly what he needed to do. Inside, he went straight downstairs to the break room. He pulled his cell phone from his pocket and called McNeely.

"I need two favors," Gordon said.

"Okay, Gordo, let's have it," McNeely said.

"First, Okunola and Kambili Adeyami. Those are my guy's brothers, and I think they're in country illegally. Can you find out if they came through Customs?"

"I'll see what CBP has on those names. What else?" McNeely was getting curious.

"I'm going to need you to open a case at OCI," Gordon said.

McNeely chuckled. Gordon was onto something, and McNeely's heart skipped a beat. He loved this part. The case was right there, right there in front of Gordon. He just had to see it. And when he did, he would have the balls to reach out and take it. Not because he had a brass set. No, Gordon would take it just because it was the right thing to do. More than anyone, more even than Gordon himself, McNeely knew this was the easy part for Gordon. This was Gordon being Gordon at his best.

Things were about to get interesting.

CHAPTER 47

In 1988, the US Supreme Court held in the case of *California v. Greenwood* that when someone exposes their garbage to the public—literally, hauling your trash cans to the curb—there was no expectation of privacy in whatever that garbage might contain and the government could search that garbage without a warrant. Thus, the "trash run" became one of the least appealing yet most effective tools of law enforcement across the country. Anything left out with the trash was up for grabs, be it a lost diamond ring or a banana peel.

A week had gone by since Gordon had seen Jummal's trash cans at the end of his driveway. It was 3:30 in the morning, and the drive to Jummal's house was a quick one. In the back of Gordon's car were four trash bags filled with crumpled newspapers—fairly light in weight, but full in volume. Once again, he eased his car into Jummal's cul-de-sac as he scanned the area for any activity. As he hoped and expected, there was none. He parked in front of one of Jummal's neighbors, turned off his car, and waited.

Five minutes passed. Then ten. No activity, no noise, and most importantly, no people. Gordon popped the trunk and eased out of the driver's seat. He quietly walked around to the back of his car and grabbed two of the newspaper-filled bags. Leaving the trunk open, he calmly walked toward Jummal's house. When he got to the end of the driveway, he put his two trash bags on the ground.

Gordon took another look around the cul-de-sac. All remained quiet, so he quickly opened one of Jummal's trash cans and pulled out three full garbage bags. With two in his left and one in his right, he walked back to his car and deposited the three bags in his trunk. He grabbed the two remaining bags filled with newspaper and carried them back to Jummal's driveway, depositing them into the empty can and closing the lid.

With a final look around, he opened the second can, pulled out a single bag of Jummal's garbage, and placed the two remaining bags of newspaper into that can, returning the lid to its closed position. Gordon hurried back to his car and deposited the fourth garbage bag into his trunk, silently shutting it.

He slipped seamlessly back into the driver's seat, flinching slightly at the sound of his engine starting. But the area remained quiet. Gordon smiled and drove away. The bags of paper he had swapped for Jummal's garbage would keep the garbage men from wondering why Jummal left empty cans at the end of the driveway. More importantly, if Jummal had to throw something out before the garbage truck came, absent a close inspection, he probably would not notice that his real garbage had been taken.

Gordon knew he could not take the garbage back to the JTTF to go through. Swayz would take his head off, and Gordon liked his head right where it was, attached above his shoulders. But the garbage in his trunk was potential evidence. He could not simply take it home. Gordon had to follow the process.

He traveled east on the Dulles Toll Road until he made it to the Beltway, the eight-plus lane loop running around the nation's capital city. He drove north before turning east again, eventually exiting at New Hampshire Avenue, one of the main thoroughfares out of DC.

This was familiar territory to Gordon. North through Hillandale, past the volunteer fire department, before turning right into the main campus of the Food & Drug Administration in White Oak, Maryland. The trip had taken an hour. Rush hour was just beginning. It was 6:00 a.m. when he parked behind the FDA Office of Criminal Investigations.

McNeely met Gordon in the parking lot and greeted him with a warm smile. There were no hugs or handshakes, as Gordon was holding two bags of Jummal's garbage in either hand. McNeely grabbed the two bags from Gordon's left hand and walked with him to the rear entrance of FDA-OCI. Inside, McNeely followed Gordon to a large conference room. Each man set his garbage bags on the table, which McNeely had already covered with a drop cloth. With only a nod to Gordon, McNeely left the conference room, shutting the door behind him on the way out. When the door latch clicked shut, McNeely blew air out of inflated cheeks. Best not to interrupt Gordon once he gets rolling, he thought.

Gordon noticed two fifty-five-gallon waste bins lined with large contractor disposal bags at the end of the conference table. He walked over and wheeled one to his side near the bags of Jummal's garbage. Donning plastic gloves, he grabbed one of the bags, said to the room, "Here we go," and ripped at the plastic of the first bag.

It was a relatively simple process. Any paper that might be of interest was separated, photographed, and laid out at the other end of the conference table. Any food-type waste was dumped into the waste container. Anything else was assessed on the fly. If he thought it might be of interest, he would keep it for later examination. Otherwise, into the waste bin it went.

It was methodical work. Not slow, but methodical. Gordon put his hands on every piece of garbage in the four bags. The bulk of the garbage was food waste, which was quickly disposed of. Gordon had laid out a small number of paper items at the other end of the table. It was not much, but he would not know what he had until he had a chance to look closely.

With the four bags emptied, Gordon wheeled the waste bin

outside and emptied it into the dumpster behind the FDA-OCI building, then returned to the conference room. He rolled up the tarp covering the conference table and folded it neatly before returning to the paper items he had separated from the rest of the garbage.

The paper pile included junk mail, a few magazines, a religious flyer you would find between your wiper and windshield in the mall parking lot, and a handful of printed pages. Junk mail, magazines, and the flyer made it to the second waste bin.

The printed pages required further scrutiny. There were several copies of a presentation related to A&A Foods that had been printed and marked up in pen. Drafts, thought Gordon, of a presentation Jummal was planning or had already made. Gordon kept those. And there was one email Jummal had printed.

He looked closely at the email. The header included the traditional "From, To, CC and Subject" lines. Gordon took note of the "From" line: Abebi_Abiona_Forever@yahoo.com. Curiously, there was no email address in the "To" box. It was blank. It looked like the email was never sent. Nevertheless, he found the narrative compelling and mysterious.

> *A test brothers to see if this will work. Its coming together now——for our sisters! We'll talk here. Cant wait. Abebi and Abiona forever!!!*

Gordon read the email again, then a third and fourth time. *We'll talk here*? Typically, Gordon's way did not allow for theoretical leaps in an investigation. He went step-by-step, painstakingly, methodically, checking all the boxes. But he made a leap this time. *We'll talk here* could mean only one thing. The brothers were coming. In fact, they were here. Gordon had seen them. They had talked and hugged and celebrated their arrival with Jummal at the warehouse. The pieces were falling into place. He still did not know what he had, exactly, but he had evidence that Kambili and Okunola Adeyami had entered the country illegally. It had started with the phone call from Jummal to Malik, then his own observation of two men arriving in the middle of the night at A&A Foods. The behavior of all three upon their arrival was further evidence that they not only knew each other, but were close enough to share an embrace. And now, there was the email intended for the brothers, but apparently never sent.

Gordon knew it was thin, but it was something. It did not exactly scream criminal activity, but maybe, just maybe, it would be enough for AUSA Jameson to jacket a case.

CHAPTER 48

When Gordon emerged from the conference room, the sun was peeking over the horizon. McNeely remained the only staff in the office, but that would change in another thirty minutes or so. Gordon sat across from McNeely's desk and his ASAC pushed a cup of black coffee toward him.

"Thanks, boss," said Gordon.

"Well, don't keep me in suspense, Gordo. What'd you find?" McNeely asked.

Gordon took a sip of coffee. "Not much, but maybe something." He passed the email to McNeely. "I think that was an email Jummal was going to send to his brothers. I'm not sure what it all means, but it looks like they were planning to talk once the brothers got here. And I think they're already here. I saw them arrive at A&A Foods last week."

"All right," McNeely harumphed. "I may be able to help you there. Like you asked, I reached out to CBP to check on..." McNeely paused, flipping a notepad on his desk to the pertinent page. "Okunola and Kambili Adeyami," he said, reading his notes. "I called in a favor and had them make it a priority. I heard back last night."

Gordon looked at McNeely, eyebrows raised, silently asking what his boss had heard from Customs and Border Patrol.

McNeely smiled, knowingly teasing his mentee and quasi-protégé. "The CBP has no record of an Okunola or Kambili

Adeyami entering this country."

Gordon slapped his hand down on McNeely's desk and jumped excitedly from his chair. "That means they're illegal. They're here and they came illegally. AUSA Jameson will open a file on that. He has to."

"Well," McNeely said, "he better, since I opened a case here and let you bring us all this garbage." He pushed the email printout back over to Gordon.

Gordon picked it up and looked at it for the thousandth time. "You mean evidence, right, boss?"

"I suppose I do, Gordo. I suppose I do. It's time to release the hounds, Gordo. You're onto something. Don't let up. I'll call AUSA Jameson this morning and we'll set up a meeting." McNeely stood at his desk. "You best finish that coffee and get to it."

"Got to do the work, right, boss?" Gordon was smiling.

"Damn right, Gordo."

Both agents took big swigs from their coffee mugs and set them on McNeely's desk.

"Thanks, boss," said Gordon as he turned to leave.

"One more thing, Gordo," said McNeely. "What's up with that email address? Apples and Angela or whatnot?"

Gordon smiled. "Abebi and Abiona," he responded. "At Yahoo.com."

"Yeah." McNeely chuckled. "Them. What's up with that?"

"Don't know yet, boss."

"Sisters?"

"Looks like."

"And A&A Foods," McNeely said flatly. "Coincidence?"

Gordon shrugged.

"What do we say about coincidences, Gordo?"

"We say fuck 'em, boss."

"Damn straight. Why don't you give your friend at NSA a shout. See if she can find anything on those names. Maybe confirm they're sisters. Dollars to donuts, they're connected to our three boys in some form or fashion."

Gordon nodded and looked down at the email in his hand. "I'll get this into evidence."

As Gordon left the office, McNeely shouted after him. "And get some sleep when you can, Gordo. Looks like you're going to be busy for a while."

McNeely sat back down and resumed his coffee intake. A few minutes passed, allowing him to walk through Gordon's case again. He was interrupted by a noise outside his office. It was his boss, Special Agent in Charge Steven Johnson.

"Morning, Pete," Johnson said, pausing at McNeely's door. "I've got donuts. I'll put 'em in the conference room."

"Thanks, Steve. I'll grab one in a few," McNeely said as Johnson went to deliver the donuts to the conference room. McNeely held his breath. He knew the conference room had been left clean, but he had not yet gone in to spray away the remaining funk from Gordon's trash run.

Johnson stepped into the conference room, put the donuts on the table and took in a deep breath. His face contorted. McNeely smiled as he heard Johnson shout, "What the hell is that stench?" McNeely opened a desk drawer and pulled out a can of Febreze.

"On my way," he shouted.

CHAPTER 49

McNeely joined Gordon at AUSA Gabriel Jameson's office. They walked Jameson through the case again, adding everything Gordon had learned from the trash run and the CBP. Jameson asked them to explain the loss-leader market once more, just so he understood the whole scheme. Then they focused on the two brothers.

Jameson frowned. "But it's who you *think* are the brothers. And I agree, they probably are, and if that's who it is, they are here illegally. But you don't really know who those two men are who arrived at the warehouse. There's no positive ID, right?" he asked.

"There's more here, sir," Gordon countered. "But I need subpoenas to see who the subject is talking to and what's up with this email account. And I can't get a subpoena unless you jacket a case."

"Where's the FBI on all this, Agent Stone? It sure doesn't seem like something the JTTF would be interested in."

McNeely interjected himself into the discussion. "Listen, Gabriel. We've known each other a long time. You've seen Gordon in action. You know he sees things differently than the rest of us. The FBI's not on this because there's no way the FBI, or sure as shit the JTTF, would touch this case. All we've got now is maybe some shady dealings in this loss-leader market, some troubling language in an email, and two likely immigration violations. But it smells bad, and it's getting worse. You know it smells bad. Hell, I opened a case at OCI just 'cause the stench on this is heavy, *and* because Gordo here brought it to me. Dammit, Gabe, this is Gordon we're talking about. He knows there's something here, but he can't get to it if he's stuck banging his head against the wall all by himself. Jacket the case. We'll get subpoenas, and Gordon will light this thing up."

Jameson realized Gordon's case was pretty thin. On the other hand, there was a lot more evidence—circumstantial evidence, he reminded himself—of criminal activity than Gordon had brought to him at their first meeting. He knew the two men Gordon saw on the loading dock were Jummal Adeyami's brothers. Of course they were. Everyone in the room knew that. But they couldn't prove it, not yet anyway. The loss-leader market angle was an interesting twist. It was not a standard fraud case, that much was certain, and there was less evidence there than there was for the immigration violations.

Jameson allowed himself the briefest moment to fantasize that Gordon was right, that there was something more here, and the loss-leader scam and the illegal immigration were leading to something bigger. Was there a terrorism link here somewhere? "Grocery store fraud," he muttered.

McNeely interjected a second time. "Hell yes, grocery store fraud. And hell yes, illegal immigration. Think about it, Gabriel. Think about the why. What's the why? Why come back and start this new business venture? Why reach out to this guy at the mosque the NSA's been watching since 9/11? Why's he using that guy to bring product to his warehouse? Our guy's already on the hook for moving ten grand to an account associated with terrorism. What if that's it? What if he's becoming a player on the international terrorism scene, raising money for God knows what? There's something here, Gabe. Gordon sees it. Let him loose and see where it goes."

Jameson took a deep breath. He made eye contact with McNeely, then Gordon, and back to McNeely. He looked down at his notes, then grabbed the edge of his desk, pushed his chair back and stood. “Agent Stone, you really came through on that application fraud case. Signed, sealed, and delivered. Wrapped in a bow so tight the defendants were racing to my office to see who could strike the best deal. I wouldn’t say I owed you, because that’s your job. But you made my job easy, and I appreciate that. So, you tell me, Agent Stone…are you going to bring the same drive to this case, the same energy, the same focus? Because right now, we’re a long way from a pretty, tight, red bow, and we’re not even in the same ballpark as a plea bargain.”

“There’s more here, sir, I know it,” Gordon said.

After another breath, Jameson extended his hand to Gordon, who reached out to take it. Both men gripped firmly across the desk.

“All right, Agent Stone,” Jameson said. “I’ll jacket a case. Let’s do it.”

The two released their handshake, and Jameson reached for McNeely, who shook the AUSA’s hand with a smile.

“Always a pleasure to see you down here, Pete,” Jameson said.

“You always make it worth the trip, Gabe,” said McNeely. “I’ll leave you two gentlemen to it. Plenty of work to do.” He smiled at Gordon and left Jameson’s office.

Gordon and Jameson returned to their seats.

“Okay, Agent Stone,” said Jameson. “Tell me what you need.”

CHAPTER 50

Gordon needed to find out who Jummal had been talking to. Subpoenas would get him a phone history on Jummal's cell, as well as email history on the email address he had discovered in the trash run. He also needed real-time information on who Jummal was talking to now. For that, he asked Jameson for PRTT orders on Jummal's phone, as well as on the Abebi_Abiona_Forever email address. Jameson simply nodded and wrote in his notebook.

PRTT stood for Pen Register and Trap-and-Trace order. These were historic law enforcement terms for physical machines that would be attached to telephone lines. One, the pen register, captured phone numbers dialed out from a subject's phone. The other, the trap-and-trace order, captured phone numbers that dialed into a subject's phone.

Wireless communications had made PRTT operations a lot simpler for the government. Equipment was no longer required because data like phone numbers and email addresses were electronically captured every time anyone made a phone call or sent an email. The PRTT order gave the government access to that data. It was simple, easy, and no one had to climb a telephone pole to install any equipment.

A court had to approve such surveillance, but the government merely had to present specific and articulable facts as to why they believed criminal activity might be happening. That was easy enough, but the only information Gordon would get from the PRTT orders he sought were the phone numbers Jummal was calling and the numbers from which Jummal was receiving calls. He could not use the PRTT orders to hear any conversations in real time, or even a later recording. The same rules applied for the email address. Gordon would get email addresses Jummal was sending to or receiving from, but not any content.

Email content or actual phone conversations required a wiretap, and a wiretap order required probable cause that a crime was being committed. Gordon knew he was not there yet. The PRTT orders were the first step.

"How about the business line at A&A Foods?" Jameson asked.

Gordon thought for a moment. Experience told him that if Jummal was really involved in something nefarious, he likely would not be using a commercial phone line to further any conspiracy. In fact, Gordon considered he had been lucky so far in that the calls he knew about were to and from Jummal's personal cell phone and not a burner. More importantly, this investigation was still largely a one-man show, and if a PRTT order on the business line was issued, Gordon knew himself well enough to know he would track every number into and out of A&A Foods. He gave himself a slight nod, internally affirming his belief that if Jummal was involved in criminal activity, he would not use the A&A Foods business line. Nevertheless, he hedged just a bit.

"Let's hold off on that for now," he said. "If it looks like he's using that line, we can come back to it later."

Step two was subpoenas. Jameson could subpoena the call history from Jummal's cell phone, as well as the history of the Yahoo email account. Gordon was not sure what he would find from the phone or the email, but he knew there was something there. The work was just beginning.

The PRTT results would be almost instantaneous. Within

twenty-four hours, Gordon would begin to receive reports of phone numbers and email addresses for anyone Jummal was in contact with, as well as the IP addresses of anyone accessing the email account and when they did so.

The two subpoenas would have to be sent out to Jummal's phone carrier and Yahoo. Gordon intended to use his status as a JTTF agent to bring full pressure to bear on the phone and email companies. This would get him front-of-the-line status and a quicker response. If Swayz found out, Gordon knew he was a dead man. The risk was worth it, he felt. A typical subpoena response might take thirty to sixty days. Add in any notion of terrorism to the subpoena, and he could potentially have the information he sought in a week or two.

While he waited for the subpoena response, he would content himself with watching the results from the PRTT order. Those results, however, were a disappointment. There were a handful of calls, all fairly short, to a seemingly random assortment of phone numbers. Other than two calls back to Nigeria to the same number, there were no other repeated calls and no calls of any significant length. Disappointing, Gordon thought, but not surprising. This was the number he believed to be Jummal's personal cell phone. Calls to set up A&A Foods and actually run the business were likely made on a commercial line. He had made the strategic decision not to track Jummal's business phone, not yet anyway. If that became necessary, they could do it easily enough. For now, he was content reviewing the traffic on Jummal's personal cell phone, however limited that might be.

It made some sense, too, as he believed Jummal's brothers were now in the country, in the A&A Foods warehouse, in fact. *We'll talk here* the email pulled from the trash run had said. As soon as the brothers arrived, there was no need for Jummal to call them, or for them to call Jummal. They were seeing each other in person every day.

The PRTT results from the email address were more

surprising. There were none. The email address Abebi_Abiona_Forever@yahoo.com had no activity whatsoever. No emails sent from or to that account at all. The account existed, but it had gone dead.

Several days brought about the same results as Gordon checked the secure PRTT website regularly. The minimal phone activity had only reduced further. Some days there was no phone activity at all. As for the email address, it remained all quiet, as if it did not exist.

A week passed, and Gordon was frustrated. He had been certain there was more here. More to what Jummal was doing, more to this case. He had been avoiding Swayz at all costs, but that would have to end at some point. He hoped the subpoena would yield better results, but with each passing day, his confidence waned.

He was exhausted, maintaining surveillance at A&A Foods to the degree he was able. He'd noted the arrival of two white refrigerated delivery trucks. One was in good condition, but while the other appeared to operate, it looked like it had been around the block once or twice. Probably rentals, Gordon thought as he took note of the tags on both trucks. Tracking the truck tags was added to his ever-growing list of things to do.

He had seen the trucks get loaded and come and go a few times. Nothing shocking there. It was a food wholesaler, after all, and it looked like the trucks were making deliveries. It had allowed Gordon to get a better look at the two drivers. From his vantage point, they certainly looked like they could be Jummal's brothers.

Gordon had begun stopping by the office after hours on his way home from surveilling A&A Foods at night. He would be the only person in the International Group area, checking for messages and mail, particularly the subpoena responses from Yahoo and Jummal's phone service provider. So it went, day after day, night after night.

Gordon spent yet another lunch hour parked down the block

from A&A Foods, waiting, hoping, something would happen. Out of nowhere, his phone rang. A generic *US Government* caller ID appeared on his phone screen. That meant it was probably work calling, likely another member of the JTTF needing Gordon's help on a case the task force was actually pursuing.

"Agent Stone, it's Liz."

Swayz's assistant. Gordon gulped. This was not good.

"Uhhhh, hi, Liz, this is Stone," was all Gordon could think of in response. This was it, he thought. I was wrong and this case is nothing and Swayz is going to fire me. Gordon flirted with the notion that after this disaster McNeely would not even want him back at FDA-OCI. He held his breath.

"I've got a couple FedEx packages for you," Liz said. "Where are you sitting these days?"

The subpoena responses. They had arrived. Swayz remained unaware. A bit of new hope returned to Gordon.

"Agent Stone? Are you there?"

"Ummm, yeah. Sorry, Liz. Uhhh, can you just leave them on your desk? I'll stop by later and pick them up."

"You got it," she said.

"Great, thanks, Liz."

"Anytime, Agent Stone. Have a great day." She hung up.

Gordon stopped holding his breath and sighed heavily. This was it. If there was nothing in those subpoena responses, he would have to come clean with Swayz and face the consequences. But if there was something—anything—that pointed Gordon in the right direction, then he would keep going. Keep doing the work.

That night, Gordon grabbed the subpoena responses from Liz's desk and took them home. He opened the response from the phone company first. The phone was in Jummal's name, and the history went back ninety days. Jummal called the same number in Nigeria every week around the same time. The calls lasted ten to twenty minutes. The number matched the Nigerian number that appeared on the PRTT report. Gordon noted there were no calls to any other phone numbers back in Nigeria. He would need to check out that number, but this was not any sort of criminal indicator. Gordon surmised this was Jummal making a weekly call home to catch up with his family.

"'We'll talk here,'" Gordon whispered to himself. The message from the email in the trash. *We'll talk here.* No phone calls. *We'll talk* when you get *here.* And the brothers were here now. Jummal saw them every day at A&A Foods. They did not need to talk on the phone because they were talking in person. They were "*here.*"

Gordon looked at the subpoena response again. A number with a 703 area code caught his attention. A number in Virginia. He had seen that number before.

"The mosque!" Gordon shouted. Abdul Malik, to be precise. The same number Jummal called from Nigeria when the NSA had been listening in. Jummal had called Abdul Malik once from Nigeria, then again when he got back to the United States.

A detailed look at everything in the package would have to wait. Gordon opened the second FedEx package from Yahoo. Would the answer to the mysterious email address be in here? The first page was a letter from Yahoo's lawyer. Gordon turned the page without reading.

The next page showed account information. Jummal had created the account while he was still in Nigeria. The account had been accessed from two phone-based IP addresses and one computer IP address. That was interesting. Gordon would have to follow up on each IP address, but his instinct told him the computer IP address likely belonged to Jummal, the account owner, and at least one of the phone IP addresses probably did too. The second phone IP address was a mystery. *Maybe I'll have to get a look at that business line after all,* Gordon thought. He did not dwell on that now, instead flipping to the next page, hoping to see email addresses Jummal had been sending to or receiving from.

The PRTT report had shown no real-time activity on the email account. The subpoena response, though, would show who Jummal had been communicating with via this email address in the past. He anticipated a list of email addresses he hoped could tell him what Jummal was up to at A&A Foods.

But there were none. Not even one beyond the single "Welcome to Yahoo" email from the provider from the day Jummal had created the account. Nothing. Not a single email sent or received. Gordon flipped back to the lawyer's letter that accompanied the subpoena response. Surely there was a mistake or there was more to come. Gordon quickly read the letter.

> *In response to your subpoena, we have provided administrative account information (who owns the account), as well as a list of IP addresses from which the account in question has been accessed and when. However, our records indicate that no email messages have been sent from or received by the named email account in your request. If you have further questions...*

It went on for another paragraph, but he stopped reading. No emails. The account had been created but never used. He shook his head. Why open the account if you're not going to use it? And why would Jummal or anyone else be accessing the account if they were not sending emails?

It was clear the brothers were talking in person now that they were in the US. But why was there nothing between them when only Jummal was in the US, apart from the regular calls to what Gordon believed was the family back in Nigeria? Is that all there was?

He had nothing.

CHAPTER 51

Gordon needed to find out what Jummal and his brothers were talking about. To do that, he needed a warrant. His pile of circumstantial evidence continued to grow, but he still could not prove anything. He suspected a lot of things: Jummal donated $10,000 to a terrorist group; the two new arrivals at A&A Foods were in the country illegally; the two men were Jummal's brothers; Abdul Malik from the mosque in Virginia had conspired with Jummal to orchestrate bringing the brothers into the country; the mosque was helping Jummal raise money through a loss-leader scam.

In an instant of reflection, a rarity for Gordon, he found himself thinking of his mother, and of a book she compelled him to read in grade school. The book was *Catch-22*, and Gordon specifically recalled Joseph Heller's famous line: *There's only one catch and that's Catch-22*. Gordon was neck-deep in a Catch-22. He needed a warrant to listen to Jummal's real-time phone calls and read his real-time emails. To get a warrant, he would need to demonstrate there was probable cause Jummal had committed a crime. But to demonstrate there was probable cause Jummal had committed a crime, Gordon needed the warrant so he could hear and see what Jummal was up to.

Gordon's suspicions were not enough. McNeely had opened a case for him at FDA-OCI, and AUSA Jameson had provided subpoenas and court orders for the PRTT orders. But jacketing a case and providing subpoenas did not require probable cause. A warrant did, and Gordon did not have probable cause. He had pushed this case and pushed it some more, but the case had not developed. He still believed the loss-leader angle was a gateway to something more sinister and that maybe the $10,000 transfer was more than a charity scam.

He was spent and exhausted, but his instincts told him there was more. His experience suggested his instincts were good and should be trusted, but he also knew he was not infallible. When you checked all the boxes and followed the process, there either was a case or there was not. If there was not, you walked away.

Gordon reached into his pocket and pulled out his phone. He needed to call McNeely and try and figure out how he could extricate himself from this mess. Before he dialed, he noticed he had a voicemail. Nora Williams from the NSA had called.

> *Hi, Agent Stone. Nora Williams here from NSA. Got some info for you that we should probably talk about. I can tell you some over the phone. You're not going to believe it. I couldn't find anything on that email address Abebi_Abiona_Forever@yahoo.com, but I did find something on the names. It's public info, so I can share it here, but there's more we should talk about offline. Anyway, when I added our guy's surname, Adeyami, to the two names in the email…BOOM! Turns out those are Jummal Adeyami's sisters. But here's where it gets interesting, and sad. Both sisters are dead. That's how I found them. They're on the list of victims of that drone strike in Nigeria a few months back that took out a school. Abebi was a teacher there and Abiona was a student, just ten years old. I'd forgotten all about that, but the names are pretty well documented. Really sad. I've got*

> *some other details as well, but we'll need to discuss those on a STE or in person. Let me know. Hope this helps. Bye for now.*

Gordon played the message again, and then a third time. He stared at the phone. "Revenge," he said thoughtfully to himself. "That's what this is about. Revenge for his sisters." Gordon had his motive. Not part of probable cause, but certainly part of his investigation. The call to McNeely would have to wait. Gordon was not done yet.

The next morning, he called Williams. She answered on the first ring.

"Agent Stone, I was hoping you'd call. We need to talk."

"Yes. Thanks for the message. That was really helpful. It sounded like you have more."

"Do I ever. Can you get to a STE?"

STE stood for Secure Terminal Equipment and was the government's way of saying "encrypted phone line that could not be tapped." If a federal agent had to discuss classified or sensitive information over the phone, it was done through a STE.

Gordon thought for a second. No way would he go back to JTTF to use a STE there. Too many eyes on him using a STE would get back to Swayz. That was a nonstarter. He could try at FDA-OCI. If McNeely was there, that should not be a problem. Otherwise, he would need to drive up to Fort Meade and visit Williams in person.

"I think I can get access to a STE, but it will take me about an hour. If that doesn't work, I'll drive up."

"Sounds good," Williams responded. "I'll be here all day. Let me know if you need to come in person, and I'll arrange to get you in the building."

"Thanks a lot," Gordon said. "I really appreciate this."

"Not a problem, Agent Stone. We're all on the same team, yeah? We'll talk soon."

Gordon disconnected and dialed McNeely.

"Gordo, how's the case? Let's hear it," McNeely said.

"Developing, boss. I need another favor."

"Anything I can do, you know that."

"Thanks, boss. Can I get on your STE today? Got some sensitive info I need to discuss with NSA."

"Sure thing. When do you need it?"

"Inside the hour. I'm on my way now."

"I'm giddy with anticipation, Gordo. Come on up."

"Thanks, boss, see you soon." Gordon ended the call. He would be a little late reporting for duty at JTTF today. As he fought the traffic northbound to the FDA, he wondered if anyone would even notice. Sometimes, being invisible paid dividends.

CHAPTER 52

FDA-OCI's office in Silver Spring, Maryland, had one STE line, which was located in a small conference room. Gordon sat with McNeely at the small table. He played the message left by Williams before dialing the NSA. McNeely sat stoically, saying nothing.

Once again, Williams picked up on the first ring.

"Stand by, Agent Stone," she said.

Both Williams and Gordon pressed a red button on their respective phones, triggering the secure status of the STE. A series of clicks and buzzes lasted a few seconds.

"Okay. Looks good here, Agent Stone. You secure on your end?"

"We're good here. I've got ASAC Peter McNeely of FDA-OCI. He's assisting on the case."

"Nice to meet you, sir. Well, Agent Stone, here's what I've learned. You recall when this started, I had the case referred to NSA by FinCEN because of a financial transfer of $10,000 into a questionable Nigerian account that was possibly associated with terrorism. Well, what we did not discuss at that time, frankly because I was unaware, was a treaty the US has with Nigerian law enforcement. Long story short, because this transfer went from a US account into a Nigerian account, we share that intel with Nigeria. Nigeria looks into it from their end, and if anything pops up, they let us know.

"Well, something popped up, and that info finally made its way from Nigeria back to the NSA. I was updating the file with the info about the sisters when I got notice of the input from Nigeria. Turns out the money didn't stop at the first account. Half of it was subsequently moved to an account of a known Boko Haram soldier. It's not much money, so it didn't set off a lot of alarms around here, but it's definitely funding that's moving into the account of a terrorist actor. Now, it still looks like a charity scam for our friend Jummal. He likely doesn't even know about this secondary transfer. *But* it is a definite and solid link to terrorism, and I thought you'd want to know."

Gordon looked across the table at McNeely. His eyebrows were raised, and he smiled at Gordon.

"Agent Stone, you still there?"

"Still here. This is very helpful. Anything else?"

"Nothing at the moment, but I'll keep you posted if anything else comes in."

"Thanks, Ms. Williams. I appreciate—"

"Call me Nora, Agent Stone. I'm happy to help. Good luck with your investigation."

"Thanks Ms., I mean, Nora. And please call me Gordon. I think you might have just saved my case."

"If it helps, it helps, Gordon. I'll get a copy of our report printed for you. It's sensitive, so may take a couple of days before it's available."

"That would be great. And thanks again."

"Happy hunting, Gordon. We'll talk again." The line went dead.

Gordon's smile matched McNeely's.

"That's going to get us our warrant, boss. We've got a revenge motive and funds going to a known terrorist group. He's raising money to support terrorism. We have to take this to the FISA Court so we can keep the information secure and still see everything."

"Hell yes you can, Gordo. But you're going to need JTTF

support for that to work. You go to the FISA Court without JTTF, and they'll kick you to the curb. You've got to get your SSA to open a case at JTTF."

Gordon frowned. Convincing Swayz to take this case would be the biggest challenge he had faced in the investigation. Swayz could just as easily suspend Gordon and kick him off the JTTF, an action Gordon knew Swayz could justify.

But Gordon now had overt contact, through an intermediary, and funds transferring to a known terrorist group, Boko Haram, not to mention the newfound revenge motive and the brothers' illegal entry. Was it enough for probable cause? He was closer than he had ever been, and with the terrorism angle developing, he probably had enough to go to the FISA Court. It should be enough. It was certainly enough to try. The biggest hurdle lay directly in front of Gordon—he had to convince Swayz. This was not a confrontation Gordon looked forward to.

"I'm going to need your help again, boss."

"Ha!" McNeely said, rubbing his hands together. "I thought you'd never ask, Gordo."

CHAPTER 53

Gordon had been lucky to stumble onto the NSA's MYSTIC system and RETRO tool to hear the one phone call Jummal had made to Abdul Malik while still in Nigeria, but he needed more. In particular, he needed a warrant from the Foreign Intelligence Surveillance Act Court, the FISA Court, tucked inside the E. Barrett Prettyman United States Courthouse in Washington, DC. He would not get in the courthouse door, however, without support from the JTTF. That meant convincing Swayz a case he had ordered closed—twice—several weeks ago had a bona fide connection to terrorism. Gordon believed he finally had that connection, but convincing Swayz would be a neat trick.

Established under the Foreign Intelligence Surveillance Act of 1978, the FISA Court's original purpose was to oversee warrant applications from the federal government when it sought to electronically surveil individuals for foreign intelligence purposes. In 2001, the USA PATRIOT Act in the aftermath of the 9/11 attacks expanded the FISA Court's authority to include warrants of subjects suspected of terrorism. When the FBI, NSA, or CIA needed to tap a phone or read an email of someone they believed to be a threat to the national security, the FISA Court is where they went to seek such a warrant, which was typically good for thirty days before requiring a renewal application.

It was time to play all his cards and see if he could convince

Swayz to get on board.

It was a dicey proposition, and Gordon knew he had to bring everything to the table if he was going to have a chance with Swayz, let alone the FISA Court. In his subterranean workspace, Gordon pushed tables together and brought in a large whiteboard. Notes, photographs, Post-its, and other documents were spread around the tables in neat, orderly piles. Gordon had reviewed it all twice, some of it many more times than that.

To crystalize everything in his head, he had to write it down. He grabbed an erasable black marker and attacked the whiteboard,. He went through it again, making changes in blue. He used his shirtsleeve as an eraser. He checked every box. Across the top of the whiteboard, Gordon wrote the following:

THEORY: Jummal using A&A Foods as front to raise money for terror activities, here or in Nigeria (home of BH), possibly through Loss Leader
MOTIVE: revenge for sisters' deaths

And underneath that, filling the board, he wrote:

1. *Drone strike destroys school*
2. *Jummal's sisters killed*
3. *Jummal travels to Nigeria*
4. *Jummal transfers $10,000 to an account associated with terrorism—believed to be charity scam*
    a. *$5,000 of that transfer is transferred a second time to Boko Haram account*
5. *Jummal contacts Malik at mosque in Va.*
    a. *Discusses illegal entry of brothers*
6. *Jummal returns to US—moves to Arlington*
7. *Sets up A&A foods in DC*
    a. *Van from mosque, using women from mosque, delivers Loss Leader product to warehouse. Items unknown at this time. Possible repackage operation for resale.*

8. *Van from mosque delivers 2 men, believed to be brothers—Okunola and Kambili*
9. *No phone calls. No emails. Believed to be communicating in person at warehouse*
10. *Trash run provides email—Abebi_Abiona_Forever@yahoo.com*
    a. *"We'll talk here" referencing brothers coming to US*
    b. *3 IP addresses accessing email account—not using*
    c. *PRTT reveals no substantive phone or any email activity*

Across the bottom of the white board, Gordon drew a big question mark. Next to it, he wrote:

Raising $$$—or something more

CHAPTER 54

As Gordon toiled in solitude in the basement of the JTTF, McNeely briefed his chain of command at the FDA Office of Criminal Investigations. His first stop was with his boss and old friend from the Secret Service, SAC Steve Johnson. Before going to see Johnson, McNeely stopped by Director Frank Sharp's office. Not to see Sharp; that would come later. Right now, he needed a second set of ears, one he could trust implicitly to be completely honest and candid with him. He needed Donna Sinclair.

"Ms. Sinclair," he called out while knocking on Donna's open door.

Donna responded with a look over the top of her glasses. "What can I do for you, Pete? Or should I say ASAC McNeely?"

"Need your wisdom and experience, Ms. Donna. Looks like Gordo might have snagged another one over at JTTF, but we've got some work to do to help him out."

"Wisdom and experience make me sound old, Pete. Try again."

McNeely stared at the ceiling, thinking. "Smarts and brains?"

"They're the same thing," Donna teased, "but points for trying." She pushed her chair out from her desk and walked around to her door. "Let's go," she said.

"Go? How do you know we're going somewhere?"

"Pete, you cross that threshold twice a year. Once on my birthday, when you bring me a card and a cake. And once at Christmastime, when you bring me a present. Both of which I appreciate very much. So, when you stop at my door and tell me you need me for my 'brains and…good looks'"—she winked at McNeely—"I know we're going somewhere."

McNeely smiled. "To the SAC's office. After you."

Donna walked into Johnson's office first, followed by McNeely, who pulled the door shut. Johnson looked up at the two of them and frowned. "Jesus," he said. "You two and the door is already shut. This can't be good."

"Language, Steven," said Donna.

Johnson silently pulled a money clip from his pants pocket, peeled off a dollar bill, and handed it to Donna. "What's up?" he said.

McNeely unloaded all the pertinent facts of Gordon's case, including how Gordon had gone rogue, disobeying orders and pursuing the case on his own. "They're not taking him seriously over there, Steve. You know how he is, but they don't. Look, if it's just some loss-leader fraud and illegal immigration, we'll wrap that up here at OCI. It'll be a win. But if this guy is raising money for Boko Haram, or something worse, JTTF has to take it. But they won't take it from Gordon alone. We need to back him up on this."

"And you've known about this, about him going rogue?"

"Yeah, for a while now. Hell, Steve—"

"Language," chimed in Donna.

McNeely pulled out his wallet and handed her a dollar without missing a beat. "You know I believe in this kid. He's got the gift. He's proven that. And Gordon believes this guy could be raising funds for terrorist activity. He needs a FISA warrant, but he can't get that without JTTF support."

"Sharp's not gonna like that you kept his conduct quiet, Pete. You know that's not a good look. What do you think, Ms.

Donna?" Johnson asked.

Donna looked at the two agents. "I've been around you two boys since you were baby agents at the Service. I've watched you learn, and grow, break cases, become leaders. I lost track of all the good you've done a long time ago, but it's truckloads. I'd trust you both with just about anything. And this kid Gordon? Pete's right, he's got the gift. In spades. He might've gone off the reservation a little bit, but you know how those guys are over at FBI. They serve up demerits for a crooked tie. Worst case is they give him the boot and you have to cover for him back here with Frank. I know you can do that. And if this is as bad as Gordon thinks, well, you're up to your eyeballs in it already. Might as well take that last step."

With little hesitation, Johnson responded, "All right. Let's go see Frank. Donna, can you get us in today?"

"Nothing on the calendar right now."

"Okay, let's do it. Pete, I'll get it started, you fill in the details. Donna, when the shit hits the fan"—he handed her a dollar—"you bail us out."

"Always do," she said.

CHAPTER 55

The three of them walked down the hall to FDA-OCI Director Frank Sharp's suite. Donna knocked on his door and let herself in.

"The boys are here, Frank," she said. "Looks like they've got something for you."

"Come on in, guys." Sharp got up from behind his desk and walked over to his conference table. "Have a seat," he said, motioning with his arm. The four of them sat. Johnson got the ball rolling, and McNeely added the details whenever a gap appeared in Johnson's narrative. Donna kept her eyes on Sharp to measure his reaction. It was not good.

"How long have you known about this, Pete?" Sharp asked, somewhat accusingly.

"A few weeks. I opened a case so he could meet with the AUSA and get a PRTT order."

"This isn't good, fellas. They're already ticked at us for giving them one agent when they asked for twenty. And now the one we've given them has gone rogue and disobeyed orders. Apparently, with our support." He glanced at McNeely. "Pete, you know that's not a good look for us. I'm not their biggest fan, but push comes to shove, we need the FBI. And you're telling me he's spent his time working on this when he's supposed to be working on terrorism cases?"

"Frank, I'm sorry about that, I truly am. But there's more

here," McNeely said. "He's found a link to Boko Haram."

"Right, but it's not your guy. Your guy was a victim in a charity scam. The guy that scammed him has the direct link to Boko Haram, not your guy."

"Agent Stone sees the link," said Johnson. "He knows there's more, but he needs the FISA warrant and JTTF support to get it. Let Pete go with Gordon and make the case over at JTTF. That's all I'm asking for," he added.

Sharp drummed his fingers on the conference table. He stopped and looked up at Johnson. "I can't do it, Steve. I'm pulling Stone out of there before he does us any more damage. We'll send over someone else, if they still want anyone from OCI. I appreciate that you two trust him, but I can't have agents going rogue on assignment at another agency, least of all the JTTF. That can't happen," he said, staring at McNeely. "I'm bringing him back today, and we'll deal with this internally. Okay, that's it."

Johnson and McNeely quietly pushed their seats back from the table.

Donna continued to stare at Sharp. "Frank," she said.

Sharp looked at her. Johnson and McNeely stopped moving.

"I know you don't know Gordon Stone particularly well. But you know me. You know Steve. You know Pete. We've all been around the block once or twice, as they say. All of us, together. We've made this quiet little office in the corner of the FDA one of the most successful law enforcement agencies this country has ever seen. And hardly anyone even knows we exist. How many lives have been saved because of the work you do, the work we all do? And that includes Agent Stone. Frank, what if we weren't talking about Stone? What if we were talking about Steve or Pete? What if it were their case? What if they couldn't break down the walls at the FBI and were doing everything they possibly could to do the *right* thing? What if one of them had gone rogue at JTTF? Would your answer be the same? Because that's what's happening here, Frank. Agent

Stone is onto something. Maybe it's a simple fraud case and that's it, but I don't think so. Steve and Pete don't think so. More importantly, what if it's not a simple case of fraud? What if this guy is laundering money for Boko Haram, or worse? Nobody wants to be on the wrong end of that, Frank."

Donna's words hung in the air.

"I can't support an agent who's gone rogue, Donna. You want me to just let it go when I can end this today?" Frank asked.

"Don't misunderstand, Frank. I'm not suggesting you let it lie. What I'm saying is you have *no choice*. You have to support Agent Stone, and you have to see this through with the FBI. If he's right, and the smart money says he is, there's something bigger going on here. Something big, bad, and dangerous. When it's done, you bring him back, give him fire and brimstone, and toss him out the back door if that's what needs to be done. But right now, today, your only play is to support him and whatever that entails, because you know, Steve knows, Pete knows, even I know that Gordon Stone is probably right. He didn't go rogue for fun. He did it because that's where the case took him. He's trying to do the right thing, Frank. And that's what you have to do, too."

Director Sharp looked at his colleagues—officially, his subordinates. Donna was right; they had all been around the block once or twice together.

"Okay," he said. "Pete, you're closest to this thing. You work with Gordon to sell it to JTTF. Bring in that AUSA, too. Get Stone his warrants so he can prove the case, one way or another. Steve-O, you and I are going to see the Deputy Commissioner of the FDA to let her know there's a storm brewing over at the FBI and it may be heading her way. Pete, Steve, thank you for dropping by. Let me talk to Donna for a minute. And Pete..."

McNeely turned to look at Sharp.

"Never again. Understood?"

McNeely nodded, then he exited the office behind Johnson. Donna remained in her seat. Sharp waited for McNeely to shut the door before he spoke again.

"Donna—"

"Listen, Frank, I'm sorry. I didn't mean to rant at you like that, and well…" She trailed off with a shrug of her shoulders.

"No need to apologize. I just wanted to say thanks. More than anyone, you keep this ship sailing on the right path." He chuckled. "I know that's a mixed metaphor, but you know what I mean. I appreciate your support, and I appreciate that you support them," he added, motioning toward the door. "And you're right. I don't really have a choice but to support Stone with everything I can muster. But I really hope he's not leading us down a primrose path."

"He's special, Frank. No one here walks the straight and narrow like Gordon Stone. I'd bet the swear jar money he's right about this." She smiled. "I'll be in my office." She turned and walked out.

Frank hollered after her. "Hey, get the deputy commish's office and schedule a meet for me and Steve."

"On it," she shouted back as the sound of her clicking heels faded down the hallway.

CHAPTER 56

Samantha Daniels was a fighter. Things were a lot better for her than they had been for her mother, who spent forty years as an executive secretary at Phillip Morris with no realistic hope of climbing higher. The sixties and seventies had changed a lot for women in the workforce, but to become the Principal Deputy Commissioner of the FDA, even an intelligent and qualified woman such as Samantha still had to fight, sometimes even fight dirty.

And Dr. Samantha Daniels had done exactly that. She finished at the top of her class at the University of Virginia, then again at medical school. With gritted teeth and an innate intellect, she forged a path through a residency at Georgetown University Hospital. Eventually, she landed at Johns Hopkins Suburban Hospital in Bethesda, Maryland, where she stayed for eleven years developing and building the region's top trauma center.

She had no tolerance for politics, so it came as a surprise when the President of the United States reached out to her to see if she might be interested in being the number two at the FDA. Despite the surprise, it took Dr. Daniels about ten seconds to say yes. In her time as a practicing physician, she had seen the good, bad, and ugly from the FDA and its collective impact on the medical community. Her trauma center was plugging along just fine, treating thousands of patients a year. But Dr. Daniels was ready to see if she could broaden her impact a little more, and she willingly entered the political arena to make that happen. Her next surprise was how much she enjoyed it. She still found much of the political side of the job distasteful, but she was a fighter, and she won more than she lost.

Her dealings with Frank Sharp and the Office of Criminal Investigations had been a refreshing change of pace from her political interactions on Capitol Hill. She knew if you stripped away the titles, Frank was a born-and-bred cop, interested in the truth, facts, and the right thing. So, when Frank said he needed to see her, she knew it was important. She scheduled the meeting for the first opening on her calendar.

Her door was open, and Frank knocked on the doorframe, letting her know he was there.

"Come on in, Frank. How are you?" she asked, motioning him and his colleague to some chairs in front of her desk.

"Doing well, Doc. Hope all is good with you and you're taking care of business up on the Hill. You remember my Special Agent in Charge, Steven Johnson?"

"Sure, sure. How are you, Agent Johnson?"

"Very well, Dr. Daniels, thanks."

"Well, Frank, I'm all yours. What disaster do you have to share with me today?" she asked with a smile.

"Hopefully preventing one. But we do have something going on with one of our agents over at the Joint Terrorism Task Force with the FBI."

"I'm intrigued."

"I assigned an agent over there a few months ago. He's been stirring things up a little bit, and is onto something that could be a pretty big deal."

"Big deal as in terrorism big deal?"

"Maybe. His problem right now is the FBI doesn't seem to be taking his case too seriously. They're kind of looking past my guy because he's not one of their own. I've been briefed on the investigation, and I'm convinced he's onto something. It's not clear exactly what—he's working on that—but we're going to pitch the case to them in the next day or two. I'm not sure how receptive the JTTF is going to be."

"Okay. And I need to be concerned about this because...why?"

"Well, if they blow our guy off, and he turns out to be right and something bad happens, really bad, the first thing the FBI will do is point their finger at the FDA-OCI. They will do everything they can to shift the blame to our guy."

"What's 'really bad?' Are people at risk?"

"Unclear, but maybe. There's evidence of money being raised for a terrorist group, though we don't know what that money will be used for. We've still got work to do on our end. But they, the FBI, may not let us do that work. And that could blow up on us."

"And if it does, they point to your agent and OCI, and that bleeds to the FDA, and the headline in the *Post* is FDA Ignores Terrorist Threat, Could Have Saved Lives. Something to that effect?"

"That's about it, Doc. Wanted you to be aware in case this goes south."

She stood up and extended her hand to Sharp. "Thanks, Frank. And you too, Agent Johnson. I appreciate the heads-up."

Daniels showed Sharp and Johnson out and retreated to her office, shutting the door. She sat quietly for a moment before nodding her head and mumbling, "Political bullshit," to herself. Reaching for her purse on the floor beneath her desk, she pulled out her personal cell phone and scrolled through the contacts until she found the one she wanted. She put the phone on speaker, laid it on the desk, and dialed.

"Federal courts desk. This is Pressman."

"Hiya, Soph, this is Sam over at FDA."

"Samantha! How are you? It's been a minute."

"I know, I know. That's on me. I want to make up for that. You available tonight? Drinks? Maybe dinner?"

"I sure can be. Where're we going?"

"How about the Old Ebbitt Grill at eight. I'll get us a reservation."

"And I'll be there. Everything okay, Sam?"

"I think so. Just might need a little cover over here and have something for you, too."

"Great, see you at eight. Shall I assume this is deep background stuff?"

"Yep. I can point you to the door, but it's up to you to open it. Does that work?"

"You bet. I'll see you tonight, Sam."

"Great! See you there." Daniels hung up the phone. "Still fighting," she said, shaking her head.

CHAPTER 57

Sharp and Johnson walked across the FDA campus back to OCI headquarters in silence. Once inside, and before they parted ways, Johnson looked at his boss and asked, "What now?"

"Now we wait and cross our fingers that Pete and Stone can convince the JTTF to take the case and not fire Stone," Sharp said.

"Can I make a suggestion?"

"Let's have it, Steve. We're past the point of no return here."

"Well, I think, and I think you agree, that they are going to have a tough time convincing JTTF this isn't an absolute clusterfuck. Hell, Frank, it's one thing for Stone to be the shop savant here at OCI. We're small, we know him, sort of. He's a little weird, but he gets results. He's brought it home for us time after time. But we've had Pete to watch over him, make sure he doesn't stray too far outside the lines. I don't think he's ever gone this far with us. Jesus, he's disobeying orders, carrying on an independent investigation, going rogue. At the FBI! Pete's good. He's really good. But we're sending him into the lion's den over there. I think there's another card to play. I don't know if it will help or not, but..."

"Go ahead, Steve-O. Let's hear it."

"I think you need to call over there, talk to your counterpart."

"Pendleton? He's a prick. You think that would help?"

"It might. Stone's boss over there is going to be pissed. Hell, he's right to be pissed. Stone disobeyed him multiple times. His boss is bound to take that personally. But Pendleton won't take it personal. Stone didn't disobey him. Maybe he won't care if one of his SSAs is pissed at Stonc. If you can sell him on the case and keep Stone's misbehavior understated, he might be able to bring pressure on the SSA to suck it up and take the case."

"Huh," Sharp said. "He is a prick, but he's not stupid. He's probably still mad at me anyway for just sending him one guy instead of twenty, so there's not really anything to lose. All right, I'll call him."

That afternoon, Sharp called Dan Pendleton, Assistant Director for Counterterrorism at the FBI. Sharp explained Gordon's case to Pendleton and said he was not getting much support from JTTF. He told Pendleton Stone was a great agent, a little strange maybe, but he trusted him and wanted to make sure the FBI was not missing out on a potentially important case. Pendleton was not particularly enthusiastic.

"Sounds like your boy went a little overboard over here, Frank," he said.

"I'm not denying that, Dan. He might have strayed off course a little, but believe me, this kid is good. I wouldn't have sent him to you otherwise. We'll take the case if JTTF doesn't, but I think he's onto something, and I think it's in your arena. I'll take all the fraud cases I can get. Hell, I'll even throw in the illegal immigration angle. But if the subject is raising money for Boko Haram for God knows what and right under our noses, well, I just wanted to make sure you had the whole picture before my guy gets bounced out of there."

"Appreciate the call, Frank, and I'll take it under advisement. I've got to run to another meeting. We'll let you know." Pendleton hung up.

He did not have a meeting. Instead, he called B.F. Dillon, an ASAC for the FBI's Washington Field Office and overseer for the DC JTTF.

"Dan," Dillon said, reading the caller ID on his phone screen. "What's up?"

"Hey B.F., I just got off the phone with Frank Sharp over at FDA. He sent us an agent a few months ago. Got assigned to Swayz in International. Sounds like he's working some case outside the lines and hasn't been playing ball with Swayz. Look, I don't care if we dump the case, the agent, or both. Let's just make sure we haven't missed something, okay."

"Sure thing, Dan. I'll look into it. Hey, is this a 'right now' thing?" he asked.

"Nothing urgent. Just let me know what you decide in a couple of days."

"Will do. Anything else?"

"That's it. If you decide you need to terminate the agent, just give me a heads-up before that happens."

"You got it. I'll talk to you later."

CHAPTER 58

Dr. Daniels met *Washington Post* reporter Sophia Pressman for dinner and drinks at the Old Ebbitt Grill, a DC landmark eatery. The two women were DC veterans and had been friends ever since a chance meeting at the Johns Hopkins Suburban Hospital. A Senator had been T-boned in a car accident and life flighted to Suburban's trauma center. At a press conference, Pressman was asking questions while Daniels was at the microphone. Pressman's questions were smart, thoughtful, and pertinent, while Daniels's answers were honest and forthright. The two paused for a chat after the press conference and hit it off immediately. They had been friends ever since, but had not spoken in a few months.

They caught up over dinner and drinks. Each ordered an espresso, and they shared a crème brûlée for dessert. The conversation then turned to business.

"So, what have you got for me?" asked Pressman.

"Well, maybe not much, but maybe something I might need a little cover for down the road."

"Do tell." Pressman smiled.

"I believe you're familiar with our Office of Criminal Investigations? In fact, I think that's the last time we saw each other. We had lunch in my office after you tried to interview an agent over there."

"I remember. Interesting guy, bit of a character. I remember he wore sneakers with a wrinkled suit. Kind of charming in his way, and cute, too. He won an award. Agent Stone, I believe. I ran into him again at the award ceremony down at EDVA."

Daniels raised her eyebrows at Pressman's recollection. "Yes, well, he's no longer with us. Turns out he was assigned to the FBI's JTTF a few months ago."

"Ohhhh, a chance to play with the big boys. And?"

"Well, there's a chance something is about to blow up over there. Looks like he's stumbled onto something terrorism related, but he's getting crickets from the FBI. I don't know the details, but I've been told that if this does blow up, the FBI is going to blame us for dropping the ball. If that happens, I'm on the Hill talking about how the FDA screwed up a criminal investigation instead of how the FDA can fix health care in this country. And that's no good for anyone."

"Special Agent Gordon Stone. You're sure it's him that's involved?"

"That's what I've been told. Is that significant?"

"Well, he's good. A little strange. I can definitely see him *not* fitting in with the FBI's buttoned-down types. Honestly, I don't think there's much I can do with what you've given me, but if you're sure Agent Stone is involved, that might be worth a few calls."

"Professionally speaking, Sophia?" said Daniels, raising an eyebrow to her friend.

"Ha!" She laughed out loud. "Yes, strictly professional. He is a really good agent based on what I've seen."

"That's good to hear."

"Plus," she added with a wink, "he is kind of cute."

Their conversation moved on.

CHAPTER 59

Gordon spent the better part of the next two days sheltered in his makeshift basement office. He had gone over every detail of his investigation and knew it backward and forward, from every angle. A confrontation with Swayz was imminent. He wasn't sure what would happen, but he knew he would be as ready as he could be. Even so, it was not a meeting he looked forward to.

It had been at least two weeks since Gordon had seen Swayz, let alone spoken to him. That was by design, of course. The less contact he had with Swayz, the better he could focus on his investigation. For all the good it had done, he thought. The investigation had brought him to a precipice, and Gordon knew he was staring into the abyss.

But he also knew he was onto something. He could almost see it, like a missing piece to a puzzle that blends in with the carpet. Except it was not a puzzle piece, it was a piece of evidence. He knew it was there, he just could not find it. A FISA warrant would help. He would find it in Jummal's conversations with his brothers, with Malik, whomever. But convincing Swayz to take the case might be an impossible task.

What Gordon did not and could not know was all the machinations swirling around him about this case. Everyone involved had their own motivations, and Gordon was privy to none of them.

Sophia Pressman called the FBI's Washington Field Office's Public Information Officer (PIO) and asked specifically about a possible terrorism case that was being *mishandled* by the FBI. So much so, that if or when it went bad, the FBI was planning to point fingers and attempt to shift blame away from the JTTF. She was intentionally vague and knew the PIO would likely not even attempt to answer her questions.

But answers were not her objective. Pressman's goal was to get beyond the Public Information Office and talk with someone in leadership at the WFO. After hearing the PIO's third response of, "We can't comment on any active investigation," Pressman decided to throw her Hail Mary.

"Listen. I appreciate what you're telling me and understand you have a job to do. But I'm telling you, if this is in the *Post* tomorrow and all I have is a 'no comment' from the PIO, that's not a good look for the FBI, or you for that matter. I'm okay if the final word is 'no comment,' but I need it from someone in leadership over there. Is that possible?"

There was a pause on the line as the PIO considered his options. Finally, he told Pressman he would try and get someone to call her later that day, but he needed time to track someone down. Pressman smiled on the other end of the call. "That's fine. But if I don't hear anything by 4:30 p.m., I'm going with 'no comment' from you, okay?"

"I understand," said the PIO. "We'll call before then."

The PIO scratched his forehead as he looked at his desk phone. He had all of the WFO leadership team on speed dial. He pressed number three, and the phone dialed ASAC B.F. Dillon.

"Hey, B.F. I just got off the phone with a *Post* reporter. She was talking about some investigation JTTF has going and made it sound like it was about to blow, and we were planning to throw anyone outside the Bureau right under the bus. This ringing any bells?"

"Pretty vague," Dillon answered, "but who knows? Continue, please."

"Well, she said we've been *mishandling* the investigation and not taking it seriously. Sounds like she's putting something in the *Post* soon. I told her 'No comment,' but she wants that from someone higher up than me."

Dillon shut his eyes and shook his head. First Pendleton and now the *Post*. What *was* going on? "Give me the reporter's info. I'll take care of it."

"Hey, thanks B.F. Just be clear about what's off the record or background only, okay?"

"Yep, been down this road before," he said.

"Got it. The reporter is Sophia Pressman," the PIO said, relaying her number.

Dillon's first call was to Sean Swayz. "Sean, Pendleton called asking about some case you're working with a TFO from FDA. Wants to make sure we're not missing something. I was going to sit on it for a couple of days, but we just got another call from the *Post* suggesting we're *mishandling* this one. This sounding at all familiar?"

"Well, I've got a guy from FDA in my shop. Gave him a knock-and-talk dog a few weeks ago. Mostly, he's just running leads for our guys."

"He turn anything up on that dog?"

"Nah, that's closed. Nothing happening there."

"Do me a favor. Take a quick look. I want to make sure before I blow off the *Washington Post*."

"Heh, yeah sure, B.F., stand by." Swayz tapped into the WFO's case management system and did a search for Gordon's cases. "Sonuvabitch," he shouted. "That sonuvabitch. He didn't close it, B.F. I told him, ordered him, twice, and it's still open. I'm done with this guy. He's out of here as of right now."

"All right, listen. Set up a meeting. Hear what he has to say. I've got to deal with this reporter. Don't do anything half-cocked just because you're pissed."

"Jesus, I might arrest him on general principles."

"Do what you gotta do, Sean. Just be smart about it. We'll

talk later."

Dillon hung up and dialed Sophia Pressman.

"Federal court desk, this is Pressman," she answered.

"Ms. Pressman, my name is B.F. Dillon. I'm the JTTF ASAC at the FBI's Washington Field Office. I understand you have some questions for me."

"I do, thanks for calling, ASAC Dillon. I was—"

Dillon interrupted. "Before we start, Ms. Pressman, let's keep this entire conversation off the record unless I say otherwise. Can we do that?"

"Well, sure, but I do need some kind of quote from senior leadership at WFO, even if it's just a 'no comment,'" she answered.

"Go ahead and ask your questions. We'll see where it goes."

"Okay," Pressman said and dove in. "What can you tell me about a JTTF investigation of possible terrorist activity with ties to the Food and Drug Administration?"

"I can't comment on any ongoing investigations. I'm guessing you already know that."

"I do. But that's just it. My sources say this particular investigation is getting buried by JTTF, but it could be a legitimate terrorist threat to the national security. There have been threats of blowback to the FDA itself if this goes bad. So, I guess my question is why would the FBI bury this case but still threaten to point the finger at the FDA if things go bad? If things can go bad, shouldn't the FBI be aggressively pursuing the case rather than burying it?"

After a pause, Dillon responded. "Ms. Pressman, those are fair questions that warrant further examination. I need some time to look into this matter. Until then, the response from my office that you can use is as follows: The FBI and JTTF do not comment on ongoing investigations. That's it. Thank you for your time." Dillon hung up.

"Fuck!" he shouted. What was going on here? He dialed Pendleton. "Dan, you got a few minutes? I need to talk to you about this FDA deal in the International Group. I think it's picking up steam. The *Post* may be running something tomorrow."

"Where's it stand right now?"

"I told them we don't comment on ongoing investigations. She had some good questions about that, since everyone but Agent Stone believed this case to be closed. Swayz is meeting with Stone today, I think. He's ready to fire him."

"All right. Can you come over at one?"

"I'll be there," Dillon answered.

When he arrived at Pendleton's office, Dillon found the PIO and general counsel were already there, sitting with Pendleton at a conference table. Dillon joined them.

"B.F." Pendleton said. "What's the current state of affairs?"

"Swayz is meeting with Stone this afternoon, maybe right now, to hear what he has to say. Because Stone disobeyed direct orders about closing this case, Swayz is inclined to fire him on the spot and send him back to the FDA. The *Post* may be publishing a story tomorrow that has the big, bad FBI burying this case, but still threatening to point fingers if it goes bad. That led the reporter to the fairly obvious question: If it could still go bad, why are we burying it? The case was supposed to have been closed weeks ago, but apparently this agent kept it open, reason unknown. I gave the *Post* the standard no comment on ongoing investigations. She seemed okay with that, but I don't know what else she's got."

"Can we answer this obvious question?" Pendleton asked.

"The case was not closed as of this morning. Swayz described it as a dog, that's why he ordered Stone to close it, twice. Stone disobeyed that order both times. If nothing else changes, the case will be closed after Swayz and Stone meet, and Stone will be sent back to the FDA."

"And if things do change, then what?"

"Then the case stays open. We still bounce Stone for insubordination. We reassign the case and close it in a week or two after everyone loses interest."

"What do we know about Stone?"

"Not much. Swayz says he's mostly been running leads for other JTTF agents."

Pendleton grunted. "The director at FDA-OCI sings the guy's praises."

The PIO cleared his throat.

Pendleton looked at him. "What's on your mind?" he asked.

"You can't fire him, sir."

"Why the hell not?" asked Dillon. "He's become a rogue agent, grossly insubordinate."

"Well, yes, that's true. But what if he's right? What if there is a legitimate terrorism case here that everyone but Agent Stone ignored?"

"It's a fair point," Pendleton chimed in. "If this guy is as good as the FDA seems to think, we have to ask, what if he's right? And if he is right and things break bad, more than one of us in this room will be looking at early retirement."

"Don't fire him," interjected the general counsel. "Not yet anyway. Keep him around. Keep the case open. Throw some resources at it. See what comes of it. If it's nothing, bounce him in six months for insubordination."

There were reluctant nods around the table.

"Okay," Pendleton said. He looked at the PIO. "You get the *Post* reporter in here ASAP. We need to talk her down from making us look like jackasses in tomorrow's newspaper. GC and I will meet with her, promise her an exclusive when the case is done, something like that." He looked at the general counsel, who gave an affirmative nod.

"B.F., get on the horn right now to Swayz and pull him back from the ledge, if he hasn't already pushed Stone off it. Let's do this right, and it all goes away in a few months."

CHAPTER 60

Swayz was seething, red in the face and repeatedly tapping the table with his index finger. He stared at Gordon, ignoring Pete McNeely and Gabriel Jameson sitting on either side of Gordon.

"Well, Agent Stone, thanks for inviting your friends. I can't imagine what they're doing here, but then again, you pretty much just do whatever you want, so what the hell, bring the whole damn FDA. It changes nothing. You are guilty of insubordination. A blatant disregard for my direct orders. I've been tasked with finding out why, but honestly, I don't really care. We'll go through this dog-and-pony show and the end result remains the same. You are gone. If I have anything to say about it, you won't be allowed to monitor a crosswalk at your local elementary school. But please, for the sake of the powers that be, explain to me why you refused to close this investigation of grocery store fraud."

"If I may," interjected Jameson.

"Counselor," Swayz retorted, "I'd really like to hear from Agent Stone if it's all the same to you. Please."

Gordon looked briefly at Jameson, then to McNeely. McNeely gave him a slight nod. Gordon took a breath and began.

"Sir, a couple of months ago, a drone strike in Ireti, Nigeria, destroyed a small school, killing approximately sixty students and staff. Included with those victims were Abiona and Abebi

Adeyami, younger sisters of our subject, Jummal Adeyami. At the time, Jummal was in New York City working at Field-Town Foods. He was a senior executive and considered an expert in the wholesale food industry in this country. The subject immediately returned to Nigeria and stayed for several weeks before returning to the United States. Before he returned to the US, FinCEN became aware of a $10,000 transfer to an account the NSA described as associated with terrorism, meaning not a direct link, but possibly related to terrorism or terrorist activities. The transfer was deemed a charity scam and Jummal was considered a victim of that scam. Subsequently, however, the recipient of the $10,000 transferred half of the funds to an account known to be held by a Boko Haram soldier.

"Before coming back to the US, Jummal contacted Abdul Malik of the Dar Al-Hijrah Mosque in Falls Church. A phone call between the two men revealed a desire by Jummal to set up a food wholesaler, A&A Foods, in Washington, DC, and to bring his brothers into the United States to help him do so. We believe Jummal sought Malik's help in bringing his brothers into the country illegally. Jummal returned to the US, but settled in Arlington as opposed to New York City, his former residence. He rented warehouse space in the District and began setting up his new venture with support of his employer, Field-Town Foods. We believe Jummal is using A&A Foods to take advantage of the loss-leader market. A mosque-owned van made repeated stops at area stores, buying up loss-leader products and delivering them to the A&A Foods warehouse. We believe Malik facilitated these transactions and utilized female members of the mosque to do so. We observed what appeared to be money changing hands between Jummal and the delivery driver on repeated occasions.

"During this period, there were several calls from Jummal back to Nigeria where he may have been planning for his brothers' illegal entry into the US. The next time the van arrived at the A&A Foods warehouse, it delivered two men. Jummal met the men at the loading dock, exchanged hugs, and escorted them inside. We believe these two men are Jummal's brothers, brought into the country illegally by Malik. We believe the brothers are living, at least temporarily, at the warehouse. Around this time, a trash run was conducted at Jummal's Arlington residence. A printout of an email was discovered that included the statement 'We'll talk here' which we believe to mean Jummal would talk with his brothers once they got to the US. The email address is a bit of an enigma, as it has been accessed from three IP addresses, but never actually used to send or receive emails.

"Sir, it is my belief Jummal may be using A&A Foods as a front to raise money for terrorist activity, either here or in Nigeria, the home of Boko Haram, possibly utilizing the loss-leader market to buy sale items in bulk and repackaging and selling them for profit. Jummal's motive is revenge for his sisters' deaths. If the JTTF were to jacket a case, that would provide access to the FISA Court to get warrants to review content of Jummal's phone calls in real time, as well as emails, that we believe will prove Jummal Adeyami is engaged in terrorist activity."

The room fell silent.

With a grunt, Swayz shook his head. "Jesus, Stone. That's all you've got? Some grocery store fraud, maybe—*maybe*—a couple of illegal immigrants, and a fucking email to nowhere? You've got nothing connecting this guy to the funds going to Boko Haram. Didn't we have this exact conversation a month ago? T for terrorism and all that. Your case is shit! And I noticed you forgot to include the parts where you defied my orders to shut this investigation down. I noticed you said 'we' a lot too. There's no 'we' here, Stone. It's you. Just you. So take your bullshit case and your friends here and get out of my office!"

McNeely raised his arm and brought his palm down hard on the table. It caused a loud "smack" and a water bottle to tip.

He stood up and leaned his massive frame across the table, his face inches from where Swayz sat.

"Back off, Swayz," he whispered with quiet menace. "You FBI types are unbelievable. You can't see your hand in front of your face without a policy telling you it's really there."

Swayz remained silent, recognizing that McNeely was not one to be trifled with.

"You've got to understand who you're dealing with here," McNeely continued. "This agent is the best damn investigator I've ever seen. His instincts are uncanny. He's proven it again and again. He sees things nobody else sees. You're too damn stubborn to recognize it and your ego is bruised because he didn't close the case when you told him to. Get over yourself, Swayz. You and your precious JTTF can either put your big-boy pants on and give Agent Stone what he needs, or you can let it slide and hope it doesn't hit the fan on your watch. That, Supervisory Special Agent Swayz, is up to you."

Swayz was beyond livid. He stood slowly, not giving an inch to McNeely. Gordon and Jameson sat mesmerized by the scene as Swayz and McNeely stared each other down, daring the other to make the first move.

On the other side of the office, the door burst open and Swayz's assistant, Liz, tumbled into the room. The four men turned to look at her.

She paused, wide-eyed. Quietly, she turned to Swayz. "Dillon is on line two. He's been trying to reach you. You need to take the call…now," she said.

Swayz shook his head, snapping out of the moment. He walked over to his desk, picked up the phone and pressed line two. There was a terse and very brief conversation. Swayz hung up the phone and looked at the three men across his office at the conference table. He seemed to deflate right in front of them.

"Looks like this case is staying open, and we are proceeding with this investigation. This grocery store bullshit is now JTTF property. Good day, gentlemen." Swayz sat at his desk looking dazed.

Without a word, Gordon, McNeely, and Jameson left the office.

CHAPTER 61

Jameson broke the silence when they made it into the hallway. "That's not something you see every day," was all he could muster. Without a word, Gordon sped off to the stairs, heading down to his space in the basement. McNeely made a hurried goodbye to Jameson and rushed after Gordon. He was worried Gordon might be headed to a breakdown, of sorts.

But when McNeely found Gordon in the break room, he was not hiding in a corner. Instead, he was digging through a file of paperwork. "Gordo," said McNeely. "Everything okay?"

Gordon did not respond, just kept flipping papers.

"Gordo!" shouted McNeely.

"Yeah, what?" he answered, looking up. Then, "Sorry, boss. Swayz was right. I can't believe I missed it."

"Swayz—What? Gordon, what are you talking about?"

"It's the email, boss."

"Gordon, stop. Take a breath."

Somewhat reluctantly, Gordon stopped and sat in one of the cafeteria chairs. He looked at McNeely. "It always bugged me about the email. He set it up before he left Nigeria to come back to the States."

"And?"

"And, I've got three IP addresses accessing that account."

"Right," McNeely said. "That's the brothers, maybe?"

"Maybe," Gordon said, almost laughing.

McNeely shook his head. "You've lost me. What's the point?"

"The point, right. Yeah, the point." Gordon stood up and went back to the file.

"Yes, Gordon, what's the damn point of the email?"

"Exactly! Why create an email account that's accessed from three IP addresses but never used? Not a single email sent from or received by that account. Ever."

"You got me, Gordo. Maybe he changed his mind. Maybe he has another account somewhere else. Maybe he's using his work email."

"Nope, it's none of those. Ah, here it is." He pulled a single page from a file.

Gordon looked down at the sheet of paper in his hand. It was a copy of the printed email he had pulled from Jummal's trash. Gordon shook his head and laughed. "Swayz was right. You heard him, 'an email to nowhere.' That's it. They weren't sending emails. They're not talking on the phone and they're not sending emails. Emails to nowhere. It's brilliant." He handed the copy to McNeely.

McNeely looked at it, then looked up at Gordon. "Gordo, I'm a pretty smart guy, but we've already established they weren't sending emails. Explain."

Gordon smiled. He gestured at the copy in McNeely's hands. "It's a *draft* email. I don't know why he printed it, but there it is. And he just threw it away." Gordon was practically giddy. "Think about it."

"A draft. A draft email...to nowhere! Sonuvabitch, Gordo! That's how they were talking to each other. Draft emails."

"Yes! Draft an email, but don't send it. No trail. No PRTT would ever see it. Maybe they had set times. Maybe they just checked at random. As long as they had the user ID and password, any of them could sign into the account from anywhere. Write a draft email, read a draft email, respond with another draft email, whatever. All on the same account. Never sent, never received. Emails to nowhere. Brilliant," he repeated. "Take a look at that copy in your hand. Read it out loud."

"A test brothers to see if this will work. Its coming together now——for our sisters! We'll talk here. Cant wait. Abebi and Abiona forever!!!"

"We'll talk here. I was wrong. Jummal didn't mean they'd talk here in the US once the brothers arrived. He meant *here*," Gordon said, pointing at the email copy. "Here inside the email account. Through drafts."

"I'll be damned," was all McNeely could say.

"I've got to get that FISA warrant," Gordon said. "It's the only way we'll see the content of those draft emails."

CHAPTER 62

Sophia Pressmen sat at her desk at *The Washington Post*. She had earned her own office a couple of years ago. She missed the raucous vibe of the bullpen, but an office allowed for privacy, and on this occasion, contemplation. The information Samantha had provided her was interesting, but woefully incomplete. She had nothing close to an actual story, though it sure seemed like there was something here.

Usually when she asked a PIO for a quote from an organization's leadership, she got an email with highly scripted language that had been vetted half a dozen times and sweated over by an attorney somewhere. If she got an actual call, it was usually from the PIO, who would read her the highly scripted quote over the phone. But this time, she got the call from the Assistant Special Agent in Charge of the FBI's Washington Field Office. This guy, she thought, was kind of a big deal.

Samantha had said she was looking for some cover because the FBI was going to point the finger at FDA when one of JTTF's terrorism investigations went sideways, and she obviously did not want that to happen. That was just normal, everyday DC political bullshit, though. That hardly warranted a call from someone of Dillon's status.

Her phone rang, interrupting her thoughts. "Federal courts desk, Pressman speaking," she said. It was the WFO PIO.

"Ms. Pressman, I have a proposition of sorts for you, all off the record, of course."

"Of course. Please, tell me what's on your mind."

"Well, ASAC Dillon looked into the case you referenced and, uh, again, this is all off the record."

"Yes," Pressman responded with an eye roll.

"Right, good. Well, the investigation remains ongoing, and ASAC Dillon's statement that we do not comment on ongoing investigations remains the FBI's position."

Very interesting. Why in the world would they call just to maintain the status quo? "That's it? That's all you've got for me?"

"At this time, yes, I'm afraid so."

"At this time. What's that mean? Should I expect another call? And if so, when? And from whom?" Pressman asked.

"Well, yes, I guess that's the whole point of my call. Ms. Pressman, we'd like to invite you in to FBI headquarters at an appropriate time, where we can discuss this case in greater detail. But as it is an ongoing investigation, such a meeting is premature at this time."

Pressman stayed quiet. This was a tap dance she had not anticipated. That could mean only one thing. There was something larger in play here than just pointing fingers at the FDA. And terrorism was on the table.

"Ms. Pressman, are you still there?" the PIO asked.

"Still here. It sounds like you're asking me to hold my story." A story that did not actually exist and certainly would not be in tomorrow's *Post*.

"I believe that would be mutually beneficial," he said.

"I get the exclusive, one day before you release anything?" she asked.

"I can certainly promise you that, Ms. Pressman."

"And what's the time frame?"

"I would anticipate bringing you in within the week, subject to change based on the investigation."

"All right. And what about the case agent? When can I talk

to him?"

"Well, that's a possibility," the PIO said, "but not until the case is closed."

"Huh," Pressman responded. "So who will I be talking to?"

"I believe you've spoken with ASAC Dillon, and we will try to make Assistant Director Dan Pendleton available as well."

Pressman almost dropped the phone. It was a big enough deal when ASAC Dillon called her to say no comment. But Pendleton was an assistant director in charge of the FBI's counterterrorism effort. He was a very big deal. What was going on here?

"I guess you've got a deal. I look forward to hearing from you in a few days."

"Have a good evening, Ms. Pressman," the PIO said and hung up the phone.

Sophia had been around long enough to know this might still turn into a whole lot of nothing, but clearly there was something going on at the FBI. And Special Agent Gordon Stone was right in the middle of it.

CHAPTER 63

Jummal looked at his brothers with a foreboding sense of grim satisfaction. They were here and the three of them were working together. If it all came together, Ireti would have a new school, and the United States would learn that its negligence did not come without cost.

He was proud of what he had created through his talents and his connections—a burgeoning food wholesale business in the heart of Washington, DC. A legitimate company that sold to high-quality stores in busy markets. He'd relied on his reputation in the industry to set it up, as well as leveraging his company's reputation. Clients were being groomed and developed. Money was coming in. Oku and Kam were fully engaged, making deliveries every day. Yes, he had done this with his brothers, but he had done it *for* his sisters.

If A&A Foods was real, he would be looking to buy more trucks, hire new drivers, legitimize Oku's and Kam's presence. But it was not real. Not really.

With the help of the women from the mosque, Jummal had collected enough loss-leader product for the plan. Diapers and infant formula were probably the two most popular loss leaders, as they were always in demand and mothers were always looking for the best deal. He was not interested in making money on loss leaders. He needed to move product that could not be tracked. The women from the mosque bought the products. Jummal would relabel and repackage the products. And once the products were repackaged, A&A Foods would distribute them to retailers throughout the metro DC area. There was a bit of an art to relabeling and repackaging, but Jummal knew how the grocery markets worked. He knew the path from the farm, or in the case of diapers and baby formula, the manufacturer, to the distributor to the retailer to the consumer, as well as anyone in the country. Monitoring those logistics had been his job. Finding efficiencies, shortcuts, preferred routes, trains, ships, and trucks was how he made his living, and he did it very well.

Perfecting a relabeling and repackaging process had been easy enough. The products he was moving just had to be convincing enough to get past the loading dock and onto the shelves. Jummal unpackaged the products, cleaned off labels, removed expiration dates and lot numbers, then put new ones on. He created new packaging with matching lot numbers on new labels, reattaching all of that to individual products. Then it was simply a matter of repackaging those containers in bulk and adding a forged lot number label that matched the lot number on each individual item.

Jummal's plan required sophistication and nuance. It demanded the products he would put back on the market appeared new, legitimate, and ready for sale to the consumer. New packaging also had the advantage of making each container untraceable.

While Jummal had perfected the repackaging operation, Kam and Oku had perfected several routes to several retailers around the metro DC area. They had met and interacted with loading dock staff at all their stops. In a short time, they had become a known quantity, trusted and reliable. Soon, that would be put to the test.

CHAPTER 64

Finally, Gordon was getting some help from the JTTF. The Adeyami case remained open and now operational support was being provided. While a warrant application to look at emails and listen to phone calls was being prepped for the FISA Court, Gordon maintained surveillance on the A&A Foods warehouse, though now with the support of operational surveillance teams.

Each time a truck left the warehouse, it was followed to its destination. And each time Jummal left for the evening, he was followed. Rotating teams maintained 24/7 coverage on the warehouse.

All of the extra manpower, surveillance, and vehicles uncovered absolutely nothing. Trucks left the warehouse, driven by Kam or Oku, and made seemingly legitimate deliveries to a variety of grocers throughout the region. Following Jummal home proved only that he drove home every night, and once there, he stayed there. A camera with a telephoto lens was able to get clear pictures that allowed Gordon to positively identify the two drivers as Okunola and Kambili Adeyami, but that was it. After they made their last deliveries, they returned to the warehouse and were not seen again until another delivery went out the next day.

Other than proof of two illegal immigrants, Gordon had nothing. A loss-leader scam? Maybe, but depending on Jummal's methodology, that might not even be illegal. And it was certainly nothing Swayz would care about. Gordon needed to figure out his terrorism case, and he needed to figure it out soon. Something was not right. He could sense it. But raising money for terrorism through a loss-leader scam made no sense. It was simply too difficult to raise substantial amounts of money quickly and required significant investment to run such a scam on a large scale. Sophisticated, complex loss-leader hustles were exceedingly rare, but most failed before they ever really got started because it was just too hard. And all Gordon had was two nights of loss-leader purchases made weeks ago by women from the Dar Al-Hijrah Mosque.

He could imagine a lot of ways for Jummal to raise money for a terrorist group like Boko Haram that were easier than a loss-leader hustle. Counterfeit products? A possibility, but that required a significant manufacturing apparatus with all the staff and equipment that came with it. He had seen no evidence of such activity at the warehouse. Drugs? Risky, but quick and easy if you already ran in those circles. Again, no evidence whatsoever linked Jummal to the drug trade.

Gordon had nothing, and his FISA warrant was still days away.

CHAPTER 65

Inside the A&A Foods warehouse, the three brothers were in constant motion. Kam and Oku spent their days delivering food and sundries in the DC metro area. They had successfully established a core clientele of twenty area grocery stores. That kept the three brothers busy and was the number Jummal felt he needed to execute the plan. Kam and Oku did not just deliver to their clients. They stopped, got out of their trucks, visited with the loading dock staff, even helped unload the trucks once in a while. They always had smiles and were quick to laugh at the banter around the various loading docks. Every delivery ended with a handshake. It did not take long for the two to become known quantities with their customers, welcomed and trusted.

While the two brothers were developing relationships with customers, Jummal kept busy in the warehouse. If the brothers were out, he would step in and take receipt of product from whatever distribution center it might have come from. But that was not his focus, and he only worked that part of the business if both brothers were out.

Most of Jummal's time was spent in a back corner of the warehouse, out of sight, working with the products that had been purchased and delivered to the warehouse through Abdul Malik and his two buyers weeks ago. These were the loss leaders. Gordon had been right about that. But what Gordon did not know was Jummal's intention. Profit did not enter

Jummal's considerations. Jummal's goal was to present his core clients with a repackaged, relabeled loss leader that would go unnoticed and be untraceable back to him, his brothers, or A&A Foods.

The women from the mosque had purchased thirty boxes of diapers from around the community and delivered them to A&A Foods. Diapers were a high-volume, high-turnover business. Retailers frequently sold them at aggressive discounts to lure mothers into their stores. It was a perfect choice for Jummal to perfect his repackaging and relabeling scheme, right down to the barcodes, utilizing equipment found in any food warehouse around the country. Once he was satisfied with his counterfeit packaging, he prepared twenty individual boxes of diapers that would not be out of place in any grocery store.

When suppliers delivered product to A&A Foods, the brothers would take box after box of items and stack-and-wrap particular items on pallets depending on what any particular client had ordered. If a grocer needed twenty cases of canned beans and corn, along with a dozen bags of sugar and forty boxes of Cheerios, the brothers would stack it all on a pallet, shrink-wrap the whole thing, load it onto one of their trucks, and Kam or Oku would deliver it to their client, on time and in perfect condition.

To test his counterfeit labeling process, Jummal took a repackaged box of diapers, placed them in the center of a pallet, and when the order came in from a retailer, he would simply surround the diapers by products the retailer had actually ordered, wrap it up and make the delivery. He did this twenty times, delivered to twenty different clients. Some were buried in coffee, some next to peanuts and microwave popcorn. It did not matter and Jummal did not care. His goal was to get the box of diapers onto the retailer's loading dock and ultimately onto a shelf without any questions or even a thought about why an unordered box of diapers had been included in the delivery. Oku made ten deliveries without incident. Kam made nine.

Kam's tenth delivery to the McLean Safeway started off like any other. He backed into the loading dock, jumped out of the truck, went around and opened the tailgate. He stood by as a twenty-something he knew as Bobby C pushed a pallet-jack across the loading dock and into Kam's truck. The two exchanged pleasantries, and Kam followed Bobby C back into the Safeway warehouse, chatting the whole way. When they reached the office, Bobby C continued on with the pallet, and Kam went into the office to get the bill of lading signed by the loading dock supervisor, Darryl.

Kam greeted Darryl with a smile and a handshake. The office was typical for a warehouse. Paperwork everywhere, a couple of phones on the desk, four closed-circuit TV monitors mounted on the wall, and a dry-erase board. The board was filled top-to-bottom and edge-to-edge with tough to decipher handwriting documenting any number of deliveries to the store. The two men exchanged small talk until Kam, again, extended his hand to Darryl.

"Good to see you, Darryl," he said. "I'd better get going before my boss starts to wonder if I'm coming back."

"Back at you, Kam," Darryl said, accepting Kam's handshake. "We'll see you next time."

Kam turned to exit office and ran straight into Bobby C.

"Hey, Kam, glad you're still here." Bobby C was holding a box of diapers under one arm. "Found these in that pallet you just delivered," he said, holding out the box. "Don't think they were part of the order."

Kam stared at the diaper box.

"Yo, Kam. You with me, bro?" Bobby C asked.

"Huh? Yeah, yeah, sorry, bud." He looked at the box. "Just trying to remember if I loaded that pallet. No clue how those got on there." Kam turned back to Darryl, still at his desk. "Want a package of diapers?" Kam said.

Darryl shrugged his shoulders. "You better take 'em with you, Kam. Don't want you to get in trouble with your boss."

"Fair enough. I'll see you."

Darryl gave Kam a mock salute, and Bobby C gave him the box of diapers. "Don't use 'em all in one go," Bobby C said.

"Fuck you, B.C.," Kam said, laughing.

CHAPTER 66

Back at the warehouse, Kam presented the box of diapers to Jummal and Oku. "What happened," they asked simultaneously. Kam told the story.

"The packaging was fine, Jummal," he said. "They never suspected for a second. It kind of felt like they just didn't want me to get in trouble. If I hadn't still been there, that box would have ended up on the shelf, no question."

"You're probably right," Jummal said, "but we won't risk it. They're off the target list. What store was it?"

"The Safeway over in McLean."

"Okay," Jummal said. "Nineteen to go."

Then, Jummal waited. He knew each box of diapers would be discovered within twenty-four hours as stockers from around the region began unloading the pallets and pushing product out to store shelves. What he did not know with any certainty is what the stockers would do once the diapers were discovered.

Nineteen stores. Nineteen boxes of repackaged diapers. Nineteen stockers.

Troy tossed the diapers into a corner of the warehouse when no one was looking. Not his problem. Marty nonchalantly carried his box of wayward diapers out to his car. "Forty bucks I don't have to spend," he said. Phillip found it hilarious there was a box of diapers hiding in a load of breakfast cereal. Of course, he was high as a kite and finding everything hilarious.

His box made it to the shelf. Lisa took the box to aisle seven, adding it to the shelf with the other diapers. Franklin dutifully took the box to his supervisor, reporting the mistake in the delivery. His supervisor shrugged and said, "Go ahead and shelve it," before explaining the concept of spillage to Franklin. And so it went.

Seventeen of the nineteen remaining boxes made it to the shelves. Jummal would never know that, not exactly. What he did know was that other than Kam's experience at the McLean Safeway, not a single of the remaining repackaged diapers made it back to him. Twenty-four hours had come and gone and not a single one of the remaining core clients had called him about the package of diapers showing up at their stores. Jummal hoped that at least ten to fifteen of the boxes made it to the shelves, to be sold to retail customers. Ten to fifteen, he thought. That would be enough. It had to be enough. He sat at the desk in the warehouse office, smiling. It had worked.

CHAPTER 67

Gordon sat in his car a block from the warehouse. He could not actually see the warehouse from this vantage point, but he could see the surveillance team set up to watch A&A Foods. Somehow, the JTTF had determined this case warranted the resources necessary to provide around-the-clock surveillance of the warehouse, the two trucks, and Jummal's residence. Gordon now had the full support, however reluctant, of the JTTF and their seemingly endless resources, though he remained stumped as to how it all came together and still felt very much alone. It could still turn out to be nothing. A&A Foods could still turn out to be a wholly legitimate food wholesaler. The one thing he knew with certainty was that Jummal's brothers were in the country illegally. How they got here and why they came at all remained open questions.

He took a breath and sighed. "What next?" he said to himself as his cell phone buzzed.

It was Swayz. "Stone, your warrant came through. Get back here and take care of this shit." He hung up before Gordon could answer.

Gordon breathed deep. This was it. If the FISA warrant did not turn anything up, this investigation would be shut down, and he would certainly be bounced out of the JTTF. He started his car and pulled into traffic. A&A Foods shrank in his rearview mirror.

"You just missed him," said Liz when Gordon arrived at the office. "He said he'd be back later, but wasn't sure when."

"Will you call me when he gets back?" Gordon asked.

"Sure thing, Agent Stone."

Frustrated, Gordon retreated to his basement. He paced the length of the room, lost in thought, waiting for the phone to buzz so he could find out what the warrant would allow him to look at. He needed evidence. An illegal immigration charge and potential fraud via a loss-leader setup did not amount to terrorist activity. The case was slipping away, and the FISA warrant was his last best hope.

His phone pinged, and he pulled it from his pocket. It was a text from Liz. *He's back* was all it said. Gordon stuffed the phone in his pocket and ran upstairs. One way or another, his fate was about to be decided.

CHAPTER 68

The FISA warrant allowed Gordon access to the Abebi_Abiona_Forever@yahoo.com email account, where he could see any activity in real time and any activity that had happened in the past but had not been deleted. It also allowed real-time monitoring access to Jummal's cell phone.

"You've got thirty days, Stone," Swayz snarled. "Bring me something soon, or it's your ass," he added.

In thirty days, Gordon's access would be shut off. If he needed more, he would have to petition the FISA Court for an extension of another thirty days. But Gordon knew he did not really have thirty days. He had burned the bridge with Swayz and was walking a fine line with the rest of the JTTF. At best, he would have to provide some real and substantive evidence in a week, maybe two at the outside, before this case was shut down for good and he was shuttled back to FDA-OCI.

An FBI tech agent showed Gordon how he could access the email account with an exclusive FBI user ID and password known only to Gordon. His presence would be masked and unknown. He could watch and read, and every input made to the account would be documented. Gordon could also tap into Jummal's cell phone at any time to eavesdrop on any call into or from Jummal's phone. Each morning, an audio file would be sent directly to him that would play the previous day's phone conversations.

Satisfied Gordon understood the process, the tech agent left Swayz's office. Swayz and Gordon just looked at each other. Finally, Swayz said, "Don't fuck this up, Stone. We're all out on a limb on this one, and I will personally run you out of here if you don't bring this case home."

Gordon did not know how to respond, so he remained silent, watching Swayz. When the silence became awkward, Swayz ordered Gordon out of his office. "Get to work, Stone," he said, dismissing Gordon.

Gordon nodded to Liz on his way out, ran to the stairs, and hustled down to the basement. He got there, his heart racing. He shut the door, plugged in his laptop, and signed on to the Abebi_Abiona_Forever@yahoo.com email.

At first glance, most agents would have been disappointed. There had been no activity whatsoever since the day Kam and Oku were smuggled into the country and took up residence at the warehouse. But Gordon was not most agents. The lack of email traffic made sense to him. The brothers were here now and there was no need to talk via email drafts. He scrolled down to the folder labeled "Drafts" and clicked it. There were forty-one draft emails dating from the day Jummal arrived back in the United States to the day his brothers arrived at the warehouse.

Gordon could not help but smile. Jummal and his brothers had left a trail after all. And why not, thought Gordon. No one but the three of them would ever see this account. He smiled wider, remembering what Pete McNeely had told him on his first-ever trash run as a new agent with FDI-OCI: "Stone," he had said, "a trash run is the most disgusting and most useful tool we have. The things people throw away."

CHAPTER 69

The email drafts started the day Jummal created the account back in Ireti. Gordon read through them all. Then he read through them a second time. The third time through, he focused on sixteen of the forty-one draft emails he thought might be pertinent to the case.

This is a test of our comm set up. Just checking to see if it will work.

Oku, I think it'll work in the drafts. Let me know if you can see it.

I can see it. Does it work.

Yes, it's working. Give Kam the account name and password, too. He can use your phone if he needs to reach me. No need to use this again until I head back to the US.

Two weeks passed until the email account was used again.

Oku, I made it. That's a long trip but everything worked out. No delays and easy connections, just took forever. Company has me set up in Arlington, Virginia. Nice little house. Got to find space for the shop starting tomorrow, then sell them on the idea. No doubt they'll go for it. It's just step one. Already missing our talks at the table. Tell Kam to hang in there. Working on getting you here when ready. Malik will make that happen. Not sure how, and may take some time, but you'll get here. I'll call the Chief in a couple of days at the usual time. You and Kam should be there. That'll make Mom happy. Best, J

Sounds good Jummal. Everyone here misses you. Not sure why, I never like you much :) We'll be there when you call Father. Here's Kam. Going to let him talk to you

Jummal, quit sending secret message and get your ass to work. I'm getting bored. Love Kam.

Oku, found a spot in DC. It's perfect for the Plan. Great location. Heading to NYC tomorrow. I know the board will buy in and then we're set. I'll give you the dates once I talk to Malik again. You'll have to get Father to take you and Kam to Lagos. He'll drop you at the airport. After he leaves, you'll meet up with Malik's people. Trip won't be as easy as mine, but you'll get here. Probably through Canada. Jummal

J, we're waiting and anxious to get going. A little nervous though. Don't like misleading Father but understand. Abebi & Abiona Forever brother! Oku

Soon Oku soon. Can't wait to see you both again. Here by myself and can't stop thinking of Abebi and Abiona and that they are really gone. Will never understand why nothing has happened. Like it never happened. Sorry brother. Getting the shop set up and getting you and Kam over here is exhausting. Then I can't sleep b/c I miss Ireti and wish I was back there still. And I miss them so much. A&A always and forever, J

Jummal, Kam says they'll live in our hearts forever, and he's right. But we can't let this stand. We're in the right. I hate it but

I know it. Good luck in New York. -O

Oku, went even better than expected. Pretty emotional telling the story to the board, but they are all in. Anything we need to get the shop up and running. It's coming together quickly now. Got to get a couple trucks and set up the warehouse. Already been calling suppliers and retailers all over DC. With my connections and Field-Town backing us, this is going to be the easy part. I think we'll have money for a new school in no time. Not much longer now. I'll meet with Malik when I get back to DC. You and Kam need to get ready. I'll share the timeline on my next call, but give you the details here. Can't wait to see you two again. Jummal

J, we'll be ready. This is great news about the shop. Excited to get the money flowing to rebuild our home. We'll wait for the call and then additional instructions here for Lagos after he drops us there. Abebi&Abiona Forever!!! Oku

Oku, here's what's happening. Like I said on the call, you need to be in Lagos a week from this Tuesday. He'll drop you at the airport, thinking I've arranged to have you pick up tickets, etc., there. If he asks, tell Father that you'll be on a special work visa arranged by me through Field-Town Foods. It's temporary and allows entry without a passport. If he asks me, that's what I'm going to tell him. Just tell him I'm taking care of it. Once he leaves, you'll need to get to the BRT Bus Station on Bayo Shadipo. Go through the main entrance. There's an info booth there. Ask for Abdullah Nafisat. You'll get directions for the rest of the trip there. They won't tell me how it all works, but that's for security. I think you'll be taking a bus ride to Accra and will catch a flight to Canada. Malik will deliver you the rest of the way. Might take a few days but you'll get here. Once you're here, I'll work on the F. Be safe brother. Kam too. I need you here and we'll execute the Plan together. Abebi&AbionaForever! Jummal

We're ready Jummal. For our sisters. For Ireti. See you soon brother, Oku

Oku, once you and Kam are on the bus to Accra (or wherever), turn the phone off. Don't turn it on again until we're face to face. J

Gordon noted that the email traffic stopped four days before the arrival of the van delivering Okunola and Kambibi Adeyami to the A&A Foods warehouse.

The information in the draft emails stunned him. Swayz was wrong. This was a lot more than illegal immigration and grocery store fraud. But Gordon admitted he was wrong too. It did not appear as though Jummal was raising money for Boko Haram or any other terrorist organization. In fact, it looked as though any money Jummal was raising was to build a new school back in Ireti.

Gordon read the sixteen emails again, then shut his laptop. He pulled out a notepad. This was an exercise Katherine had used with him many times. "If something isn't making sense, stop what you're doing and write everything down from memory," she had said. "The important stuff is in there, in your head. It just gets cluttered when there's too much information floating around. Shut everything down. Pull out a paper and pen and just write. The important stuff will find its way onto the page."

Gordon shut his eyes, forcing himself to focus on the draft emails. He opened his eyes, picked up a pen and began to write. It only took a few minutes. He looked at his notes.

"The Plan." There's a plan. What is it?

"Don't understand why nothing has happened, like it never happened." They're mad about something. The sisters?

Why go to such lengths for illegal entry? Not just to earn money for a new school. Something else is going on.

"We're in the right." Motivated. Angry. Frustrated.

"Abebi_Abiona_Forever" name of the account. Used a lot by all of them. They're mad about their sisters. Is this about revenge?

"For our sisters." Sounds like revenge.

"We'll execute the Plan together." ??? The plan again. What are they up to?

"Once you're here, I'll work on the F." F??? What is F?

Revenge. Could it be that simple? Maybe. Probably. But how? *The Plan. F.* Gordon shuddered. He was not sure what it all meant or how it would come together. But he knew if he was reading these draft emails correctly, Jummal was planning a lot worse than fundraising for a terrorist group halfway around the world.

The draft emails made the illegal entry case against the brothers, with Jummal and Abdul Malik as co-conspirators. And the drafts dripped with a revenge theory. What remained unclear, however, was how they would take their revenge. If he took this to Swayz, it would not be enough. Swayz would execute search warrants today, interview the parties, and be done with it, probably as a simple illegal entry matter.

"How will they take their revenge?" Gordon asked himself. Not by reselling product in the loss-leader market. There had to be more. Unfortunately, none of the draft emails mentioned Boko Haram. That link was cold. The brothers, however, were here to help Jummal raise money for a new school *and* to implement their "plan" for revenge. "Whatever that is," he mumbled.

"F," he said, rubbing his chin with his left hand.

CHAPTER 70

A week went by with no further input into the Abebi_Abiona_Forever account. Gordon reviewed phone traffic on Jummal's cell every morning, but nothing was turning up there either. There had been a single call home to talk to his parents at the usual time, but nothing that helped his case. It appeared Jummal was talking to his brothers in person at the warehouse, or not at all. And with the brothers sleeping there, the JTTF had been unable to wire the warehouse for surveillance.

AUSA Jameson got him a Pen Register Trap-and-Trace order for the A&A Foods business line, but all the calls on that line had been to or from phone numbers associated with legitimate food industry businesses. Monitoring that line as well seemed a bit desperate to Gordon.

He made his way into JTTF headquarters early on Monday morning. He wanted to listen to any recorded conversations from Jummal's cell before heading over to A&A Foods to support the surveillance there. He had nothing. No further draft emails, no phone calls of any evidentiary value, and he still could not hear inside the warehouse. He was about to play the cell phone recordings from the previous day when his own cell phone buzzed. It was Swayz.

"Stone, I need a briefing on your case in five. My office." He hung up.

Gordon groaned. This was not going to be good. His case had been reduced to an illegal immigration case. That was all he had. Swayz was going to love this, he thought. Gordon shook his head. "If it's not there, it's not there," he mumbled. Maybe he did not have a case. Maybe, in the end, Jummal had ideas but could not ultimately act on them. Maybe it was nothing more than what the evidence pointed to. For the most part, A&A Foods appeared to be a legitimate wholesale food business. The white van and the women from the Falls Church mosque had not been seen in weeks. The brothers were in the country illegally, but just making deliveries on behalf of A&A Foods. Maybe it was time to move on.

Gordon finished his briefing for Swayz, who stared at him blankly.

"That's it," he said. "How about that? After all this, we're stuck with two illegal immigrants. Jeeeeesus, Stone." Swayz whistled. "You are fucked." Gordon could not disagree. "You've got 'til Friday and then I'm shutting this bullshit down." Shaking his head, Swayz added, "I can't believe we went to the FISA Court with this crap. What a waste of time."

Swayz's smug satisfaction was lost on Gordon. "What happens Friday?" he asked.

"You find something, and we'll hit the warehouse and wrap this up. You find nothing, and I'll dump you and this grocery store bullshit fraud and immigration case right back to the FDA. Or maybe we'll just execute the search warrant anyway. Either way, I'm done with this case, and I'm done with you. That'll be all, Stone." Swayz turned away from Gordon, pretending to work on his computer.

"Friday, then," said Gordon. He stood up and left.

Once more alone in his basement bunker, Gordon still had to be Gordon. He had to check all the boxes. He had to complete the process. If he was wrong about this, so be it. McNeely would take him back without question. Gordon could live with that, but he was not prepared to give up just yet. There was more work to be done. He noticed he had left his laptop open and on. The screen to play Jummal's cell phone audio from yesterday was still open. Gordon grabbed his earphones, plugged them into his laptop and hit play.

There were two calls from Sunday. The first was a ten-minute chat with his parents in Nigeria. There was nothing of substance on that recording. The second call was brief, less than twenty seconds. It revealed little, but changed everything.

Hello Malik, this is Jummal.

Jummal, how are you. I have not seen you at the mosque recently. Is everything okay?

All is well, thank you. The time has come for my brother.

Yes, very well. Say no more, just like we discussed. Two days, okay?

Okay, two days. Thank you, I'll see you at the mosque.

CHAPTER 71

The time has come for my brother.

Gordon repeated the phrase over and over again. What did it mean?

The time has come.

"Ominous," said Gordon aloud. The call was Sunday. Today was Monday. Two days meant tomorrow. Something was happening with one of the brothers tomorrow. Gordon made a few calls. Additional surveillance teams were sent to the warehouse, the mosque in Falls Church, and Jummal's residence. Any vehicle leaving the warehouse was to be followed. Anyone leaving the residence, followed. Activity at the mosque would be observed and recorded. If a vehicle needed to be followed, that decision would be made on the fly. It was now or never, thought Gordon. At a minimum, twelve JTTF agents were involved, sometimes more. Only a skeleton crew remained at the office. Nobody, least of all Swayz, was happy.

On Monday afternoon, Jummal left A&A Foods. That was unusual for two reasons. Usually, Jummal did not leave until early evening. And usually, he went straight home. On Monday afternoon, however, he left at 3:50 p.m. and fought the beginning of DC's rush hour all the way to Falls Church, where he parked and walked into the Dar Al-Hijrah Mosque, disappearing for forty-five minutes before emerging, getting back into his car, and driving home.

There was no way to confirm what Jummal was doing at the mosque, or who he was meeting with, though Gordon had a pretty good idea—Jummal and Malik were meeting about one of the brothers.

The time has come for my brother. What it all meant remained just out of reach.

On Tuesday, Gordon joined one of the surveillance teams observing the warehouse. The two delivery trucks sat motionless and unattended at the loading dock. Jummal had arrived before Gordon was at the scene, and his car was the only other vehicle on site.

The hours crawled by. The surveillance teams rotated to keep everyone fresh. Gordon would simply leave the back seat of one vehicle and climb into the back seat of the replacement when it arrived. He was going nowhere. The warehouse appeared closed for business all day, until around 6:00 p.m., when three pizzas were delivered and Jummal appeared at the front door to pay the delivery man. Another four hours crept by with no activity, until a familiar white van pulled into the loading dock. It was the van from the mosque. Gordon knew it was coming, as it had been followed by one of the surveillance teams observing the mosque. The van backed into the loading dock.

The three brothers appeared on the loading dock. Multiple hugs were exchanged until the driver climbed out of the van and interrupted the brothers, pointing at his watch. With a final hug for Jummal and Kam, Oku hopped down from the loading dock and climbed into the passenger side of the mosque van, which then pulled away.

Gordon allowed a few seconds to pass before ordering the surveillance vehicle he was sitting in to follow the van. "The time has come for my brother," he whispered. The van did not return to the mosque, nor did it go to Jummal's house. Instead, it worked its way through the quiet DC streets, then headed south on I-395 before exiting northbound on the George

Washington Parkway. The van took the GW Parkway to its terminus, where it joined the DC Beltway, the massive eight-lane loop around the capital city. When the van left the Beltway and continued north, Gordon understood. *The time has come* for this brother to bug out. Oku was going home.

Malik had arranged to take one of the brothers out of the US and back to Nigeria, through Canada, just like the two of them had come in a few weeks ago.

Gordon called Swayz at home. It was after midnight, early Wednesday morning.

"This better be good, Stone," a sleepy Swayz said.

"Sir, we're north of Frederick, tracking one of the brothers. He's northbound in a van from the Dar Al-Hijrah Mosque. Looks like he's trying to head home the same way he came in. I think we need to keep on him, sir."

"Thanks for that insight, Stone. What do you propose? We should follow him into Canada? Pull him over and bring him in. This ends now."

"I don't think we should, sir. This is the first movement we've seen from either of the two brothers since they got here. If we bring him in, we'll be exposed. It's too soon for that, sir."

"Jesus Christ, Stone," Swayz said. "You've got nothing more than illegal immigration on this case, and you're letting half your case get away. Bring him in and finish this." He hung up.

Gordon shut his eyes and hung his head. If they pulled the van over now, his investigation would be over. It was not time. He had not connected all the dots. He had not completed the process. They might never find what Jummal was really up to if they stopped the van now. They needed to let Oku go, because if Oku was leaving his brothers, leaving the country, that meant one thing—the Abebi_Abiona_Forever account was going to start seeing draft emails again, soon.

"You all right back there, Stone?" asked the agent driving the car. "Looks like our boy is bugging out. Dollars to donuts says he's Canada bound."

"I think you're right. Let's follow him to Pennsylvania. If he's still going north by then, we'll call it a night."

"You're going to let him go?"

"Yes," Gordon said, "I believe I am."

"Your case," said the driver matter-of-factly.

They followed the van north on Route 15, even continuing into Pennsylvania. Gordon ordered the car to turn back when they reached Gettysburg. He turned in the back seat, staring out the rear window as the van carrying Okunola Adeyami left his line of sight. He faced forward again and let out a deep breath. He had disobeyed Swayz *again.* He made eye contact in the rearview mirror with the driver, who just shook his head before turning his attention back to the road.

The surveillance team sped south toward Washington. Gordon had the rear seat to himself and sat stoically. He did not question his decision to let Oku get away. Swayz would never understand, he knew that too, but this case was not over

Gordon pulled his laptop out of his bag. He set it on his lap and opened it, accessing the Abebi_Abiona_Forever@yahoo.com email. He clicked the draft folder open, and there it was. Oku had left the warehouse only a couple of hours ago, but already there was a new entry in the drafts folder.

CHAPTER 72

Oku had been gone only a couple of hours, but Jummal's heart was heavy. With a grim determination, he signed into Abebi_Abiona_Forever@yahoo.com. He paused briefly as he typed his sisters' names. Would they approve of what he was doing? "Of course not," he answered aloud. But they would not understand, he internalized. They would never know what was taken from him and the rest of the family, or what was taken from Ireti. They could not know the feeling of something so cherished being taken away, never to return. They would never know or understand the pain and suffering of their brothers, their parents, and the rest of their village. But it was a pain Jummal could share with those who inflicted it upon him, and his family and village. He would share it, and those responsible would feel it.

Jummal hit the "compose" button and began to type.

> *Oku, you have been brilliant! That we could do this all together has eased our torment and even brought some joy to me and I hope you and Kam too. And now your going home. Resume your place by Father's side. Take care of Ireti. We'll be in touch. A&A Forever!!! Jummal*

Jummal clicked "save as draft" and signed out of the email

account. He checked the time. It was after midnight, early Wednesday morning. He needed to talk to Malik, but that would have to wait. Right now, his thoughts were of Oku heading back to Nigeria to see their parents and help continue to rebuild Ireti. He shook his head and let out a breath. It was a pathetic attempt to rid himself of this melancholy, but there was work to be done.

CHAPTER 73

Gordon read Jummal's email again. It confirmed that Oku was heading back to Nigeria, and with him, half of Gordon's illegal immigration case. That was okay, though. Swayz was right about one thing. You do not work at JTTF to investigate illegal immigration. But Gordon was right, too, about letting Oku go. The draft emails had started up again already, and the other two brothers were still here and working on something. "*We'll be in touch,*" Gordon mimicked.

Gordon thanked the two FBI agents after they dropped him off at JTTF. He drove home and managed a few hours' sleep before reporting to the International Group late Wednesday morning. When he got there, Swayz was apoplectic.

"You let him go!" he shouted. It was an accusation, not a question. Gordon could only stand there and take it, and hope it would not last long.

"You're done, Stone. Fucking done. Liz, get Dillon on the phone. Tell him it's urgent. I'm ending this now, Stone. You're done with the FBI and JTTF. Pack your shit and get out. Bring your case files up to Liz. I don't want to see you, you insubordinate sonuva—"

A "ping" sounded from Gordon's pocket, interrupting Swayz's screed. Gordon automatically retrieved the phone from his pocket and examined the screen.

"Jummal's making a call," he said. "I've got to listen to this."

Swayz just stared at Gordon, unbelieving that the target of his ass-chewing interrupted him to listen in on a phone call. He was speechless.

Gordon entered a password and hit the speaker button. After a couple of electronic clicks, a voice said, "Hello."

CHAPTER 74

An abbreviated night's sleep had not shed the melancholy from Jummal. Already, he missed Oku. But Kam was still here. Kam would finish this to whatever bitter end it might take them. Kam had grown sullen and surly over the past weeks. Instead of the melancholy Jummal felt, Kam found strength in the mission, his anger focused and deliberate, almost unfeeling. Jummal felt badly for Kam. He hoped one day, after this business was done, Kam could find his old self again and enjoy laughter and his brothers' company at that picnic table behind the house in Ireti.

But it was by no means clear that would ever happen again, even if they did make it back. Jummal discreetly wiped a tear before it streamed down his cheek. "Enough," he said under his breath. "Kam," he shouted. His brother looked over from across the warehouse. "I'm going to call Malik. I'll be in the office." Kam waved in acknowledgment.

Inside the office, Jummal picked up his cell phone and dialed.

"Hello."

"Malik, this is Jummal."

"Jummal. How are you? Things went well last night, yes?"

"Yes. Very well. Oku is on his way."

"Excellent, excellent. I bid him safe travels."

"Thank you, Malik." Jummal took a breath. "About the fent—"

"No, no. No, no," Malik interrupted. "Not over the phone."

"Yes, right, sorry."

"Listen, Jummal. I can help you, but..." Malik hesitated. "Are you certain? This is big stuff. You must be certain. You are crossing the Rubicon, I think, yes?"

Jummal closed his eyes. He did not speak.

"Jummal?"

"Yes, I'm here," he said. "Yes. The answer is yes."

"Okay," Malik replied, no hesitation this time. "I'll have it for you next week. Anything else?"

"No, no thank you."

The call ended. Jummal set the phone down. He realized he had been standing and pacing for the entirety of the call. He sat and closed his eyes again. "Madness, madness," he mumbled, holding his head in his hands.

CHAPTER 75

Gordon stared at the phone. "*About the fent*," he whispered as he put the phone in his pocket. He looked at Swayz, who appeared to be gearing up for another round of ass-chewing. In a move that left Swayz gobsmacked, Gordon held up his palm, facing his Supervisory Special Agent. A non-verbal command to stand down. "*About the fent*," he said again, louder this time.

An icy silence followed as the two agents stared at one another. Swayz eyes were cold and filled with menace. Gordon's eyes were blank and unfocused, lost in a thousand-yard stare. Swayz could have had horns and been chewing on a human leg and Gordon would not have noticed him. He might as well have been on the moon. Gordon was doing Gordon, consumed with the process. Checking the boxes.

"*About the fent. Fent. Fent. Fent.*" He closed his eyes.

Swayz remained silent, contemplating whether Gordon had lost his mind.

Gordon opened his eyes, this time really looking at Swayz. "Fentanyl. You can't shut it down, sir," he said. "It's drugs. He's got a shipment of fentanyl coming in next week."

Gordon looked to the door of Swayz's office. Liz stood there silently. He looked back at Swayz. "I have to go," he said.

Swayz just watched as Gordon left, then looked at Liz. She raised her eyebrows, turned on her heel, and shut the office door behind her.

CHAPTER 76

Gordon walked deliberately to his break room, hit the lights and shut the door. He had to think. He began to pace.

Drugs? Maybe Jummal was raising money for something nefarious. You can make a lot of money selling drugs. Certainly more lucrative than a loss-leader scam. But risky. Very risky. And there was no evidence of any sort of drug history with Jummal. It's not his area of expertise. And fentanyl. Why fentanyl? Is that where an aspiring drug dealer would start? With fentanyl? That didn't make any sense. What's he up to?

Fentanyl, Gordon knew, was a super-charged pain killer—a hundred times more potent than morphine and forty times stronger than heroin. It provided a similar high to heroin, but was significantly more lethal, and much cheaper—two dollars for a dose of 100 to 400 micrograms. It was often used to cut heroin in order to stretch product and chase a bigger high. Typically, it came in powder form. Dissolved easily in liquid. Illegally manufactured fentanyl was incredibly dangerous. An amount as small as a few grains of salt could kill you.

Could Jummal be building a drug operation in the A&A Foods warehouse? An operation already so advanced it was using fentanyl? No. Gordon was not buying that scenario. Nothing in Jummal's history or any of the activity they had seen at the warehouse indicated a sophisticated drug operation. But if not that, then what? Drugs were a dangerous business, and what was the motivation? Raising money for terrorism had already been ruled out. Was Gordon wrong about that? No, he thought, no chance. Selling drugs to raise money for terrorism would require significant backing and support from an established player to make that work. There had been no evidence whatsoever of anything like that.

No evidence, that is, except for Malik at the Dar Al-Hijrah Mosque. Could Malik have finagled his way into the drug business right under the nose of the NSA? They had been listening since 9/11. There had been no indication of any activity in the drug trade. But Malik could certainly know people in that line without being an active participant.

"*About the fent—*" Jummal had said.

"*Not over the phone,*" Malik responded.

Malik was discrete. He was smart. A middleman? Maybe, thought Gordon.

Illegal immigration, a sliver of fraud, and now illicit drugs. The introduction of fentanyl into the investigation gave Gordon one thing he needed. More time. But he remained no closer to linking Jummal to any sort of terrorist activity. Swayz may have been thrown for a loop, but Gordon knew he was only down, not out. Gordon still had to put it all together somehow. He had to get back to the work.

CHAPTER 77

Jummal insisted A&A Foods maintain their normal delivery schedule. Kam did not like it, but grudgingly went along with his oldest brother. Jummal knew the more *normal* it was for a retailer to receive a delivery from A&A Foods, the better chance of the plan's success. So legitimate deliveries continued. Jummal helped when he could, replacing Oku as the second delivery truck driver. But he had other work to do as well, which meant from time-to-time Kam had to double up on deliveries.

Hard work was nothing new to Kam. It's what he knew from his life in Ireti. Making deliveries to markets? That was nothing, even with the occasional double shift. What frustrated Kam was the pace. Planning and getting product and repackaging and making labels and more planning and test deliveries and buying supplies and still more planning. Kam felt like he was standing still and growing old, unable to leave the warehouse except to make deliveries. Oku was gone, and Jummal just kept making plans. Everything had to be perfect for Jummal. Kam just wanted to finish the job. He wanted to make them pay for taking his sisters and then go home, a balance restored.

Jummal knew Kam was wired for action. Meticulous preparation was his bailiwick, but Kam was a coiled spring. Instead of exploding, Kam complained and cursed. Jummal let him, knowing that Kam needed the release. But Jummal would not rush the plan. All of it—A&A Foods, his brothers, the deliveries, working with the mosque, the loss leaders—was deliberate and intentional to give the plan the best chance of success. And they were almost there.

When Kam would go off on a rant about the food or sleeping at the warehouse or any number of things, Jummal would tell him, "Soon, brother. We are near the end and soon we will be home with Oku."

Jummal had stopped mentioning his sisters, except in the recent emails he had put in the draft folder to communicate with Oku. Talking about them might have helped allay Kam's frustrations, but it only brought more melancholy and more questions to Jummal.

With Oku on his way home to Ireti, rather than leave Kam by himself at the warehouse, Jummal started sleeping there as well. He was not at all clear if this helped Kam or only added to his frustration, but he knew if they made it back to Ireti, they would speak of this time together as a fond memory.

Jummal's thoughts turned to Ireti and his parents. Initially, the plan allowed that they would all make it home. After the job was done, he would send Kam home, then quietly shut things down at A&A Foods, turn it back over to Field-Town Foods, and return to Ireti to start life anew and ultimately become the village chief. Not a happy ending. He was not so naïve, but a survivable ending. He was only beginning to recognize that getting home grew increasingly unlikely with every step forward toward executing the plan. How could they reasonably hope to emerge from all this unscathed? Even if they all made it back to Ireti and lived out their lives, there would be scars, and plenty of them. Oku would be okay. It was one of the reasons he was sent back early. Kam? Kam was a question mark. While not overly emotional or burdened with big-picture intellect, Kam had changed.

In the beginning, he followed Jummal because he was the eldest brother, the future chief, and that is what you did. He was enthusiastic and eager to please. But the realities of the plan had worn him down, stripping the happy-go-lucky veneer to its base foundation that included anger, frustration, even contempt.

Jummal believed Kam would revert to his old self after a month or two back in Ireti. At least that is what he told himself. He also told himself that he, too, would make it back. He would become chief and fulfill his destiny. But he knew it was a lie. Even if he made it back to Ireti, how long would it last? When would they find him and take him away? Could he even live with himself with what he had done? Questions on top of questions.

Answers were few, but the plan itself allowed him brief moments of escape from the tortuous introspection. He made deliveries. He made occasional trips to the house in Arlington. He went to the bank. Fentanyl was cheap, but it was not free. Jummal knew there were cameras everywhere, but he allowed himself to believe that if their plan worked, maybe no one would ever think to look at any closed-circuit video. Nevertheless, and unaccustomed to cloak-and-dagger field work, he found himself with his head down, shoulders hunched, and coat collar upturned whenever he was aware of a closed-circuit camera.

He went to a drugstore, where he spent hundreds of dollars on syringes, superglue, and 30-gauge needles—strong enough to get the job done, fine enough to go unnoticed. It was a big order. If questioned, Jummal would explain he was diabetic and going on an extended trip, so he needed a large supply. Nobody asked.

On Sunday, he went to the Dar Al-Hijrah Mosque for the last time. There, he met privately with Malik.

"As-salamu alaykum," Jummal offered to Malik.

"And to you as well, Jummal," he responded. Malik managed a modest smile, but Jummal was stoic. "You are troubled?" Malik asked. "Questions of faith, perhaps?"

"Questions, yes," Jummal answered. "But not of faith. It's

the path I have chosen. I am unsure if it's the right path. If I'm doing the right thing."

That got a laugh from Malik. "Well, I'm no imam. But based on the services you've asked of me, I know you are right to question your path. Alas, I have no answers for you. Those can only be found inside yourself." Then with a chuckle, "Or perhaps in this building," he said, gesturing to the breadth of the mosque.

"What I can tell you with certainty is that the matter with your brothers—getting them in and out—is nothing. Unlawful entry into the country is nothing. But the drugs, well, that's something. I don't know what you are up to, Jummal, and I don't want or need to know. But I'm not a fool. You ask me for fentanyl, I get you fentanyl. Not easy, but not hard. Not my preferred line, but I know enough to know what it is and how to get it for you. And I caution you, Jummal," he said, grabbing Jummal by the shoulders. "This is a dangerous, dangerous path. You are right to question yourself, and I will pray you find the right answer."

Ever stoic, Jummal could only nod.

"You have the money?" Malik asked.

"Yes, of course," Jummal said, handing over an envelope.

Malik tucked it inside his jacket pocket. "Very well. I'll have it delivered next week."

"Thank you. Kam will need to leave soon, and quickly, as we discussed. I'll let you know when?"

Malik nodded. "Of course. That is taken care of. I will wait for your call. Be well, Jummal. You are wise to question."

Jummal nodded. As he turned to leave, Malik called out to him, and Jummal turned back. He looked forlorn, his expression long and tired. "Yes?"

"This is a one-time only arrangement with the fentanyl. I don't like this business and next time, if there is a next time, I will not help you."

"I understand," he said glumly and turned away, knowing

that no matter what happened, he was unlikely to see Malik or the Dar Al-Hijrah Mosque again.

The one area Jummal found solace, where he could escape the questions that taunted him relentlessly, was the one email he allowed himself to write each night for Oku updating his brother on the day's events. The draft emails were short and to the point, but Jummal found he could mention his sisters and not feel distraught. He could discuss the plan and not feel crippled by the entirety of it. He did not know if Oku was getting the emails yet, as he was likely still in transit back to Ireti following routes unknown to Jummal.

When he wrote, he was reminded of the times with his brothers at night at that picnic table where the plan was born. They were all still innocent and pure then, driven by the excitement and satisfaction of *doing* something. Jummal could almost laugh at that. It was only months ago, a time filled with tragedy and sadness, but he knew he had never been closer to Oku and Kam than those weeks at the picnic table, grieving the only way they could. And planning. Always planning, never questioning.

That came later.

CHAPTER 78

With an angry and befuddled Swayz at the office, Gordon knew his time would be better spent in the field. On Thursday, he drove to the warehouse with a relief surveillance team. There were still teams at Jummal's house, the mosque, and the warehouse, all with backup support so that if any of the players moved, they could be followed.

The only movement on Thursday was Kam and Jummal making deliveries. They traveled to all the usual spots, engaged with the staff at the retailers, delivered whatever they were delivering, and went on their way. The only difference between today's deliveries and hundreds of others that had been observed was that Jummal was driving one of the trucks, stepping in for Oku.

It was tiresome, tedious work. There were no phone calls to listen to and no draft emails since the previous night. That email provided little new information, just a brief update from Jummal to Oku.

> *Oku you are missed. Kam is ready to move on. Soon I think. I'll be driving your truck when I can. I'll let them know I'm your older brother. That should help. Ha! Just realizing you probably won't see this until your home. Malik is going to come through with the F so done with*

> *that part. Safe travels brother, J A&A Forever, I miss them so*

A relief team came around dinner time and Gordon went home. All he could do was watch and wait. Before he went to bed, he checked for phone calls or emails. No calls, but Jummal had drafted another email for Oku earlier that night.

> *Lots of deliveries today. Almost a normal shop. A different time it could have been agood deal. Sleeping at the shop to be with Kam. He's ready to blow. He gets madder I get sadder. Try not to think about A&A during the day as there is much to do. I hope this is right. Wondering where you are on your journey. Be well, J*

Gordon slept in fits and was up at 5:00 a.m. on Friday. Another day working surveillance with a team that did not really want to be there. The day was interrupted when Jummal emerged from the warehouse. Gordon joined the team that followed him to a bank. He did not go in, but withdrew cash from an ATM outside the bank. The agents in the front seat chuckled as they watched Jummal flip up his collar and hunch his shoulders, trying to hide from the camera staring at his face.

"Pretty smooth operator there, huh, Stone," said the driver.

Gordon did not understand and ignored him. He was wondering why Jummal needed cash today. Last night's email was enough to establish a pattern. Jummal had reached out to Oku Tuesday, Wednesday, and Thursday nights. Oku had not responded to any of Jummal's messages, but that was probably because he was not home yet, taking whatever circuitous route was necessary to elude authorities and make it back to Nigeria safely. None of the emails said anything about a trip to the bank or needing cash. Friday night's email was no help.

> *Oku, it's late Friday. I'm thinking you'll be home soon. Very happy for you. It's been a long week. Busy again tomorrow, but the Plan moves ever forward. It's dark days here. Can't stop thinking of A&A and just very sad. Hope this is right. Kam barely speaking to me. Angry and ready to do the job and get home. I pray it's that easy but fear it won't be. J*

"What plan and what job?" Gordon practically screamed inside the break room in the basement. It was Saturday morning, and no one was here. The surveillance teams had been deployed, and Gordon knew Swayz would not be in the office on a Saturday. Gordon needed to focus and think without interruption. He could do that here, in his basement. There had been no further emails and no phone calls. If the pattern stayed accurate, a new draft would appear later Saturday night.

He was still in the break room at 5:30 p.m. when his phone rang. It was the surveillance team at the warehouse.

"Agent Stone," Gordon answered.

"Hey Stone, this is Baxter." Gordon recognized the name from the International Group at JTTF. Baxter was FBI. "Our relief just showed up, so we're shutting down."

"Anything happening?"

"Pretty slow day. Our guy went to Walgreens around twelve-thirty. Came out with a couple of bags and straight back to the warehouse."

That got Gordon's attention. "What did he buy?"

"No idea," Baxter said.

"Any chance you followed him inside?" Gordon knew the answer. It was not protocol to follow the subject into the store. You stayed with the vehicle. Nevertheless, he wanted to scream.

"Hey, Stone, he was in, he was out. We followed him back to the warehouse. That's it."

Gordon clenched his fists and squeezed his eyes shut. "What store?" he asked through gritted teeth.

"Walgreens. Uh, I don't know. It's like four or five blocks north," Baxter said.

"I know it. Thanks for letting me know." Gordon ended the call.

First the bank, now the drugstore. Why? Why now? Maybe he was just getting some supplies since he was staying at the warehouse. But he could have brought stuff from his house. Packed a bag, toothbrush, work clothes. That is what most people would do. So why go to Walgreens? What was so important he had to buy something today?

Gordon knew he was probably overthinking a simple trip to the drugstore. There were a thousand reasons to go to Walgreens on Saturday afternoon. He also knew it was going to bother him until he found out for sure.

Saturday night's email was short and fairly vague, but this time, there was a response. Oku, it appeared, had made it home.

> *Almost there Oku. Just waiting on the F. Kam still grumpy. We both want it to end. Respond when you can. A&A Forever, J*

> *Jummal, I made it. A long but uneventful trip. Thanks for the messages. Keep sending if it helps. Kam just needs to come home. He'll be okay. I know it. Mother and Father are well, as well as can be. They were really happy when I made it home. Mom still crying. You will be here soon brother! Ireti still sad. People lay flowers every day still. A&A Forever Jummal! O*

Gordon sighed. *Just waiting for the F.* The fentanyl was coming, Gordon knew. And whatever Jummal's plans were, they were happening soon. Gordon was running out of time.

Sunday found Gordon in the back seat of a car down the street from the warehouse, where absolutely nothing was happening. No deliveries were going out. No shipments were coming in. It was so quiet the teams pulled back another block so as not to arouse suspicion.

Around 1:30 p.m., Jummal emerged from the warehouse and left in his car. Gordon ordered his car to follow. They kept their distance, as there was not much traffic, and they did not want to be discovered. Jummal did not go to the bank or a drugstore, or even his house. Instead, they followed him to the mosque in Falls Church. When Gordon realized Jummal was heading for the mosque, he called ahead to the teams in place there. As soon as they could see Jummal's white Elantra, the mosque teams took over. That team circled the mosque and observed Jummal arrive and enter. The vehicle Gordon rode in peeled off and returned to the warehouse.

After thirty minutes, the mosque team called Gordon. Jummal had come out and was getting in his car. Gordon instructed the mosque team to follow him. Unfortunately for Gordon, Jummal just drove back to the warehouse and disappeared inside. The mosque surveillance team waved at Gordon as they passed them on the street and returned to the mosque.

It was a seemingly uneventful trip, but Gordon knew all this activity meant something. Where there had been little to no activity, now Jummal was running errands all over the place. He was staying at the warehouse. He was still drafting emails to his brother back in Ireti. An illegal and dangerous drug was in the mix. Whatever was happening was happening right in front of them. And now a trip to the mosque. For what? The fentanyl? To get Kam out of the country and back home?

And the purchase at the drugstore still troubled Gordon. Could Jummal have just forgotten to bring toothpaste from home, or was it something else? It was a loose end, and Gordon hated loose ends.

Sunday's emails served to increase Gordon's fear that something big was happening. And it was happening soon.

> *Oku, went to mosque today. Met with Malik. That's done. I am unsure if this is right. Kam is certain. I wish I thought like that. Such certainty and confidence. Still very angry though. I try not to think to much about it, but you know me. It is killing me O. I just don't know. Wish you were here to talk though it all. What would Abebi and Abiona think? I wish this was not so hard. I've found tears again thinking of them, every day, all the time. They're right there, just out of reach. There is strength in that. Strength to see it through to the end I think. A&A Forever, J*

> *I feel it too, Jummal. I think of them often and they give me strength. Of course there is doubt. That is you being you. It is not perfect b/c they are not coming back. It is a good plan. A strong plan. I know you will make the right decision and I will support you all the way. A&A Forever, Oku*

CHAPTER 79

On Monday, Gordon went into the office. He made a meager attempt to check in with Swayz, but Liz informed him Swayz was out for the day. "Thanks," Gordon said. "Ummm, just tell him I checked in, would you?"

"Sure thing," Liz said with a knowing smile.

Gordon retreated to the basement. No field surveillance today. Gordon felt like a wave was cresting. When it broke, he would determine where he needed to be, and he would get himself there. Gordon would spend the day hoping the FISA warrant would become more fruitful and provide him with more substantive evidence. Was this a terrorism case? Gordon still thought it could be, but he did not have evidence to support that. Not yet. He had some sort of drug case, maybe, though he was not sure if Jummal had picked up the fentanyl during yesterday's visit to the mosque or if it was coming in later. Worst of all, and a thought he tried not to dwell on, was that all he truly had at this point was an illegal immigration case, half of which he had allowed to leave the country. Swayz would love that.

Gordon signed into the Abebi_Abiona_Forever account. His cloned phone for listening to Jummal's calls was on as always, but it had been quiet for days. Nevertheless, today he would watch and listen and pace and think. Even though he had not slept much the past few days, Gordon was not tired. He was invigorated. One way or another, this case was coming to a head. And until it did, Gordon would follow every process and check every box.

Reports trickled in from the warehouse. Both trucks had checked out in the morning and made multiple deliveries at the usual retailers. The same routine followed at each stop. The driver would get out, engage with the staff on the loading dock, deliver the product, and drive away to the next stop. Nothing whatsoever out of the ordinary.

Both trucks were back at the warehouse by 1:00 p.m. The surveillance team reported that Kam and Jummal exited the trucks and went back inside. There had been no activity since then. There had been no new emails and no phone calls. Gordon was getting a bit stir-crazy. Nothing appeared to be happening, but at the same time, he knew everything was happening. He could not pace in the break room any longer. He got in his car and headed to the warehouse. Maybe he would follow a delivery truck around town if there were any afternoon deliveries. He had to do something.

On his way, Gordon stopped and pulled into a vacant streetside parking space. He put his car in park but left the engine running. He pulled out a notepad and began flipping through the pages. Walgreens. It was probably nothing, but it was doing something, so he decided to take a shot and see if he could find out what Jummal was buying at Walgreens. It was ten minutes away. Gordon pulled back into the street and made his way to the store.

It was a little after 2:00 p.m. when he got there. Gordon identified himself and asked to see the manager. A clerk escorted him to the back of the store. He introduced himself and sat on the lone wooden chair in the manager's cluttered office.

"What can I do for you, Agent Stone? I didn't report any shoplifters today," he said with a chuckle.

Gordon gave a half-hearted smile. "No, I'm not here about

that. I need to see your surveillance video from around twelve thirty on Saturday. At the registers."

"Sure thing. They're set up in the closet down the hall. Let's go see."

The two men stood and walked down the hall. The manager opened the closet with his key and exposed a computer rack and half a dozen closed-circuit monitors.

"Registers are on monitor one," the manager said. "Controls are right underneath. Do you know how to use the machine, or you want me to rewind for you?"

"Nope," Gordon said. "I'm all set. I can take it from here."

"Okey-doke. Good luck. I'll leave you to it."

"Thanks," Gordon said, already with one hand on the machine. He spun the dial, taking the recording back to 12:20 p.m. on Saturday. He hit the play button and watched.

At the 12:24 p.m. mark, he saw Jummal approach the register with a full basket. Gordon could not tell what Jummal was buying from the angle and clarity of the video. He looked at the other monitors. Gordon had looked at a lot of security video throughout his career. It was always hit-and-miss. He scrolled them all back to 12:20 on Saturday and tracked Jummal's movements through the store. While there was coverage throughout most of the store, it was not good. The cameras were mounted high, and on the walls instead of in the ceiling. They were zoomed way out to cover more territory at the cost of any detailed video. There was not enough detail to even guess what Jummal had purchased. He could not even see where Jummal had stopped and pulled something off a shelf. Questioning the usefulness of the security cameras at all, he went back to the manager's office.

"Just a suggestion, but you might want to add a few cameras, put 'em in the ceiling over the aisles. The ones you have don't really show you a whole lot."

"Ummmm…okay, sure. I'll get right on that," the manager said.

"Good. I need you to tell me who the cashier working Saturday afternoon was."

The manager looked at the dry-erase board across from his desk. It was the staff schedule, and the weekend lineup was still there. "Looks probably like it was Felipe Simms. Is he in trouble?"

"No, but I'd like to talk to him. Is he around?"

The manager grimaced. "No such luck, Agent. He worked the weekend but was headed down to Richmond to see his grandma or something." The manager looked back at the dry-erase board. Gordon followed his eyes.

"Looks like he's due back at work later next week. Should be in on Thursday, if you want to catch him then."

This whole episode was bothering Gordon. Like finishing a puzzle and finding a piece missing. Then again, it could be Jummal needed toothpaste and Gordon was just wasting time. He pursed his lips and decided.

"Thanks for your help," he said. "It can wait."

Gordon was agitated. Yes, he thought, it was probably nothing. But he was bothered not knowing what Jummal had purchased. He was also bothered that he would have to wait to talk to the cashier. His process was stalled. There were boxes that needed to be checked, and Gordon could not check them.

But he would. He would check the boxes. He had to.

He decided to forgo a visit to the warehouse and just head back to the office. A call to the warehouse surveillance team revealed there had been no more deliveries. All was quiet. The trip to Walgreens was a bust, but it had killed some time. Time during which, apparently, absolutely nothing was happening. There was nothing for him to do except wait. He paced, checked for emails, checked for phone calls, but there was nothing. He imagined Swayz storming through the door and shutting him down. He imagined being heckled by a gauntlet of FBI agents as he was escorted out of the building, not quite measuring up to their standard.

The waiting was brutal. Gordon allowed himself the briefest fantasy of simply walking up to the warehouse entrance and knocking on the door, being let in by Jummal, and just asking him what he was doing. That got him to smile a little bit and laugh at himself. Maybe he should call Katherine, his therapist. She would probably have some choice words for him.

The minutes ticked by ever so slowly. At 5:00 p.m. and with no sign of Swayz, Gordon went home. As soon as he got in, he turned his laptop back on and signed into the email account to see if any drafts had appeared during his drive home. They had not. He left his computer on and nibbled on some leftovers for dinner. However, he found he was not very hungry and went into his living room, sitting on the couch. He thought about watching television, but decided against it. Instead, he stretched out and closed his eyes. Just for a minute.

It was 4:30 a.m. Tuesday when he woke up, still dark outside. He had slept soundly and was wide awake, so he took a shower and got dressed. "I guess I needed some sleep."

Gordon checked his computer to see the email drafts from Monday night and was surprised when there were none. That was odd. For six days running, Jummal had input a draft email to his brother Oku. But last night there had been nothing. Not from Jummal. Not from Oku. He called the overnight surveillance team at the warehouse, but they had nothing to report. As far as they knew, both Kam and Jummal were in the building. Nothing had come in or gone out since Monday.

Gordon went into the office early and hooked up with the relief surveillance team. Another day in the back seat of a car, watching a warehouse and waiting for something to happen. Gordon shrugged. This was the job. This was the work.

He picked up coffee and donuts, and they made the drive to the warehouse. It was another exceedingly slow day. Not even any deliveries, as the trucks sat unmoving at the loading dock. The overnight crew was confident no one had slipped out in the night. They had eyes on the building the whole time. Nevertheless, the place was eerily silent this morning, and remained that way through the afternoon into the early evening.

Then, at the height of the evening rush hour, Gordon took a call from the surveillance team at the mosque.

"Agent Stone, we've got movement on our favorite white van. Same tags as the van that made previous trips to A&A Foods. We're following, but it looks like the van is headed your way."

"Stay with it," Gordon said. "If they come here, peel off and head back to the mosque. Otherwise, stay on the van."

Thirty minutes later, the familiar white van showed up and backed up to the loading dock next to the delivery trucks. It was the same van that had brought Kam and Oku to the warehouse several weeks ago, then taken Oku north on his way back to Ireti last week. The same van that had shuttled the women around even longer ago. But it was not the same driver. Gordon recognized the new driver immediately—Abdul Malik.

Gordon's phone buzzed. "Van's all yours, Agent Stone. We're headed back to the mosque."

Gordon and the two agents in the front seat were on high alert. Everyone was wide awake and focused. If this was an exit strategy, the case could be wrapped up tonight. They watched, impatient after the day's inactivity. Malik got out of the van and climbed the small set of stairs up to the loading dock platform.

Jummal appeared on the platform and exchanged words with Malik. Malik was carrying a plain manila envelope. He pinched the edges and reached into the opening, pulling out what appeared to be a small plastic bag and showed it to Jummal. Malik then replaced the bag inside the manila envelope and handed it to Jummal. He gave Malik a nod, which Malik returned with a hug. He held Jummal by the shoulders, looked him up and down, and nodded. When Jummal responded with another nod of his own, Malik released him, took the steps down from the loading dock, got back in the van, and drove away.

"You want us to go with the van?" the agent behind the wheel of Gordon's car asked.

"Nope," he said without hesitation. "We'll stay right here until the relief team comes."

It was only twenty minutes before the relief surveillance team showed up. The two drivers acknowledged each other, then Gordon's driver turned to face him. "Where to?"

"Back to the office. Let's call it a day."

"Sure thing. So, what was that?" the driver asked.

"Not entirely sure, but I suspect that was a delivery of fentanyl."

"Hmmm," was all the driver said.

Later that night, at home and eating a late dinner, Gordon's computer pinged. He had been waiting for this. Another draft email. Hopefully of significance, but regardless, it had been a good day. Things were indeed starting to happen. He opened the email and read.

Malik came through. Got the F. Moving quick now. Ready soon. Still unsure, but Kam smiled today. First time in a while. J

Confirmation, thought Gordon. Fentanyl had been delivered to Jummal at the warehouse. But, *Ready soon.* What did that mean? Was there a drug deal about to go down? Could he possibly be distributing narcotics through his food deliveries? Possible? Sure. Definitely possible. Likely? Gordon just could not believe that. The only indicator of a drug distribution enterprise was a single delivery of fentanyl. The only deliveries from the warehouse had been groceries and dry goods to various retailers in the metro DC area. But drugs? Who of any of the recipients behaved in any way like a co-conspirator in a drug ring? None of them. "Drug dealers don't hug," he said.

If it was a drug conspiracy, it was the most well-hidden,

expertly organized, and effective conspiracy in the history of illicit drugs. It could not be that, Gordon concluded, but *something* was most certainly going down. He was re-energized with this latest development. The case had taken a giant leap forward today. To what end, he did not know. But he was going to find out.

CHAPTER 80

Wednesday brought Gordon back to the warehouse, this time in his own government-issued ride supporting the existing surveillance team. He felt things might happen fast today, and he wanted to be able to move quickly and on his own. Where to and when would be determined, but today, he thought, was the day. He would have answers today.

When Kam appeared on the loading dock, Gordon's pulse picked up. It was happening.

But the answers did not come, only more questions. Kam simply loaded a truck, shut the door, climbed into the cab, and drove away. A team followed him. He made the same stops he had been making for weeks. The same routine. He did not stray from his scheduled deliveries.

But Jummal was a no-show. The second truck sat at the loading dock all day. Jummal was nowhere to be seen, presumably still in the warehouse. For the first time, Gordon considered sending a team in and bringing this investigation to whatever end he found inside the warehouse. At worst, he had a weird combination of possession, fraud, and illegal immigration. Even all together, that did not amount to all that much. It certainly did not warrant all the expense and aggravation the JTTF had gone through with multiple surveillance teams working 24/7 for more than a week.

Best case, they were about to catch Jummal in the act of an

elaborate drug ring set up to raise funds for Boko Haram. The evidence did not really point to that, though. Gordon saw something here, but after all the convincing, all the arguing, all the persuasion, all the work, he still was not sure what he saw. It was all there in front of him. He just could not put the pieces together.

He would not enter the warehouse today, he decided. But he would, soon.

CHAPTER 81

Jummal woke with the sun on Wednesday. He had a long and busy day ahead, and an early start was necessary. In a far corner of the warehouse, fifteen boxes of the loss-leader product he had settled on for the plan had been stacked. A table was set up with a few bright lights strung overhead. A single chair rested empty, next to the table. On the table was a box of syringes, a glass measuring cup, a bottle of water, a stainless-steel spoon, a package containing three sets of rubber gloves, a package of white surgical masks, safety goggles, and four small tubes of Krazy Glue, all laid out in a neat and orderly fashion. Sitting on the chair was the envelope Jummal had been given by Malik.

Jummal thought of Kam and let him sleep. This part of the plan was his alone. He would not share it with Kam. He was the oldest. It was his responsibility, his burden. It would be long and tedious work well suited to his meticulous nature. And then there was the guilt. A weight growing heavier every hour, every minute. He would not put that on Kam. This part he would do alone.

Jummal shook out a folded sheet and laid it over one end of the table, then took the envelope out of the chair and placed it on the sheet. He ripped open the package of rubber gloves and struggled to put a pair on. His hands were shaking. He closed his eyes and gritted his teeth, forcing himself to calm down. He fumbled with the package of surgical masks, cursing at himself for putting the rubber gloves on first. Last were the goggles.

He approached the envelope with some trepidation, paused at the end of the table, then with more confidence than he felt, opened the envelope and pulled out a Ziploc bag with a single small glass vial inside. Inside the vial was a gram of white powder. So, Jummal thought, this was fentanyl. Such a small amount, it looked like nothing. But even Jummal knew it was more than enough. He set the Ziploc bag down on the sheet and tossed the envelope aside.

He walked around the table and retrieved the measuring cup and bottle of water. He opened the water bottle, pouring a bit more than 300 milliliters into the measuring cup. Sitting in the chair, he leaned over the table and carefully pulled open the Ziploc bag. He gripped the small vial inside with two fingers and pulled it out. Slowly, he unscrewed the cap. His hand shook as he set the cap aside, and again, he forced himself to settle down. Carefully, he moved the vial and held it over the measuring cup. Jummal held his breath and tipped the vial, its minimal powdery contents dumping into the measuring cup. He tapped the vial gently on the side of the cup, clearing it of any residue. Still holding his breath, he replaced the cap on the vial, placed the vial back into the Ziploc bag, and set it down on the table.

Finally, he took a breath. Then, holding the spoon at the end of the handle, he lowered it into the measuring cup and began to stir, slowly and deliberately, watching as the fentanyl powder dissolved into a lethal solution. Satisfied the powder had liquefied, he removed the spoon, tapping it against the side of the cup, and placed it into the Ziploc bag with the vial. He sealed the bag and pushed it across the table.

Jummal shut his eyes and exhaled. It was indeed going to be a long day. Opening his eyes, he stared at the measuring cup. Just a third of a liter of fentanyl-laced solution. *That should be enough,* he thought. "It has to be," he said aloud, leaning back in his chair.

"A lot of work for so little," a voice behind him said.

"Sonuvabitch!" Jummal shouted as he jumped from the chair, banging into the table. The solution in the cup sloshed about as Jummal just stared at it. None spilled. He almost wished it had. He turned around, pulling off the goggles and mask. "Damn you, Kam!" he yelled at his brother.

Kam sneered. "Damn us all, brother."

"I'm pretty sure you have some deliveries to make, yes?"

"What's the point? Let me help with this."

"No," Jummal answered, louder than he meant. "This job is for me. We have deliveries scheduled this morning. That's your job. We can't start missing deliveries now, not this close to the end. It has to appear normal."

"Normal." Kam practically spit the word out. "I've been making the same deliveries for weeks. It's fucking bullshit, Jummal."

"Exactly," Jummal. "The same deliveries, day after day, week after week. So, if you miss a delivery today, people will notice. People will ask questions next time you show up. We can't have questions, Kam. This won't work if people are asking questions. Now load the damn truck, make the damn deliveries. Don't run any lights and don't speed. You do your job, I'll do mine, and we can go home."

Kam stared at his brother. "It's fucking bullshit," he repeated before crossing the warehouse to get his delivery truck ready for the morning's run.

Jummal watched him walk away, then stretched his arms, releasing the built-up tension. He paced back and forth in front of the table, constantly checking to see if the measuring cup was still there, half-hoping it magically was not. He stretched his neck. Twisted his torso. Shook out his arms. He returned to pacing, maintaining a rhythm back and forth, checking the cup with a sideward glance at every turn. The pacing was hypnotic, not moving forward and not moving back, time standing still. Knowing he must continue. The plan must happen. Yet, knowing he wanted to walk away.

Somewhere, off in the distance, a truck's engine turned over. To Jummal, it was a beast waking from a long hibernation. It startled him out of his self-induced trance, and he realized it was Kam setting off to make his deliveries. Keeping up the appearance of normalcy. Kam had not said goodbye.

The warehouse was eerily silent.

Alone now, Jummal began carefully unpacking the fifteen boxes of loss-leader product stacked on the warehouse floor at the end of the table. He was careful not to tear the boxes, as they would need them for repackaging later. The boxes contained six thirty-two-ounce plastic bottles, with tamper-proof plastic seals wrapped around the cap and neck of each bottle.

Jummal removed the bottles, ninety in all, and lined them up in neat rows until one end of the table was full. He took a long, slow walk around the inside of the warehouse. This next step was a big one. *Can I do this?* he asked himself. Part of him hoped his circuitous path around the warehouse floor would last forever and he would just keep walking. He knew he was kidding himself. He had to do it. And he had to do it now.

He cut back across the floor to the table and opened the box of syringes. One hundred individually wrapped syringes with needles. He unwrapped each one and created a haphazard pile of them stacked next to the measuring cup with the fentanyl solution. Then, for the second time that day, he put on a surgical mask and safety goggles, added the rubber gloves, and sat back down in the chair. He picked up a syringe, removed the safety cap from the needle and tossed it aside. He stuck the tip of the needle into the liquid and pulled back on the plunger, filling the syringe with three milliliters of fentanyl solution. He carefully placed the full syringe on the sheet at arm's length, grabbed another empty syringe from the pile, and repeated the process. Then again, and again.

Finally, the cup was empty. One hundred syringes filled with fentanyl solution laid out in precise rows on the sheet. Jummal stood and stepped back from the table and removed the goggles, mask, and gloves. He stretched his neck from side to side and shook his arms out, steeling himself for what was to come next.

Could he do it? Should he do it? Jummal had no answers. He only knew he *had* to do it. Abebi and Abiona were dead. The girls' school destroyed. Ireti devastated. From that calamity, the plan had been born at the picnic table at his parents' house in a small Nigerian village and had brought him to this point. Had brought his brothers to this point. Jummal wanted to weep. Wanted to scream. Kam would be back soon. He had to keep going.

CHAPTER 82

With gloves, goggles, and mask back in place, Jummal began. A thirty-two-ounce bottle in one hand and a full syringe in the other, he carefully inserted the tiny needle into the neck of the bottle. Ever so gently, he depressed the plunger on the syringe, sending three milliliters of fentanyl solution into the bottle. He withdrew the needle, set the empty syringe down on the table, and grabbed an open tube of superglue. Squeezing the tube, he pushed out the tiniest dollop of glue and placed that dollop onto the tiny hole made by the needle.

He examined the bottle. The sealed hole was, for all practical purposes, invisible. You would have to be looking for it to have any hope of actually seeing it. And no one, Jummal thought solemnly, would be looking for it.

When he was about halfway through the bottles, Kam returned.

"Deliveries are done, brother. It's time to make them pay," he said casually.

Jummal stopped what he was doing. "Kam, do you even understand what we're doing here? What we're about to do? The *magnitude* of what we're about to do? Can you feel *anything*?" he pleaded.

"Fuck them," he said. "They took my sisters. They took my village. They took my life. And why? Why would they do that? We'll never know. No one responsible will ever tell us why

Abebi and Abiona had to die. 'Do I understand what we're doing?'" he mocked. "Yeah. Fuck them. Fuck you, too, Jummal. They have to pay."

A heavy silence hung between them. Jummal turned back to the table and picked up the next bottle, staring at it for a moment. Without looking at him, Jummal told Kam, "Get to work on the labels. Each box needs one. No trace."

With a grunt, Kam left to go print out the new labels.

Hours crawled by. It was dark when Jummal applied a dab of superglue to the last bottle. He shut his eyes and shuddered. Then he stood up and walked across the warehouse floor, shedding his gloves, mask, and goggles. He made it to the opposite side of the warehouse before he put his head in his hands, driving the heels of his palms into his eyes. He gulped his next breath. And then he cried. When he looked up, his eyes were red and his cheeks wet.

Kam was there, shaking his head. Jummal collected himself.

"Labels are ready," Kam said.

"Get the boxes packed up and resealed. Put the new labels on. We'll load the trucks tomorrow morning," Jummal said. With a sigh, he straightened up and walked to the office. They did not speak again that night.

Kam's face had frozen into a permanent scowl. He repackaged each bottle into a newly labeled box of six, resealing all fifteen boxes. His work was diligent and with purpose, his expression unchanged until the last bottle was packaged and the last box sealed. Kam looked at the neat stack of boxes and grunted with satisfaction. They appeared untouched, as if straight from the original manufacturer. Only then did he allow himself a modest grin. He thought of Abebi and Abiona and whispered, as if to them, "It is time."

In the office, Jummal sat and stared out the window to the warehouse floor. He'd watched Kam pack, seal, and relabel all the boxes. He wanted to feel satisfaction. The job was nearly done, the plan nearly executed. But he felt none. He was despondent, guilt-ridden. For an instant, he envied Kam. Kam, the strongest of them, had grown only stronger working here at A&A. His face had been grimly set with tortured purpose for weeks. But Kam's face did not concern him most. The stern looks he could not shake, could not find relief from, were from his sisters' faces. They were in his dreams and haunted every waking moment. "What?" he whispered. "What do you want?" Jummal felt their spirits reaching for him. In his mind's eye, he reached back, but he was grabbing at the wind as he slid inch by inch into the abyss. He was lost.

He had no concept of how long he stared out the office window. Minutes? Hours? Had he fallen asleep, passed out? He was not certain. Kam was nowhere to be seen, but a stack of sealed and labeled boxes was there. Waiting.

He abandoned the view from the window and shifted focus to the computer on the desk. It was on. He signed in to Abebi_Abiona_Forever@yahoo.com.

Okunola, it's ready. We're coming home.

CHAPTER 83

"Shit," Gordon said to himself as he literally scratched his head.

It's ready.

What's ready? Whatever it was, *we're coming home* meant it was happening soon. All they'd seen today was a single truck making routine and seemingly legitimate deliveries.

It was late Wednesday night. "Thursday," he whispered. "Tomorrow," he said louder. "It's happening tomorrow. Whatever *it* is."

Gordon reached out to all the surveillance teams currently deployed and left messages for the teams in relief. He pulled back surveillance from Jummal's home, as well as the mosque. He needed everyone at the warehouse. Whatever was happening was happening there, or at least starting there. Thursday was going to be an interesting day.

CHAPTER 84

Jummal never left the office. He managed some sleep in fits and starts, sometimes seated at the desk, sometimes on the floor. Probably even a little as he paced around the office. He was emotionally spent. The ramifications of what he was about to do haunted him. He was desperate and broken. How did he end up here? He had instances where he almost felt euphoric, but they lasted only seconds and were only because the plan neared completion. Any euphoria was quickly abated by the overwhelming anguish he felt.

What are we doing? What am I doing? he asked himself over and over again. He could not rid his mind of his sisters' beckoning faces. They reached out to him continuously, and the effort to push them from his mind was exhausting. "We are doing this for you!" he shouted, pleading with them.

But Abebi and Abiona refused to give him the affirmation he so desperately sought. They offered no comfort at all, but instead filled him with unrelenting guilt for what he was about to do.

CHAPTER 85

Thursday morning, Kam watched his brother through the office window. When they made eye contact, Jummal stared right through him. "*Mumu*," Kam said. *Fool* in his native pidgin.

Kam turned from his brother and walked away. He looked at the stack of repackaged boxes. "*Mumu*," he said again. Shaking his head, he moved toward the stack and began the process of loading the delivery trucks himself.

Jummal emerged from the office and walked to the loading dock where Kam was dutifully loading both trucks. Despondent, Jummal told Kam to stop. Kam ignored his older brother and kept loading.

Here and now, after all the time, money, and energy that had been expended, the enormity of the plan hit Jummal's body and soul. He managed to stumble back into the warehouse, into the office. He sat at the desk and put his head down. In an instant, he was sound asleep.

Two hours later, Kam reached across the desk and shook his brother awake. The sleep had worked its magic. Jummal was awake and alert. He rubbed his eyes and looked at Kam.

"The trucks are loaded. Thanks for your help, by the way," Kam said.

Jummal just looked at his younger brother.

"You look better, Jummal. Good thing, too. We're ready."

Jummal was silent. *I will be chief,* he told himself. He would assume his father's position in Ireti. He would channel this all-consuming grief to the good of the village. He would rebuild Ireti, make it whole. For the first time in weeks, the dark shroud hanging over Jummal lifted. His true purpose was renewed, his mind clear. He stood and walked to the loading dock.

Kam followed. "Finally," he said.

Jummal turned to Kam. "This," he said, gesturing to the delivery trucks, "is not what a village chief does. It's wrong, Kam, and I can't do it."

"*Mugu fuck*," Kam shouted. *Stupid fuck*. "Let's go. It's time."

"No, Kam. We cannot." Jummal walked back into the warehouse.

"Fuck!" Kam screamed, his fists clenched, beads of sweat forming on his brow. He took a deep breath, then another. Finally, he turned and followed Jummal back inside. He caught up with him on the warehouse floor and grabbed him by the right shoulder, spinning him around. The brothers stared at one another, and in an instant, Kam released a powerful slap to Jummal's face.

Jummal recovered quickly but did not respond.

"You fucking pussy. This was your plan, Jummal. Your plan. *The plan.* It's too late to back out now."

"No, Kam, it's not. This is not what Abebi and Abiona would want. We can't do this."

Kam reared back again to deliver another blow, but Jummal caught Kam's arm mid-swing. "Enough," he said. He released Kam's arm and turned toward the office. He made it a few steps before Kam tackled him from behind.

Jummal defended himself, but Kam's attack was unrelenting. He had Jummal on his back and straddled him, delivering blow after blow. Jummal kept his arms up in a defensive posture, but soon enough, his face and Kam's hands were bloody.

Jummal's strength was waning. He would not be able to defend himself much longer from his enraged and stronger brother. He pulled up his right knee, delivering a glancing blow to Kam's groin. It was not incapacitating, but forced Kam to roll to Jummal's side. As Jummal got to his feet, Kam reached for him. It was not over yet.

With nowhere to go, Jummal stumbled across the warehouse floor to the back corner, just trying to put some distance between himself and Kam. It was not enough. He made it to the table where he had prepared the fentanyl solution only hours ago before Kam caught him again. Stream of consciousness cursing flowed from Kam as he dove at Jummal. There was a painful crunch as Jummal's midsection made hard contact with the table. The two of them crashed down on top of the table, splitting it and falling to the floor.

"This is not who we are," shouted Jummal.

"No," Kam shouted back, "it's not who *you* are." Kam continued his assault. He had taken too many steps down this dark path. He had to see the plan through.

Jummal felt himself losing this fight. He extended both arms, reaching for anything that might help him stop Kam. His right hand found the now empty glass measuring cup in which he had dissolved the fentanyl powder. He grabbed it and swung up wildly, making contact with Kam's head. A gash opened up above Kam's left eye. Blood flowed freely.

"I can't let you go. I can't let you do this," Jummal screamed, tears filling his eyes.

Kam's eyes began to refocus. The blow to the head hurt, but he would not let that stop him. "I love you, Jummal," he said. "But you're weak. I'm going to finish this."

Jummal was running out of energy. Kam's continued blows were taking their toll. He realized the measuring cup was still in his hand. With his last ounce of energy, he swung once more at Kam. Not as strong as before, but a blow to the same spot over Kam's left eye, spraying blood. Kam roared with pain and anger. Whatever beast lurked inside him was unleashed, keeping him conscious, finding a way to survive, to win. To finish the job.

Kam was no longer in control. The beast was in charge now, and it reached to the floor, finding a leftover syringe. The beast removed the protective sleeve covering the needle, drove the needle into Jummal's neck, and depressed the plunger to the hilt, delivering an ungodly dose of fentanyl solution into Jummal.

The world stopped.

Kam rolled off Jummal and pulled his head and shoulders onto his lap. Jummal stared up into Kam's vacant eyes, not fully comprehending what just happened.

"I'm sorry, brother," said Kam. "You were not meant for this, but I will finish the job. Oku will lead Ireti into the future. Our sisters will be avenged. Abebi and Abiona. Forever."

Jummal heard the words but could not respond. He felt himself sliding away. The metallic taste of blood was joined by the sensation of a gooey foam filling his mouth and running down his cheeks. His eyes never shut. He did not move again.

The beast returned to its cage within, and Kam stood. A grim determination rose with him. This had to happen. He left his brother's side and walked to the office. There was a first aid kit there. He needed to bandage his forehead and clean himself up. He had deliveries to make.

CHAPTER 86

It was nearly noon when Kam emerged once more on the loading dock. More than one surveillance team member saw what looked like a bandage over his left eye. They watched as Kam got into a delivery truck and drove away. Gordon ordered two teams to follow the truck. There was no sign of Jummal.

Once again, the surveillance teams watched as Kam made his usual deliveries. The banter increased as the various retailers asked about Kam's injury. Other than that, there was nothing unusual about any of it. The deliveries appeared legitimate. Notes were made of all the stops. None of them were new and all the recipients were familiar.

Surveillance teams followed Kam back to the warehouse. Gordon watched him go inside. The second delivery truck remained parked. When Kam emerged from the warehouse again, every JTTF member watching would have predicted that Kam would get into the second truck and make another round of deliveries. Only Gordon was not surprised when, instead, Kam got into Jummal's car and left the warehouse for the last time.

Okunola, it's ready. We're coming home.

Gordon knew that whatever this was, it was happening. Now. He ordered two teams to follow Kam. He stayed put.

Jummal was the answer, and Jummal remained inside the warehouse. Gordon would wait as long as it took.

CHAPTER 87

Kam was on edge. Adrenaline had pushed him through the deliveries, but the realization he had killed Jummal now slammed home and sapped his remaining energy. Had that really happened? Had he killed his brother?

He parked the truck at the loading dock, next to the one Jummal was supposed to use for the rest of the deliveries, and went inside. A fleeting glance to the back of the warehouse confirmed what he knew to be true. Jummal's body was there, right where he left it. Kam shuddered. The beast that had been born at the picnic table outside of his parent's house had been nourished and had grown during his time in the United States. He had felt it inside him, telling him to kill his brother, to complete the plan.

Only one truckload had been delivered, but it was enough. It had to be. He dismissed any thought of making the second round of deliveries. Now, he had to get out of there, could not stay a second longer. He knew Jummal had made arrangements for him through Malik to get home, but he had no idea how that was supposed to happen. He knew Oku had been taken north toward Canada, backtracking the way they had come in so many weeks ago.

He could not figure it out here. He had to move. Grabbing Jummal's computer from the office, as well as his car keys, he packed nothing else. He left the warehouse through the loading dock and did not look at Jummal. He did not pause to lock up. He would not be back.

Moving quickly, he climbed into Jummal's car and left. Where he was going and what he would do were unknowns. At the moment, the only answer was to go north, so he did. He drove through DC, careful to obey lights and not speed. He found his way to the George Washington Parkway and took that north to the Beltway. He continued north and took I-270 toward Frederick, Maryland. Farther and farther away from the warehouse. He fantasized that maybe it was all a dream, knowing it was not. It took him ninety minutes to reach Frederick. He pulled off the highway and found a cheap motel, checking in for one night. He needed sleep. He needed a new plan.

CHAPTER 88

Two JTTF surveillance teams tracked Kam all the way to Frederick. When he checked into a motel, they reported back to Gordon.

"Stay on him. Let me know if there's any further movement," Gordon instructed. "He's trying to go home." *We're not letting you go,* he told himself.

Day turned to night, and the warehouse stayed quiet. Gordon was frustrated. He had been certain Jummal would act today, but the only action was from the brother, who was now holed up in a motel in Frederick.

With nothing happening, Gordon decided to check another box. With orders to keep him informed of any activity, Gordon left A&A Foods and drove to Walgreens. Felipe Cruz was supposed to be back at work today. Gordon wanted to close the loop on Jummal's drugstore purchase, and he needed to get away to think things through.

At Walgreens, he arrived just as Felipe was punching out for the night. Back in the manager's office, Gordon showed Felipe a picture of Jummal and asked whether he remembered this man from the day before he left town.

Felipe did not hesitate.

"Yes, I remember him," he said. "He bought a bunch of stuff, but I remember the syringes, the needles. You know, like for a diabetic. But he bought a measuring cup, too, and gloves and masks. That's drug shit, isn't it?" Felipe asked. "I stay away from that stuff, man. Killed my cousin. I rang him up and didn't ask any questions, bro," he explained.

Gordon thanked Felipe and walked out to his car. *Syringes? What kind of drug operation is this?* Sitting in the parking lot, he pulled out his phone and dialed McNeely.

"What's up, Gordo?"

"I'm stuck, boss. Everything told me this was happening today, and stuff happened, but we're all quiet again tonight. I've got a brother up in Frederick at a motel, probably trying to get home through Canada, and all's quiet at the warehouse."

"Where are you? What are you doing?"

"I'm at a Walgreens."

"Walgreens?"

"Yeah, our subject stopped here the other night to pick up supplies. I thought it was a little strange given the timing of everything, so I wanted to see what he bought. Turns out it was hypodermics, like a diabetic might use. Except I don't think they were to treat diabetes. He also bought a measuring cup and gloves and some surgical masks, like he was using them as part of some weird drug operation."

"Personal use, maybe?" suggested McNeely.

"Maybe, but there goes the whole money-raising theory. And why fentanyl? Nobody in Jummal's position buys that for personal use. That's for cutting."

"So, you've got some fentanyl, some needles, and some other paraphernalia. But you haven't seen any dealer-level volume, and personal use is a no-go?"

"It just doesn't sit right. The only drug we know about appears to be a fairly small amount of fentanyl. There are no indicators of a drug operation. There's no history. There's been no drug-related traffic into or out of the warehouse, outside of the one fentanyl delivery. And if it's a drug op, I can see bringing the brothers in to set up the operation, but why the loss leaders? Why go down that path?"

"Well, the loss leaders are what your subject knows. He's in the grocery business. Maybe that's how it started, but it wasn't enough money. Or it wasn't fast enough. Anything ever come of that?"

"Just a handful of buys and deliveries of goods to the warehouse several weeks ago. Seemed like it stopped before it started. It never made any sense that it was a loss-leader scam. I'm still not sure what he was buying."

"Well, what are the most popular loss leaders? What's always in demand that people buy a lot of and are always looking for the best price on?" McNeely asked.

Gordon thought before he answered. "Diapers, toilet paper, paper towels, baby food..." Gordon trailed off.

"Whatcha got, Gordo?" McNeely asked. "Baby food?"

"Yeah, baby food."

"Like the creamed crap, comes in the little jar?"

"No. The liquid kind. Filled with all kinds of baby nutrients. Goes straight into a baby's bottle." Gordon went silent again. McNeely let him.

Loss leaders, needles, syringes, baby formula, deliveries...fentanyl. All the lights in Gordon's brain came bursting on at once.

"Holy shit, Pete!" It was the first time ever he had called his boss by his first name. "He's doctoring baby formula. I gotta go."

Gordon never heard McNeely telling him to "get back to the work." He had already hung up and was dialing Swayz.

McNeely allowed himself a smile. "Goddamn," he said. "Gordo has done it again."

Swayz picked up on the first ring. "International Group, this is Swayz."

"Sir, it's Agent Stone. I need authority to breach the warehouse and a hotel up in Frederick. We've got to go now, sir. It's happening now."

"Approved, Stone. You better be—" The line went dead. "Asshole," muttered Swayz.

Gordon called the warehouse team lead first. "Take it. I got the green light from Swayz. Secure the warehouse right now. I'll be there in ten."

"Now? You sure. Nothing's happening here."

"Do it!" Gordon shouted. "Now!"

The team lead did not have to be told a third time. The teams were prepared and ready. They would have the warehouse secured in about two minutes.

Gordon called the team lead at the Frederick motel.

"Hey, Stone. What's up?"

"Arrest him now."

"Okay. I'll get the manager to let us in."

"No, kick it. We can't wait. Go now."

"You tell Swayz?"

"Yes, it's approved. Take him now."

"You got it. We're on our way in."

Gordon dropped his phone in the passenger seat, started his car, and sped back to the warehouse.

CHAPTER 89

Inside his motel room, Kam grew more frantic and desperate with each passing minute. Stupidly, he had brought Jummal's laptop but not his phone. He did not know Malik's number and had no way to reach him for help getting out of the country. He had no clue how he could possibly do it on his own. He would not go back to the warehouse. Jummal was there, and he was not interested in revisiting that place ever again.

He paced back and forth across the small room. He had a little cash. No gun, only a box cutter he had used to repackage the tainted baby formula. He'd used the credit card Jummal had given him to keep the trucks running to get the motel room. That was it. Any other resources he might have had were dead on the floor of the warehouse. He was as alone as he had ever been. He twirled the box cutter in one hand and considered his options.

He saw Jummal's laptop on the bed and an idea struck him. *Oku will know what to do.*

Kam set the box cutter down on the bedside table and opened the laptop. He signed in to the Abebi_Abiona_Forever@yahoo.com account for the first time, remembering the password Jummal had required him to memorize. He did not stop to read all the correspondence between Jummal and Oku. Instead, careful not to reveal too much of what had happened, he typed up his own draft email to Oku. Satisfied it said what it needed to say, he signed out of the account and shut the laptop. All he had to do now was wait for Oku to respond.

As Kam breathed a sigh of relief, his pulse slowing for the first time in hours, he lay down on the bed, starting to breathe a little easier.

And then the door to his room exploded.

Federal agents rushed through the motel room door, guns raised. Within Kam, the beast re-emerged, sealing his fate. It was too late for him. He had killed his eldest brother. He would not go home.

In one motion, he leapt up, grabbing the box cutter. The agents screamed at him to drop the weapon. Kam let the beast take over. "Abebi and Abiona," he said, over and over again, louder and louder, until his screams of, "Abebi and Abiona!" joined the cacophony of the FBI agents' shouted orders. He did not—would not—drop the box cutter. Slowly, he raised his arms, simultaneously pushing the box cutter's blade out with his thumb. He stopped screaming. The agents did not. The beast told him to smile, and Kam did. Then he charged.

Two of the four agents in the room fired. Eight bullets found their target. Kam's lifeless body fell to the bed. It was over in seconds.

CHAPTER 90

The team at A&A Foods breached the warehouse, but discovered they were too late. Jummal was dead. The area was secured, and a forensic team was requested and on its way. While they waited, they began to inventory everything in the warehouse, starting in the back corner.

When Gordon arrived, he rushed in from the loading dock and saw the crowd gathered at the back of the warehouse. He began to make his way to them when his phone pinged. It was the Frederick team lead. Gordon stopped and took the call.

"What do you have?"

"Nothing. Just a laptop," the team lead answered. "He tried to fight his way through us."

"What? What happened?"

"He's gone, Agent Stone. We had to take him down."

"Fuck," Gordon shouted. He hung up and continued across the warehouse to the group gathered at the other side.

Gordon saw Jummal on the floor. He was clearly dead, but Gordon was looking elsewhere. The broken table, syringes spread around the floor. The glass measuring cup beside Jummal's body. A rubber glove, inside out as though pulled from someone's hand, rested on the ground by the table, lying across a pair of safety goggles. By itself, up against the wall, was a Ziploc bag. Gordon carefully stepped over to the Ziploc. Inside was a small vial with a white powdery residue. "Fentanyl," he whispered.

There was only one thing missing, thought Gordon, and it scared him. Not a single bottle of baby formula could be seen in the warehouse. He approached a gaggle of agents standing around, waiting to be told what to do. “Come with me,” he said, and took off at a run back out to the loading dock. Gordon pointed to the second truck. They had seen it get loaded, but it had gone nowhere. With Jummal dead, it was no wonder.

“Get in that truck. See what’s there. Let me know what you find ASAP. Got it?”

The agents nodded and went to work.

With Jummal and Kam dead, Gordon would have to piece the case together from what he had. There was only one more place to look. He pulled out his phone and logged into Abebi_Abiona_Forever@yahoo.com. There was a single draft email that he had not seen before.

> *Oku, it’s Kam. It’s done. Finished last night and delivered this morning. Most of it. It got messed up. Jummal is gone, Oku. He’s gone. I’m trying to get home. Love you brother. Take care of Ireti. Kam*

Gordon went pale. He stepped over to the truck. “What’ve you got?” he hollered.

An agent stepped to the door. “Looks like five pallets, shrink-wrapped. Mostly dry goods.”

“Dry goods? Any baby formula?”

“Not that we can see. We’re starting to break down the pallets. See what else is there.”

“Okay, do it fast. Who followed the deliveries the other truck made this morning?”

“I was there,” the same agent said.

“Did you record where all the stops were?”

“Of course. Got it right here.” He pulled out a small notebook and handed it to Gordon.

A voice from inside the truck shouted, "Got something here." Gordon stepped inside the truck. "Buried inside a pallet of paper towels. It's a box of baby formula. Looks like six bottles."

"All of you, stop what you're doing and come with me. Bring that box. Now."

Gordon ran back inside with the three agents from the truck following him.

Inside, Gordon ripped the box of baby formula open. Six thirty-two-ounce bottles inside the box. Gordon pulled out one bottle and held it up in front of him, studying it. He turned the bottle over and around, looking at the entire package. He saw nothing. Gordon shut his eyes. "Think," he said to himself. *A syringe with fentanyl used to taint a bottle. How would I do it?*

With his eyes still shut, he gently ran his hands over the entirety of the bottle of formula he held. His JTTF counterparts looked at him, sharing awkward glances. Gordon's thumb stroked across the neck of the bottle just below the plastic wrap, sealing the cap onto the bottle. He opened his eyes. "There!"

"Agent…Agent…" Gordon motioned to the agent he had spoken with earlier.

"Panowicz, Agent Stone. I'm Panowicz."

"Sorry, right, Agent Panowicz. Come look at this." He showed Panowicz the bottle.

"What am I looking at here, Stone?"

"Look there, just under the wrapping at the top. Look at it, then feel it."

"Yeah, I see it. Can feel it too; a tiny raised dot."

"Let's check the other bottles."

They pulled the other five bottles from the box. Each one had a tiny, clear raised dot just below the packaging on the bottle top.

"Everybody listen up," Gordon shouted. "Gather 'round. Okay, this is no longer a search, but is now a rescue. The deliveries made this morning likely contained boxes of baby formula tainted with fentanyl. They used a syringe to inject it into bottles like this one." He held up the bottle from the truck. "In the neck of the bottle, you'll find a tiny raised bump. It's a hole made with a syringe, then sealed with something."

"We found a couple used tubes of Krazy Glue," said one of his colleagues.

"That's what it is. They punctured the necks of the bottles, injected a fentanyl solution, and sealed the hole with superglue. No one would ever notice unless they were looking for it. The tainted formula would have been delivered inside a pallet of something other than baby formula. It was made to look like a packing mistake. Some of those packages may have made it to the shelves already. You all know what fentanyl can do. We've got to track each one of those deliveries and recover all of it or babies are going to die on our watch. That can't happen.

"Agent Panowicz has all the locations where deliveries were made this morning. How many stops, Panowicz?"

Panowicz opened his notebook. "Ten," he said.

"Okay, I need ten teams hitting each one of these retailers. Find out exactly what they accepted on delivery and find out where it went. Every bottle of this stuff must be accounted for. It looks like they hid one box on each pallet. Each box has six bottles of formula. That's sixty bottles of baby formula tainted with fentanyl. Find 'em all. There are lives on the line, people. Infant lives. Do not accept any pushback. If you have to shut down a store to track a case of baby formula, do it. We've got to get it all."

For the first time since the surveillance teams had been assigned, a real sense of urgency swept through the agents. A commotion ensued as the group split into new teams and were each assigned a delivery address. Within three minutes, all the teams were moving out.

"Check in regularly with me on your progress," Gordon said. "Go."

Despite being in panic mode, the teams did not show it. They moved methodically and with purpose, all recognizing what was at stake. They had to find the tainted infant formula before babies across the mid-Atlantic region started dying.

CHAPTER 91

One-by-one the calls came in. Of the ten deliveries Kam made, none of the stores had rejected the infant formula. The retailers had all accepted the deliveries without question. They knew Kam. They knew A&A Foods. A stray box of baby formula did not turn any heads. The forged packaging had worked and gone completely unnoticed. Three boxes remained on the loading docks of the stores to which they had been delivered, left there by stockers busy shelving something else. One box was in the loading dock office, where a stocker had brought it because he thought he would get in trouble if he put it on the shelf. Five more boxes had been greeted with shrugged shoulders by their respective stockers and made it to the shelves, but had not been sold. Another hour or day, and all of the tainted formula would have found its way to store shelves and put up for sale to an unknowing consumer market.

The JTTF's efficiency had been impressive. Nine boxes, a total of fifty-four tainted bottles, had been recovered without incident. All with the telltale small, clear, raised dot where Jummal had injected the fentanyl solution and sealed the hole with superglue.

Only one box—six bottles—remained unaccounted for.

CHAPTER 92

Mattie Boons was tired. She had done a double shift to make some extra money and was just leaving the hospital after sixteen hours. The thought of seeing her husband and little baby Jen after a short ride home made her smile. She called her husband to let him know she was on her way. He told her they were out of formula and asked if she could stop at the store and pick some up.

Mattie groaned, but smiled and said it was no problem. It was on the way and would only delay her commute by a few minutes. Her husband dutifully told her to forget it, that he would go out later and pick some up. Mattie assured him it was no problem and that she would make it a quick trip.

She pulled into the Arlington Safeway, still in her scrubs and Crocs—the tried-and-true uniform of the double-shift nurse. In the Arlington Safeway, she knew exactly where to go. She turned down the familiar aisle, but when she got there, the shelves were empty. Her brand was out of stock. She considered something else, but thought better of it. She did not want to upset little baby Jen's tummy. "Shit," she said out loud.

"Can I help you?"

A stocker she had not noticed was across the aisle a few feet behind her.

"What? No. Sorry," said Mattie. "The baby formula I like is sold out. I'll just have to go somewhere else."

"My mom's a nurse," the stocker said. "I know that look. Just off a double?"

"Yeah," Mattie said. "You got that right."

"Well, hang on a sec. Let me see if there's any in back."

"That'd be great," Mattie said. "I really appreciate it."

He returned a few minutes later with a box in hand. "This just came in today." He pulled out his box cutter and sliced into the box, quickly placing the six, 32-ounce bottles of formula in the open space on the shelf.

"You're a lifesaver," she told the stocker, grabbing two of the bottles. "Have a great night."

CHAPTER 93

Gordon left the warehouse and rushed to the Arlington Safeway, where agents had only recovered four of the six tainted bottles.

"Shut it down," he told the agent on scene he was speaking to as he made his way to the store. When he arrived, agents guarded the door and a line of customers were getting angry waiting to be let out.

Gordon went straight to an intercom and broadcast for the whole store to hear.

"Ladies and gentlemen. This is Federal Agent Gordon Stone. We apologize for the inconvenience. We have a problem with some infant formula that we need to get a hold of. If you have or are trying to purchase infant formula, please see one of the agents at the front of the store. If not, tell the agents at the door and you are free to leave. Thank you."

Soon enough, it was readily apparent that no one in the store possessed the two remaining bottles. In a matter of minutes, the store was empty of customers. Gordon approached the manager.

"We need to see security footage right now."

"Sure thing. It's over here behind customer service."

Unlike the drugstore, the Arlington Safeway had modern, quality cameras expertly mounted to observe all activity throughout the store. Gordon was able to see the entire interaction between Mattie and the stocker. "Nurse's scrubs," he said.

He turned to the manager. "How do I see the parking lot footage?"

The manager showed him, and Gordon went to work. He synced up the time and scrolled through each of the eight parking lot cameras. It took until camera #5 before he found Mattie getting into a white Honda Civic. He tracked the Honda out of the parking lot until he was able to get a clear image of the tag number.

Gordon called the FBI's Washington Field Office dispatcher. He identified himself and said, "I need an expedited address on a Virginia vehicle tag."

"You got it, Agent Stone. What's the tag number?"

"Sierra-Tango-Kilo dash 8-7."

"Virginia plate Sierra-Tango-Kilo dash 8-7," the dispatcher repeated. "Running it now."

"Thanks."

The seconds crawled by as Gordon waited. Finally, the dispatcher broke the silence with a Virginia address that was linked to the tag number. A stream of JTTF vehicles and agents raced from the Arlington Safeway to Mattie Boons's Virginia home.

Gordon did not arrive first, and when he got there, a breach team had guns drawn and stealthily approached the house, waiting for Gordon's "go" order. He ran from his car toward the front door, passing the breach team and shouting, "No guns. This is a rescue."

Gordon arrived at the front door with the breach team on his heels. He pounded on the door, shouting, "FBI." There was no response, and Gordon did not wait. He grabbed the heavy iron battering ram from an agent behind him. He drew the ram back, building momentum, then drove it into the lock area of the Boons's front door. The door gave way in a splintery explosion. There was no sign of anyone, but jazz music could be heard coming from the back of the house. Gordon tossed the ram aside and sprinted in that direction, followed by the breach team. He found Mattie's husband on his way from the kitchen to check out the noise. When he saw Gordon, his mouth fell open, and his full glass of wine shattered on the tile floor.

"Where's your wife? She's in danger," Gordon shouted, holding up his badge.

Mattie's husband gathered his wits. "This way," he said and led Gordon to the nursery.

Mattie sat on a rocking chair. Little baby Jen was cooing in her lap. Mattie was bouncing her and making airplane noises. Baby Jen was all smiles, her eyes glued to the bottle in Mattie's other hand, getting closer and closer.

"Stop!" Gordon screamed.

Mattie froze. Baby Jen stopped cooing. Gordon took two steps across the room and gently relieved Mattie of the bottle. Gordon let out a long breath.

"Sorry about that," he said. "And, um, we'll get your front door fixed. She hasn't had any of this, no?" he asked, referencing the bottle.

Mattie could only slowly shake her head, unclear on what was happening.

"How about you, did you test it at all, for temperature, anything like that?" Gordon asked.

Mattie shook her head, mumbled, "Straight from the bottle."

"That's good. I'm going to need the other bottle you purchased as well."

Mattie managed a nod, but remained seated, unmoving.

"Let me get rid of these guys," Gordon said. He walked through the house, instructing the agents to head out. "Back to HQ, everyone," he said. "We're all set here."

Gordon returned to the nursery, where Mattie's husband was on one knee next to the rocking chair. Gordon allowed himself a seat in the stuffed chair beside them. He looked at the Boonses, a happy family, and proceeded to tell them what just happened.

When he was done, he promised he would follow up with

them tomorrow, then walked to his car. The boxes were checked, the process complete. Potentially, hundreds of nameless, faceless, infant lives had been saved. Gordon was unsure what came next between him and the JTTF, but he was ready for his next case...almost.

CHAPTER 94

Early Saturday morning, Sophia Pressman's phone rang. She was not working and almost let voicemail get it. Instead, she rolled over with a grunt, opened her eyes and picked up. It was the public information officer from the FBI's Washington Field Office. She was invited in for a noon meeting with ASAC Dillon and Assistant Director of Counterterrorism Dan Pendleton.

That was a surprise. Pendleton was a player, in line to possibly be the next Director of the FBI. She told the PIO she would be there.

When she arrived, she was met at security by the PIO, who escorted her upstairs. Inside Pendleton's office, she found Dillon, Pendleton, and someone from the FBI's general counsel's office. This meant only one thing. Something big was going down. Noticeably absent: Special Agent Gordon Stone.

Pressman was not one to be intimidated by the trappings of high office in Washington, and she threw them all for a loop when she asked, "Where's Agent Stone? I was promised access to Agent Stone when this case was resolved." She was taking a shot here. She had no idea whether the case had been resolved or what Stone's role had been. Clearly, however, she had struck a nerve. Dillon and the PIO shifted uncomfortably in their seats.

Pendleton broke the uneasy silence. "Ms. Pressman, I'm Dan Pendleton. It's a great pleasure to meet you."

"The pleasure's mine, Assistant Director Pendleton, but I'm

not entirely clear what's going on here."

"Well," he said, "there have been developments in the case you've been discussing with the Washington Field Office. It has reached a certain level of completion, and we are preparing to go public."

Pressman bristled and stared at the PIO. "I thought we had an arrangement."

"Yes, Ms. Pressman," Pendleton intervened. "We stand by our agreement, and you will get your story. But I'm going to need you to wait a few more days."

This was not a problem for Pressman, as she still had no story. She leaned in anyway. "Why should I? I've been sitting on this for weeks already."

"Well, and this is all off the record, of course."

"Of course," she agreed.

"Ms. Pressman, I've got two bodies and ninety bottles of baby formula laced with fentanyl. Agent Stone...well, he's a goddamned hero. You'll get your story, but we need a few days to wrap this up with a nice tidy bow. You'll still get it, twenty-four hours ahead of the rest of the world, and Agent Stone will be made available for an exclusive interview as you see fit."

Pressman could barely contain her excitement. She wanted to say, *"Holy shit, you're damn right I'll wait a few days."* Instead, she stoically offered, "You deliver what we discussed, and I'll hold for a few more days, no problem."

"Then we're in agreement. Thanks for stopping by, Ms. Pressman. Enjoy the rest of your weekend."

CHAPTER 95

Less than a week went by before Pressman heard back from the PIO. He had arranged a meeting with Agent Stone, who had been given authority to discuss the case, along with Swayz and the PIO. Sophia did not like the fact Agent Stone would have two babysitters at the interview, but she knew the game.

Gordon was not an easy interview. His comments were detailed and specific but lacked any feeling or color. He was more "subject exited the vehicle," than "guy got out of his car." But, she noted, he completely ignored Swayz and the PIO, and their presence appeared to have absolutely no impact on Gordon whatsoever.

She found his awkwardness charming and his lack of awareness that he was a certifiable American hero made him one in a million in Washington, DC. A successful man in DC with absolutely no ego was a rare bird. And Gordon's attention to detail and thoroughness of technique was a reporter's dream. Pressman would have to do little actual reporting because Gordon's story was rife with detail and missed nothing. The color and feeling she would figure out later. Maybe it was already there, because it was a great story. Because of Gordon, potentially hundreds of infant lives had been saved.

The article made the front page of the *Post*. Gordon hated the attention. He had checked the boxes and wanted to move on. He refused any other interviews and let Swayz and the PIO deal with the media. He just wanted another case.

Like the news of the drone strike, interest in the story waned after a couple of weeks. The next big story was always close by, waiting to chew up yesterday's news. Gordon stayed on at the JTTF. Things were moderately better. He got a couple of real cases, but never truly fit in with the International Group. That was fine with him. He worked his cases in his basement break room, helped out when he could, but mostly worked on his own. He and Swayz kept their distance.

Gordon thought about calling Sophia. While he did not particularly like being interviewed, or being on the front page of *The Washington Post*, she had treated him fairly and had always been nice to him. Maybe a cup of coffee would be nice. He mustered up the courage to take a shot, but when he called and got her voice mail, he hung up without leaving a message.

Three months went by before Gordon got the news he had been nominated and selected for the Director's Award, the FBI's highest investigative honor. He shuddered at the thought of attending the FBI's annual awards ceremony.

Because of her front-page story, Sophia received a formal invitation to the ceremony from the Washington Field Office PIO. She responded affirmatively, thinking it might be a chance to get a few minutes with the Director of the FBI. And, she admitted to herself, it would be nice to see Special Agent Stone again too.

At the ceremony, Gordon's discomfort in these situations once again compelled him to revisit the Pokémon technique in order to calm himself down. He was getting better at it, though, he thought. His leg was not bouncing. He had kept his eyes open and was not mumbling the names out loud. It seemed like he had only just started his recitation when the FBI Director called him up onto the stage to receive his award. After the ceremony, he once again retreated to a quiet corner during the reception. He heard someone shouting his name and reluctantly looked across the room to see the FBI Director heading straight for him.

The Director usually had a commotion that followed him wherever he went, and the accompanying noise made it hard to hear. He leaned in to Gordon so that he could be heard and asked, "Why aren't you working for me?"

Gordon mumbled something about the JTTF and being detailed from FDA-OCI.

"No," the Director interrupted. "I mean, why aren't you an FBI agent?"

"Well, um, sir, I tried to be. To do that. But, well…Asperger's," he blurted out, looking down at his black Vans. Gordon thought he really ought to invest in a pair of dress shoes.

The Director looked at Gordon, scanning him from head to toe. Gordon looked up tentatively and made eye contact. For a moment, they held each other's stare, Gordon not knowing what to do, the Director assessing him.

The Director leaned in a second time. "I think we can find a spot for you."

ACKNOWLEDGMENTS

As with all worthwhile ventures, this book does not happen without the help and support of many, many others. In no particular order, but with a great deal of gratitude and appreciation, we, the writers, would like to thank the following people: Lisa Burnett and Jeanne Weiland, our wives as well as our first readers and editors. Their extraordinary patience, sound advice and guidance, and never-ending encouragement made Silent Killer possible. Our editor, Elizabeth White, who saw something special in Gordon Stone and perfected our portrayal of his story. We'll see you again soon, Elizabeth. Our readers: Mitch Yockelson, Andrea Kropf, Sally Seppanen, and Dennis Chapman, who each brought a new, different, and unique perspective to Silent Killer that gave us real hope that we had a good story on our hands. Our various subject matter experts: Roger Cressey, Jeff Thorpe, Bob Ekey, and David Stebenne who taught us, advised us, corrected us, and ensured Silent Killer, while a work of fiction, was as real as it could be. Artist extraordinaire Xing Burnett for the eye-catching cover art. And to the numerous unnamed others who gave a hand along the way, thank you all.

Photo Credit Mary Kay Palmer

TRACY BURNETT began his law enforcement career as a Deputy Sheriff at the Palm Beach County, Florida Sheriff's Department. His next stop was with the Drug Enforcement Administration where he became a special agent and went through training at the FBI Academy in Quantico, Virginia as well as DEA US Army Ranger Training. That began a 25-year federal law enforcement career leading investigations on behalf of the US Departments of Justice, State, and Defense, among others, working both domestically and around the globe. Tracy now works as an Adjunct Professor for the School of Public Affairs in the Key Executive Leadership Program at American University in Washington, DC.

Photo Credit Mary Kay Palmer

ROSS WEILAND was a journalist in New York City before attending law school and joining the US Navy's Judge Advocate General's Corps in 1998. He served as a prosecutor, criminal appeals attorney, and civil litigator in the Navy before transitioning to federal civil service where he spent 21 years in the Office of Inspector General community as counsel, investigator, and senior executive at the National Archives, Department of Defense, and NASA. Ross now works as an administrative executive supporting oversight and law enforcement in the private sector in Washington, DC.

On the following pages are a few more great titles from the Down & Out Books publishing family.

For a complete list of books and to sign up for our newsletter, go to DownAndOutBooks.com.

Girl in a Dumpster
A Holland Taylor Mystery
David Housewright

Down & Out Books
April 2025
978-1-64396-402-7

Henrietta Weller wakes up one morning in a dumpster with no memory of how she got there. P.I. Holland Taylor discovers that the woman was a victim of a sophisticated kidnapping ring that is targeting the daughters of Minnesota's rich and famous—and infamous. He insists that the FBI be informed.

However, a financial guru and fixer for the families demands that the incidents be dealt with and forgotten. Until there's another kidnapping. And another. And Taylor and his partner Freddie are forced to take matters into their own hands—no matter what the cost.

It's Not Even Past
Anna Scotti

Down & Out Books
June 2025
978-1-64396-409-6

A brainy young librarian must rely on Witness Protection to keep her alive as she jumps from one alias to another, always just a step ahead of her murderous ex and his cartel henchmen.

Forced to keep a low profile by taking menial jobs in random locations, "Cam" solves murders from the foothills of Montana to the gritty streets of L.A. as her rational, intellectual persona slips away and a streetwise, world-weary woman takes charge.

Calypso Blue
A Len Buonfiglio/Caribbean Mystery
Brian Silverman

Down & Out Books
June 2025
978-1-64396-394-5

Bar owner and ex-New Yorker Len Buonfiglio, a hero in his hometown, flees his family and the city for what he hopes is a quieter, idyllic life in the tropics. But when Lord Ram, a world-renowned Calypso performer dies, Len is called in to quiet damning rumors about the man's death.

In his search for the truth about Lord Ram and dealing with the very dangerous mess Maurizio has brought with him, Len soon learns that even on a sunny tropical paradise there is no escape from darkness.

The Gorgon of Los Feliz
Nolan Knight

Down & Out Books
July 2025
978-1-64396-397-6

The Gorgon of Los Feliz is Cameron Kilbride, a bisexual female in her early twenties, newly evicted, hustling a living by rolling tourists on the fringe of Hollywood, stealing cars—*anything* to get by. Enter the affluent Stevensons; Richard and Mauve have lost track of their troubled daughter, Tiffany, and fear she has fallen back into pills, last seen on tour across America with a psychedelic rock band. Desperate to reel her back home, they employ Cam, who makes it her life's mission to find Tiffany for a handsome reward. When she finds their daughter, things soon go haywire, forcing her to steal the girl's identity to bilk her inheritance; however, once she procures this troubled life, the sordid characters in Tiff's world begin to haunt her every step.

Made in United States
North Haven, CT
12 August 2025

71604141R00210